BLIND LANDING

Blind Landing

BLIND LANDING

Sydney to London
dead stop

An Aviation Mystery

By

Tony Blackman

ISBN 978-0-9553856-1-2

First Published May 2010
© 2010 by Anthony Blackman.

Published by Blackman Associates
24 Crowsport
Hamble
Southampton SO31 4HG
UK
www.blackmanbooks.co.uk

Previous books by the same Author

Fiction:-

A Flight Too Far
ISBN 978-0-9553856-3-6, 0-9553856-3-6
Published Blackman Associates

The Final Flight
ISBN 978-0-9553856-0-5, 0-9553856-0-1
First Published 2006
Published Blackman Associates

The Right Choice
ISBN 978-0-9553856-2-9, 0-9553856-2-8
First Published 2007
Published Blackman Associates

Flight to St Antony
ISBN 978-0-9553856-6-7, 0-9553856-6-0
First Published 2008
Published Blackman Associates

Now You See It ISBN 978-0-9553856-7-4
First Published 2009
Published by Blackman Associates

Non Fiction :-

Flight Testing to Win (Autobiography paperback)
ISBN 978-0-9553856-4-3, 0-9553856-4-4

Vulcan Test Pilot
ISBN 1-904943-888 hardback
ISBN 978-1-906502-30-0   paperback
Published Grub Street June 2007/2009

Tony Blackman Test pilot (Autobiography revised and hardback)
ISBN 978-1-906502-36-2
Published Grub Street June 2009

Author's Note:-

The time frame for this book is set about five years ahead of the present day and is based on the concept of the new satellite navigation systems being used for landing. A block diagram of the system used in the aircraft is included as an appendix for the technically minded.

This book is not a 'flight of fancy' since the design building blocks for these satellite landings are already in place and aircraft are already making approaches using satellites in good weather. However such landings will have to be closely monitored and some of the safety implications are discussed in the Analysis at the end of the book.

This book is a revision of an earlier book published four years ago but it has been completely revised to bring the technology up to date.

May 2010

Acknowledgements:-

This book could not have been completed without the support of Nick King of Air Services Australia who ensured that I was familiar with the latest developments in the Air Traffic System. I also had help from Tobin Berry of the UK National Air Traffic System at Swanwick, Richard James on the crash recorders and Chris Payne on aircraft operation. In addition Charles Masefield and Andrew McClymont gave me invaluable advice in the drafting of the Analysis at the end of the book.

I also received help from Kevin Hindle and also many people in the aviation industry; Robert Foulkes helped in writing the original version of this story. I hope I will be forgiven for not naming the many others who helped me in a variety of ways.

Any errors remaining in the book must be laid entirely at my door.

To Margaret, without whose ideas, enormous help and continuous encouragement this book, like all the others, would never have seen the light of day.

Anthony L Blackman OBE, M.A., F.R.Ae.S

About the Author

Tony Blackman was educated at Oundle School and Trinity College Cambridge, where he obtained an honours degree in Physics. After joining the Royal Air Force he learnt to fly, trained as a test pilot and then joined A.V.Roe and Co. Ltd. where he became Chief Test Pilot.

Tony was an expert in aviation electronics and was invited by Smiths Industries to join their Aerospace Board, initially as Technical Operations Director. He helped develop the then new large electronic displays and Flight Management Systems.

After leaving Smiths Industries, he was invited to join the Board of the UK Civil Aviation Authority as Technical Member.

Tony is a Fellow of the American Society of Experimental Test Pilots, a Fellow of the Royal Institute of Navigation and a Liveryman of the Guild of Air Pilots and Air Navigators.

He now lives in Hamble and spends his spare time writing books and designing and maintaining databases on the internet.

CONTENTS

DRAMATIS PERSONNAE

Peter Talbert	**Aviation Expert, Narrator of Book**
Ahmed	Hijacker
Anne Moncrieff	Surveyor with Safety Regulation Group, Civil Aviation Authority
Bill Baker	Chief Training Captain, NWIA
Bob Furness	Head of Air Accident Investigation Branch
Brad Wentworth	A 798 Captain, Royal World Airlines
Brian Tucker	Flight Magazine Air Correspondent
Carol Trentham	Wife of Richard Trentham
Catherine Mercer	Frank Mercer's Wife
Charles McGuire	Inquiry Member, Professor, Software Engineering at Imperial College
Charles Tumbrill	First Officer of crashed aircraft, killed on flight.
Chuck Osborne	Daily Telegraph Air Correspondent
Diana	Peter Talbert's wife
Dick Tremlett	En-route Captain crashed aircraft
Dora	Peter Talbert's domestic help
Eva Pearson	Liz Ward's room mate
Evan Evans	RWA Expert on 798 Landing Systems
Francis Thomas	Royal World Airlines Engineering Director
Frank Mercer	Surviving First Officer on fatal flight
Fred Longshaw	A First Officer on a Royal World Airlines flight to Sydney
George Nesbitt	An en route RWA Captain to Sydney
Glen Lawrence	NWIA/United Electronics Engineer
Harry Hodgson	Captain of crashed aircraft, killed on flight
Harvey Gates	Approach Controller, Heathrow
Humphrey Barton	Tower Controller, Heathrow
Jack Chiltern	Managing Director, Royal World Airlines
Jane Franklin	Times Air Correspondent
Janet Crowburn	Chief Counsel for the Attorney General
Jeff Templeman	Inquiry Member, Chief Engineer, Britannia
Jill Stanton	John Chester's secretary
Jim Akers	Aeronautical Correspondent of Financial Times
Jock Mansfield	NWIA Training Captain
John Chester	Chief Pilot, Royal World Airlines, wife Jane
John Fairlane	Counsel for CrossRisk Insurance
John and Julia Marchant	Peter Talbert's Neighbours

Josh Wilson	An en route First Officer to Sydney
Justin Lockyer	An RWA 798 Captain
Lance Stephens	NWIA Electronics Engineer
Liz Fairlane	John's Wife
Liz Ward	Operations staff, NWIA
Lord Justice Thomas	Head of Court of Inquiry
Mandy Arrowsmith	Peter Talbert's Solicitor Girl Friend
Marcia Hodgson	Captain Harry Hodgson's wife
Martin Foster	Senior Inspector, Air Accident Investigation Branch in charge of crash investigation
Matt Thompson	Head of Maintenance, NWIA
Michael Noble	Seattle Editor of Aviation Week
Mike Mansell	Partner in CrossRisk Insurance
Paul Franconi	Daily Mirror Air Correspondent
Phillip Trotter	Chief Ground Instructor of NWIA
Ray Robson	Captain of the Royal World Airlines 798 before fatal flight.
Rex Williams	John Chester's deputy, wife Margaret, daughter of Jack Chiltern
Richard Tremlett	RWA First Officer killed on flight
Richard Trentham	Deadheading Cathay Pacific Pilot, killed on flight
Sir Robert Applegate	Chief Constable of the Metropolitan Area
Robin Turnsmith	AAIB investigator
Roger O'Kane	Avionics designer, Independant Transport Aircraft Company
Sam Falconer	Captain on Talbert's first Royal World Airlines flight to Sydney
Ted McIntosh	Peter Talbert's solicitor
Ted Richmond	Senior Operations Staff, NWIA
Tim Forrestal	Solicitor for CrossRisk Insurance
Tip Brewster	NWIA Shift Supervisor
Tom Gardner	American Airlines Training Department
Tony Giles	RWA 798 First Officer before fatal flight
William Parnell	President, Independant Transport Aircraft Company, builder of 798 airplane

ACRONYMS

Acronym	In full
AAIB	Air Accident Investigation Branch
ACARS	Aircraft Communications Addressing and Reporting System
AFDAS	Approach Funnel Deviation Alert System.
ATIS	Automatic Terminal Information Service
ATC	Air Traffic Control
BAA	British Airports Authority
CAA	Civil Aviation Authority
Category III	Visibility less than 100 meters called 'Category 3'
DGAC	French Directorate of Civil Aviation
DME	Distance Measuring Equipment
EASA	European Aviation Safety Agency
FAA	Federal Aviation Administration
FMS	Flight Management System
GAPAN	Guild of Air Pilots and Air Navigators
GBAS	Ground Based Augmentation System
Galileo	Galileo European Satellite System
GLOSNASS	Russian Satellite Positioning System
GPS	Global Positioning System
GSA	European GNSS Supervisory Authority
HUD	Head Up Display
ILS	Instrument Landing System
INMARSAT	International telecommunications company
IRS	Inertial Reference Systems
ITAC	Independant Transport Aircraft Company
LAAS	Local Area Augmentation System for GPS
Microspot	Makers of the MMR in the 798
MLS	Microwave Landing System
MMR	Multimode Receiver
NTSB	National Transportation Safety Board
NWIA	New World International Airlines
PAI	Pacific Aerospace Insurance
Qinetiq	UK Defence Firm
RVR	Runway Visual Range
RWA	Royal World Airlines
SAE	Society of Automotive Engineers
SRG	Safety Regulation Group, UK CAA
TCAS	Traffic Collision Avoidance System
WAAS	Wide Area Augmentation System

Great Circle Route
Sydney—London
Flight RWA 573

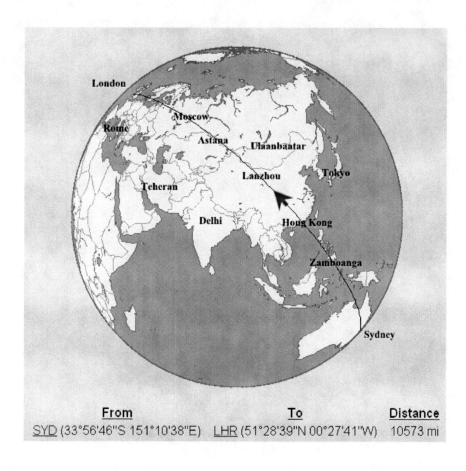

From	To	Distance
SYD (33°56'46"S 151°10'38"E)	LHR (51°28'39"N 00°27'41"W)	10573 mi

Map produced using Karl L. Swartz mapping web site

Blind Landing

IN THE BEGINNING

Eva

"Final Call Sydney Heathrow."
The announcer in the international terminal repeated her message.
"Final Call RWA 573. Non Stop to London."
Eva, waiting with the Royal World Airlines cabin staff at the glass screens for the aircraft to be ready, watched the passengers coming to the gate. This was her first international training trip though she had made quite few flights under instruction on New World International Airlines Australian internal flights.

The glass doors slid open and she went with the chief steward and the other attendants to the upper deck of this new enormous very modern jumbo aircraft to prepare for the passengers. She had been allocated to observe the operation of the upper business compartment and, as they went in to the galley behind the first class section, she was surprised to see that there were already two men on the aircraft, who clearly weren't crew, sitting at the front of the business section. They were sitting next to one another on a pair of seats in the centre of the compartment and were both wearing formal double breasted grey suits; she was puzzled when the cabin staff ignored them as if they weren't there.

She watched the cabin crew checking that all the food compartments were secure and then helping the passengers to their seats as they came aboard. The ground staff left and she helped close the forward upper entrance doors. She heard the engines starting and then felt the aircraft being pushed back and starting to taxi. She checked that the escape slides were set to automatic.

The Captain warned the cabin crew that they were about to take-off and she sat down next to another stewardess by the port aisle looking aft at the business passengers. As she strapped herself in she glanced at the two men she had noticed earlier and something about them made her feel uneasy. She wasn't a Roman Catholic but to her surprise she felt herself wanting to make the sign of the cross.

PROLOGUE

Richard

Richard knew he was dying. He could feel his consciousness slowly slipping away. The whole thing was like a nightmare. One moment he was sitting in the jump seat on the flight deck of the world's most advanced airplane about to land at Heathrow and the next moment he was in terrible pain, lying in hospital, with the world spinning around. He tried to remember what had happened but nothing seemed to make sense.

He could not see the room clearly but he could just make out Carol and was relieved that she was there, though he could barely say a word to her. What a homecoming. He was aware of people rushing in and out of the room, looking after him, but he realised it would not be for long.

Though everything was a blur, the flight somehow kept coming back to him. He remembered Harry arranging for him to travel back from Sydney as supernumerary crew. He had been wanting to see the 798's advanced flight deck ever since it had gone into airline service and so he had leapt at the chance when Harry invited him. The 747s he was flying were quite new, but seemed archaic compared with the 798. He had read about the aircraft in the newspapers and magazines, especially those articles by his old colleague Peter Talbert.

Carol had just come into the room again but she seemed far away behind the flight deck. The pain in his shoulders from the shoulder straps was terrible and he tried to loosen them. It had been a wonderful flight until the hijackers arrived. How on earth had they got on board? And onto the flight deck past the marshals? They had somehow forced their way through the flight deck door, both carrying some peculiar looking guns, pointing them at Harry and at Charles, the first officer. Harry had been magnificent controlling the madmen and the aircraft at the same time.

The hijackers had a crazy scheme of getting the Government to give them some al-Qaeda prisoners and then take-off again for the Middle East. Ahmed, the leader, was talking about blowing the plane up if the prisoners were not released. Surely they had not got a bomb? Perhaps it was all bluff. Richard had known, and surely Harry must have done, that they would never have been allowed to take-off again but Harry played along with Ahmed, the leader, arranging the refuelling on the runway. As if to make matters worse, the headwind from Sydney had been stronger than forecast so they did not have too much fuel and the weather at London was freezing fog. Richard had felt so sorry for Harry to have to carry this burden but he was powerless to help.

Now Carol seemed to be walking through the instruments towards him and bending over him. He tried to move but he couldn't and he knew it wasn't really the shoulder straps stopping him. He seemed to hear air traffic control talking. Harry had turned the speakers off but Ahmed had insisted that they should be turned back on again. He remembered wondering if it was going to be possible for Harry to fly a Category III approach and land the aircraft in freezing fog without it crashing when the hijackers were interfering and interrupting him all the time. He knew the autopilot would be flying the aircraft but the system was not infallible and needed monitoring.

Poor Harry, he seemed only to have one display in front of him and he was continually having to switch from the vertical display to the horizontal one. Charles didn't seem to be having a problem. Richard remembered that he also had had a display and some instruments in front of him but they did not seem to be much use for finding out what was happening. Air Traffic had told them they could not use the MLS on 27L for landing which Harry had wanted as it was out of service but he had known it was permitted to use the Galileo satellite navigation system. He could see Harry's displays as the aircraft lined up with the runway and flew down the glide slope. Ahmed started talking to Harry and Harry told him to be quiet.

Suddenly he remembered what he wanted to tell Peter. Something that Peter needed to know. He felt himself saying "Peter Talbert. Get Peter. I want to tell him …"

Richard woke up with a start. He must have dropped off into a coma. The pain in his leg was terrible. Carol was still there and so was the flight deck. They were close to landing. He remembered feeling worried as his experience with the American GPS for approaches and landings had not been all that good but Peter Talbert had written that the latest Galileo system was first rate and very closely monitored for errors. Nevertheless he had felt that it was going to be very difficult for Harry to be able to manage with Ahmed standing there with his gun distracting him. Harry and Charles had seemed very confident even though Ahmed kept interfering. They were down to 100ft now and he looked again at his instruments and then at the hijackers. He tried to yell 'Pull up, Pull up' felt himself bracing, there was a crash and he realised that he was being moved from his bed.

Sometime later Richard woke again. His right leg was completely numb. This time the flight deck had gone. He could see Carol and there was Peter standing next to her. He made a supreme effort to talk.

"Peter. The hijacker…" Peter was leaning forward. "I wanted to tell Harry…"

He felt himself slipping away.

CHAPTER 1

Blind Landing

"Heathrow broadcast – the airport is now closed. I say again, the airport is closed. Speedbird 6328 route direct to Ockham, climb flight level 100 and join the hold."

I was driving in thick fog, trying to get home from Bournemouth. I didn't have far to go to my house in Kingston and I was looking forward to getting back. As I often did, I was listening to the conversation between aircraft and ground controllers on my VHF set. I had had the receiver specially fitted to my rather elderly BMW at what was, in my view, an extortionate cost but I reckoned I could offset it against my tax.

"Speedbird 6328 climbing to level 100 to Ockham to hold. What's the problem? We are Category III."

The transmission from the London Approach transmitter was only just audible, even though I was only a few miles from Heathrow but the aircraft were loud and very clear. Clearly the fog I was experiencing covered Heathrow as well since the aircraft mentioned Category III weather conditions. Like the British Airways pilot I wondered what the problem was and why the aircraft was not allowed to land.

"Speedbird 6328 call Director on 119.2 with cleared level"

"119.2 Speedbird 6328"

It was strange that Approach did not advise the aircraft of the reason for diversion.

"RWA 372. Please advise your desired alternate."

"Roger. RWA 372 calling company."

"RWA 372 thank you – quick as you can please."

I switched to Royal World Airlines Operations frequency.

"RWA Operations this is 372. Just been told Heathrow is closed. Why? What do you want me to do?"

"Ops to 372. Confirm Heathrow is closed. Request diversion to Stansted. We are arranging a gate for you."

It was odd that RWA operations did not tell 372 what the problem was either. I would have liked to have known as well. The fog if anything was getting worse and there was now ice on the road. Perhaps the airport authority had decided that they needed to treat the runways.

"Operations, this is RWA 573. Have you arranged the refuelling?"

"We're still doing that. You are having to be refuelled by tankers instead of by hydrants on the stands. We are making sure that they have enough fuel for Karachi and that they can get to your parking position on the runway."

"573 understood."

If the reception had not been absolutely clear I would have thought I had misheard the aircraft transmission. It did not make sense.

"RWA Ops This is 573. I have been asked to establish whether the prisoners have been released and are waiting at the airport?"

"573 please stand by. Will advise."

There was only one explanation I could think of. The aircraft must have been hijacked. But that was virtually impossible these days with such high security at the airports. I wondered where 573 had come from. What a dreadful situation. If the aircraft was going to land at Heathrow it was no wonder the airport was closed.

There was a short pause.

"RWA Ops I have been told to remind you that the hijackers are going to blow up the aircraft if there is any delay to their instructions which I passed to you"

"573 this is RWA Ops Copied."

I wanted to retune my VHF receiver to London Approach but I was frightened I might miss something. However there was nothing more on the RWA Ops channel so I switched to the Approach frequency just as I was entering my drive. I decided to stay in the car until 573 had landed. I left the engine running to keep warm.

"Speedbird 756 Heathrow now closed. Do you want Stansted or Gatwick?"

"Gatwick please 756"

"Speedbird 756 maintain flight level 70 and turn left heading 240 degrees. Maintain 220 knots. Expect to hold at Biggin."

Clearly there was a real emergency for this hijack. I wondered how many other people besides me were hearing this appalling situation unfold.

"Director RWA 573 reaching 4,000."

"Roger. Cleared procedural Galileo final approach 27 left"

"RWA 573 we'd prefer to use the MLS."

I sympathised with the pilot. I always preferred radio beams physically defined in space to virtual centre lines calculated by software.

"Sorry RWA 573 the ATIS is incorrect. The MLS is out of service. What are your intentions?"

There was a distinct pause.

"RWA 573 request Galileo approach 27 Left."

"You are cleared for Galileo approach and to descend on the procedure. Maintain heading and call the Tower on 118.5"

"118.5 RWA 573"

I switched to the tower frequency just in time to hear 573's call.

"Tower RWA 573 ten miles 27 Left. Confirm GBAS OK."

Blind Landing

"RWA 573 Heathrow Tower. You are clear to land 27 left, wind calm RVR 20, 30,20 GBAS showing OK"

"Roger RWA 573"

The weather was definitely Category IIIC. The three transmissionmeters measuring the runway visual range along the length of the runway all agreed visibility was at the best 30m. I just couldn't imagine what it must be like doing an automatic landing in fog while being hijacked, presumably with a pistol being held to my head. It was clearly going to be a completely blind landing. Furthermore, I did not understand why the aircraft was having to use Galileo, the European Satellite System, instead of the Microwave Landing System, MLS. The pilot was very sensible to have rechecked that the Ground Based Augmentation System, GBAS, which augmented the accuracy of the Galileo satellites, was working correctly.

"RWA 573 two miles to go. You appear to be below the glide slope."

"Heathrow Tower RWA 573 copied please check wind speed."

The Tower did not answer immediately then,

"573 from Tower, the wind is calm. You...."

Another aircraft came on frequency and blotted out whatever the Tower was trying to say. All I heard was

" 564 confirm Heathrow closed"

"Lufthansa 564 from Heathrow Tower. Airfield closed leave frequency immediately."

The Tower controller tried again

"RWA 573 ."

Again there was a transmission blotting out the Tower, I suspected Lufthansa was acknowledging Tower's instruction and asking for a frequency. The controller tried again but the transmission again clashed with another aircraft transmission, presumably Lufthansa.

"573 you still appear to be low on the glide slope."

"I say again Lufthansa 564 from Tower. Heathrow closed. Change to London Approach 119.2 immediately. 573 abandon approach."

"573 I repeat abandon approach."

But there were no more transmissions from 573. The controller incredibly had told the aircraft to abandon approach; he must have thought the aircraft was very low or, more likely, the warning system in the Tower had operated. The silence was frightening. I wound down my car window and I thought I could hear sirens in the distance. I looked at my watch. It was 10.30. It had taken me over three hours to get home from Bournemouth instead of my normal two.

I collected my things from the car, unlocked the front door, cancelled the alarm and went into the house, full of trepidation. Something terrible had obviously happened. It would have been pointless rushing to the airport. I dropped everything and switched on Radio 5.

It was too late to ring Mandy, my girl friend who I had just left. I knew she went to bed early when she was working the next day since her train left at 6.30 am. That was why we had had a very early meal and I had left soon after seven having lingered much longer than we had planned and had very nearly broken our unspoken resolution about where I should stay the night.

I had driven back to my house in Kingston on an emotional and sexual high, trying to listen to some of Andrew Lloyd Webber's older songs on my CD but having to keep switching the CD off in order to concentrate on the almost impenetrable fog, made much worse by the freezing conditions. It was a very scary drive trying to allow for the vagaries not only of the weather but the other foolhardy drivers on the road and I was very thankful for my satellite navigator. In the end I had switched the music off and decided to listen to my VHF receiver to hear how the fog was affecting the Heathrow traffic.

As usual Radio 5 was talking about soccer though I did wonder sometimes whether there wasn't a bit too much coverage of football on the BBC. Suddenly the guy leading the discussion said there was breaking news and passed us over to the newsroom.

"It has just been reported that an aircraft has had an accident trying to land at London Airport. Apparently the aircraft has touched down very early on the A30 to the east of the airport. Crash crews, fire engines and ambulances are trying to get to the aircraft."

There was nothing more and soccer once more reigned supreme. I turned the volume down only slightly so that I would hear the inevitable upgrading of the news on the accident. I was horrified. Unless a miracle had happened the accident was likely to be a terrible disaster. I dreaded to think of the likely loss of life. Already people would be wondering how the accident could have occurred. The hijacking was clearly a critical factor.

Automatically I went into my office, and turned on my computer. Aviation was my business. I had spent the first fourteen years of my working life flying for Britannia Airways, until the doctors discovered a heart murmur which had never troubled me but which they considered made it impossible for me to keep a licence. In truth it didn't worry me too much since I didn't want to spend the rest of my life as an airline pilot. I was able to get my loss of licence insurance and with my degree in electronic engineering I was attempting to earn my living as a consultant in airline safety matters.

I had been becoming increasingly concerned about the design of modern flight decks and the way the pilots were expected to rely on the electronic displays to show the action required if systems malfunctioned. Furthermore, in order to get the best economically out of an aircraft there was no direct connection between the pilots' controller and the flying controls; computers interpreted the pilots requirements and moved the control surfaces to get the best performance out of the aircraft. Of course the pilots could practise all the likely emergencies on simulators but it was always the unexpected malfunctions that concerned me. I was visiting airlines explaining to the pilots some of these issues and also attending conferences and often presenting papers where these matters were discussed.

I went to the Royal World Airlines web site and found the flight details of RWA 573. It had taken off from Sydney at 0930 local time and had been due in at 2230. There was no other information on the web site.

I thought about the conversation I had heard with air traffic. The voice sounded very familiar. I felt I should have recognised it. Perhaps the voice, presumably the Captain, was a member of the Guild of Air Pilots and Air Navigators, as I was, and we had met.

It was puzzling that the aircraft had been allowed to land at Heathrow. The standard Air Traffic Control instructions were to divert all hijacked aircraft to Stansted. Not that there were any hijacked aircraft these days. Security was always far too good. I wondered again how the hijackers had got on board since the Sydney security was extremely tight. It was going to be important to discover not only why the accident happened but how the breach of security occurred.

I heard the news of the accident being reported again on Radio 5.

"Further details have emerged on the accident to an aircraft that occurred trying to land at Heathrow. The weather was extremely foggy and very icy. The aircraft was an Independant Transport Aircraft Company 798 belonging to Royal World Airlines flying non-stop from Sydney to London, flight number RWA 573. There are believed to be about 500 passengers and crew on board. The situation is confused because it is understood there was a hijacking alert coming from this aircraft. There are reports of considerable loss of life at the scene of the accident."

The news reader had said that the aircraft belonged to Royal World Airlines and was one of the new super jumbo four-engined Independant 798s. I knew the aircraft fairly well because I had written a technical article on it for the Financial Times when it was first certificated. It had a maximum capacity of about 750 people when flying on the Sydney-London route against the normal headwind. It was made by the Independant Transport Aircraft Company, ITAC, based near Seattle and could carry over 1,000 people when flying short distances with the maximum number of seats, a fact which I found slightly disturbing imagining the understandable panic if there was ever a need for rapid evacuation.

ITAC was a relatively new airplane manufacturer started by ex-Boeing engineers and marketing executives. As the competition from the European Airbus company had increased, Boeing had found it harder and harder to compete. The launch of the new Airbus aircraft had accelerated the decline of Boeing in the commercial airliner market and the firm had had to lay off a considerable number of engineers in the Commercial division of the company. These engineers, realising that the Boeing overheads were crippling the company, had persuaded some venture capitalists in the State of Washington, many of whom had made a lot of money locally out of Microsoft, to start the Independant Transport Aircraft Company. The new firm had managed to get a lease of some ground on the airfield at Everett, where the large Boeing aircraft were assembled, and had built a huge new hangar. The design office was in a rented building in Renton near the Boeing facility and nearly everything was subcontracted so that all the parts came together for the first time at Everett. The headquarters of the new company was in Kirkland, just north of Bellevue. Almost every facility they needed was rented to avoid the need for excessive amounts of capital and this was made possible because of the surplus capacity available in the United States commercial aerospace industry. This technique really kept the costs down and Boeing were having a hard time competing with the new company. Even Airbus in Europe, with the subsidized launch costs from the various national Governments concerned, was feeling the strain. This was the first major accident to an ITAC manufactured aircraft and would be an enormous blow to the company.

It was 11.30 by now and I was feeling tired but it was difficult not to stay up and listen to the details of the accident unfolding; however I had just decided that I had better go to bed when the phone rang.

"Peter, Jim Akers here."

Jim was the aeronautical correspondent of the Financial Times and it was thanks to him that the FT had commissioned me to write the article on the 798 some months earlier. "Hope I didn't wake you up. Have you heard the news?"

"Yes, Jim. I was actually listening to the aircraft talking to RWA Ops as it was coming in. I couldn't believe what I was hearing on the hijacking."

"What do you mean? You actually heard the aircraft talking to the ground?" Jim was a newsman through and through. I think he felt he had struck oil. "What happened?"

"Well, apparently the hijackers had asked for some prisoners that they wanted to be released and taken to the airport, ready to be loaded on to the aircraft. It was then going to take off again for Karachi."

"How do you know all this?"

"I just heard the aircraft requesting confirmation that the prisoners would be available and that the refuelling arrangements were in hand."

"Was it confirmed?"

"The refuelling was. The Captain said that he had been told to remind Ops that the aircraft would be blown up if there was any delay to the carrying out of the hijackers instructions."

"Peter, perhaps that was what actually happened? No wonder the aircraft crashed." Jim paused. "It was Category IIIC weather wasn't it? That must have made matters worse."

"Yes it was. The MLS was out of service and the aircraft was using the Galileo satellite system to make the approach."

"What do you make of it all?"

"I don't know. We shall have to wait until AAIB investigates the matter. The real issue at the moment, Jim, is what is happening at the crash site? How bad was the accident. How many people have lost their lives?"

"You're quite right." Jim sounded slightly chastened. I think he realised that his curiosity for the cause of the accident had got ahead of the mayhem and carnage that must exist on the A30. "I understand that there are some survivors, Peter."

We didn't carry on much longer. I guessed that Jim, having listened to me, wanted to update his article on the accident in the FT.

Radio 5 was talking about the accident again. It sounded as if the soccer had been kicked into touch and the accident had taken over. The announcer said that the situation was completely confused because apparently some terrorists had somehow got on board the aircraft with weapons and overpowered the crew. The story was that the hijackers had been planning to get the Government to release some prisoners, believed to be from al-Qaeda, and then to take-off again for somewhere in the Middle East. They were going to blow the aircraft up on the ramp at Heathrow if their orders were not obeyed. Consequently, the police, army, and fire services had all been alerted, ready for the landing.

The point was made that the accident couldn't have happened at a worse time. The roads had been very busy as it was the Monday night at the end of the Christmas/New Year holidays and people had been returning to start work the following day. Making an approach to Heathrow, the aircraft had apparently dived into the ground before reaching the airport. The visibility had been reported as less than 30 metres. It had crashed on the road causing a lot of casualties, not only in the aircraft but also to people travelling in cars, before sliding into a new cargo shed just beside the road and to the left of the approach lights; this had caused the whole front of the aircraft to concertina, but it wasn't clear whether there had been an explosion, either before or just after the impact. There were several hundred people in the aircraft, the exact number was still being investigated. It was clear that a lot of the passengers had been killed though apparently there were a significant number of survivors near the back of the upper cabin who had either been thrown clear or had managed to scramble out of the wreckage. Nearly all the survivors had had to be taken to nearby hospitals. Work had already started in identifying the victims.

The news reader went on to say that it was probably the worst air disaster ever in the history of UK aviation, worse even than the accident to the Pan American 747 at Lockerbie many years earlier, though of course not to be compared with 9/11 deliberate wrecking in New York.

The newscaster explained that because all the Heathrow rescue services had been on stand-by in the airport next to 27L runway, it had taken only a few minutes for the crash crews, fire engines and police to get to the crash, though they were hampered by the appalling visibility. The rescue teams had been working non-stop, assisted by the armed services who had been drafted in to help, but everything was complicated by the fog which was still very thick. Things were made even more difficult by the need for the security forces to cordon off the area and check for weapons and bombs. Even the survivors had to be security checked which made things harder for the ambulance crews and the hospitals. It was going to take a long time dealing with all the injured. The Air Accident Investigation Branch inspectors, AAIB, were already on the spot looking for the crash recorders and examining all the wreckage and they were getting specialist help from the security experts who had apparently appeared on the scene from nowhere.

I switched the radio off. It was well after midnight. I went to bed and went straight to sleep. It seemed only moments later when the phone rang, waking me up before I was ready. I stretched out, rolled over and lifted the phone off its hook. Even after four years it seemed strange not to feel Diana's warmth on the other side of the bed. I sensed through the curtains that it was still very dark outside.

"Peter?" It was Mandy, her voice vibrant, urgent, catapulting me from deep sleep to extreme awareness. "There was a terrible accident last night. An aircraft landing at Heathrow crashed on the road outside the airport. I've just heard the news on the radio. The passengers included the Foreign Secretary and two or three of his staff. Apparently the aircraft had been hijacked in some way and all the emergency services at the airport had been alerted and were waiting for it to land. Did you hear about it last night on your way home?"

"What time is it? I've only just gone to sleep."

"It's alright for some! It's 6.30 already. I'm on the platform waiting for the train."

"Mandy. Yes, I did know about the accident. I was listening to the VHF in my car. But I didn't know about the Foreign Secretary." I told her about my journey home and the Jim Akers telephone call.

"Look I've got to dash. The train is coming. I'll call you later. Bye."

There was what might have been a perfunctory kiss and she was gone. I rolled over and switched on the radio, the announcer was just giving the headlines. There was to be a statement on the accident by the Prime Minister on radio and TV at 9 o'clock. Telephone numbers to call were given out so that worried families could find out if their relatives were on board, whether they were in hospital, whether their bodies had been found or if they were still missing. These same families might well be needed to help in identification so it was very important indeed that all people who were concerned rang in.

Listening to the news reader, it was clear that the Police, the British Airports Authority, the Fire Services and the local hospitals had all done a marvellous job dealing with the horrendous problems caused by the accident. The Police had set up an Accident Operations Room, conceived and planned several years previously by the Department of Health and Safety with the help of all the local authorities, the British Airports Authority and the rescue services and it seemed to have been extremely effective. Less immediately obvious to the uninitiated was the speed with which Air Traffic Control had reacted. The announcer said that Heathrow was now open again using the northern runway but that the weather was still very foggy.

The rest of the news followed and then the producer went back to the accident story. In the middle of the night one reporter had managed to find a survivor who had received only minor injuries though the reporter remarked that the man had a bandage on the side of his head. The man sounded dazed and it seemed to me that he should have been in hospital, not talking to the reporter. I always felt that no-one should be expected to give an interview in such a situation but the reporter clearly had no such reservations. I wanted to switch the radio off but the survivor's description was so graphic and heart rending that I found myself listening.

"The flight from Sydney was fine." The man sounded very hoarse. He coughed. "I was sitting in a window seat in the middle of Upper Class. We could see the ground most of the way and then the stars as it got dark."

He stopped again and we could hear him spluttering. Why he carried on I could not imagine. Perhaps talking about what had happened helped him.

"I heard a strange noise up front like a muffled explosion of some sort and then about four foreign looking people got up and went through the curtain. Almost immediately afterwards the Captain announced that the aircraft had been hijacked and that no-one was to move from their seats. He said that we were going to land at Heathrow and the situation would then be sorted out."

There was a pause and the man started coughing uncontrollably for a few seconds. Surely this interview would be cut short. I found it hard to believe that, apart from anything else, the security people would allow the interview to be heard. The survivor tried again.

"We were told to remain in our seats, I could see everyone around was as worried as I was. Two swarthy looking men with beards appeared at the front of the two aisles carrying what looked like pistols of some sort. Then cabin staff appeared from the galley behind us and tried to quieten some of the passengers who were panicking."

Another long pause and sirens could be heard in the background. The man seemed to pull himself together.

"No more announcements were made. The cabin staff made certain we were strapped in for landing. Everything was very smooth. As we descended, I heard the landing gear go down and then we suddenly went into cloud. Then, just before the crash I saw some lights, caught a glimpse of a house incredibly close, then a car and an enormous bang."

We could almost hear him shudder. He coughed again, this time very loudly. I was certain that that must be the end of the interview but somehow the man struggled on.

"The next thing I knew I was lying on the side of the road."

Apparently someone had helped him into a nearby house immediately after the crash. As he told his story he could be heard bursting into tears. It was appalling. Nobody should be subjected to that sort of interview. The interviewer started to say something but I had had my fill and I switched off the radio but not before I heard his last few words which I found it impossible to blot out.

"I could hear cries for help and frightened shrieks of pain from the wounded and the ringing of mobile phones. There were flames coming from what I took to be the wreckage. It was like a nightmare. Everything was in fog. I could smell burning and there was ice on the ground. I felt numb, lying on some grass. I thought I was in Hell already."

CHAPTER 2

Carol

As I started to get up I saw that the windows were covered with condensation in spite of the double glazing. I cleaned a patch of moisture away and could just see the house next door had some lights in the windows where John and Julia Marchant were clearly already dealing with the new day. It would not be long before John got the car out and headed for Reading, closely followed by Julia taking their two children to school. I did not envy them driving in the fog. At least there was some benefit to my working from home, even it was very lonely at times.

I got dressed into some casual trousers and a pullover, and wandered downstairs. In the kitchen I emptied the coffee machine and made myself a drink. Tuesday was one of Dora's days and hopefully my invaluable but rather loquacious help would deal with all the mess I had made. Ideally, I would have liked her to come more than twice a week but I could not afford the money to pay her nor the time she seemed to need to discuss her family problems. The smell of fresh coffee was reassuring of normality as I wandered into the hall to get the paper.

The Times was by the front door and I picked it up. 'HIJACKED AIRCRAFT CRASHES' was right across the front page and 'DISASTER IN FREEZING FOG' headed another column discussing the weather. It seemed to be a fact of life that every time an aircraft crashed, the eyewitnesses said the aircraft had exploded or was on fire just before it hit the ground. Perhaps in this case for once it might even be true. I scanned the paper rapidly. Clearly, at the time the newspaper was going to press there was still so much confusion that the reporters had been unable to get a full understanding of the situation but it was expected that the loss of life would be horrendous and that at least three hundred people had been killed. The papers had managed to discover somehow before they went to press that the Foreign Secretary had been a passenger and that the airport had been on security alert just prior to landing. The survivors of the crash had been rushed to hospitals by ambulance but the paper said that it was still proving extremely difficult in view of the very thick fog.

It was obvious that the reporters had not been able to get particularly close to the wreckage themselves due to the weather and also the security cordon which the army had managed to put round the crash site fairly soon after the accident. Because of the fog, helicopters could not be used to rescue the wounded. It must have been a desperate situation though the police seemed to have had excellent liaison with the security forces. I shuddered involuntarily. What a terrible mess and how appalling for the all the dependants and the survivors.

I went into the front room and turned the television on. The Chairman of the Civil Aviation Authority was being questioned and doing a very good job of standing up to the grilling he was receiving. I always admired the way politicians and public figures kept their temper when being subjected to probing from interviewers who, it seemed to me, were sometimes as much interested in making a name for themselves as for informing the public. Presumably in the current situation the Civil Aviation Authority Chairman could not refuse to be interviewed and, as usual, he did a first class job. He pointed out that it was going to be very difficult to establish the cause of the accident since it was known that there must have been at least one hijacker on the flight deck giving instructions to the captain during the approach and landing. He added that the Secretary of State for Transport was of course responsible for investigating the cause of aircraft accidents in this country and no doubt he would be making a statement.

The interviewer asked if the 798 was really safe and the Chairman patiently explained that questions like that had no meaning since safety in any field, be it aviation, nuclear power stations, food production or indeed in any industry, was a matter of acceptable risks and probabilities. The only certainty in life was that we were all going to die. With regard to the 798, the aircraft had a valid UK certificate of airworthiness but it had actually been certificated by the European Aviation Safety Agency, EASA, based in Cologne. In the unlikely event that safety questions of the 798 needed to be addressed, then these questions would have to be addressed to the EASA since aircraft certification was no longer the direct responsibility of the UK Government and the Civil Aviation Authority; European law made the ratification of the EASA type certificate mandatory.

The newscaster gave up trying to get incautious statements from the CAA Chairman. Because of the fog the TV reporters had been unable to get any eyewitnesses. Luckily, the survivor from the aircraft who had given the interview in the middle of the night must have gone to hospital or to bed and was no longer available. The BBC had managed to find one or two people who lived close to the accident and who had arrived on the spot soon after it occurred. Their stories were horrific and I was not sure that getting these people to tell their experiences on TV actually helped in any way but merely encouraged the ghouls. Luckily, when the security forces had cordoned off the whole area, the media producers and their reporters had been prevented from raking over the wreckage. Of course it was understandable that this crash, as with other crashes in the past, was a subject of great interest but in reality nothing was ever gained by trying to guess instantaneously the cause of an accident before it had been thoroughly investigated. In this case, with the Foreign Secretary on board and with terrorists as well, it was clear that the actual sequence of events that led to the crash was going to be even more complicated than usual to determine, and there seemed little chance of there being a survivor who would know what had happened.

I knew from the experience of listening to the media dealing with other disasters that there would be hastily convened discussions purporting to give an in-depth analysis of the situation. The producers would have been scouring the country for aviation experts and the interviewers would then be bullying them, asking what they thought had happened. Sure enough, an expert appeared saying that this was the first time for many years that terrorists had hijacked an aircraft instead of blowing it up or destroying something on the ground like the Twin Towers in New York. He was not clear why the hijackers had wanted the aircraft to go to the Middle East, but guessed that they wanted to take the released prisoners to some safe country. He gave his opinion that this was a strange thing to want to do, since even militant Muslim countries would not be keen to accept the aircraft with the hijackers and al-Qaeda people on board. However, if the airplane still had passengers they might be forced to let it land though it was most unlikely that they would free the hijackers and the terrorists that they had rescued.

A security expert was then interviewed and he made the point that even if the aircraft hadn't crashed it would never have been allowed to take-off again from Heathrow. Another security consultant speculated on how the hijackers had got on board with weapons, and wondered whether the weapons and bombs had been loaded by a member of the ground staff at Sydney. The interviewer asked whether it was dangerous to use a gun in an aircraft and he was told that the weapons were probably the very special small calibre air pistols now used by aerial hijackers which could kill but, because the bullets were very soft, the range after coming out of the body was very small, thus making it unlikely if used carefully that the bullet would affect the aircraft significantly or go through the aircraft skin unless it was fired at the skin deliberately. It amazed me that that sort of information was allowed to be broadcast for everybody to hear.

One thing was obvious in all the confusion. It was clearly going to be necessary to find out exactly how the hijacking had caused the crash. Of course there might be some other explanation but the coincidence of a freak accident whilst a hijacking was taking place seemed unlikely. Since almost all the leading players, flight crew, hijackers, and witnesses would almost certainly be dead, it was going to be incredibly difficult to establish what had really happened. This accident sounded dreadfully like the one that those of us in the business had hoped would never occur, a super jumbo crashing killing nearly all its passengers. Finding out the how and the why it had happened was going to be more difficult than anyone might imagine. Luckily, the emergency services had planned for the worst case scenario and their work had to be done regardless of the reason for the crash. For them, the cause of the accident was irrelevant.

Because air transportation was so safe, it was only occurrences like hijacking or an unlikely combination of circumstances which resulted in aircraft accidents and it usually required great detective work by the accident investigation experts to discover what had actually gone wrong.

I turned the television off and went into the office, still thinking of the evening before. Mandy, my current girl friend, had produced a splendid meal and we did not hurry. I had planned to leave much earlier but it was after seven by the time I had got away. For the first time I realised that Mandy must be playing a much larger part in my life than I had previously thought, or indeed cared to admit even to myself. We had met a few months earlier travelling across the Atlantic to Seattle when I was visiting both Boeing and the Independant Transport Aircraft Company, while she was going on to Portland to deal with some business on behalf of one of her clients. We were gradually getting to know one another but were being very cautious in developing a relationship as we had both been hurt by affairs in the past. I think we felt there was a possibility that our increasingly frequent meetings could develop into something more enduring. We had not yet consummated our relationship but clearly the time could not be too far away.

Mandy was a hard working partner in a small firm of solicitors in the City but she lived in Bournemouth because she liked sailing in her spare time. She travelled up to London every day by train leaving at 6.30 and was lucky if she got home before 8 o'clock in the evening.

Mandy was not dissimilar physically from Diana, but then in my experience men often chose a second partner rather like their first and I was no exception. She was quite tall, maybe 5 ft. 9 in. but still comfortably below my 5 ft. 11 in. She was very trim, not running to fat and her breasts jutted out provocatively, the way I liked, though my alter ego was always reminding me that lasting relationships are in the mind, not in the body. Mandy's hair was light but not blonde. She kept her hair short and businesslike, as one would expect in a solicitor's office. She wore glasses most of the time since she was long sighted, but I noticed that she always wore contact lenses when we were going out.

It was now 9 o'clock and I switched on the television set on the shelf over my computer. The Prime Minister came on and briefly repeated the details of the accident. He confirmed that the loss of life was indeed the worst in British aviation history, worse even than Lockerbie.

"We are still investigating the exact circumstances of the flight but we know that some people who we have reason to believe were terrorists, attacked and killed two passengers in the upper sleeping compartment of the 798. The Foreign Secretary was on board returning to London and his body has now been identified. The hijackers seem to have entered the flight deck area together with the Foreign Secretary, held the crews captive, and then Captain Hodgson was ordered to land normally at Heathrow. After landing, the aircraft was to be refuelled and the terrorists were demanding that the six named al-Qaeda terrorists we captured two months ago were to be released from prison and taken out to the aircraft. The terrorists then intended that the aircraft would take-off again for somewhere in the Middle East where all the passengers would then be released. As a result of this message which was sent by satellite to Royal World Airlines flight operations, all the security and crash services were either standing by for the aircraft to land or on their way through the fog.

"As you all know the aircraft crashed on the A30 and then caught fire. There may have been an explosion either just before or just after the impact and this is being investigated. I have declared a state of emergency in view of the security aspects of this crash and because the aircraft has crashed on the A30, very close to houses and vital airline operational buildings at Hatton Cross. I hope to be able to relax the emergency very quickly once the fog has cleared and the police and security forces have the situation completely under control.

"As usual the Air Accident Investigation Branch will carry out its normal function to discover the real cause of the accident, helped in this special case by the security investigators. I need the co-operation of all who are involved to help the families who have been so tragically, unexpectedly and suddenly bereaved. There is no need for anyone except the people concerned with the accident to go to the accident site and I have asked the police to use their emergency powers to remove summarily any people near the accident who have gone just to look or to take pictures or videos. I must remind you that many of the victims came from overseas and I have sent a personal message of sympathy to the Australian Prime Minister since I understand there were many Australian nationals on board. I want you all to co-operate with the police and the authorities to get the situation back to normal.

"If anyone has any special information about the accident which might help in the investigation of its cause, would they please call this special number at 10 Downing Street, since I am personally committed to finding out exactly what happened and to ensuring that nothing like it can ever occur again."

The telephone number appeared at the bottom of the screen. I sympathised with the Prime Minister. This accident was going to make his normal heavy workload even heavier. It would be a testing time for him and inevitably he would be judged by how he responded to the crisis.

Of course, it was all very well for the Prime Minister to be determined that a similar accident would never happen again but it would all depend on the accident investigators finding out what had actually occurred. Aircraft always have accidents however hard the manufacturers, certification authorities and regulators try to prevent them and planes were liable to have hijackers and bombs on board, however rigorous the inspection. In all probability this accident would have been caused by interference in some way from the hijackers with the flight crew during the landing in fog. Hopefully, the crash recorders would yield some vital clues.

Aircraft were always at their greatest risk from accidents when they were landing and having hijackers on the flight deck was bound to be a recipe for disaster. Everything had to be right for a safe landing and, however hard the regulating authorities tried, one could never allow completely for the unpredictability of the human pilot in the control loop. In this case, the weather conditions were clearly at the limit for a safe landing so the presence of hijackers would have made the situation that much harder for the crew. Thankfully, judging by the number of people reported killed, the Independant 798 had not been full since it could carry many more people on inter-continental flights, much more in fact than the previous world's largest aircraft, the Airbus A380.

For me every aircraft accident was very important. Since I had stopped flying two years previously and become a consultant to the airlines, I had been analysing all airliner accidents and discussing them on the training courses I was giving. Some of these accidents were very relevant to the way pilots interfaced with the six or more flat panel displays on the modern flight deck. It seemed to me that it was necessary to emphasise the need for the pilots to keep a critical awareness of the aircraft's control systems and not get lulled into a false sense of security by the superb suite of flight deck displays and computers which had taken the place of the specialist navigators, flight engineers and radio operators who used to help the pilots.

After the second World War it took five flight crew to take forty or fifty passengers across the Atlantic; now two pilots could take nearly a thousand people across the world much more efficiently and safely. However, the modern aircraft was incredibly complicated and the pilot's job could only be done by relying on computers, both to fly the aircraft efficiently and to manage the vital systems like the electrics, the hydraulics, the fuel and the air conditioning in normal flight and when the systems malfunctioned.

Most of the time nowadays pilots had very little physically to do actually flying the aircraft, once the computers had been loaded with the flight plan; their job was to watch the aircraft being controlled automatically half way round the world along the planned flight path until it had landed and was rolling along the runway. The pilots' main task en route was getting the clearances that were required to enable the aircraft to follow the optimum flight path. The problem was that there were more and more aircraft flying the routes, not at identical speeds; it was a considerable task chasing the local air traffic centres for new altitudes or for changes in routing

It was very difficult earning a living trying to persuade the airlines that their pilots needed to do more training than the minimum amount required from the aircraft manufacturer and the regulating authorities. I had to convince the airlines that I understood more about the aircraft systems and the way their crews reacted than they did and that spending money with me would improve the total airline performance. Safety was always a difficult thing to sell because achieving it was seen as a cost, spoiling the airlines' profits. To be fair, good airline management realised that it was vital to have a reputation for safety, since there were always plenty of other airlines from which the travellers could choose if there was a feeling that an airline was unsafe. The airlines knew that discounting the ticket prices would never make western world passengers travel in aircraft or with airlines that had an unsafe reputation. The problem for me was always that the flight training staff in the big airlines did not like having outsiders doing their work or telling them what to do. Still, I was managing to get some work from some of the larger flag carriers.

The telephone rang. It was the Chief Pilot of Royal World Airlines, John Chester, on his direct line. Understandably, he did not waste any time in coming to the point. He wanted us to meet as soon as possible, but not in his office. He had to go into London to brief his Chairman and I suggested we met in the Royal Ocean Racing Club for a sandwich. He said that he would probably be able to get there sometime after one o'clock and rang off. Though I was very curious as to the reason why he wanted to talk to me, I decided not to add to his problems by wasting time asking questions.

I had got to know John well some years back when we were both members of the Technical Committee of the Guild of Air Pilots and Air Navigators, GAPAN, and also of the Society of Automotive Engineers S7 Flight Deck Committee. He had had to leave the committees when he was promoted within the airline but we kept in touch and I think it was largely because of him that his training staff gave me some work, explaining the problem of trying to get the right relationship between the pilot and the computers which controlled the aircraft. We had both seen this very important human factor problem coming and had both been nervous of very clever technical pilots who encouraged the aircraft designers to make too many fancy alternatives available to the airline pilots. John and I belonged to the 'keep it simple' school of thought.

I tried to finish the proposal I was writing for American Airlines to provide training in Dallas for their senior training personnel but my mind kept returning to the accident and my conversation with John Chester. I could not stop trying to work out what had happened to cause the disaster. I switched on the television set again. The newscaster was interviewing the Chief Constable who was explaining about the Emergency Accident Operations Room and the co-ordination required to deal with the fire brigades, the traffic handling, the army, the security people, the AAIB investigators, and the ambulances which were getting survivors to the hospitals as well as the dead to the mortuaries, all in the fog.

The interview was followed by a talk with the Chief Airport Fire Officer. He gave a very low key understated description of the devastation and carnage at the scene of the accident which somehow, because of its very restraint, was the more disturbing. The TV cameras had at last managed to get on to the airfield's southern perimeter road so that it was just possible to see the scene of the accident through the fog over the top of some buildings. The pictures were unbelievable. Wreckage of parts of aircraft could be seen everywhere, one of the engines was standing on end and there were still a lot of fire engines and ambulances on the scene. The cameras zoomed in to show a body without a cover being carried away to the back of a nearby ambulance. It was a terrible sight and must have been immeasurably worse for those people actually there and for the anxious relatives and friends watching and waiting at home. I switched the set off and almost immediately the telephone rang again. Mandy had reached the office and, despite all her appointments, had found time to call to hear my reactions.

"I've made it but quite a few haven't. Some managed to get in from the south west by taking wide detours. I think the fog is clearing slightly and it isn't freezing any more."

She sounded breathless. I was not too surprised about the number of people who had managed to get into work despite the problems. Life is about survival and people are always very resourceful in times of difficulty. Because the accident had taken place the previous evening a lot of drivers had had time to make contingency plans.

"However," she carried on, "I expect the time-table in the courts will be affected. Many of the judges will not have been able to make it unless they live in town." She paused. "But Peter, what do you think happened?"

I could think of nothing useful to say. I knew nothing and hated speculating.

"It's too early to say yet. Almost anything might have happened with hijackers on board. They could have shot the pilot, they might have exploded a bomb, the pilots could have had their attention diverted and made a mistake. The problem is that the accident will almost certainly be due to the hijackers in some way if not completely, but it may not be straightforward, which is going to make finding the exact cause very difficult. Aircraft are so safe that accidents inevitably occur only when there is a most unlikely combination of circumstances. I may know a bit more later on as John Chester phoned and we are meeting at the RORC."

She latched on to that straightaway.

"Be careful when you talk to John. Don't offer advice unless he is going to be your client. If he called you then there must be something worrying him which he knows and you don't. Listen and learn all you can. Don't volunteer."

"I'll do my best."

As usual she was giving good advice, but she was not so emotionally involved as I was. She was in a competitive business with her own clients but she had the enormous advantage of the support of her partnership. I was a one-man band, struggling to make ends meet and she was concerned that I was not commercial enough. She felt that in my eagerness to help to find the reasons for the accident I would offer gratuitous advice and might spend a lot of time helping John and others without any reward. She knew, faced with the need to find out what had gone wrong, that I would find it very difficult not to enter into long discussions to solve the problem and I appreciated her concern. Lawyers were trained to be commercial however harrowing the circumstances, but Mandy knew I found this a difficult concept.

"I'll call you later when I get out of court though I expect in the circumstances they will defer the hearing."

I finished my proposal to American, made an airmail package for the post office and then went into the kitchen. Dora was probably on the wrong side of fifty and had been married twice. She had had two children from her first husband, who had died from a heart attack, and they were now grown up and both working somewhere in London. Fred, her second husband, had left home fairly soon after they got married but not before helping to conceive Jenny. Dora was having to bring up Jenny on her own and was not able to get Fred to send her money regularly. She looked after her figure and had not let her appearance run to seed though things were clearly pretty difficult for her. She worked long hours as a domestic help to make ends meet. Inevitably, she immediately started asking me questions about the crash but I avoided saying anything, since I knew that anything I did say would be noted and quoted at the Fox and Hounds later in the day while Jenny was doing her homework. I pleaded ignorance.

It was quarter to eleven by now but I had a little time in hand so I went back into my office, switching the TV on again while looking for some technical papers I had on the 798. The announcer was giving an update on the crash. One crash recorder with all the flight information had been found but the second one with flight deck voice recordings was still missing. RWA were bringing Australian relatives of the killed and injured to London as quickly as possible. Independant had managed to get some specialist crash investigation engineers on the regular RWA flight out of Seattle the previous night, the moment they had heard about the accident. They had also chartered a special flight to bring more engineers to London and the team was headed by William Parnell, President of the Independant Transport Aircraft Company.

Like all aircraft companies, Independant had always responded immediately to the few incidents that had occurred to their aircraft. This particular accident would be especially important for them, even though it was bound to be due in some way to the hijacking. The aircraft type was comparatively new and did not have the millions of flying hours behind it like Boeing airplanes, the 737s, the 757s, the 767s, the 747s, the 777s and the 787s. RWA was one of Independant's biggest customers and only had a few Boeing and Airbus aircraft. Airbus were trying very hard to persuade RWA to support Europe and buy their latest stretched A380 from Toulouse. Independant, and of course Boeing, were watching the situation closely and trying to match the Airbus salesmen. The cause of the accident had to be found straightaway to prevent Airbus or Boeing taking advantage of Royal World Airline's bad luck. No wonder Parnell was coming over to talk to the Chairman and Managing Director of the airline.

I turned the TV off and found the papers which Independant had given me when I was writing my article on the 798. There was a magnificent data dump of material weighing about 10 lb. which, splendid though it was, unfortunately made it very difficult to find anything. Realising the problem, Independant had thoughtfully also provided me with a summary book. The 798 was fairly conventional in design though using a lot of carbon fibre in the structure. The only new development on the flying side was that the electrical cables connecting the flight control computers to the control surfaces had been replaced with fibre optic cables, but this technology was now well established on military aircraft. The design and inter-linking of the computers, called the system architecture, made sure that no conceivable electrical failure would result in loss of control. I could see nothing unusual in the 798 which might give cause for any concern. I devoutly hoped that the accident had been due to the hijacking and it clearly was the most likely cause. I guessed that that would be the prayer of the whole of the aerospace and airline industry.

I put the papers in my brief case with a writing pad and went up to the bedroom to change into a standard grey suit, white shirt, blue tie and black shoes. Formality was essential to enable an efficient interchange of information to take place without getting side-tracked into other matters. Soft shoes, slacks and a polo necked pullover might keep the wearer warm and comfortable but I always felt that such informal dress did not create the right atmosphere for important exchanges of information. Everybody had to have a uniform to inspire confidence and to enable work to be done as quickly as possible. It seemed to me that offices that had relaxed the rules, certainly when dealing with other organisations, regretted it later.

The phone rang again.

"Peter, it's Carol Trentham. Remember?" I remembered alright. She came straight to the point. She hadn't changed in that at least during the years since we had last met.

"I'm worried stiff. Richard hasn't called me. Can you find out if he was on the plane?"

For a moment I was speechless.

"Peter, are you there?"

"Yes, Carol. I can hear you. Tell me what has Richard been doing?" I first knew Richard Trentham when we were both junior first officers on Britannia Airways. Later he had had the opportunity to join Cathay Pacific based in London flying the Airbus A330 and he had leapt at the chance. We had not seen each other for some years though he was also a member of GAPAN.

"He's been flying for ten days operating between Hong Kong and Sydney and he told me he was hoping to find a way of dead heading back to London for some leave. He should have left yesterday. I'm so frightened, Peter. I fear the worst. I'm sure he's dead. I took the children to school in Amersham this morning without saying anything. What am I to do?"

"Have you called Cathay in London?"

"Yes I did. I called flight operations the moment I heard the news at seven this morning. They're trying to find out but they haven't called me back. Can you call Royal World Airlines to find out for me? I must know."

I hesitated again trying to make up my mind what to do for the best. I had known Carol long before I met Richard.

"Look, by chance I am just going in to London to meet John Chester, he's the chief pilot of Royal World Airlines. I'll have a word with him and call you from London. Will you be at home?"

"Yes. I'll be here until about three when I have to collect the kids. Forgive me for calling you but I know I can rely on you to help." She gave me her number and rang off.

I felt appalled. The accident was bad enough but suddenly to find I was deeply involved was devastating. I had not seen Carol for some time but some relationships can never be forgotten. I knew in my heart of hearts that Richard was dead, or seriously injured at the very least. He would have called Carol the moment he had heard about the accident if he had still been in Sydney. What a terrible mess.

I had met Carol in my first year at Cambridge. We were both at Trinity but she was reading oriental languages while I was doing electronic engineering. I noticed her during dinners and started chatting her up. She was a very attractive redhead and I was smitten but it was clear to me that I was not her only admirer and she, very understandably, played the field. However, I discovered that she liked listening to classical music. I took her to several concerts and we had supper afterwards. Nothing developed, probably because we both shared rooms in college with other students.

She agreed to be my partner at the May Ball in June at the end of the academic year. About a week before the dance we were talking and she asked me what time the Ball finished. I said dawn. She looked me in the eye and said she would like to visit the new motel at Newmarket and why didn't we stay there for the night of the ball. Carol was my first real encounter with a girl. I had never made love before though I suspected she had. I could barely contain myself. We arrived at the hotel early. She had chosen well. The staff did not even look at the guests checking in.

We kissed slowly at first and then more seriously. I felt her hands undoing my belt, undoing my trousers and stroking me. She showed me how to excite her. We made love as we were getting undressed to change for the Ball, then used the shower together. It became touch and go whether we would get to the Ball but somehow we did. We danced all night in a dream and got back to the motel at 4 o'clock. We took all our clothes off and went to bed exhausted. The chamber maid knocked on the door at 10.30. I rang down and arranged a late check out. We took full advantage of the two hours extension and arrived back at College at three feeling rather tired. It occurred to me how marvellous it would be to be able to perform now as I did then!

In fact our relationship did not continue for much longer as I was committed to going sailing all summer and, when we returned in the Autumn, I stupidly agreed to do some rowing for the college second eight which cramped my spare time. Carol was not too pleased and disappeared in a huff. I did not mind too much as I was having to work quite hard and there were other girls at college who were not so time consuming, even if they were not quite as exciting.

CHAPTER 3

The Chief Pilot

I looked at my watch. I was going to miss my train unless I got a move on. It was no use taking the car as I might not be able to find somewhere to park. I collected my brief case, put on my overcoat and gloves, said good bye to Dora and almost ran to the station. The train was on time in spite of the fog and I only just caught it. It was not full and I was able to do some more thinking about the 798 as the train travelled to Waterloo. I caught the Bakerloo line to Piccadilly Circus and then walked along Piccadilly in the grey mist until I reached Green Park. Walking was one of my favourite activities in order to keep reasonably fit and I enjoyed looking at the shops and the people. The park had the feel and smell of winter with the dead leaves lying on the ground as I went down the tarmac walk and then turned into the tunnel which led to the top end of St. James Place and the RORC. I entered the key code, pushed the door open and went upstairs.

John Chester was not due for another twenty minutes and he could well be late. I ordered a tomato juice, picked up the Financial Times and sat down in the corner. The Club was not very full and nowadays I did not know many people there. I had joined in my youth when I was at Cambridge reading electrical engineering and spending all my spare time racing in the Channel. When I started flying for a living and got married, there did not seem time for racing and, anyway, Diana had never been very keen on sailing though we had sailed over to France once or twice. In fact, it was because I was not well known in the club that I thought it was a good place to meet up with John. I had avoided suggesting the Royal Air Force Club, which would inevitably be full of mutual acquaintances who would have tried cross questioning John the moment they saw him.

Looking at the FT, I saw that Jim Akers had written a very good article about the accident and all the implications, perhaps not altogether surprising after our talk at midnight. Still, how it was possible to put together articles of such quality at such short notice always baffled me since I never wrote anything unless I had researched it very carefully. In his article Jim had suggested that the chances were that, because air transportation was so safe, the accident was almost certainly due to the hijacking.

Jim also touched on the legal issues. If the cause was due to some form of hijacking then the claimants might find it very difficult to get money from the airline, though they would try and prove negligence when the passengers were being loaded and, therefore, name the Sydney airport authorities as co-defendants in the case. If the cause was not due to hijacking, then of course it was the airline and/or the aircraft manufacturer which would be sued in the event of an accident and, conceivably, the defendants could include the certificating authorities. However, one of the points made in this article amplified the point made in the interview I had watched with the Chairman of the Civil Aviation Authority; because the 798 was certificated by the European Aviation Safety Agency, passengers or their dependants could no longer make a case against their own Governments for failing to certificate an aircraft properly but would have to try to take legal action against either the EASA or against the European Commission itself, which inevitably would be fraught with difficulties. Whether the cause of the accident was proved to be due to some form of terrorism or not, it looked like a legal minefield with rich pickings for the lawyers whatever happened.

Someone switched the television set on in the bar in time for the news headlines. The recorder with the flight deck voice recordings still had not been found. The police were diverting all the traffic down the Causeway and along the A316 to the Clockhouse Lane roundabout. It was going to take a long, long time to collect all the wreckage from the A30 and the surrounding area. The death toll had risen to 383; it was very high in spite of the relatively slow speed of the aircraft on the approach because of the impact with the cargo shed. It was still not known if there had been an explosion. There had been 530 passengers and crew on the aircraft, mostly UK nationals but, as the Prime Minister had indicated, there were quite a lot of Australians. There was also some doubt on exactly how many people had been killed on the ground by the aircraft but it looked like somewhere between thirty and forty. The whole thing seemed unbelievable since aircraft travel was now so incredibly safe but, when an accident did happen to a large, long range aircraft, a lot of people were likely to be killed. It was indeed the nightmare accident that we had all feared.

John arrived looking his normal distinguished self. Immaculately dressed, no-one would have guessed he had been up most of the night. How he managed it I didn't know. John was just over 6ft with very dark wavy hair which somehow had escaped any dilution with grey, notwithstanding he was on the wrong side of fifty. It occurred to me that he must be using some hair colouriser, but men I noticed never discussed these matters. I had decided the best thing to do was to ignore the suggestion of a sandwich and to take him straight into the dining room where I had booked a table at the far end, out of the way. John, not surprisingly, looked very serious and I decided to let him start the ball rolling. He did not want a drink and we both ordered soup and the grilled plaice. There was a couple fairly close to us, luckily seemingly more

41

interested in themselves than in anything else. There was also a crew of four near the door way out of earshot.

"The exact cause is a complete mystery, Peter, but it's almost certainly due to the hijacking by terrorists." he started. "However, I wanted to talk to you because I am worried that the accident might be due to the pilots having done the wrong thing for some reason, maybe connected with the hijacking or maybe not. You're giving lectures to our training courses so you're probably as knowledgeable as anybody on the flight deck/crew interface. Harry Hodgson was in charge and he was one of our most experienced Captains."

I gulped. No wonder I thought I recognised the voice. We both knew Harry socially as well as professionally since, as I had guessed, he too was a member of GAPAN. He paused as the waiter, a new one I did not recognise, brought the soup over. John took a roll and buttered it but he did not really notice what he was doing. He was reviewing the whole situation and describing it to me with great precision. I listened carefully but did not comment.

"Nothing unusual had happened on the early part of the flight according to our flight operation department's log except that the Captain's Navigation Display failed. There had been the normal position reports from the crew, using the INMARSAT communication satellites, which backed up the automatic satellite position reports that the air traffic centre at Swanwick had sent to us as they got them. Because we took your advice Peter on making the crew log on when they take over on the flight deck we know from the ACARS messages that Harry flew the aircraft for the first six hours and then presumably he went to one of the two pilot's sleeping cabins in the flight deck area and in front of the VIP area. His first officer, Charles Tumbrill, left the flight deck shortly afterwards and went into the other cabin. The other crew, Dick Tremlett and Frank Mercer, took over and flew across Asia. Later Harry and Charles went back on the flight deck for the rest of the flight.

"By the way, the aircraft had the latest type of recorder, so there should be a record of the last four hours of the flight when they find it instead of the earlier two hours of recording on the older cockpit voice recorders.

"The weather en-route was reported to be good though they had been flying into a stronger headwind than had been forecast. They did not have as much fuel as expected when they flew over Warsaw but our operations department released them to go on to Frankfurt. The weather in London was Category IIIC, indeterminate cloud base, freezing fog and a visibility of 20 metres. About three hours before landing Harry reported that they had been hijacked.

"Apparently he was being told to land at Heathrow as planned and then the aircraft was to be refuelled immediately so that they could fly on to somewhere in the Middle East. Meanwhile the Government were to collect the six al-Qaeda prisoners they had captured recently and take them to the aircraft. We did not know where the aircraft was supposed to be going and so we calculated the fuel to Karachi. Once the prisoners were on board the aircraft, it was to depart straightaway. If the authorities tried to prevent the aircraft taking off then the terrorists said that it would be blown up on the ground. About the same time as Harry was talking to our operations, Eurocontrol advised London Approach that the aircraft was transmitting the emergency hijack code.

"Our operations then rechecked the fuel on board at Frankfurt and cleared the aircraft all the way to London. They should have had about 70 minutes fuel left as they started their final approach on 27L, just within limits for diversion to Manchester where the weather was good."

The waiter took our soup dishes away. I decided to keep my questions back so as not to disturb the flow.

"Charles made a routine report to Operations and then switched back to talk to Air Traffic. About fifteen minutes before landing Harry said that he was being told to check that refuelling was available, that the prisoners were at the airport and that a flight plan was being prepared for Karachi. I had arrived on the scene by then and I told our dispatcher to confirm that all was ready, though Air Traffic would be able to advise on the whereabouts of the prisoners to be uploaded. There was no point in telling him what was really planned and in any event we didn't really know in detail, since the police were giving instructions to the British Airport Authorities on where the aircraft was to be parked. Harry said that he would call after landing and the next thing our Operations knew was a report from Air Traffic that there had been an accident and Operations could get no reply from the aircraft, Alfa Juliet by the way."

I knew from the time when I did some lectures to the first RWA crews that the Royal World Airlines ten 798s had been registered G-RWAE to G-RWAN so that G-RWAJ, Alfa Juliet as it was colloquially called using the phonetic alphabet, was not particularly new. Clearly, there was going to have to be a lot of investigative work done correlating the communications between Air Traffic and the aircraft and also between Royal World Airlines flight operations department and the aircraft.

"John, after Harry had said that they were going to land at Heathrow, were there any other communications about the hijacking?"

"No, none at all. From that point onwards during the approach the flight seemed to be routine. Harry presumably was concentrating on the landing, though it must have been incredibly difficult with hijackers there."

"Do we have any idea at all if anything unusual happened during the approach."

"Not really, Peter. The aircraft seems to have kept to the runway centre line but something must have happened to make it go below the glide slope. Our problem now is that all the communication tapes have been impounded by the AAIB and it is going to take some days before the whole flight path can be ascertained. But that's not going to tell us what went on inside the aircraft. Let's hope they find the cockpit voice recorder soon and that it is not damaged. We have to find out what happened."

"What sort of approach was he doing?"

"We don't know for sure, Peter, and Air Traffic won't talk to us but the Microwave Landing System, MLS, on 27L was out of service for some reason. He would have had to select the Galileo Satellite System for landing, not really desirable in fog, though it is certificated and seems to work well."

He paused expectantly, clearly waiting for me to ask some more questions. Mandy's advice was ringing in my ears and I decided not to probe too deeply. I decided not to tell John about the Tower controller querying the aircraft's height. It would soon be a matter of public record and meantime I wanted to think about the significance of the Tower's transmissions.

"John, you don't need me to tell you that the problem here is going to be very different from most accidents just because of the hijacking. Normally, if nothing obvious is found wrong then the simple thing is for everyone to blame the pilots but this time it could be the hijackers. Obviously pilots can make mistakes because they are careless or because they are misled by the information presented on the flight deck or, in this case perhaps, because they are being distracted from what they are doing. This investigation is going to be very difficult unless there is some stroke of luck to indicate the cause or it can be proved to be due to the hijackers. It could be a lawyer's dream."

"You're right of course," John said. He was hesitating and I wondered if he was hiding something from me. Since the cause must surely be due to the terrorist hijackers, why on earth had John called me to meet him? He must know something he hadn't told me. I felt sure that he had had second thoughts about what he was going to tell me. Perhaps his boss Jack Chiltern, Royal World Airlines Managing Director, had warned him not to discuss anything outside the airline. Perhaps there was a security angle to which I was not privy. The waiter brought our grilled plaice and the conversation stopped as we ate our meal.

"When did you eat last?" I decide to change the subject for a moment and noticed that John had started to eat as if he was very hungry.

"I had a sandwich at about midnight last night. We were just about to have a late dinner when the phone rang telling me about the hijack. Somehow I haven't had much time for anything else except coffee. And an occasional biscuit" He smiled, glad to get away for the moment from the worries that surrounded him. "I got three or four hours sleep in the office but the phone never stopped ringing. I had to speak to Marcia, Harry's wife, told her that there was still hope, but not much. She took it very bravely but it seems so hard." He swallowed for a moment and managed to compose himself again.

"Also I had to speak to the other families, all very difficult. The media have been terrible and we had to take our phones off the hook. The direct line to Operations came into its own. Mind you the MD wasn't too pleased when he wanted to talk to me and couldn't get through. I had to give him my mobile number." He grinned.

"The police at Hounslow with their accident centre are acting as the central reporting point and relaying the information on to us. We have a copy of the passenger/crew manifest which we are trying to keep up to date."

"Do you know which passengers were the hijackers?"

"No. We have no idea but the fact that they wanted to go somewhere in the Middle East suggests they were Muslim terrorists, almost certainly al-Qaeda. We believe that some of the hijackers were seated on the upper deck near the front, Upper Class. I've no idea if they were all killed but the security people will sort that out. Goodness knows how they got the weapons on board."

"You must have had a job getting here."

"Well yes. Luckily, my office on the North side of the airport is some way from the crash and so I managed to get out using the northern perimeter road, get home, see Jane, shower and change before coming into Town to see Jack. I hope I will be able to get back to the Office but it is going to be quite difficult. My driver is an expert on all the side roads so I suppose we will make it. How he got me into work this morning I don't know. The A4 and M4 were completely blocked with traffic trying to get into London."

He came back to the present.

"Peter, I'm very worried about this whole thing, not just because of the accident but because I was one of the strongest advocates for the aircraft. If the accident is not due to the hijackers then I might be in some difficulty. You see, in order to keep the total package price to a minimum and the Independant bid competitive, I persuaded the Board that we should have almost the identical technical specification for the aircraft as United and American Airlines and this was not too popular. The Chairman seemed to want to be the launch customer for the latest larger version of the Airbus A380 on the grounds that we ought to be good Europeans and clearly the Department of Industry felt that this would be the correct thing to do. The MD, as always, wanted an easy life and would have gone along with the Chairman.

"I argued that all my pilots were used to the Independant flight decks and that the Airbus flight decks might be safe enough but were not as safe as the Independant aircraft. I really believe that Peter, but think how it would look if this was pilot error due to the Independant design philosophy. Francis supported me because the whole of the company's engineering maintenance system was based on the Independant concept. Changing to Airbus would have been very expensive and would have been confusing for the engineers. The operating economics of the two aircraft were very similar, so Jack and the Chairman couldn't very well overrule us. It was a very close run thing because Airbus were criticising the electronic architecture on the aircraft. At the final meeting a couple of the non-execs. started pushing the Airbus."

John stopped, looking very concerned and worried with what he had just told me.

"Well John, the hijacking is bound to have had an influence on the crew when they were making the approach. I think you're worrying unnecessarily."

I didn't say anything more. Francis Thomas had been the RWA engineering director at the time the 798 decision was taken but he had retired two years ago. I knew that Rex Williams, John's deputy, would love to take over from John and the fact that Margaret, his wife, was Jack Chiltern's daughter would probably not spoil his chances. I suspected that Airbus had been trying to persuade Rex as hard as they could. Certainly, he and his wife were always going to France on holiday and visiting Toulouse!

I could just visualise the Royal World Airlines Board meeting when the agenda item for the 798 decision had come up for discussion. The Board would have already had all the supporting papers but there would have been a presentation by the finance director explaining the financial implications of purchasing a new aircraft. There would have been a summary paper highlighting the pros and cons of the larger A380 and the Independant 798 and then the non-executive directors would probably have started probing. John and Francis would have explained why they favoured the 798. It was anyone's guess how hard Airbus had been influencing the various Board members but from what John had said it was pretty clear that at least some of the non-executives had been talking to them. Stories were legion on the way aircraft decisions were made by airlines all round the World.

In some countries buyer's commission was an accepted way to proceed since the decision makers expected to be rewarded for their choice. In the Western World such payments were frowned upon as bribes, but payments are not always made with money and it is unlikely that some form of reward had not been made for aircraft decisions in the past, both in the USA and the UK. The problem was that the prize for winning was so great, the cost of each aircraft so high and the value of the reward needed to sway the decision maker's choice was relatively so very small. Of course with a large Board no single person ever made the decision, but that did not prevent the aircraft manufacturers from trying to influence the situation.

John took his telephone out of his pocket and switched it on to get the messages. He listened for a few minutes as the waiter took our plates away. He made one or two notes and then he dialled a number. "Jill, how's the office?"

Jill Stanton at the other end, a devoted secretary of a certain age, started to give him a run down. "OK. I will be about an hour if the traffic permits." He turned his phone off.

"I just have time for a very quick coffee," he decided. We went into the bar and helped ourselves. There were a couple of seats free by the library. "Thanks for listening to me, Peter. I may have some work for you depending on how things are looking. We will just have to wait and see how things develop.

"By the way, you should know that we have just heard that one of the survivors miraculously was the off duty first officer, Frank Mercer. He's unconscious but let's hope he gets better and will be able to help."

I grabbed my moment. "Look John. I don't think you knew Richard Trentham. He's in the Guild and he works for Cathay. We were pilots together on Britannia. His wife has been on the phone to me. Richard was due home to-day dead heading from Sydney and he hasn't called. How can I find out if he was on the plane?"

He looked really upset and passed me his card.

"Call my secretary, Jill Stanton. This is my direct line. She'll know what to do. I'm so sorry"

John collected his brief case and went downstairs to where his car was waiting. I watched the Jaguar drive down past the Stafford and turn left towards St. James. The problem for John, now that he was so senior in the organisation, was that he was under pressures which most of the workers didn't appreciate. I felt a bit mean adding to his burden by mentioning Richard. The pay at the top may be good but the hours are long and the responsibilities are enormous. John was good at delegating as much as he could, but he knew that in the end he was responsible. Of course some managers seemed to manage by delegating everything and

47

never being responsible for anything. I always felt his boss, Jack Chiltern, came into that category, as he was very adroit at making sure that the buck never stopped with him. In my experience, many chairmen and managing directors of large public companies, however competent they were, had qualities in order to get to the top which did not endear them to their fellow men.

After John left I helped myself to another coffee. I wasn't sure whether to ring Carol first or John's secretary. I decided I would try John's secretary and called her from my mobile when I got downstairs in the lobby. Jill told me she would look at her copy of the passenger manifest. I gave her Richard's name. She came straight back telling me that he had been on board the aircraft as supernumerary crew but that his body had not been found; he might be in one of the hospitals. She added that the bodies of Harry Hodgson, Charles Tumbrill and the other 798 Captain on the aircraft had been found. She sounded desolated.

I called Carol. The phone rang and rang but there was no answer. I tried Mandy.

"Where are you?" she said "I've been calling you and they told me in the RORC that you had left."

"I'm still in the RORC, just about to go home."

"How did you get on with John? Did he ask your advice?"

I didn't feel like giving her a run down on the conversation just then. I needed to explain all the many nuances.

"Why don't you come round to my place to-night? It will save you a long journey and I need to talk. Have you got any spare clothes with you?"

"Oh yes. I always keep some in the office. OK. I'll be round about 6.30 to 7." She paused and then carried on. "I'm looking forward to seeing you." The phone went dead.

I collected my briefcase and caught a cab to Waterloo. The fog which had been thinning as I went into lunch had lifted into a mist and the visibility was about 800 yards. I felt a sense of urgency to get home and do some work but could not define what was driving me on. I was back by 3.30. Dora had left and the place looked spotless. I called Carol. A strange female voice answered. I gave her my name.

"Oh thank goodness you called. I'm Susan, a friend of Carol's. She has rushed off to Ealing General Hospital. Richard was on the plane and is very seriously injured. I've collected the children but I don't know what to do as we are all going away on a skiing holiday to-morrow morning."

I seemed to remember that Carol's children were about ten and eight years old.

"Susan, Carol is bound to call you. Doesn't she have any other friends locally? Try and get something organised for to-night and get them to school to-morrow." I gave her my number to call in an emergency.

The news was still full of the accident. The accident investigation authorities needed to collect every piece of wreckage and mark carefully where it had been found so that the flight trajectory of the aircraft could be worked out. It was going to take a long time since even the smallest piece of wreckage and electronics could be very important. They were getting a bit worried because the cockpit voice recorder had still not appeared. There was no way that the A30 would be open for a day or so, even though troops had been called in to help collect the wreckage. It was mentioned that the AAIB would be using a special hangar at Farnborough which used to belong to the Defence Establishment Research Agency for assembling the wreckage.

Jill Stanton rang to give me the news I already knew. Richard was very ill at Ealing. I asked her how he was but she did not know. I rang the hospital. It took ages to get through. The lines must have been jammed with calls. At first they would not tell me Richard's condition but when I explained the situation briefly the girl on the phone told me that Mr Trentham was critically ill. I rang off; there was nothing more I could do but pray, something I did not normally do.

The phone rang.

"Peter." It was Carol sounding desperate. "He's alive but there's not much hope. I'm going to stay here over night. I've spoken to Susan who has agreed to look after the kids this evening and her eighteen year old daughter is going to sleep in the house to-night. They're off in the morning so I don't know what I am going to do. My mother lives in Edinburgh and is not very fit and Richard's parents are both dead. I will have to get back by the end of school to-morrow whatever happens."

"Carol, call me the moment you have any news. Phone me to-morrow morning in any case and let me know how you are getting on." She rang off.

I did not know what I should do to help. I could bring her kids over here for a day or so but I had had no experience of children and anyway they really ought to be with their friends. Surely she must have other friends who could look after them. Apart from our early infatuation, we had not kept in touch. I was shattered when Richard had first introduced me to his new wife in the car park at Luton Airport but instinctively neither of us said anything at the time. Richard had met Carol when she was a management trainee with Britannia but she left when she had her first child. Carol and I had met several times while we were at Britannia but after Richard left we did not see each other again. I decided that Carol would have to sort it out to-morrow, by herself. She should get her mother down. I did not want to get involved again.

49

Blind Landing

It occurred to me that I had not checked the mail. It was mostly bills and computer companies selling hardware and software. There was an invitation to take part in a symposium on the modern airplane flight deck at the Royal Aeronautical Society, 4 Hamilton Place, which pleased me. It was six months off but it would need a lot of work.

On a shelf in the study I found my Jeppeson radio navigation approach charts. I took out the MLS and Galileo approach plates for 27L at Heathrow and marked where the 798 crashed on the chart; it was actually right on the centre line for the runway but about 500 yards short of the correct touch down point. The instruments on the flight deck would have shown that the aircraft was on the runway centre line all the way down until it crashed. However, the instruments should also have shown that the aircraft was about 150 ft. below the correct glide slope. The weather of course was very poor but that should not have mattered. What really had happened? Surely whatever went wrong must have been due to the hijackers? It was difficult to think of any other explanation.

Though I could not stop thinking about the crash it was really not my business, even though John Chester had drawn me into the action. He was only keeping me on line as an insurance policy, possibly using me as a sounding board. Mandy had told me just to listen, but she did not know about Richard, or Carol for that matter. I realised that I needed to be careful how I introduced Carol into the conversation with Mandy. Least said soonest mended had always been one of my maxims but I was the world's worst dissembler.

CHAPTER 4

Mike Mansell

I must have dozed off in the sitting room. The TV was on, the local London news just finishing and there was a banging on the door. I recognised the imperious knocks. Mandy had arrived.

"You made good time. What train did you catch?"

"I didn't work overtime to-night, everything was so disorganised because of the crash. Clients didn't turn up or they wanted to leave early so, what's sauce for the geese is sauce for the gander or something like that. Anyway," she suddenly turned serious "I wanted to see you and hear how you're getting on."

"What was the weather like? Has it cleared any more?"

"The fog's now quite patchy but the *Evening Standard* says it will be gone completely by the morning."

I helped her off with her jacket and once again saw two of the reasons why I found her so attractive. She had a magnificent figure and knew it. She stretched knowing that I would immediately pull her towards me. I could feel myself pressing against her. Suddenly she broke away.

"Let's be sensible. We have a lot to talk about. What time did you book the table for?"

She was right of course, about not rushing anything, as she was right about a lot of things, but from where I was standing it seemed a pity. On the other hand there was something to look forward to.

"Eight o'clock at Simon's. I ordered oysters, lobster and shrimps in that order!"

She grinned, took her bag upstairs to change and shouted down as she climbed up the stairs "To-day's only Tuesday and I have to work to-morrow. You'd better check that they've got salad and sole meuniere." She came back and looked down at me. "You are not accompanying me looking like that, I hope." She turned and went into the spare room and probably always would in this house, whatever our future relationship might be. I should have moved when it became obvious that Diana wasn't coming back but it hadn't mattered until Mandy came along.

Upstairs, I concluded that a shower might be a good thing in the circumstances, bearing in mind I could hear Mandy using the shower in the spare room. A slightly less formal suit than the one I had been wearing in London seemed also the order of the evening. After a quick shave I went downstairs to wait but not for long. Mandy would win first prize for a quick change act against all comers. Diana had always seemed to take an eternity to get ready. Perhaps Mandy's legal training and her ability to switch quickly from one subject to another was relevant. Anyway, whatever the cause the result was always very agreeable.

She entered the sitting room radiating a smell of some exotic French perfume. I could never tell which one was which since they all had the same effect on me. She was wearing a fawn cashmere dress, buttoned all the way down the front which showed her figure off to perfection. I hoped her clients were not affected the way I was. Of course they had to endure the severe spectacles which reassured me slightly. To-night however the spectacles were nowhere to be seen. Besides her other attributes, Mandy just had to hold the world record for inserting contact lenses.

"Where's my Kir?" she announced quickly as I approached her, almost as a defence mechanism. "It's the minimum reward for such a quick change."

"Good idea." I went into the dining room to get the drinks from the dresser and on my return she was watching the Channel 4 news. The accident seemed to be the only subject. Everything else in the world seemed to have been put on hold. A new Foreign Secretary had been appointed. The missing recorder had still not been found. The A30 might be opened on Thursday morning. Sadly, two more survivors had died.

There was one new piece of information from Sydney. A dead body, murdered by a bullet in the head, had been found in the Hyatt Regency car park. It was suspected that the body might be associated with the hijacking as the bullet was a special soft type found in the latest pistols that hijackers used. Significantly, there were no papers on the body to aid identification.

The news reader showed an interview that had taken place earlier with William Parnell. He had started by sympathising with all the relatives and people affected by the accident. As befitted the President of the Independant Transport Aircraft Company his words somehow carried the conviction of someone who really cared, unlike a lot of politicians.

"At this stage clearly no-one knows for sure whether the cause of the aircraft loss was due to the hijacking. However, I can assure you all that my company will do everything in its power to help in discovering the true reason for this terrible accident and to ensure, as far as we can, that nothing like it ever occurs again."

The interviewer tried to get Parnell to speculate on the cause of the accident but he would have none of it.

"Your AAIB is probably the best of its kind in the world and we must all help them to find out what happened. To try to second guess the cause would be very stupid. We must be certain that we find the right answer. Neither you the media, the travelling public, the world's airlines nor we, part of the world's airline manufacturing industry will be helped by rushing into the wrong answer."

The interviewer attempted to get Parnell to agree that if Independant was to blame then they would meet all the claims.

"No useful purpose will be served by discussing the issues you are trying to raise. Claims are a matter for the courts, not for discussion on the television."

The interviewer kept on trying to speculate but was no match for Parnell who had been trained in a hard school. Mandy switched the set off.

"If we get hooked on these interviews we will never get out."

"Did you notice the smooth way Parnell tried to include Airbus and Boeing in the equation, suggesting that the cause may read across to all aircraft as well as to Independant."

"Tell me about it. These guys really earn their money. They don't run monopoly utilities. They know what true competition means. And look at the way he side stepped the issue of whether Independant would pay the claims. Which reminds me. We have a lot to talk about. Come on, Peter. Let's get the show on the road."

I had chosen Simon's because we would not need a car and could drink without worrying about whether we were over the limit. The downside was that we had to leave early to allow for a fifteen minute walk. We put on our coats, I set the alarm and locked the door.

As we walked along the street Mandy started to chat.

"I don't know whether it is significant for our relationship but our firm has been retained by General Electric."

"I shouldn't think so. They supply the engines of course, but it is most unlikely that the accident was due to the engines. Hijacking must be the obvious reason. If it was due to the engines then there would have been conversations between the crew and air traffic and the media would already know all about it. In my opinion, this accident is almost certainly going to be due to some effect of the hijacking."

"You should know. I hope you're right because somehow I feel you are going to get drawn into this thing. I don't want there to be a conflict of interest. It seems to me that my firm will have to be at the inquiry for a start and who knows what will happen after that. There are bound to be claims, because the existing Warsaw Convention passenger insurance amount of $150,000 is still pitifully small. If there were any US citizens on board, the claims would start in the USA so Independant and GE had better be prepared, let alone Royal World Airlines. This thing could rumble on for years."

Mandy must have been psychic about my involvement. She did not even know yet the detail of my conversation with John Chester and certainly not the Carol/Richard Trentham dimension. One thing for sure, I had no intention of mentioning Carol to Mandy unless I was forced to.

Blind Landing

Luckily we reached the restaurant and were shown to our table, conveniently to the side of a quite small dining room. Simon, the owner came up and asked what we wanted to drink.

"I'll stay with Kir," decided Mandy without hesitation, but I decided to have a Scotch since the Kir was a bit too sweet for my taste. Simon returned with the drinks, some water for my whisky and the menus. There was a complete silence as we studied the options. I looked round as I added the water to my Scotch. The room was quite full of diners which must have been good news for Simon.

"Have you decided?" I asked and shut my menu.

"Yes. I shall have crudités and grilled sole with sauté potatoes. What about you?"

"Salad niçoise for me and I'll join you with the sole." We put down the menus as a signal to the waiter.

"OK. Let's hear about John Chester."

I started to explain what John had told me, but she interrupted me.

"But the security forces would never have allowed the aircraft to take-off again."

"Yes, the hijackers obviously realised that there would be a problem and so they told Harry to tell Heathrow that the aircraft would be blown up with everyone on board killed if they weren't allowed to go. Clearly the recorder with the cockpit voice recordings is going to be absolutely crucial because, if there are no clues there, it really will be a mess. Let's hope they find it soon. I'm sure we are going to learn something from the crews' conversation.

"The weather was Category IIIC, blind auto-pilot landing, so they would not have seen anything until just before they hit the ground. John is very worried because if the accident is not due to hijacking then he may be involved personally. He was one of the chief advocates for choosing the 798 over the new larger version of the Airbus A380. He felt that the flight deck design was basically safer than the Airbus and he was supported by Francis Thomas who was Director of Engineering at the time. To cheer him up I told him that in the circumstances anything might have happened. The design of the flight deck would almost certainly be irrelevant.

"One problem for John is that at about the time of the Board Meeting, Airbus was saying that they did not like the electronic architecture of the 798. It was not in accordance with the latest specifications of the Airlines Avionic Committee."

"Who are they, for goodness sake? Does their opinion matter?"

"Well, the committee is very influential and is a collection of all the major airlines, together with aircraft and avionic equipment manufacturers. There has to be a very good reason for a manufacturer to go against the committee's recommendations. Airbus felt the aircraft was designed to a standard that was less safe than the standard to which the Committee had agreed. Of course, at the time everybody dismissed the Airbus remarks in the immortal lines of Mandy Rice-Davies 'they would say that wouldn't they'. However, now there's an accident Airbus can say 'I told you so!'"

"But it's the hijacking."

"Maybe, but not proven yet. Remember some of the Board would have preferred the Airbus. If the accident is shown to be due to poor flight deck design, inadequate safety provisions or bad interfacing with the pilots then John's job could be on the line. Margaret Williams can't wait for Rex to take over from John."

"Surely all planes are designed to the same rules. Aren't they all equally safe?"

"You know it's not quite as simple as that. The rules are pretty well the same both in the USA and in Europe but manufacturers can meet the requirements in different ways and Airbus, Boeing and Independant are always looking for a competitive edge. On the flight deck the new aircraft are full of digital computers and the pilots are really managers of all the different systems, electrical, navigation, auto-pilot, hydraulic, air conditioning and many more. The days of the pilot actually pulling and pushing the flying control surfaces himself are long since gone."

"But the flying controls are operated by the pilot when he, or she, is actually flying the aircraft?"

"Well yes, but the pilot is not actually strong enough to move the controls. The control surfaces are moved by motors signalled from the flight deck. The pilot can tell the controls what he wants by moving the control wheel but, depending on the actual flight conditions, the computers modify what the pilot selects so that there is not always a fixed relationship between the position of the pilot's control wheel and the position of the control surfaces. The computers know best."

Mandy pulled a disapproving face.

"What a horrible thought."

"Everything's fine when all the computers are working correctly and getting the correct input data, but it can be a very different story when things start to go wrong. Pilots are trained to deal with all the emergencies which the designers can think of, but I always get worried about how the flight crew will react to emergencies which no-one has thought of. The problem is that when things are going normally, the pilots don't have all that much to do actually flying the aircraft since all the routine functions are performed automatically. The pilots' biggest work load en route is probably dealing with Air Traffic, getting the cruising altitudes and routings that they want. From that point of view things are not getting any easier since the number of aircraft on the long haul routes is steadily increasing."

"You make it sound as if the pilots are just managers, not pilots at all."

"That's just my point, Mandy. They really don't have to do a lot of actually flying the aircraft and for well over 99.9% of the time the systems are working correctly.

"The difficulty is that the pilots have to be incredibly knowledgeable to understand all the systems, but the control of the systems is, most of the time, done automatically so they are not exercising their knowledge. For most of their working life the pilots are doing a very humdrum routine task and the real test only comes when things go wrong. These days, pilots can be trained on emergencies in flight simulators which are really superb and incredibly realistic but the problem here is that the pilots know that they are going to be given emergencies during the training flights so it is somewhat artificial and anyway, as I said, how do you practice for a real emergency that no-one has anticipated?"

I was getting too enthusiastic on my pet subject and speciality but luckily the waiter appeared with our starters and I was able to stop. Mandy however was clearly listening very intently, subconsciously filing the information away for her legal briefs. She started eating absent-mindedly and then stopped.

"Look. You're getting carried away. The aircraft was hijacked and crashed and you can't resist wondering if there was some abstruse fault in the aircraft design." She waved her finger at me. "I think it will be very interesting to see if the dead man found in the Hyatt in Sydney has any connection with the flight. It would have been better if the crew had been trained to deal with hijacking."

"They are all trained in dealing with hijackers. It's just another emergency they have to cope with."

She paused as she was about to carry on eating.

"Tell me, what was John Chester getting at about preferring the Independant over the Airbus?"

"Well for a start, in the Airbus aircraft the engine throttles do not move when the engine power is being controlled automatically. You can have the throttles fully forward as you would when taking off but the engines can actually be at flight idle. The only way you can tell how much power is being applied is by looking at the engine instruments and possibly by the noise, but these days that's not much of a clue. Airbus made this change to save weight but both Independant and Boeing considered that the visual cues from the moving throttles actually helped the pilots control the aircraft better. So in the 798 the four throttle levers between the pilots are always in the correct position for the amount of power being applied and they move even when the speed or power is being controlled automatically. I think John liked that."

"But Peter, surely the government authorities who approve the aircraft must know if the Airbus system is alright and if it is, surely that's an end to the matter."

"You would think so, but some people think that the European regulating authorities, now the EASA, tend to support European industry."

"What does EASA stand for? You people talk all the time in acronyms. How anyone is meant to understand you I just don't know."

"I bet you are just the same in the legal profession. It's just not practicable to keep repeating whole collections of words to describe a single element, be it organisations like the European Aviation Safety Agency, the Federal Aviation Administration or a radio aid for navigation like the Global Positioning System which we call GPS for short; at least the European system is called Galileo and there is no confusion. Seriously though, you've made a very good point. I know what, I'll give you a list of all the acronyms.[1] You really will need my list if you get involved with this case.

"Anyway we digress. The point is that commercial competition between the manufacturers is intense, so the regulators really feel the pressure from their local industry. In the example I have given you, the French authorities approved the Airbus throttle arrangements and everybody else validated the approval, even the FAA. There have been one or two Airbus accidents which some people attribute to the throttles not moving, but all the accident investigators concerned have given the concept a clean bill of health. In my view the system seems to work and even if having the throttles moving does make for a safer aircraft, the Airbus system is safe enough and that's all that matters."

I paused. "Look let's hope all this discussion is quite irrelevant. The situation is that there were some hijackers on the flight deck. As Jim Akers wrote in the FT to-day, it would be incredible if some very unlikely rare fault occurred on the aircraft on the very day the aircraft was hijacked."

"You're almost certainly right. But it's going to be so difficult to sort it all out."

"Look if we carry on talking like this, my love, we will never finish the first course and our fish will be ruined. Let's have five minutes silence."

Mandy said nothing but ate the rest of her crudités, chewing every mouthful very carefully. She looked as if she wanted to ask me a load of

---

[1] See page 12

questions but I kept on raising my finger to my lips which clearly did not please her. She finally ate the last mouthful and looked at her empty glass.

"I wish you weren't so rude. All I wanted was another Kir," she said primly. I waved to the waiter who brought another Kir and I asked for another whisky to keep her company. The drinks arrived followed almost immediately by the fish, which clearly had been waiting for some time while we were talking. We started to eat but Mandy could not hold her questions back.

"Are there any other differences between the aircraft that I would notice if I went on to the flight deck?"

"Well yes. There is one big difference at the moment between the Boeing and Independant aircraft on the one hand and the Airbus fleet of aircraft on the other. The pilot on the Airbus flies with one hand using a small 'side stick controller' to fly the aircraft while the pilot on the 798 has a conventional two handed control wheel. The point here is that all the latest aircraft including the 798 use either electrical or fibre optic cables, instead of steel cables, between the flight deck controls and the control surfaces, so the pilots' control forces can be very light indeed. As I said, the controls surfaces are actually moved by large motors situated at the surfaces themselves and that's why there is no need for a conventional and heavy control column. On an Airbus the pilot with a side stick has an unrestricted view of the instruments and navigation displays."

"Well if the side stick controller is so good why won't Boeing and Independant use it?"

"Good question. In my opinion for three reasons. Firstly, they are very conservative and the side stick controller is a relatively new concept which in their opinion has not been validated. Secondly, Airbus thought of it first and the others don't like being 'me too's'.

"The third point is that with a side stick controller the pilot not flying the aircraft has no idea where the other pilot has put his controller since the two controllers are not tied together mechanically. In other words he can't be certain what the operating pilot is trying to do. On the 798 the two wheels move together all the time so the 'safety pilot' is 'in the loop' which is very important in the opinion of the protagonists of the Boeing/Independant solution."

"But what happens in an emergency? Can you have an emergency in the flying controls?"

"Bingo. You have asked the $64,000 question. Airbus have put an enormous amount of work into ensuring that if anything goes wrong with the pilot flying on one side of the aircraft, the other pilot can take over. It is all done by computer logic. The regulating authorities including the FAA are convinced that the Airbus solution is safe but the US aircraft manufacturers and some airlines don't like or trust the idea. They believe in the conservative approach when dealing with safety issues. But in fact, some manufacturers are trying to connect the two side stick controllers which might make Boeing and Independant change their minds. "

As usual I could not help being impressed by Mandy's grasp of any subject she put her mind to. She was a historian for her first degree but she always grasped the key points straightaway, however technical the subject.

"As I said, Airbus was very concerned about the 798 avionic design. However, neither the FAA nor the EASA were convinced by the Airbus arguments and agreed to certificate the aircraft. Only time will tell if they should have done."

By mutual agreement after we finished our fish, we decided to have coffee back at the house. I called for the bill, helped Mandy on with her coat and as we walked slowly back home Mandy carried on questioning me.

"Peter, you've told me why John is worried. Did you learn anything else?"

"Yes, two things. Firstly, the off duty first officer is alive and in hospital, unconscious. Let's hope he will be able to shed some light on the situation. The other thing is that I'm sure John didn't tell me everything. My guess is that he was going to give me a complete run down but, perhaps after talking to Jack Chiltern, he decided not to confide in me. Perhaps there is some security implication. I suppose I'll find out eventually what it is he's holding back. However there is one thing I haven't told you or anyone else for that matter."

Mandy looked at me and I clearly had her full attention.

"I heard the exchange between the aircraft and Air Traffic just before it crashed. The Air Traffic Controller told the aircraft it was going low. Apart from me at this moment of time only the air traffic controller and now, presumably, AAIB will know what was said."

"Surely it will soon be a matter of public record."

"Yes I expect so. In fact the controller was having trouble trying to tell the aircraft that it was low on the approach because a Lufthansa aircraft kept interrupting."

"How did the controller know the aircraft was low?"

"Very good question. They have an alerting system; the aircraft transmits it's altitude and there is a box in the Tower which calculates the position and altitude of the aircraft relative to the runway approach path being used and if the aircraft is not in the right place the controller gets a warning from this box. The system is based on an earlier system called AFDAS, Approach Funnel Deviation Alert system. Presumably it gave the controller a warning."

"Another acronym."

"Yes but it could be very significant."

"I do see that. You are quite right not to tell anybody at the moment." She looked at me accusingly. "That FT man you spoil keeping him briefed doesn't need to know."

"Jim Akers. Absolutely. I haven't told him and I'm not going to."

As usual as we arrived home I went in first to cancel the alarm. I shouted to Mandy when it was safe for her to come in. I was always very careful not to set off the alarm inadvertently, ever since a friend of mine went into the living room before I had cancelled the alarm. The central monitoring station got the alarm call immediately and they had rung the house to check, but the noise was so great we did not hear the phone in time before the answer phone took over. In no time flat the police were around and quite rightly gave me a hard time. This time there was no mistake and Mandy came in and went upstairs to her room. I went into the kitchen and started to make the coffee. My mobile phone rang.

"Peter, it's Carol. Richard is alive but he has had to have his right leg amputated. I don't think he really knows what is going on. He is full of drugs." I could hear her choking at the other end of the line. I felt terrible. She had no real family to support her and with her mother not very strong, life was suddenly treating her very cruelly.

"Mother is managing to get here somehow, thank goodness and the children are staying with friends. I'm virtually living at the hospital. The people here are just wonderful. I barely know what I'm doing."

Mandy wandered into the kitchen to find out what was going on. She took over making the coffee but was clearly listening, certainly to my end of the conversation.

"Carol. Is there anything I can do to help?"

"Not really. I just had to talk to someone who understands. I'm not very optimistic. Anyway I'm not sure Richard could adjust to just having one leg and not being able to fly."

"Don't talk nonsense. Of course he'll be able to manage. Look at all the people who only have one leg and lead normal lives." I tried to reassure her but I don't think either of us was convinced.

"Carol, give me a call to-morrow when Richard has recovered from the operation and let me know how he is."

Mandy eyed me thoughtfully as the coffee drained through the filter into the pot. So much for my idea of not telling Mandy about Carol.

"Who was that?"

"Carol Trentham, Richard Trentham's wife. Richard and I were pilots together at Britannia before Richard went off to join Cathay. He is based in London but was operating Hong Kong - Sydney last week. He was dead heading back to London on Flight 573. Carol called me this morning worried as hell and then later she let me know that Richard had been found and was alive. You probably gathered that he has had to have one of his legs amputated and she is doubtful whether he will survive. What a mess."

"That's terrible." There was a pause. "You didn't mention that she'd called," she said almost accusingly. Nothing got by Mandy.

"I forgot. It didn't seem that important and everything else drove it out of my mind."

Mandy said nothing, to be put in the 'to be continued' folder. We took our coffee into the living room and sat down, close together, on the settee. She must have put on some more perfume while I was talking to Carol. I put my mouth on her neck and smelled the fragrance. She turned towards me and took my hand in hers. Her hand grasped mine as I turned the TV on to the News at Ten and then put it at the top of her thigh. She then took her hand away and reached for the controller to turn the TV off but stopped suddenly as we both realised that there was an interview with Bob Furness, head of the Air Accident Investigation Branch. Bob was explaining the procedure for investigating accidents and how important was the analysis of the two crash recorders. We relaxed for a moment and started to drink our coffee.

"We have not yet found the recorder with the cockpit voice recordings but it can only be a matter of time. We do have the other recorder with all the flight information. The 798 meets the very latest requirements for recording the critical flight data which can shed light on possible causes of accidents. However the analysis will take a long time. We need the help not only of the airline but also of the aircraft manufacturer and of course the security and explosive experts.

"In parallel with this work we are collecting every piece we can of the aircraft and looking for evidence of bomb damage. We are laying all the pieces out in a hangar we are using at Farnborough and we are 'rebuilding' the aircraft. We have had a lot of experience of similar work in the past starting with the Comet fatigue failure accident many years ago. The position of each piece where it hit the ground is important since this can show if the aircraft started to disintegrate before it hit the ground. We log the position of every part before it is moved and 'reassembled' in the hangar."

"But surely Mr Furness this is going to be a straightforward case of the hijackers interfering with the crew?"

"Possibly, but if so we still need to understand what exactly happened."

The interviewer raised the subject of voice recorders. Would the public be able to hear the conversations of the crew.

"You are quite right to mention the voice recorder. The remarks on the recording between the crew will be absolutely vital in helping us to find out what went wrong. Deciphering what has been recorded however is not as simple as it sounds." Bob paused to stress a point. "It is our policy in the United Kingdom only to let the absolute minimum number of necessary specialists listen to the recording. For a start it can be quite difficult to understand what is being said and a lot of what is said is very often quite irrelevant to the accident. If the recording got into the wrong hands a lot of unnecessary grief could be caused to the dependants of the crew and passengers."

For once the interviewer did not question this point as I expected.

"What would happen if you couldn't find the voice recorder?"

"We will find the recorder. It's just a matter of time. When we know the cause of the accident we will let everybody know. Meantime I would ask you to help us by not interfering with our work. You must realise that the work of inspecting the wreckage is incredibly harrowing and upsetting to my inspectors and they need your support."

I switched the set off.

"He must be getting a bit impatient, not yet having the cockpit voice recorder." Mandy remarked.

"You're right. It shouldn't be taking this long. It's a pity it is not underwater because it has a special beacon if it is submerged."

We sat up and drank our coffee. Mandy put her cup down and then took my cup and saucer from me and put it safely out of reach. She turned to me and as she came closer I could smell the fresh perfume again. Slowly and gently she made it clear that life had to go on in spite of tragic accidents. She ran her fingers through my hair and down my body and I could feel myself reacting. This was going to be our first time and we had to learn how the other would respond. I started to unbutton her dress and helped it off her shoulders. I realised why Mandy had gone upstairs. She was not wearing a bra, or anything else for that matter. I held her breasts in my hands and caressed her nipples as we started to kiss. We both froze as the telephone started to ring.

"Let it ring." she whispered in my ear. "The answering machine can deal with it."

"It won't. I haven't switched it on."

"Well it's your decision." But the way she stroked me made it almost impossible for me to leave.

Everything stopped while the phone seemed to ring for ever. The caller finally gave up and all was quiet. We both relaxed and tried to continue where we had left off but the noise started again. Mandy took her hand away and moved back slightly so that I could get up to answer the phone.

"Peter, it's Mike Mansell here."

I sat down as I knew it would be a long conversation. Mike was a partner in CrossRisk Insurance and I had advised him once before in an accident claim which had looked like a clear cut case of pilot error. Mike's firm had been retained by the airline concerned. It had been a tricky case and the engine manufacturer had been trying to say the crew drills had not been carried out correctly and a very expensive engine had been damaged. I had been able to show that the drills in the Flight Manual had not covered the particular case in question and that the airline was not responsible. I had saved Mike's company over a million pounds and they were very grateful. They even gave me a percentage bonus which had kept me going between other jobs.

I had got to know Mike quite well. He was slightly older than I was and he had never married. Not, I judged, that he had not had lots of opportunity with quite a few delightful girls, but he always seemed to shy away when he reckoned he might get 'caught'.

My telephone chair faced Mandy who had not bothered to pull her dress back up. Her breasts seemed very prominent and I found it very difficult to concentrate. I put the phone down and turned the chair round so I could not see her.

"Peter, are you still there." Mike asked as I re-lifted the handset.

"Yes, it's OK. I was just getting a chair and some notepaper. Go ahead. How can I help you?"

"Look, I'm sorry I'm calling you so late. I hope I'm not disturbing you?" I made no reply. I did not dare look at Mandy.

"Are you there?"

"Yes Mike, please go ahead."

"You may know that we recently got the contract from Royal World Airlines to supply insurance cover for any passenger claims that might occur from flight crew negligence. RWA did not want us to insure the hull, that was already being done by Hull Claims Insurance but Hull Claims didn't want to be involved with claims resulting from 'pilot error'. They felt that pilot error was still the most frequent cause of accidents and required a specialist organisation. Well Peter, we have just had an internal company meeting and we are very concerned that the claims from this particular accident could bankrupt the firm. We laid off a lot of the risk of course but we feel that the magnitude of the claims will be unprecedented, particularly when all the legal fees are taken into account.

"Of course I'm not for a minute suggesting the accident was due to pilot error. The accident is almost certainly due to the hijacking. It's anybody's guess at this stage, but the nature of the accident suggests that if it's not a bomb or something like it then pilot error is clearly a possibility and we might then be liable. I recommended that we should ask you to advise us and everybody agreed. They hadn't forgotten the last job you did for us. What do you think?"

"Well, I think you're probably worrying unnecessarily. However I think you're right to be prepared. Mike, I think I'm free to accept your offer but I'll have to check with John Chester since he half hinted when I saw him at lunch to-day that he might have a job for me. To be honest I think he changed his mind about using me but I had better check with him in the morning. In any event his interests and yours should be identical."

"Great. I feel much happier already."

"Mike. Let's get one thing straight. If I help you I am only interested in finding out the truth, hijacking, maintenance fault, pilot error or whatever. This accident could conceivably have been caused by pilot error but of course, bearing in mind all the safeguards that are currently built in to protect modern aircraft, I feel that the hijacking must have caused something to go wrong. For example, the hijacker may have prevented the crew from flying the aircraft correctly. Clearly in that case it wouldn't have been pilot error. It's not going to be easy working on the job because, as you know, everything is in AAIB's hands at the moment. If they think it's pilot error, the chance of getting anyone to believe anything else is going to be very small and there are no witnesses, except possibly the other first officer, Frank Mercer, if he survives. However, it certainly looks like a bomb or possibly hijacking and as far as the manufacturer, Independant Transport Aircraft Company, is concerned either would be an ideal solution.

"Another thing, if you do want me to help, you must realise that if I'm going to keep abreast of the situation I shall have to do a lot of work and travelling using all my contacts and it 's going to cost you. Your money will probably be wasted. I will do everything I can to help you but I don't want to mislead you."

Mike Mansell didn't hesitate. "I know that and in this case my company is prepared to pay you not only your normal per diem fees and expenses but a lump sum percentage bonus as we did last time if we judge by your actions that you have saved us from having to pay up the many millions of pounds that will be due if the fault is found to be due to pilot error."

"OK. I don't like being mercenary in situations like this but this accident is on a scale that no-one has encountered before and there are many ramifications that are going to complicate the legal issues. Send me the normal contract letter and also another letter which shows that I am acting as your consultant. I may need it to convince people that I have a right to be involved. I will confirm I can take the job when I have spoken to John Chester. Bye."

I put the phone down and stood still for a moment thinking about the conversation. I suddenly realised that Mandy had come over from the settee and I could smell her perfume again. I decided to turn off the answering machine. She was standing behind me and starting to remove my clothes so we would be on an equal footing. I turned to make it easier for her. Mandy came very, very close and Mike Mansell seemed to go a long, long way away.

CHAPTER 5

The Leak

I woke up with a start in Mandy's bed. As I had suspected she had not wanted to sleep in the room that Diana and I had shared, even though the bed had been changed a long time ago. The last thing I remembered before going to sleep was asking Mandy how she could have been so sure that we were going to make it that night. She murmured that I was being very silly, it was standing out a mile. I told her that as a solicitor she should not exaggerate; she told me not to be coarse. But she was right in one way. I was never very good at hiding my feelings.

There were noises downstairs. It was already 7.15. There was a smell of coffee and bacon. I leapt out of bed to find out what was going on. I got some trousers from my room and went downstairs. As I had anticipated, Mandy was sitting at the kitchen table tucking into a bowl of cereal, a plate of bacon under the grill, brown toast in the toaster and coffee already made in the pot. She was dressed in her lawyer's uniform but without her jacket. She was wearing her glasses and reading the Times.

"Good Morning, Ms Arrowsmith, did you sleep well?" She said nothing for a moment but finished her cereal.

"Good morning, Mr Talbert. I trust you had a good evening?"

"It was like the curate's egg, thank you. Good in parts. I've come to consult my lawyer. Would you advise me to have some coffee?"

"Very definitely."

I poured myself a mug of coffee and moved another chair to the table. Mandy looked at her watch. It was nearly time for her to go.

"Peter," she said breaking the lawyer/client relationship, "From what I heard on the radio they've found the recorder with the cockpit voices. The security people unearthed it while they were checking for bombs and it's now on the way to Farnborough for AAIB."

"Strange that it was not found earlier." I looked at the time. "You're going to be late. You must stop eating and run."

She agreed and dashed to get ready. She returned with her jacket and I helped her and kissed her neck on the way. She leant back to show approval but quickly turned round.

"For once I wish you were dressed. You could have taken me to the station. I must go home to-night," anticipating my next question, "I've some things to do. I'll call you from the office later on when I see what's happening."

She turned back again and kissed me slowly, on the lips.

"Oh Peter. While I remember, I enjoyed last night. We must do it again sometime."

She rushed out with her bag before I could answer and I watched her hurrying down the street being barked at by next door's dog. I collected the clothes I had been wearing last night from the living room and went upstairs to get dressed. It was just as well that Dora had not been coming to-day, though I supposed she would not have been surprised. I had no plans to go out and in some ways it was a relief that Dora wasn't going to come.

I logged on to the Internet and looked at the FT. Jim Akers had an article saying amongst other things that at the time the paper went to press the second recorder had not been found. He pointed out how vital it was not only to find the recorder but that it must work properly. He also pointed out that if something had gone wrong then it must have been at the last moment. Jim favoured the crew being distracted by a highjacker when landing in critical conditions. If this proved not to be the case then it would be necessary to investigate how it was possible for the aircraft to be actually well below the correct flight path and the crew to take no action. Was there something wrong with the landing system they were using? Jim went on to discuss the procedure in the UK for dealing with cockpit voice recorders. He pointed out how everything on the recording was confidential and how normally not even the transcript was ever written down in the final AAIB accident report. In the United States excerpts from the transcript were sometimes made available as a matter of public record but even there the actual recording was never played publicly.

I decided to ring John Chester to ask whether he minded my being a consultant to CrossRisk Insurance. Jill Stanton answered his private number.

"Captain Chester is not available at the moment. Can I help you?"

I told her of the need to speak to him as soon as it was convenient and she undertook to pass on the message.

"How is your friend in hospital? Is he alright."

I explained about the loss of his right leg and that it was unlikely that he would survive. She sounded very sad. My story was just one of so many she was dealing with. She had a very difficult job. In my study I went through my letters and started tidying up. Doing nothing for twenty four hours always left a lot of odd jobs to be cleared up. The phone rang.

"Peter? It's Carol. Richard's very bad I'm afraid but he suddenly said he must speak to you. It was very strange. It seemed more important to him than anything else." She paused trying to get a hold on herself. "He is able to recognise me but nothing else. Can you come over straightaway? I'm so afraid. If you don't come immediately it may be too late."

"Of course. Which ward is he in?"

"He is in the Hossack Ward. Park your car in the visitor's park and you will see the sign to the Ward. When you get there you must ask for sister. He is on the critical list but you are being allowed in because I have explained the situation to Matron. You may have to wait because he is in great pain and on drugs. Anyway you will see me there. See you soon."

I got the car out, locked up the house and drove as quickly as I dared to Ealing General. I managed to find room to park the car and went to the Hossack Ward which was on the first floor. The swing doors must have operated a buzzer and a nurse came out of the side office. She looked me up and down.

"Can I help you"

"I've come to see Richard Trentham who is on the critical list. His wife has just called me and said that she had spoken with Matron and it had been agreed that I could go in when it was judged possible."

"Oh I don't know anything about that. Let me get sister."

She returned with another nurse, no older than herself but wearing what must have been a sister's uniform.

"You are Mr Talbert?" I nodded. "Well Mr Trentham is very, very ill but has moments of consciousness and he has been asking for you. You had better sit down in the waiting room but it may be a very long wait."

I did as she asked and picked up the papers. It was impossible to concentrate but I tried to make myself read an old copy of Country Life. There was an article on houses in Brittany and it all seemed a million miles away. I suddenly became aware that I was not alone. Carol had appeared. She was an elegant and striking woman in spite of the surroundings. She looked very tired but she had obviously taken care with her appearance in spite of the world falling apart around her.

"Peter. It's been a long time." She held both my hands in hers and looked at me. I felt slightly uncomfortable, perhaps unsure of myself. "Thank you for coming. To be honest I'm not very hopeful. He has been asleep for an hour or two. If he comes round and can talk they are going to call me. If it seems alright and he still wants to talk to you I will call you."

"OK Carol." We said nothing, perhaps both of us remembering happier times in the past. "Can I get you some tea, coffee? Have you eaten to-day?"

"A cup of coffee would be nice. There is a machine on the next floor. To tell you the truth I haven't had breakfast. I've got a few biscuits in my bag." She produced an unflatteringly large ladies' bag which obviously contained all her emergency requirements.

"Look. I'll get some coffee and we had better go out somewhere."

"Peter. I can't. I never know when Richard is going to come to. They bring me some food from the canteen when they can."

I went downstairs and managed to make the machine deliver some coffee with milk and without sugar. As I climbed up the stairs Carol rushed down to meet me. "Quick. Richard wants to talk to you."

We went into the ward and passed many patients. It was not visiting time and the nurses were doing all the various things which were needed in a very busy ward. At the far end we went into a room which I realised was reserved for patients who were critically ill. I was horrified when I saw Richard but I hope I did not let my feelings show. He had a bandage on his head and both of his shoulders seemed damaged. One arm was in a sling and the other arm was positioned for a drip. His eyes were open and I could see that he recognised me. I could barely hear what he was saying. I leant right up to his mouth.

"Peter. The hijacker…" He coughed and shut his eyes. I waited. He opened his eyes again. He had obviously forgotten he had spoken. He stopped and then seemed to make a supreme effort "I wanted to tell Harry…" He coughed again and then he seemed to go into a coma. I decided to leave which obviously pleased the nurse. Carol stayed behind.

I went back to the waiting room and tried to escape once again to Brittany but there was no way that Country Life could hold my attention. Presumably Richard must have been sitting in the crew rest area and seen one of the hijackers. Had he seen the lights out of the windows? I began to sympathise with the AAIB inspectors who have to go to the accidents. When one is surrounded by death on all sides one takes a very different and sometimes emotional view of what needs to be done to prevent another accident. Safety may be a statistical matter to the aircraft designers and the regulators but if one is present at the accident, it all seems very different. AAIB had a history of recommending modifications to prevent accidents but in truth the only thing that would really prevent accidents would be to stop flying, and that would never happen. The fact is that people are prepared to accept accidents providing they are not too frequent because they believe it will never happen to them.

I thought about what Richard had said. It didn't make any sense. What did the hijacker do? What did he try to tell Harry?

Carol appeared. It was all over. "He's dead". I put out my arms to comfort her and she burst into tears. I held her as she sobbed uncontrollably for a minute or so. Then she quietened down.

"I'll take you home."

"But I can't leave my car here."

"Don't worry. We can sort that out." I spoke to the sister to make sure she knew how to contact Carol. We went down to my car and I drove her back to Farnham where she lived. It seemed to take forever. The traffic was terrible. We said nothing.

When we finally got to her house she gave me the keys and I opened the front door. It was about 3 o'clock by this time. "Have you got any food in the house?"

"There's some food in the fridge and also in the freezer compartment. But I don't want anything. I think I'll go to bed."

"Carol. Your best bet is to eat something. Get the children home. You'll have to go on living. After all Richard has been away a lot and the children are used to a life without him, most of the time." I knew I was being hard but I really believed that though she had to grieve, she must not give way.

She looked at me and nodded miserably. I found some bacon and eggs in the fridge and turned the grill on. Carol pointed to a cupboard which had saucepans and a frying pan. She went upstairs.

I checked my mobile. John Chester had phoned and also Mandy. Mandy was busy with a client so I left my number. Jill put me through to John Chester.

"John, it's Peter. How are things going?"

"Not too well. How I can help you?" He was obviously up to his armpits in problems.

"Only a quick one. Mike Mansell of CrossRisk Insurance wants to retain me as a consultant to help them. Is that OK? You mentioned you might want me to act for you."

There was a pause.

"Yes. That's fine. Whatever. After all RWA insures with them." He clearly was not too pleased at this development but could not really stop it. I wanted to know what was troubling him but it seemed he was not about to tell me. "Keep in touch. I'd like to know how you get on." He rang off.

I started cooking the bacon and scrambling the eggs. I found some rather stale bread but felt it would be OK for toasting. Half way through Carol appeared. She had changed into sweater and trousers and looked very smart in spite of everything. She had not let having two children spoil her figure. She laid the table and when it was ready we sat down to eat.

I think she managed to eat a lot more than she expected. In fact she cleaned her plate. There was some bacon left over but she refused to have any more. "You're right. I had better get hold of the children. They've got to know."

She went over to the phone and called the friend who was looking after her children. She had to explain about Richard first which obviously she found very hard. She managed to arrange for the children to come over after they had had tea.

"Carol. You need to get some food. I'll take you shopping and get you home before the children return. Then I'll get your car back from Ealing." She nodded her agreement.

We went to Sainsbury's and got a trolley. I had to prompt her to get the things she needed. I told her again, Richard may have died but life had to go on. The children needed to be fed. She bought bread, fruit, milk and a host of other things. She had very little money but paid with a credit card. I made her use the cash dispenser outside before we got back into the car.

As we got back my mobile started to ring.

"Peter? It's Mandy. Where are you?" she asked tersely.

"Mandy. I'm at Carol's. Richard has just died. He wanted to say something to me and I went to the hospital. I was only just in time. He started to tell me but he couldn't get the message out. He died a few minutes later. I wish I knew what he wanted to say; I think it must have been important."

"Poor Carol."

"I'm trying to help her. We've been shopping and the children will be home in a moment. Then I've got to go by train into London and out to Ealing to bring her car back from the hospital."

"Where are you now?" She sounded a lot more understanding but still suspicious.

"Carol lives in Farnham."

"Well I shall be here until quite late and then I shall be off to Bournemouth. Call me to-morrow and maybe we can meet up."

"Fine. See you soon." We said our goodbyes but they were not too extravagant. However sympathetic Mandy might have been she clearly didn't want me to spend too much time with Carol, who had been following the conversation but said nothing.

I rang for a cab to take me to the station and got Carol to give me the keys of her car. The cab came within ten minutes. I waved goodbye and was on my way. It was a miserable journey. When I got to Waterloo I bought the Evening Standard and took the underground to Ealing, reading the paper to catch up with what had been happening. The Secretary of State for Transport had decided to call a press conference the following afternoon. It was an unpleasant journey what with the rush hour, standing up most of the way and the difficulty of getting a cab to the hospital. It was gone 8.30 before I got into Carol's car.

The drive home was uneventful and I got to Carol's house by 10 o'clock. The children were still up looking very subdued. There was not much I could say. I embraced Carol sympathetically and said good-bye. "Keep in touch. Anyway I'll call you." I got in the car and drove off.

I got home about 11.30. It had been a long day and I didn't feel I had accomplished much. I went straight to bed and dropped off to sleep but the day hadn't finished. I saw Richard Trentham with all his bandages standing over me, next to the bed. Carol was next to him, holding yesterday's Daily Telegraph. He looked through me with sightless eyes and shook his head, frowning, and I could hear him repeating 'I wanted to tell Harry…'. I tried to speak and nothing came out so I reached to grab him but he disappeared. Carol bent over as if to kiss me and I tried to escape by rolling over. I woke up covered in perspiration. I felt afraid and I didn't sleep very well after my dream; my mind kept trying to guess what Richard had been trying to tell me and, much more important, what he wanted to tell Harry. I finally dozed off as it was getting light.

***

My alarm went off at 7.30. It was set to prevent oversleeping though usually I was awake well before it went off. Thursday was Dora's second day and I always liked to be down well before she arrived at 8.45. I got up, showered and went downstairs. The phone rang.

"Peter, I've just got into the office. Have you seen the paper?"

"No, my love, not yet."

"Well you'd better get hold of the Telegraph for a start. Their air correspondent, Chuck Osborne, has got a story about the crash recorder and the pilots' conversations. Apparently they'd been on a party at a beach the night before the flight."

"A leak? From AAIB? It's unheard of. There's never been a leak."

"Well there's been one now."

"Anyway even if the leak is accurate and they'd been out the night before it wouldn't matter. They would have slept on the aircraft before the landing."

"Well don't shoot the messenger. Get your bottom out of bed for a change and buy some newspapers."

She rang off. The Times was there and I glanced hurriedly through it while I had breakfast. There was a short article by a reporter mentioning the story and saying how deplorable such a leak was. The news item went on to mention that it was strange that the crew had noticed nothing wrong on the approach before the aircraft hit the A30. I dropped everything, got the car out and bought the Telegraph and the FT at the local newsagent.

Back home I read the Telegraph where Chuck Osborne had a large article on the front page. 'DID PILOTS' PARTY CAUSE ACCIDENT?' screamed the headline. Osborne told how he had managed to get an exclusive chance to read a transcript of the flight deck conversations. Up to now everybody had thought that the accident was due in some way to the hijacker alert, but was there another explanation? Osborne went on to say that the he understood the recording was rather noisy but it was quite clear that before the start of the approach there had been a discussion about a beach party the night before they left. The aircraft then carried out a normal approach. Air Traffic Control had told the aircraft it was below the glide slope but apparently the Captain said later 'we are on the glide slope but we seem to be descending rather quickly'. Then he called the control tower and asked for a wind check. At 100 ft. he said he still couldn't see the loom of the lights. The first officer said the instruments showed they were on centre line, at just below 20 ft. there was an 'Oh my God', apparently there was then a noise of engines followed by a crashing noise and nothing.

I was appalled. How on earth did the Telegraph get hold of the story and, if it was anything like true, what had been going on? My mind was racing. It did not make sense in several ways. The paper was quite oblivious to the damage that might be being done by running the story. There was a leading article justifying the right of the public to know and saying thank goodness for the integrity of the media, conveniently not mentioning any dirty tricks that they had probably carried out in order to get the story.

I switched on the radio just in time to hear the news headlines followed by an interview with Flight Magazine's air transport correspondent, Brian Tucker.

"Presumably Mr Tucker you will have read the story in the Telegraph this morning about the accident to the 798 and the voice recorder. Have you any comments?"

"Yes. I did read the article and let me say that if the story is true, the whole aerospace industry will deplore that any information that was on the voice recorder has become public knowledge. Accident investigation relies on complete confidentiality whilst the investigations are going on and it is quite improper and most unhelpful if anything leaks out. No doubt the AAIB will be investigating the source of the leak."

"But Mr Tucker, the fact is that the news has leaked out. Can you understand why the crew did not see that something was going wrong?"

"We must all be very careful in accepting the Telegraph's story as being true and, equally as important, a lot of very important details will almost certainly have been missed out, such as what the hijackers were doing. The article said that apparently the quality of the recording was poor which underlines the problem. Only when all the pieces of information are assessed can any sense be made of the causes of the accident. We have no idea, for example, if a bomb went off which might have caused the aircraft to come down below the glide slope. Clearly, if it was not a bomb then it will be very important to explain why the crew thought they were on the glide slope and yet landed half a mile short."

"The story is that the crew had been out partying the night before. Would…"

Brian interrupted. "It is quite disgraceful that personal conversation on the recording should be discussed in this manner. Anyway what did or didn't happen in Sydney is quite irrelevant since the flight lasted 22 hours and the crew had had a long rest before coming on duty to land the aircraft. Bunks are provided in the flight deck area to ensure the crew off duty get a good rest. The last thing the crew would be thinking about would be about partying when there were hijackers on board."

The interviewer interrupted Brian. "But once the story is out people are bound to discuss it and consider what happened in Sydney. You must realise that."

"It is precisely for this sort of reason that it is so important that information on the cockpit voice recorder should be kept absolutely confidential. There has been a terrible accident and, whilst people are bound to speculate at this time, it does not help for the media to rake over private matters and it will be very hurtful to the families of those concerned."

The interviewer clearly didn't give a damn to any hurt he might be causing to Marcia Hodgson. I turned the TV off feeling sick with disgust over Osborne in particular and the media in general. Dora was in the kitchen and I wandered in to get some more coffee.

"Isn't it terrible about the accident? What did the hijackers do to make it crash?"

"Dora, we don't know anything about what happened. We've got to wait for the accident to be investigated properly by the AAIB."

"And the crew out partying the night before."

"Dora, the flight lasted 22 hours. Whatever happened in Sydney would not affect the landing in London."

"If you say so, Mr Talbert" she said, completely unconvinced but I was sure that she was expressing what would be a general view. It would not make my job any easier convincing the Inquiry that there was no pilot error, in the unlikely event that that proved to be the issue.

"By the way. There is no need to change the sheets on the spare bed. A friend stayed the other night and might be staying again."

"Very good sir. I've put the clothes she left on the bed." I felt that I could detect a knowing smile under her impassive face.

It was 9.15 in the morning UK time. It would be 8.15 in the evening Sydney time. I looked up the number in my database of Bill Baker, Chief Training Pilot of NWIA. I had done some work for NWIA a couple of years before on the Boeing 747-8 and had met Bill Baker then, as he was Chief 747 pilot at the time. New World International Airlines was a rapidly growing Antipodean airline very much in competition with QANTAS and, like QANTAS, seemed to be known only by initials. Luckily I had Bill's home number as well as his office number.

In no time the phone was ringing and a female voice answered. I asked for Bill explaining that I was calling from England.

"Oh I'm so sorry. Bill's not here. This is Mary, his wife speaking. Bill is still in the office."

"No problem, Mrs. Baker. I've got his number. I'll call him there." I rang off and tried the NWIA main number in Sydney. The operator put me through to Bill's office after giving me his direct line in case we got disconnected before he answered.

"Bill, you're working late! It's Peter Talbert here, calling from England. You remember I did some work for you some time back."

"Of course I remember. How are you doing, Peter? What's the news?"

"Bill, I am getting involved with this terrible accident at Heathrow. Were any of your people on board?"

"I'm afraid so. We've lost a Captain and two first Officers re-positioning to London. You know there were 49 Australian passengers on the flight, 35 killed and 14 survivors all in hospital, so it really is a national disaster. I must say that to us the whole thing looks like the hijackers interfering with the crew in bad weather. If it was a bomb it must have gone off very late on the approach. We've all heard about the voice recording of course. How on earth did that get out?"

"I don't know but I hope for Bob Furness's sake at AAIB that he's found and plugged the leak. I'm so sorry to hear about your people. We've got to find out what happened. By the way when do you get your first 798?"

"In about six months time. I've got two of my senior training captains in Seattle right now learning about the aircraft and our first course starts in just over a month. Somebody told me you're lecturing to the RWA training courses. Is that right?"

"Yes. The 798 has a very interesting systems configuration and flight deck."

"How would you like to come out and help plan the course in detail and give some talks on the significance of the latest crew/flight deck interface?"

"Are you serious, Bill? You know I'd like that very much. However I'm rather busy at the moment otherwise I'd come out to-morrow."

"Actually to-morrow would be a bit soon anyway, Peter. This accident has got a lot of us thinking hard. We don't really believe that the accident was due to pilot error and we don't think there is anything wrong with the 798 design. Our current view is that the hijack was responsible in some way. However, we need to make absolutely sure that our pilots are as properly trained as they can be. We want to be quite clear about the latest pilot interface issues on the flight deck and the system design. I can't help feeling that your input will be well worthwhile. I need to talk with my captains when they come back. I'll let you know."

"Bill, that's fine, I look forward to hearing from you. But let me tell you why I called. NWIA does all the servicing for Royal World Airlines?"

"Yes we do. Why?"

"Do you think you could find out for me if there were any allowable deficiencies when the aircraft left for London? Did all the electronics work when they left?"

"You bet. I'll contact Matt Thompson, head of maintenance and call you back. Anything else I can do for you?"

"Not really. What is your media making of the story about the party the night before?"

"Not much so far, all the talk is about the hijacking. As I said the accident is really terrible for us since the death toll is so high, not to mention the injured. The papers are concentrating on the family aspect of the tragedy. Understandably they don't seem to be pursuing the party story, perhaps because they feel, as we do, that it's not relevant. Anyway, you know as well as I do that there are scores of beaches and restaurants in the Harbour. We've had a heat wave for the last few days and it would probably be easier to find what the crew had been up to if they'd been downtown or had stayed in their hotels and hadn't gone down to the beaches!

"Besides, all people can talk about here, after the accident, is the cricket. There is a test series on with the West Indies at the moment. Everybody feels that accidents will always happen and that sport must go on. If there is going to be any investigation of night life and parties, it will be reserved for the two cricket teams."

"Well Bill, that's a bit of good news. It's bad enough for the families as it is without adding a sex scandal."

"OK Peter. No worries. I'll let you know the moment I get anything from Matt."

"Thanks. Call me any time, day or night. Leave a message on my answering machine to call you if I'm not in. All the best."

The phone went again.

"Peter? I'm in a mess. I'm going to need money and I don't know what to do. I called the Cathay Office. They were very sympathetic and said they would call Hong Kong but I must know how I'm going to be placed."

"Carol, don't you have a solicitor who can help you?"

"Yes, but he's in Hong Kong and he's Chinese."

"Well you had better get hold of a solicitor in London. Look I've got to call my girl friend who is a solicitor and I'll ask her who she recommends. I'll call you back as soon as I can."

Mandy was in the office but it seemed to be forever before she came on the line. I was pretty certain that we'd had eight of Vivaldi's four seasons on the tape before she answered.

"How's everything going?"

"Not short of work. I understand from GE that the inquest is starting immediately but the coroner is only interested in making positive identification of the bodies. He's not going to get involved in investigating the cause and second guessing the AAIB. He is determined not to get into the problems that have occurred in other accidents where a lot of people were killed and mistakes in identification were made."

"Well, my love, he may be lucky there because what fires there were, were put out very quickly. Of course if there was a bomb, that would make life impossible for the coroner but the fact that there were some survivors makes me think there wasn't an explosion. We'll hear soon enough. Just as well the Australian families are coming over to help. However, it is still going to take a long time with so many bodies. I'm afraid that there may have been quite a few bodies severely harmed due to the aircraft hitting that building."

"The Coroner has also let it be known to the interested parties that after the identification he is going to adjourn the inquest indefinitely until the results of the AAIB investigation are known. That means we won't have to be involved for months."

"Well I can't wait until then. I need to keep ahead of the gossip and get some real facts. I'm not sure yet how to do that but I'm working on it. I spoke to Bill Baker of NWIA in Sydney this morning and asked him to check on the aircraft serviceability state on departure.

"Australia is clearly treating the accident as almost a national tragedy. They're also assuming, as I think most of us are, that somehow the hijackers caused the accident. He did tell me some good news. Apparently there's a heat wave in Sydney and also a cricket test series so that the beaches have been crowded and the reporters are so busy that they don't seem to be pursuing the cockpit voice recorder story. Let's hope it stays that way."

"How did you get on last night?"

"I managed to get Carol's car back and got home about 11.30. I went straight to bed and had a dream in the middle of the night. It was like a nightmare. Richard was next to me reading the Daily Telegraph. I tried to grab him and he disappeared." I stopped, deciding not to mention that in my dream Richard was not alone. "I was soaked in perspiration. It took me ages to get back to sleep and…"

"Write down exactly what happened. The mind works even when one's asleep. It may be important."

"Look, I need your advice. Carol is very worried financially. Obviously Richard was insured but Cathay in London can't help her, goodness knows when she will hear from head office and their solicitor is in Hong Kong."

"She had better get a UK solicitor straightaway. I'm sure there won't be a problem but it needs to be made clear to Cathay that she is well represented."

"That's what I told her but who should she get? Should I give her the name of my solicitor? Or can your firm do it? Can you recommend someone?"

"No she had better not use your solicitor. To be honest with you I wouldn't like that arrangement. Our firm doesn't do that type of work. Where did you say she lived? Farnborough?"

"No. Farnham."

"Let me think about it. I'll call you back in a few minutes. I need to talk to you some more anyway."

She rang off.

CHAPTER 6

Jim Akers

It was clearly one of those mornings. The phone never seemed to stop ringing. This time it was Bill Baker.

"I spoke to Matt. He said you were the second person to ask him about allowable deficiencies to-day. Someone from the AAIB had called him, it was an inspector but he didn't leave his name."

"Well what was the answer, Bill?"

"There were no deficiencies reported. The aircraft had landed with two defects. One of the Captain's main instrument displays, the Navigation Display was not working and one of the Multimode Receivers was giving a GPS System warning. The ground crew checked the display but could find nothing wrong. However NWIA doesn't allow a 'ground checked and found serviceable' entry in the log book and so they put a replacement display in the Captain's position. It worked fine and they sent the reported defective display to be checked in the avionics shop.

"The Multimode Receiver fault was more of a challenge. As you know the three receivers control all the equipment that can be used for automatic landings. The fault was confirmed on the ground when satellite landing was selected. The avionics engineer on duty decided to change the Multimode Receiver which proved to be the right solution. He ground checked the system and everything seemed to be fine."

"Thanks very much. If you hear anything else you think I ought to know, please call me straightaway."

"Peter, wait a moment. I told you this 798 accident has got us all worried. I've now spoken to my guys in Seattle and we would like you to come out when they've finished their course in about a month to advise on our training courses. At the moment you're much more up to speed on the aircraft than my guys. You can put yourself down for some lectures as well on the initial courses. If you'd like to block off the last full week in January or the first week in February and we can decide nearer the time."

"OK. That's fine. We'll be in touch."

I sat down for a moment and thought over my conversation with Bill. For a start I could use the money working with NWIA though it was a pity in a way I wasn't going out right away since at this stage of the investigation I could probably spare the time. By going to Sydney I would have been able to talk to the servicing people who had dealt with the display on Alfa Juliet and, who knows, I might have found out some more about the 'party'. I needed to know if it was important or not. The phone rang yet again.

"There's a firm in Aldershot called Trethowan and Parker. Tell Carol to ask for David Smith. I knew him at law school and have had some dealings with him professionally since. Tell her to mention my name.

"Incidentally Peter, when are we meeting next? In case you have forgotten it's Thursday to-day. Why don't you come down and spend the week-end with me? We could go sailing or something. It could be fun."

"That's sounds a super idea. What are you doing to-night?"

"I'm having a quiet evening with a friend."

"That's a pity. I was going to suggest you came round here."

"I'll need an awful lot of persuasion to change my mind but you've talked me into it. I'll be with you to-night at about 7 o'clock, clients permitting. By the way we'd better not go out as I've got no clothes left."

"OK. That sounds exciting. It's definitely not a problem. I'll cook you a meal and, by the way, you can collect the clothes you left behind."

"Ah. I knew there had to be an explanation when I couldn't find them."

I sighed. "Well, I had better deal with Carol."

"Can't you deal with Carol over the phone?" I began to think she did not want me to see Carol.

"I'll try. I should be able to. However, it must be rotten for her, all alone with the kids and no family support except a frail mother."

"OK Peter, but she has been living in London by herself ever since Richard went to work with Cathay. She can't be that helpless."

I thought about that. Maybe I should be a bit careful not to be dragged into helping Carol, but I felt I ought to do something.

"Peter, are you listening to me?"

"Oh yes. Your advice is always good but I feel involved and that I ought to help."

"Well be careful." The phone went dead.

Carol's mother answered the phone when I got through, not sounding too strong.

"Is that Peter Talbert? Carol's told me so much about you. Thank you for helping her. This really is a terrible business. Carol's out shopping at the moment. I'll get her to call you. I don't think she slept much last night." She rang off.

My next call was to Mike Mansell. He was clearly worried.

"What about that business of the party, Peter? I know the crew had plenty of time to sleep on the plane but a lot of people won't like it."

"We don't know really if there was a party but I agree it won't help the cause. The problem is that we have no idea what was on the recording and the AAIB are not about to help us. However, the chances are the hijackers interfered with the pilots or perhaps a bomb went off, though I must say that it doesn't look likely at the moment."

"You're right. I'm probably worrying unnecessarily. Keep in touch."

Jim Akers came on the line. "How about lunch at Rules and then coming with me to the Press Conference? I've told them you'll be with me and I'll bring a press pass for you."

Rules in Maiden Lane was one of my favourite restaurants. However my upbringing, what the Americans called 'Mid Western ethic', felt that a working lunch at a place like Rules was decadent. I normally went there for a pre-theatre dinner. Diana used to like it and Mandy did too, though I never mentioned to Mandy that I'd been with Diana. I decided to be decadent.

"Fine. What time?" We agreed 1.15.

I went upstairs to change and Carol came on the line. I told her the name of the solicitor that Mandy had given me.

"Thanks for that, I'll contact them straightaway. Why don't you come over for dinner this evening?"

"Carol, I'm sorry I can't. I've got too much on investigating the accident. I'll try and call you to-morrow. Have you enough money?"

"Oh yes. I'm fine for a bit but I need to know Richard's insurance position."

I did not like the way she seemed to be depending on me but I felt I had to do everything I could.

"Anyway call me if you need help. Bye."

"Yes, I will. Thanks so much Peter." She sounded dreadful.

I accelerated and just made Rules at the appointed time. They showed me straight to the table where Jim was already waiting. The place was absolutely full and nobody seemed to be dieting or on the wagon. If there was an economic recession, it wasn't at Rules. We read the menu and the waiter sent our order on his machine down to the kitchen.

"Not much hard news about the accident, Peter. We don't know yet what the hijackers did or even if there was an explosion. The story about the party seems to be irrelevant."

"I hope you're right but I think it's too early to say. By the way, I liked the bit in your article yesterday on the 798 and the aircraft being the largest aircraft certificated by the new European authority. I have a concern in that area since the European Aviation Safety Agency seems to be law unto itself. There's no outside technical body seeing if they're doing a good job as the Airworthiness Requirements Board in the UK used to do interfacing with the Safety Regulation Group of the Civil Aviation Authority. In my experience an organisation that is not supervised in some way and is not being challenged technically, gets into bad habits. Anyway that's for the future I'm sure, not to-day's problem."

"But Peter, the European Aviation Safety Agency works very closely with the Federal Aviation Administration and they can't get very much out of step without everybody knowing. Both authorities have to certificate the other country's products."

"Of course you're right, Jim. But the competition between Airbus and the US manufacturers is enormous and both regulating authorities get pressurised by their indigenous manufacturers to relax the rules. In the UK we never used to yield to pressure. We had a reputation for being quite impartial in setting safety standards, wherever the aircraft was made. The UK authorities were as hard if not harder on the UK manufactured aircraft as on the foreign ones being imported into the UK. On balance I think the UK system was better than the EASA."

"I think you're fussing too much. In spite of this accident, look at the magnificent low accident rate that has been achieved world-wide, not just on UK aircraft. We gave in on abolishing our special UK requirements because we could not justify having them from a safety viewpoint." Jim emphasised his point. "In fact the new Regulations are probably stricter than they need be due to the influence of the UK."

"It's not quite as simple as that. Certification authorities very often don't even apply their own rules properly. You know full well that the UK has, on many occasions, had to insist on special requirements for certain imported aircraft because they felt that the original certifications by the FAA and others were not good enough. The most famous case I seem to remember was when SRG said that the FAA let the Boeing 747-400 through without proper venting in the cabin floor in non-compliance with their own regulations. SRG pointed out that if a cargo door had blown open in flight, the floor would have collapsed and the aircraft crashed. The UK imposed a special condition."

I paused and considered the situation.

"Look, I'm not saying that EASA certificated aircraft are unsafe. I'm just saying that the UK can no longer add its own safety requirements."

"Well you may be right but unless the accident rate goes up sharply it looks as if the UK may have been over zealous in the past and was the odd one out."

I said nothing. Jim was almost certainly right. Perhaps the UK had been too strict. As Jim inferred, the proof of the pudding was in the eating and air travel was probably still the safest form of transport. It was things like hijacking that ruined the statistics, not bad certification standards. However I decided to raise another issue.

"Jim, forget what has happened in the past. I think the situation is more serious than people realise. This terrible accident should make the regulating authorities consider carefully what should be the statistically acceptable level of risk for these very large aircraft. Should a higher standard of safety be demanded? The unpalatable fact is that all aircraft crash but these large aircraft carry so many people that perhaps the current safety level is not good enough."

"The manufacturers won't like that, Peter, and you can't very well change the rules now."

"Yes, you're right there but what could be done now is to consider whether there is any way of demanding safer operating rules. For example, should there be three flight deck crew instead of two on these large aircraft? Is it reasonable to expect two crew to be able to fly the aircraft and control all the aircraft systems if things go wrong? Should there be a flight engineer to deal with the systems and let the pilots get on with operating the aircraft?"

"Peter, you've got a good point there." He thought for a moment. "But wouldn't there have to be two flight engineers on a long flight?"

"That's a real problem, of course. However, it's managing the systems when things start going wrong that really concerns me."

We started to eat our meal and while the waiter was clearing away our first course Jim asked the point which was worrying everybody.

"What do you think happened? Why did the aircraft crash? It just doesn't make sense to me. I'm sure the hijackers didn't want it to crash."

"Perhaps not, but when you start intruding on the flight deck during an automatic landing in freezing fog you're asking for trouble. Let's hope it was a bomb but if Osborne's story about the recorder is to be believed, it would seem unlikely. By the way, I've checked with NWIA and they said that the plane was fully serviceable when it left Sydney.

"But Jim we can't ignore what is probably a key factor in the accident which is the weather when it tried to land. The fog was very thick but that shouldn't have been a problem for the crew or the aircraft. It was equipped with the latest blind landing equipment. However, I hope that someone organised a check on the GBAS after the accident in case it was faulty, assuming of course that they really were doing a Galileo approach." Jim raised his eyebrows querying what I had just said. "You know, the augmentation system which allows the Galileo satellite system to be used for Category III approaches. Of course we haven't heard the recording ourselves but despite what Osborne has said, the hijackers were there and must have been talking to the crew during the last part of the approach. Perhaps the flight deck microphone didn't pick their voices up."

I thought for a moment.

"Mind you, it's a bit much when we have to rely on Osborne. It's strange isn't it, if Osborne is right, that the crew didn't know something was wrong with their approach? I don't believe in the bomb theory but it does make the bomb explanation more likely. Hopefully we will learn something this afternoon."

Jim changed his approach.

"Do you think that the crew really get a rest in those 798 bunks? They look very comfortable but it would not do for me."

"I suspect it depends on the person. It must be much harder for the cabin crew because their accommodation is less spacious, but on the other hand their performance is less flight critical. The pilots are much better off up front and it should work. In my view, the crew that does the take-off should not do the landing but the senior Captain likes to do both and RWA management have gone along with it."

"What do you think of the 798? How does it compare with the A380?"

"You know I've only flown the aircraft in the simulator, but they both seem very good to me from a pilot's viewpoint. I can't speak for the economics. My concern is that the flight control computers in both aircraft are a vital part of the pilot's control function and are needed to get the required performance safely. Independant claims to rely less on the computers than Airbus but I'm not sure whether this is really true. We must not forget that the systems are controlled by software as well. We are completely in the hands of the aircraft and software designers just as much as the regulatory authorities, the FAA and the EASA, to ensure the safety standards are good enough."

The conversation stopped for a bit while we ate our main course. I only hoped it would not send me to sleep during the press conference.

Jim told me he was trying to get another article out to-night. He really needed a new slant and I guessed he was thinking of using the issue of higher safety standards for the new large aircraft. We finished our meal and were walking down to the Strand to get a cab when I saw a large headline on an Evening Standard billboard. *'MINISTER CALLS PUBLIC INQUIRY ON CRASH.'* I bought two papers as we took a cab to Marsham Street in Victoria. Jim looked at his copy.

"So that's why the Secretary for Transport called the press conference, Peter. He's decided to call a Public Inquiry. Do you know what that means?"

"I'm amazed. There's been some fairly recent legislation from the European Commission which prohibits individual countries having their own public accident inquiries. We used to be able to have them of course. Strangely, I think there was one on the Trident landing at Heathrow many years ago, clearly déja vue. The Commission are going to be very unhappy with the UK Government."

"Well the UK is not particularly enamoured with the EC at the moment so it may be quite convenient politically to strike a blow for freedom. Anyway, what's the effect of having an inquiry?"

"The inquiry effectively replaces the AAIB, Jim."

"That doesn't seem very sensible. They're the experts."

"Well we're going to hear all about it."

We arrived at Marsham Street and identified ourselves. We were given our passes and then ushered into a large room that Jim told me was always used for briefings. The place was packed and I saw Chuck Osborne from the Telegraph on the far side of the room. The Secretary of State appeared at about 3.30 and to my surprise he was accompanied by an uncomfortable looking Bob Furness. The Minister looked very grave.

"I've asked you to come here to-day because this is the worst aviation accident that has ever occurred in the UK. As you will have heard, I have decided to call a Public Inquiry. The effect of this is that I shall be appointing a Chairman and two other members to ascertain the cause of the accident. The AAIB will continue their current investigation but will now operate under the instructions of the Chairman since other investigations will be required into the hijacking, into the way the emergency was handled and there will also be security issues to be considered. To help some of you in your research in this matter, I'm having copies of the modus operandi of the Inquiry prepared so that you will be able to see the procedure that we shall be following. They will be available to you when you leave.

"I'd like to leave that subject for the moment and talk about the accident. I believe that it is important to keep all of you as fully informed as we can. As you know the plane was hijacked. We have found the bodies of the two guards who were travelling with the Secretary of State who had been shot. The aircraft carried two captains and two co-pilots and we understand that at least two hijackers were on the flight deck threatening the crews during the approach and landing. The emergency services were alerted before the aircraft started the approach and I'm sure that you are all aware that the emergency rescue services have and are doing an outstanding job. In addition, the local hospitals have responded to the demands of this accident superbly. The total death toll so far is 385 passengers and crew and 38 people in vehicles and on the ground. There are 101 people still in hospital and of those 27 are still on the danger list. The total number of people on the flight was 530.

"With regard to the cause of the accident, we are still investigating whether there was an explosion on the aircraft, but we now think that it is most unlikely that the accident was caused by a bomb. We feel it is far more likely that the hijacking interfered with the proper performance of the crew and the AAIB have been investigating the matter and will continue to do so, but now under the instructions of the Inquiry. I am, of course, extremely unhappy that there has been an apparent leak of information from the cockpit voice recorder and Bob Furness here, the Chief Inspector, is investigating how the leak occurred. The leak is particularly unfortunate because of the security implications. It is important that there are no more leaks and that we try to protect the bereaved as much as possible. I ask you all for your help.

"The facts on this accident are quite clear. The weather was very foggy and the aircraft was cleared for an approach using the Galileo European Satellite System. As you all know, it crashed half a mile short of the runway on the A30. Bob Furness will now give you some more details."

Bob went to the lectern, pulled out some notes and started his briefing.

"You will appreciate that we have a lot of work to do just to check the basic facts even before we try to discover what went wrong. What I am about to tell you is all preliminary information which will need corroborating."

Bob put up an approach plate for Galileo on runway 27L at Heathrow on a large screen.

"We believe that the crew were properly licensed and current in their required proficiency ratings. The aircraft had been serviced overnight in Sydney by NWIA. The aircraft was fully serviceable as far as we know at the start of the flight but the Captain's Navigation Display failed during the flight. The aircraft was hijacked nearly three hours before landing but the crew carried on flying very professionally. The aircraft was equipped to carry out automatic landings and appeared to couple automatically to the centre line and glide slope correctly. The local air traffic controller at the time confirms that the aircraft was on the centre line but at two miles he thought that the aircraft was low on the glide slope and warned the aircraft. The Captain then asked the tower for a wind check. The controller passed the wind which was calm. The controller was still worried about the aircraft's altitude and tried to transmit his concern to the aircraft but unfortunately there was another aircraft already transmitting on the frequency and the controller's transmission was blocked. By the time he was able to transmit, the accident had happened.

"We are analysing all the radar traces, VHF radio transmissions and the like and this will take some time. All we can say at the moment is that the aircraft was seen by the controller to be slowly going below the glide slope. You should be aware that the controller in fact has no responsibility to warn the crew in these matters though, once he was convinced that there was something seriously wrong, he did try to give a warning. In fact he told the aircraft to abandon the approach but by then it was too late.

"If it is confirmed that there was not an explosion, then the Inquiry will have to try to solve the problem of why the crew thought the aircraft was tracking the glide slope whilst in fact it was well below the correct flight path. It is very important that we find out what was the influence of the hijackers. The investigation is in its early stages but we wanted to share with you the current situation.

"Regrettably in one newspaper there has been a report of what was said on the cockpit voice recorder. However, without giving you any more details I can confirm that the crew did notice a slightly faster rate of descent than normal which would easily have been explained by a light following wind. There is nothing more I can tell you at this stage. My inspectors are working flat out reconstructing the flight, trying to assemble all the wreckage and trying to understand what went wrong. We have not yet analysed all the recorder traces in order to check on the navigation equipment."

Bob Furness remained standing and was joined by the Secretary of State who took over the briefing.

"Ladies and Gentleman. We are prepared to try to answer questions as far as we can."

Jim Akers asked the first question.

"Secretary of State, I thought that the EC had altered the rules affecting the investigation of accidents and that member states were no longer allowed to have Public Inquiries for accidents."

"That is debatable. In this case there is more to be investigated than just the accident, which is why the Government has decided to call this Inquiry."

Jim persevered.

"Secretary of State, can you tell us who the Chairman is going to be?"

"I have asked Lord Justice Thomas to be the Chairman and head the Inquiry and I am delighted to say he has agreed. We have not yet appointed the members and, of course, I want to consult Lord Justice Thomas when making the appointments. The members will be experts who have the appropriate knowledge and experience to understand all the likely issues to be investigated in this terrible accident."

Jim wasn't about to give up.

"Why couldn't you have left the investigation to the AAIB? They have an international reputation for their expertise and professionalism."

"As I said earlier, this accident has wide implications, and we feel we must leave no stone unturned to investigate all the threads leading to the accident and, of course, to find the cause. It is already very clear that the solution may be quite difficult to find."

Paul Franconi from the Daily Mirror raised a new subject.

"Secretary of State, I thought UK registered aircraft all carried marshals these days. Shouldn't they have prevented the hijack?"

"Paul," the Secretary of State was being unusually friendly I thought. Maybe they knew one another socially or, perhaps more likely, he didn't like the question. "It is not Government policy to discuss whether marshals are carried on aircraft."

"But Minister," Paul was not about to be put down, "it is obviously very important to know if there were marshals on board and, if so, why they did not prevent the hijack."

"Paul, I think we should leave that to be investigated by the inquiry."

There was a distinct murmuring amongst the audience. The reporters obviously didn't like being fobbed off. The Minister clearly knew more than he was going to disclose.

A reporter from the Independant then asked if there was any connection between the body found in the Hyatt car park in Sydney and Flight 573. The Minister said he had no information on the matter and quickly took the next question. I thought he looked a bit uncomfortable and I made a mental note to pursue the matter.

The Daily Mail man, who was next, focussed on the new information about the air traffic controller and the indicated heights. How did the controller know the aircraft was low on the glide slope? Bob explained that the aircraft height shown on the display came from the aircraft transmitting the information. There was no easy way of determining accurately if the aircraft was on the glide slope except by looking at the position of the aircraft shown from the secondary radar and only large errors are discernible.

One reporter asked about the Navigational Display and Bob Furness mentioned that the Display was a brand new one which had just been fitted before the flight in Sydney. The reporter queried whether it was significant that the display had just been changed. Bob said that this point was being looked at since it was possible the problem may have been an aircraft fault. The same reporter went on to query if anything else was changed in Sydney. Bob said that a Multimode Receiver was changed in Sydney but as there were actually three such receivers, any single failure would not be critical.

Questions were then asked about the safety of the aircraft and how it was certificated. The Secretary of State confirmed that this aircraft was approved by the European Aviation Safety Agency and that the UK had no independent jurisdiction in this matter. There seemed to be some surprise when this was explained since, despite Jim Akers article in the FT, most of the reporters thought that because the UK had issued the Certificate of Airworthiness for the aircraft on the UK register, the UK was responsible for the 798 type certification. The Secretary of State explained that the UK had no alternative under European Commission rules but to validate the 798 type certificate.

One reporter tried to discover if there was a conversation about girls and parties on the cockpit voice recorder and the Secretary of State became extremely stern and told the reporter that any such conversation, had it occurred, could have nothing to do with the accident since the flight had lasted 22 hours and that the crew had rested in the middle of the flight.

The press conference came to an end after about an hour without anyone really being any the wiser. Jim and I left and caught a cab to Waterloo.

"Well you've got a subject for your article in the FT to-morrow."

"Yes but I'm not sure about this Public Inquiry. It's likely to hinder AAIB's investigations, not accelerate them."

"Jim, I don't think the Minister had any alternative. He was getting bombarded with questions from MPs, the accident happened in the middle of a hijack and the leak of the voice recorder conversation cast doubt on the reliability of the AAIB. It's never happened before and let's hope it never happens again."

"You say that, Peter, but not releasing the voice recorder transcript enables the investigators to be secretive. We want to live in an open society with freedom of information and yet the recordings of the pilots' conversations are all hushed up. Let's face it, it's an unholy alliance between the Establishment and the pilots' unions."

"Well I admit there's something in what you say but you have to appreciate that there's bound to be a lot of stuff on the pilots' recordings which has absolutely nothing to do with flying but everything to do with private conversations, for example criticising the airline management, praising the attributes of cabin staff and, in this case, apparently talking about a party. If rules for the use of the voice recorder cannot be agreed then the pilots won't fly." Jim was shaking his head. "OK. You don't agree. It'll make another good discussion item for your article to-morrow." I carried on.

"Jim, are you going to mention the marshals. I thought the man from the Mirror had a good point."

"Yes, you're right. It is definitely worth a word or two."

We stopped discussing the Inquiry and started discussing the conference we'd just been to. We agreed that the new information about the air traffic controller thinking the aircraft was low on the glide slope was interesting but did not help in finding the cause of the accident. The analysis of all the recordings, not just the pilots' microphones, would be very important indeed and we would just have to wait until this had been done. I told him I was looking forward to reading the FT in the morning and got out of the cab. Jim carried on to Southwark Bridge. However I decided not to tell him that the warning system in the Tower clearly had not gone off or Bob would have mentioned it.

Blind Landing

In spite of my mind whirling trying to make sense of what had happened I remembered to buy some fillet steaks, new potatoes and salad when I got to Kingston before going home.

CHAPTER 7

John Fairlane

I met Mandy at the station at 7.15. She looked tired. It had obviously been a long day. We drove home in silence and she held my spare hand. That was the nice thing about having automatic transmission.

"I'm going to relax in the bath. It is breaking one of my principles but it will have to be your bathroom because I fancy using the Jacuzzi. You can run it and then start cooking the steaks. Leave the doors open to encourage me to come down. I've had no lunch. I could eat a horse."

"Well you won't have to unless the shop is liable for prosecution under the Trades Descriptions Act."

She went upstairs into the spare room. While I was waiting I put the grill on, got the steaks out of the fridge and then I laid the table in the dining room which I had seldom used since Diana had disappeared. I put the steaks under the grill and cooked them until they were both medium rare. They looked and smelt delicious with just a touch of garlic.

Mandy must have known when to appear from the smell. She was wearing a very thin blouse and short skirt.

"I thought you didn't have any clothes."

"Well I haven't as many as you think."

I inspected her more closely.

"I see what you mean. How do you expect me to eat?"

"Well you can start off with the food and then we'll just have to see."

She sounded very confident, with every reason as far as I was concerned. She took the salad and I took the steaks and we went into the dining room and sat down, adjacent rather than opposite one another. I tasted the wine. It was good and I poured it out.

"Well what have you been doing to-day?" she asked.

"I had lunch at Rules and went to the Secretary of State's press conference."

"I don't know how you can sit there stuffing steak if you've had lunch at Rules."

"It's not easy but I'm doing my best. I did have the foresight not to make a pig of myself and I walked back from Kingston station which helped a little."

"Well, I didn't walk anywhere and I don't intend to. You'll have to carry me up to bed when the time comes."

"You're on. Let me know when."

"That must be your decision. I've made all the decisions I intend to to-day."

We ate our steaks and steadily drank the wine.

"Shall I open another bottle?"

"I said 'no more decisions' but my advice to you is that we might both regret it. I am liable to go straight to sleep."

"How about dessert or cheese?"

"No just coffee. I'll help you clear up."

The phone rang just as I realised that once again I had not taken the receiver off the hook. I unclasped an arm and was able to reach the phone.

"Peter, it's Carol."

Mandy suddenly stiffened and moved away. I looked at her face and it was clear that she was not pleased.

"Carol. It's late. I'm up early in the morning. Can I call you again later? What's the problem?" I hope I did not sound as cross as I felt as I saw Mandy disappearing.

"It's Tristram. He's throwing temper tantrums and blaming me for Richard's death."

"Carol. This sort of thing is right outside my experience. You need psychiatric help. Why don't you go to your doctor first thing in the morning?"

"I'm sorry to pester you Peter. But there's no-one else I can talk to. You're right I'll do what you say." She sounded very unhappy and I felt I'd been rotten. "Good night."

I put the phone down and went into the living room. I felt very guilty being so abrupt with Carol. The living room was empty. I could understand Mandy's annoyance with the telephone call but surely she must know that all I was trying to do was to help Carol carry on living. I couldn't believe that someone as sensible as Mandy could be jealous.

I collected my things and went upstairs. There was no light in the spare room and I did not dare go in uninvited. I cursed Carol, but most of all myself for not remembering the telephone.

***

My alarm went off at 6.15. I got out of bed and knocked on Mandy's door.

"This is your wake up call."

"Thank you." That was all.

I went downstairs and put the coffee on and made her a cup of tea. I knocked on the door.

"Come in." Mandy was sitting up in bed watching me with the sheet firmly up to her chin as I entered her room.

"Thank you. You'd better get a move on."

I went into the kitchen and prepared breakfast. Mandy appeared shortly afterwards looking like a smart solicitor, wearing her glasses.

"Can I leave some stuff for Dora to wash?" She sounded slightly less frosty. As if there might just be hope.

"Be my guest. It will give her something to talk about in the pub. I haven't done any bacon if that's alright with you."

"That's fine. We weren't short of food last night." She helped herself to cereal and I passed her the carton of milk.

"Don't start relaxing standards, Mr Talbert. Where's the jug?"

"It needs washing."

"So?" She took the carton and helped herself.

I put the toast on and we settled down to breakfast. I heard the paper arrive, collected it, passed the main paper to Mandy and kept the business section. She looked at her watch.

"We'd better go. Can we leave the dishes for Dora?"

"Not to-day we can't. But there's another help here who may be able to manage. Go up and get your things. I'll get the car out."

I opened the garage, backed out to the front of the house and locked the garage door. Mandy came down and I put her bags in the car, then set the alarm and double locked the front door. We did not say much as we drove to the station. I got out and gave Mandy her bags.

"See you to-night, Mandy."

"Don't bet on it. Call me later."

Back at home I had a shower and got dressed. I had bought the FT and the Telegraph at the station and read Jim's article about the Inquiry and the press conference. He clearly had reservations about not being able to read the transcripts but on balance agreed that confidentiality was probably the correct approach. The article also criticized the Secretary of State for not saying if there were marshals on board the aircraft. I turned to Chuck Osborne in The Telegraph where he had mentioned the conference but then, incredibly as far as I was concerned, added that reliable sources close to the accident investigation were beginning to think that the accident might be due in some way to an error by the pilots and not due to the presence of the hijackers. Analysis of the Distance Measuring Equipment beacon, DME, showed quite clearly that the aircraft was very low on the glide slope. The phone rang and I went into my office.

"Peter, it's Mike Mansell. Have you read the papers?"

"Yes, thanks. You sound incoherent."

"Chuck Osborne has clearly got the AAIB building bugged. Bob Furness must be going mad."

"You're right. I can't remember anything like this happening before. It's just as well the Secretary of State called a Public Inquiry. I should think Thomas will be reading the riot act to Bob. Amazing."

"This could be very serious for us. What can you do, Peter?"

"I'm not sure at the moment. Things don't look too good, I admit. The only thing that gives me any hope is that Harry Hodgson was a first class pilot and wouldn't do anything stupid. It's so easy to blame the pilots but, in this case, perhaps there's a lot more to it. Don't get downhearted, Mike."

"I'll try not to but the omens are not propitious. When are we going to hear who are the members?"

"I would have thought we should hear to-day, before the week-end."

Mike rang off and I decided that I didn't know enough detail about how the RWA 798s used the Galileo Satellite System for approaches and landings. I called Jill Stanton and asked to talk to John Chester. She put me straight through.

"Thanks for talking to me, John. How are things going?"

"As well as might be expected. Did you read that rubbish by Osborne?"

"Yes I did but surely he must be reflecting the attitude in AAIB?"

"I suppose so, Peter, though how he knows what's going on is beyond me. It's about time Furness took over the investigation himself instead of leaving it to the senior inspector in charge. Obviously, there are lots of people in the AAIB who are concerned with the investigation and clearly so far Furness hasn't found the leak."

"Anyway John, Harry wouldn't have done anything foolish, whatever the pressure from the hijackers."

"I know that, you know that, but the aircraft has crashed and, if Osborne is to be believed, it was well below the glide slope while the crew did nothing." He stopped. "Anyway Peter, how can I help you? You're working for our insurers so hopefully we're on the same side."

"I'd like to learn a bit more about the Galileo installation on your aircraft. Could I talk to your expert?"

"Of course. The man you need to talk to is Evan Evans and if he doesn't know all the answers he'll put you onto someone else who does."

John gave me Evan's number and told me to call him in a few minutes after he'd briefed him. I thought about calling Mandy but decided it might be better to wait a bit. The mail didn't look terribly interesting but I did a bit and then called Evans.

"You don't know me, Mr Evans. Did John Chester call you and explain that I needed to understand certain details about the Galileo installation on the 798?"

"Yes Mr Talbert. I gather you're representing one of our insurance companies. How can I help you?"

"Well if you're prepared to talk on the phone perhaps you could run through how the Galileo satellite system is used for making approaches and landings on the 798. I want to be absolutely sure that my understanding of the system is correct. Assume I know nothing. Will that be alright?"

"Fine, though I suspect I'll be teaching my grandmother to suck eggs. Well as you know both the microwave landing system and instrument landing systems, MLS and ILS, transmit a horizontal centre line for the runway in use and a 3° glide slope angle for landing. The MLS and ILS radio receivers on the aircraft just listen to the signal modulation as it is called and can tell straightaway where the aircraft is relative to the centre lines of the runway and glide slope. The desired centre lines, both vertically and horizontally, are determined by the siting of the ground antennae. On the 798 there are three receivers to guard against failure, all in one box. OK?"

"Yes, fine. That's what I like about ILS and MLS, no software."

"Right. Now the Europeans decided they wanted their own navigation system and not be dependent on the United States Global Positioning System. They would have liked to have called it the Galileo Positioning System but obviously the acronym conflicted with the United States GPS so they were forced to use just Galileo."

"Evan, that could have been incredibly confusing."

"Anyway, approaches using Galileo, or any satellite system for that matter, are done very differently from MLS and ILS. On the 798 there are three separate Galileo satellite position receivers housed in one box. The output from each receiver is fed through a selector switch into a separate Multimode Receiver, MMR and each MMR has a world database of airfields and runways. So each MMR compares the aircraft's position from its satellite receiver with the runway and glide slope centre lines calculated by the software."

"Sounds great, Evan, as long as the database information is OK."

"Well Peter, good point and somebody must have thought of that. At each airfield there is a Ground Based Augmentation System, GBAS, which transmits the latest runway information so that for a Cat III approach the MMRs use the GBAS transmitted runway position; however if there is a big difference between the MMRs runway position and the GBAS's runway then the aircraft is prevented from making the approach. Of course the beauty of using satellite positioning for approaches and landings is that the airfield does not need to have MLS transmitters for each runway. The deviations of the aircraft from the computed centre line and glide slope are sent to the auto-pilot and to the displays in just the same way as for MLS."

"Presumably there are three Galileo receivers and MMRs to get the required integrity for automatic landings just like there are three MLS and ILS receivers?"

Blind Landing

"Yes that's quite right, and the avionic manufacturers have put the three receivers in one box. The pilot selects whether he wants to use the MLS, ILS or Galileo for the approach and the MMR sends the deviation output, computed in the case of Galileo, to the flight deck display and to the automatic flight system. The accuracy of the Galileo signals have to be improved for a Category III approach and so the GBAS transmits the necessary information to enable this to happen as well as the runway information."

"If I understand you correctly the GBAS is the European equivalent of the United States Global Positioning System LAAS, Local Area Augmentation System?"

"Yes, that's exactly right. Both satellite navigation systems need augmenting to get the required accuracy for precision approaches, particularly for Category III though I don't think LAAS sends out runway positions."

"You make it sound straightforward but goodness knows how the experts ensure the software integrity for the system. Presumably from what you say there is a choice of satellite systems which can be used for landing, GPS and Galileo?"

"Yes, that's so. However, Royal World Airlines decided they didn't trust the United States GPS system and in any event GPS Category III approaches were not certificated when the first 798 was delivered because the new GPS satellites were not yet in orbit. I think the long term aim is for the MMR to use satellite positions from the Russian System GLOSNASS, GPS and Galileo so that position will be so accurate GBAS won't be required. However at the moment GLOSNASS is not used at all."

"Are the Airbus and Boeing aircraft organised the same way?"

"No, Peter, they are not. Technology changes at a frightening pace, as you know and 798 took advantage of the latest advances. It is the first to have this method of organizing the satellite navigation systems. One good thing about the design is that it keeps the two different satellite systems in step."

"What about for ordinary navigation, Evan?"

"Well in the case of the 798 the two systems are kept entirely separate but either GPS or Galileo can be selected for en route navigation on the MMR controller."

I couldn't think of any more immediate questions though I knew there would be some the moment I rang off.

"Evan, thanks so much. I need to think about what you've just told me."

"If you need anything more give me a call."

Thinking about things, it seemed to me that whichever positioning system was used, satellite approaches could only work safely for Cat III conditions if the database information for each runway was absolutely 'immaculate' and that was the beauty of GBAS. The other blindingly obviously point was that the whole system was completely dependent on software. I was used to automatic flight systems and Flight Management Systems using a lot of software but not to the idea that ordinary radio receivers also needed software.

I got myself some soup and wondered what to do next. The phone rang.

"Peter, I'm sorry I was unreasonable about Carol. You're quite right to try to help her. How is she to-day?"

I felt a wave a of relief that Mandy had realised the pressure I was under.

"I don't know. I haven't called her and she hasn't been in touch. Perhaps I should. But I don't want to encourage Carol to depend on me." I paused. "Mandy, what are you doing this week-end?"

"Well that depends. I'm catching the 6.10 to Bournemouth and going home. After that I haven't decided whether to go to the yacht club, ring up a friend or wash my hair."

"I could help you wash your hair."

"I'm not convinced that would help but you could come round and try."

"I'll meet you at Waterloo at the platform entrance and if that fails I'll catch the train anyway and meet you at the station exit. Do I need to buy the shampoo?"

"No, only dinner."

The line went dead and I decided to call a French restaurant that I knew she liked in Poole. If her car wasn't working we could always go by cab. It was close to the yacht club so we could have a drink there first if we wanted. I went upstairs to put a few things in a bag when Mike rang again.

"They've just announced the members. The first one is Jeff Templeman, Chief Engineer of Britannia and the second one is Professor Charles McGuire, professor of software engineering at Imperial College."

"Good Lord. Templeman is OK but I'm not sure about a software professor. They always try to say that everything needs more testing. However, to be honest it's probably a very shrewd move to make him an assessor. I'm just beginning to realise how much software might be a factor in this accident, it seems to be everywhere. By the way, do we know anything about the Inquiry?"

"That was the other thing I was going to tell you. The Inquiry is going to have a preliminary meeting next Thursday to determine the procedure with a view to starting it quite soon. Everybody who wants to be party to the proceedings must notify the Treasury Solicitor if they have not done so already."

"Next Thursday? That sounds very soon. Have you told the Treasury Solicitor you want to be there?"

"Yes, we have. You're right, it seems incredibly early but the Inquiry wants to get things started. The Inquest starts on Monday but that is going to be confined to identification at this stage. Of course, with so many dead identification is going to be a real problem. The Coroner is taking special measures to speed things up. Obviously the Coroner and Lord Justice Thomas have been talking and there seems to be no reason why a lot of the facts can't be established and recorded in the first part of the Inquiry even though the reason for the crash is not known."

"What about AAIB? What are they doing?"

"Presumably they're under orders from the Inquiry and continuing with their investigation. Now Peter, we need to have a meeting with our solicitor, Tim Forrestal, and our counsel John Fairlane. Can you manage Monday at 11.00?" I agreed. "Fine, come round to my office and then we'll go round to John's."

I looked at my watch after Mike had gone and then tried to speak to Carol. Her mother answered the phone, Carol was collecting the children. I said I'd call sometime over the week-end but that I was not going to be at home. I finished packing, remembering to put in the stuff that Dora had done, and went downstairs just in time to pick up the phone.

"You won't know me, Mr Talbert. My name is Anne Moncrieff." The voice was very French but the English was perfect. "I'm currently employed by the Safety Regulation Group at Gatwick as a surveyor but at about the time of the certification of the 798 I was attached to the EASA certification team from the French equivalent of your CAA, the DGAC. I had some reservations on the way the EASA team were handling the certification."

"Ms Moncrieff, how did you get my name?"

"Because of my job I know a lot of the electronic engineers in the airlines and I had discussed my reservations with Evan Evans some time ago. I wanted to talk to someone and he suggested I talk to you."

"Have you spoken to AAIB?"

"I tried to but I didn't seem to be getting anywhere so I've written to the Chief Inspector."

"That's good. Bob Furness will contact you, I'm sure."

"I read your article some time ago about the aircraft in the FT. I know you've been retained by the insurers. Is there any chance that we can talk?"

"How are you placed on Monday?"

"I'm working at Gatwick."

"Well could we meet at lunch time? No, that won't work. How about at the end of the day?"

"If you could come to Gatwick we could meet at the meeting point in Terminal 2 at 5 o'clock."

"Fine. I'll be wearing a grey suit, carrying a black briefcase and I'm in my mid thirties."

"I shall be wearing a blue jacket and trousers and I'm probably a few years younger than you."

"Good. We should be able to recognise one another. But give me your mobile number in case I need to cancel."

The phone rang as I put it down. Mandy was on the line.

"Bad news I'm afraid. One of my clients in Edinburgh is in trouble with the police and needs to see me this evening; almost certainly I'll have to go with him to-morrow to the police station. If I don't stop I can get the 17.30 shuttle."

"But what about our week-end?"

"We've got something to look forward to."

"But what about your hair? It needs washing."

"It's going to have to wait. I'll call you when I know what's happening. Must fly. Bye."

She was gone and so was our week-end. I wondered whether it was a wealthy client or an altruistic mission or maybe both. I called the restaurant and cancelled the meal and then went upstairs to unpack. It had been quite a week. Perhaps a restful week-end doing nothing might be a good thing. There seemed to be no way I could help Mike Mansell which was worrying me. I secretly agreed with Osborne's alleged view of the AAIB; the chances were that with hijackers in the cabin the pilots' attention was diverted and didn't notice the approach was going wrong. It was strange Ms Moncrieff calling me. I wondered what she wanted but it would have to wait until Monday to find out.

***

The week-end passed very slowly. I'd made no alternative plans following Mandy's unexpected departure. I did some work and tried to catch up with the many periodicals which I received, since it was vital for me to keep up to speed on what was happening or the march of technological progress would pass me by. New ideas were always emerging and it was important to watch which ones fell by the wayside and which were adopted by the industry.

Blind Landing

I'd recently subscribed to cable TV and tried to find something decent to watch but apart from sport there was mainly a choice of old films. Mandy called on Saturday afternoon.

"I've finished at last. I'm catching the 7.30 shuttle and I'm going straight home."

"Shall I come down?"

"To be honest Peter, I shall have to spend to-morrow sorting myself out. Give me a call to-morrow afternoon and we'll try and synchronise our diaries.

"It wasn't our diaries I had in mind."

"Sometimes I think you have a one track mind " There was a pause. "Never mind, looking forward to hearing from you to-morrow."

On Sunday the papers arrived and I scanned the Times. Not much about the accident so I decided to go out and buy the Telegraph. Sure enough Osborne was giving the readers the benefit of his views on the accident. In fact, apart from reiterating the alleged AAIB view that the accident was probably due to pilot error, there was nothing particularly new.

I pondered over the dead body at the Hyatt in Sydney. The Secretary of State had looked uncomfortable when he was questioned and there was no mention of the body in the Sunday newspapers. It may have just been a coincidence but the description of the bullet did suggest a hijacking pistol had been used. I wondered whether there had been a security clamp down on the media. If there was, then I needed to know. I called Jim Akers.

"Jim, I've been thinking."

"Peter, it's Sunday and I'm at home resting."

"Come off it. You guys never rest if there's a story."

"A story? That's different." Jim suddenly sounded interested.

"Well I wouldn't call you on a Sunday to pass the time of day. The dead body at the Hyatt..."

Jim interrupted me.

"Oh, I knew you'd notice the Secretary of State's rapid reply." He paused. "Go on."

"Well I wondered if the media was having it's future read by the Government? A D-notice perhaps?"

"You're quite right of course. The guy was meant to be on the plane but we've been told not to mention it."

"Why not?"

"That's just what we would like to know. I wanted to chase it up and investigate who the fellow was but my editor told me not to. My guess is he was a marshal and a hijacker took his place."

"So much for freedom of information."

"I agree but there's not much we can do."

100

I rang off. If Jim wasn't going to do anything then I would have to. The explanation of the murdered man could significantly affect the hijacking. Perhaps Mandy would have some ideas on where to start digging for information.

After lunch I called Mandy and we agreed to meet the next day at the Archduke next to Waterloo at 6.30. I'd be back from Gatwick by then and she would have finished work.

It wasn't too bad a day for January and I drove down to the river and went for a walk. On Monday I went up to town and arrived at Mike Mansell's in plenty of time.

"What sort of a week-end did you have, Peter?"

"Very quiet, unfortunately. My girl friend had to work in Scotland. How about you?"

"I went down to my little cottage in Wiltshire. Also very quiet. A change from London."

"What's the plan for to-day?"

"Well we need to brief our counsel John Fairlane and also Tim Forrestal our solicitor. Tim of course will be going to the preliminary hearing on Thursday and I thought we should give them some background to the accident. What did you think of Osborne's piece in the Telegraph?"

"I don't think it said anything new, did it?"

"I agree but from our point of view it's very bad news if that is the AAIB view. Anyway, let's go and see Tim."

We walked along to Lincoln's Inn where we were shown our way to John Fairlane's chambers. We waited briefly and then Fairlane appeared and introduced himself. He was 6ft 2in grey haired, thin and very distinguished. He spoke precisely and slowly as I expected from a QC.

"Let's go into my office and talk this thing through. Tim Forrestal, your solicitor is here already." We followed into a large room which had a partner's desk covered with papers in an orderly manner. He invited us to sit at a conference table where Forrestal was already in position. We shook hands. Tim was a bluff man, 5 ft. 10 in. wearing a brown suit and not my immediate idea of a solicitor. He started to summarise the situation.

"We have a unique legal situation. This is the first aircraft accident since the EC altered the accident investigation procedures. The Secretary of State for Transport has directed that a Public Inquiry shall be held and replace the normal investigative procedure carried out by the AAIB. This is against the latest EC rules. However the AAIB investigation is still proceeding but is now under the control of the Chairman and members of the Inquiry. The responsibility for determining the cause is now shifted from the AAIB to the Inquiry. In order for this to be done the Secretary of State has appointed Lord Justice Thomas as the Chairman to lead the

Blind Landing

Inquiry and has appointed two technically able members to help the Chairman; as you know they are the Chief Engineer of Britannia, Jeff Templeman, and a software professor, Charles McGuire from Imperial College."

John Fairlane interrupted. "Tim, I'm still not clear why the Secretary of State called the Inquiry, especially as the EC rules don't permit it. Why couldn't he have let the AAIB carry on as normal?"

"Well the reason for the Inquiry being called is not of course relevant to our discussion, but the generally accepted view is that the Secretary of State was forced to have the Inquiry because of the security implications which are outside the remit of the AAIB. It is very convenient therefore, with such public interest in such a terrible tragedy, to have a public inquiry. The Attorney General has given notice that the main Inquiry will start next Tuesday."

"But that's ridiculously soon." John interjected.

"Yes, it is. But the Inquiry wanted to get the non-critical evidence out of the way while it was still fresh in the witnesses' minds. The inquest will still be on but it won't matter. It will be adjourned once all the identification of the bodies is complete but, of course, with so many bodies to be identified the inquest is going to be a very long one. The Inquiry preliminary meeting being held this coming Thursday is to determine the procedure and to check who wants to be represented and thus become a party to the proceedings.

"The obvious organisations will be Royal World Airlines, Independant, the aircraft manufacturer, the National Air Traffic System which provides aerodrome control at Heathrow and the ground installations for both the ILS and Microwave Landing System. Then there will be the consortium who control the Galileo European Satellite System and the manufacturer of the local augmentation system, GBAS; also General Electric who make the engines. I suppose the pilots' and controllers' unions will also wish to be there. We shall be making an application to be a party to the proceedings because we are so involved financially and because only by so doing can we cross examine the witnesses. In addition, we shall probably wish to call witnesses as is permitted in the legislation. We cannot rely on Royal World Airlines to protect us since the hull is insured elsewhere and we need to look after our own interests. I imagine their hull insurer will be present and I anticipate that Microspot, the maker of the multimode receiver, MMR, may also wish to be represented. I suppose that the Police and the Emergency Services will ask to be represented as a matter of routine but really it is unnecessary for them since it is quite clear that they did a magnificent job.

"The order of the Inquiry will be determined at this preliminary meeting and also a likely calendar to be followed. I anticipate that I will be at this meeting and the discussion we are having to-day will enable me to make the necessary request for time and witnesses. I expect that the first few days of the Inquiry will be spent hearing evidence from the Police and the Emergency services in order to satisfy everyone that everything that could have been done was done. After that it would seem logical for the chief inspector of the AAIB to be called followed by the senior inspector allocated to the accident. What the Inquiry looks at after the AAIB evidence may well depend on us. By the way, the Inquiry will almost certainly be in two parts. The first part, as I said, will be to try to establish what really happened. The second part will be to permit the assessors to get further evidence to establish why it happened, and to determine the true cause of the accident so that the Inquiry can write its report to the Minister. This report ought to include how the hijackers got on board and how the leak got out from the AAIB."

I indicated that I wanted to speak and Tim nodded to me.

"Tim, the way the plane was hijacked could be important. Apparently the media are under a D-notice over the body that was found in the Hyatt car park in Sydney. He was on the passenger list. We really need to find out who the person was."

"What do you suggest."

"I'm not sure but possibly that's how the hijacker got on board, pretending to be a marshal. If John threatens to ask some questions, we might be let into the secret."

John Fairlane joined in.

"That's exactly right. Tim, it seems to me that the Inquiry may well want some of the evidence held in private in view of the hijacking. As you say, they must discover how the hijackers got on board, what weapons they were carrying and how these weapons escaped the inspection of the ground staff in Sydney, but they may not want all that information to be public knowledge."

"Yes, John, I'm sure you're right. I expect they'll tell us on Thursday how the Inquiry will be organised. With any luck, by the time the AAIB evidence is over it may be an open and shut case of hijacker interference." I made it clear that I was uncomfortable with relying on that happening. "Peter here clearly doesn't agree with that rather optimistic hope and he may well be right. So what I think we have to do this morning is to review what we believe happened to Alfa Juliet and to decide the witnesses we need. We need to judge what the AAIB and other expert witnesses are likely to say and whether we feel there is going to be a conflict of opinions."

"Thank you Tim." John Fairlane took over the running. "That's very helpful. It seems to me listening to what you've just said that it is going to be very important to know what we expect the AAIB to say and so I think we should start there. Mike, any views?"

"Well, there have been a succession of inspired leaks about what the AAIB have been thinking in the Daily Telegraph, which seems to have a source giving them information. The first leak was the voice recorder transcript and the significant point here is that if the Telegraph report was right, there was nothing really to suggest that the crew should not have been able to carry out and complete the approach and landing. After that first leak, the report stated that it was the view of the inspectors that the accident was due to pilot error. Presumably, the inspector is going to tell us why they think that."

John turned to me. "Peter, I think it is time you explained to us the procedure that the pilots would have adopted in making the approach. I should have thought that the aircraft would have been designed so that pilot error just is not possible."

I settled down as I realised that this meeting was going to take some time if I was going to explain how the aircraft made the approach.

CHAPTER 8

Anne Moncrieff

Tim, Mike and John were all looking at me. I drank some water, took a deep breath and started slowly. I pointed out that the phrase 'pilot error' is not as simple as it sounds. Pilots can and do make mistakes but the most common pilot errors are due to poor aircraft design, normally due to a bad interface between the pilot and the displays. Sometimes errors are due to a lack of understanding of a too complicated aircraft. Normally these errors occur only if there is a malfunction of some type. It is always necessary to be on one's guard because it may be that the manufacturer of the aircraft, for competitive commercial reasons, will not acknowledge that the aircraft itself could have been better designed.

"The problem is complicated because not all pilots have equal ability. An aircraft has to be capable of being flown by the world's worst airline pilot. The facts are that there is a huge range of ability and modern aircraft are incredibly complicated. Who is to judge when an aircraft is so complicated that it is unreasonable to expect the below average airline pilot to fly it?"

John butted in as he realised I was about to continue.

"Come on Peter. Answer your own question. Who is to judge what is satisfactory so that pilots will not make mistakes?"

"In the short term the regulation authorities. That is the Federal Aviation Administration or the European Aviation Safety Agency. There is of course a bible of Airworthiness Requirements with which the designer has to conform. However, life is not that simple. Things are not just black or white, right or wrong. When the aircraft manufacturer applies for the aircraft to be certificated, judgements have to be made on acceptability, decisions have to be made on whether the aircraft is too complicated for the below average airline pilot. If a wrong decision is made then accidents will almost certainly occur. That is why it is so important for every accident to be investigated wherever it happens in the world and for the real cause of each accident to be established."

I looked around at them all. "This is easy to say but very hard to do because when an accident happens in a remote place it is invariably the aircraft manufacturer and the regulation authority of the country where the original type certificate was issued who are asked to help the local accident investigation authorities and it could be that commercial pressures will try to prevent the true cause of the accident from being established."

John came in again.

"Surely it is in everyone's interest to establish the truth?"

Blind Landing

"You know much better than I do, John, that truth is a matter of opinion, depending on where you happen to be sitting. Wasn't it Pilate who said 'What is truth?' and he wasn't jesting. It is vital that the true cause of an accident is established so that any necessary modifications are carried out."

"I'm not sure I understand what you are saying about modifications, Peter."

"Well the normal situation is that if there is an accident due to bad design then changes will be required to prevent the accident re-occurring. Obviously, manufacturers have mixed feelings over this since they will invariably have to pay for any changes and of course they don't like that. So the regulatory authority must ensure that any necessary modifications are declared mandatory."

John indicated that he had got hold of this point and had finished taking the note. I carried on.

"Let's talk about Alfa Juliet. The aircraft had flown all the way from Australia and had enough fuel, but only just enough, to meet the minimum requirements of being able to land or divert to Manchester where the weather was good, then being able to carry out a holding pattern near the airfield for 45 minutes before landing. RWA Operations therefore told the captain that he could carry on to Heathrow as planned where the weather was bad, in that there was an indeterminate cloud base and the visibility was 30 metres. This sort of weather is classified as Category IIIC for landing and, in the case of Alfa Juliet, this meant that the approach had to be made by the automatic flight control system. The pilots had a supervisory role so that if anything went wrong they would initiate what is called a missed approach procedure and the automatic flight system would apply power to the engines and climb away from the airport. Yes, John?"

"Surely the pilots have to take over sometime during the landing?"

"Yes, the procedure is that the pilot flying the aircraft disconnects the automatic flight control system after touch-down when the aircraft is going sufficiently slowly to be able to steer it by reference to the centre line runway lighting.

"Now returning to Alfa Juliet, Hodgson apparently did all the correct checks and coupled the aircraft to the Galileo satellite system for an approach on runway 27 Left. However, for some reason the aircraft went below the correct 3° glide slope and it crashed. I'm not sure whether we're going to be allowed to listen to the recording but the AAIB have and, according to Osborne in the Telegraph, they think that the accident was due to pilot error. This means that they have discounted the effect of the hijackers. I'm very unhappy about that because it is bound to be

106

difficult to judge what effect having a knife or pistol held at the pilots' throats will make on their ability to perform correctly."

John looked at me. "Surely we're going to be able to hear the recording?"

"A good question. I believe Tim must insist that we be allowed to hear the recording, possibly at Farnborough or possibly at the Inquiry but I can't believe that the Inquiry would want that because the recording would then be a matter of public record and that would not be acceptable in the UK."

"Would you be satisfied with the transcript, Peter?" Tim was obviously reviewing how to play his input at the preliminary hearing. "It ought to be possible to get hold of that."

"I'm not sure you will be allowed to have it but to answer your question, the transcript may be good enough but it obviously would be better to hear the recording played in real time." I looked at him. "Can't you press the Inquiry to play the recording?"

"We can try. Whatever happens we'll use the first part of the Inquiry as a fact collection opportunity." John was summing up. He obviously needed to get on with some other work. "I'll get everything we need from the witnesses and then Peter, you'd better advise us what you consider is our position and what else we need to establish. Tim, let me know how things go on Thursday."

The meeting was over and we chatted in the lobby before going our different ways.

"I'll call you on Thursday Mike and then you can tell Peter how I got on." Tim was complaining, half to himself. "I can't see why, if the Inquiry goes into private session, we can't listen to the recording."

I butted in.

"As long as everybody is searched for private voice recorders before they go in, Tim, it might be alright, but let's face it, if the press were there it definitely would be a non-starter."

Mike and I went back to his office.

"What do you think?"

"I don't like the feel of this thing, Mike. As we said earlier, the chances of having a pilot error accident at the same time as a hijacking is extremely slight unless the two events are inter-related. How would your policy stand up if the pilots made a mistake because of hijackers pressure?"

"I don't know but I would have thought we would get away with it. However, it would be expensive because we might be taken to court." He paused. "Come on, let's go and have a sandwich."

We went into Covent Garden and watched the world go by.

"I didn't tell you Mike. A lady called me up on Friday in connection with the certification of the 798. Apparently there was a problem and she wants to tell me about it. Perhaps it might be relevant. She sounded French with a very English name."

"When are you seeing her?"

"I'm going to Gatwick in a moment. She's employed by the Safety Regulation Group down there."

"Well good luck. We need a break."

"It's early days yet, Mike. We don't know what the hell happened on the flight deck. If Osborne has seen the transcript then we certainly must see it as well but reading it won't be good enough, we must hear the recording."

I went down to Temple and caught the circle line to Victoria. At Gatwick I was a bit early and went to Terminal 2 arrivals and had a cup of coffee. At ten minutes to five I wandered over to a position where I could watch the meeting point. Looking around I could see a lady dressed as per specification with a brief case, also watching the meeting point. She looked over, saw me and grinned. I went over to her.

"I'm Anne Moncrieff." I suppose I looked surprised. "My family name was Delange but my husband's name is Moncrieff."

I gave an inward sigh of relief. Mrs. Moncrieff was not unattractive and I wanted no complications with this witness.

"How pressed are you for time, Mrs. Moncrieff? Can I get you tea or have you time to go over to the Hilton for a drink or a meal."

"Anne, please." She came to a rapid decision. "Well my husband won't be home until 8 o'clock to-night. We live in Croydon. It will be quieter at the Hilton."

I led the way and we walked through the car park to the Hotel.

"Drink or food or both?"

"Let's sit by the bar. We can talk there."

We wandered over and sat down.

"Anne, I used to be a pilot and am now a consultant on flight decks. I have been retained by an insurance company to help them over the recent 798 accident."

"You are a journalist as well, Mr Talbert. I read your article some time back on the 798."

"Please call me Peter." I carried on. "Well not a journalist, though I do occasionally write for the FT and other periodicals on technical matters."

The waiter came over. She chose a glass of white wine and I asked for a Scotch and water.

"I know of course that the 798 was hijacked, Peter, and that therefore the accident could be due to that. However, the weather was very bad and it occurred to me that it was just possible that the hijacking was irrelevant."

"You are quite right to be concerned. Until the Inquiry gets under way we'll have no idea of why the accident happened."

"Let me tell you a bit about myself. I have a masters degree in electronic engineering specialising in aircraft systems, obtained at the Paris École Polytechnique. My first job was with DGAC in Paris, the equivalent of your SRG here at Gatwick. I was sent to Hoofddorp in Holland to get experience. I was attached to the EASA team certificating the 798 and I was lucky enough to be sent over to Independant in Seattle with the certification team. We had endless presentations and I was especially interested in the satellite navigation and landing systems and, in particular, the way they were installed." She paused, picking her words carefully. "To be blunt, having heard the presentations, I did not like the way the Galileo and GPS receivers were installed, I did not like the standard of the software inside the Multimode Receivers, and I did not like the way the flight path deviation was presented to the pilots."

I couldn't help smiling.

"That's seems fairly comprehensive, Anne. What did you do?"

"Forgive me, but I am now going to have to tell you a lot of information that you probably know already in order to explain the problem I had with the EASA certification team."

"Don't worry about it. Just tell me the story as it happened."

"Well, firstly the GPS and the Galileo receiver boxes provided by the manufacturers had provision for three separate receivers on three separate cards within the box and the outputs from each card was fed into a different Multimode Receiver. Each MMR then computed the necessary steering commands to drive one of the three channels of the autopilot. This arrangement was to give the required integrity for automatic approach and landings. I felt that the three satellite navigation receivers should have been segregated into three separate boxes to achieve the required standard of safety but the manufacturers of the boxes had convinced both the FAA and the EASA that it was not necessary because of the particular power supplies being used and the way they had been arranged within the box. One of the reasons they did this, I am sure, was because they had to have a receiver to receive the GBAS augmentation information and they only needed to have one augmentation receiver if all three navigation receivers were in the same box."

Our drinks arrived which gave me time to make some notes.

"Very well. My next problem related to the Multimode Receiver. As you well know the box is full of software to calculate the steering command to the autopilot and this software has to meet a certain safety standard which is set by the regulation authority, in the case of the 798 by

Blind Landing

EASA. This standard had been agreed with the FAA to be category B for the software of the Multimode Receiver. I felt this was not of a high enough level since the Multimode Receiver did all the computation for the autopilot during a blind landing and a failure could be catastrophic. In my view, the software level should have been set at Category A. but I suspect the box manufacturers did not want the extra cost of preparing the documentation."

"That's all very understandable but what was wrong with the flight path deviation information, Anne?"

"Well it is all to do with the display of the deviation information to the pilots. In the case of the 798, the pilots are shown the same deviation from the desired flight path on the approach as is passed to the auto-pilot. Therefore, if it was incorrect for the auto-pilot then it would be incorrect for the pilots looking at the displays. The fundamental point here is that there was no independent method for the 798 pilots to check if the deviations being calculated for the auto-pilot were being done correctly and, therefore, for the pilots to check if the aircraft was on the correct glide slope and centre line. I had real reservations about doing it this way with the satellite systems, because of the intricacy of the software. I felt that the pilots must not be completely dependent on the MMR and auto-pilot software when carrying out Category III landings, but I was told to shut up and stop raising difficulties."

"Anne, let me be the devil's advocate. There are three Multimode receivers, not one. Doesn't this deal with some of the problems you are raising?"

"No, Peter, I'm afraid not. In my opinion only a completely separate reference system which the pilots could look at in fog conditions when the auto-pilot was flying on Galileo would be adequate. Of course as you are well aware, a forward looking device that could see through fog, displayed on the head up display, would be a possible solution but such systems don't work very well yet and no such equipment was fitted to the aircraft."

"But there is an MLS indicator which the pilot can look at on the left hand side of the centre instrument panel if he is doing a satellite approach."

"Yes, Peter. That's just what Independant said but such a display is not mandatory doing a Cat III approach and in this case there was no MLS"

"What happened after you made these comments?"

"In the evening I was told that I was an observer, fresh out of training, no experience and I was not a contributor to the technical discussions. If I had any comments I could write them down and give them to the team leader when we got back to Cologne. So I stopped asking questions and continued making copious notes during the briefings. When I got back I did write a report showing that, when all my concerns were taken together, the RWA aircraft could not meet the overall required safety standard during a Category III approach. I pointed out that in my opinion Independant had only done the display installation the way they had because it would have been very difficult to present deviation information on the displays independently from the auto-pilot without a lot of extra complication and expense.

"I was called in by my team leader and asked to withdraw my report and I refused to do so. The next thing that happened was that I was called from Paris administration and they told me that they had been reviewing their manning requirements and how would I like to go to Gatwick and become an electronics surveyor. It was obvious that I had caused great embarrassment to the certification team of the EASA and they wanted to get rid of me.

"My English needed a lot of practice so I decided that I would not make a fuss and accepted the posting to Gatwick. In fact it was not long after that that I met my husband to be and we got married quite soon afterwards. He is an executive with Britannia at Gatwick so it was all rather convenient."

"Anne, did you keep copies of your correspondence?"

She smiled at me as if I was out of my mind and opened her briefcase.

"Here is a copy of my report and another letter asking them to confirm that they had my report on file. Needless to say there were no replies."

"Did you do anything when the 798 crashed? You must have been very concerned."

Again she gave me another look as if she could not believe I could be so stupid.

"Here is a copy of the letter I wrote to the AAIB the day of the crash. Again I have had no acknowledgment. In fact I sent the letter again, recorded delivery to the inspector in charge of the 798 accident and the letter was delivered."

She gave me another set of papers.

"As you know, Anne, there is going to be a Public Inquiry fairly soon. Are you available as an expert witness if you are needed?"

"Yes. I would be delighted. You and I know that for some reason the crew were below the correct glide slope and because of the installation they were unable to see this."

"Anne, I believe your comments may well be very relevant. We'll know a lot more when we are allowed to hear the flight deck voice recorder and know what the hijackers were doing. Like you I do not believe what we are being told in the press, that the accident was due entirely to pilot error. Apart from anything else the hijackers must have been influencing the proceedings. We need to find out what really happened and, if necessary, convince the Inquiry members.

"However, there is one thing that occurs to me. Airbus criticised the avionic design of the 798 when they were trying to sell their aircraft. Was this the point they were criticising?"

"Strangely, not at all. They were getting at much less critical parts of the system."

"Thanks for that. Hopefully the Inquiry will soon be under way and these matters can be discussed."

Anne gathered up her things and I gave her my card.

"If you change jobs or move please let me know."

She gave me her card and we said goodbye. I caught the next train back to Victoria, went to Waterloo and went upstairs to a table in the Archduke. Mandy appeared a few minutes late. We embraced.

"Sorry if I still look like a solicitor."

"You look lovely and you know it. And your perfume is exquisite as usual."

"You noticed."

"I notice everything about you. It's lovely to see you, I've been looking forward to it all week-end."

"I should hope so. If we're being honest, so have I." She squeezed my hand underneath the table and then moved her chair next to mine and not opposite so she could rest her hand on my knee. "Where have you been, Peter."

"I've been having a drink with a twenty five year old attractive young lady."

"I'm not sure I like the sound of that."

She drummed her fingers on my knee.

"Well she managed to find time for me between leaving SRG at Gatwick where she works and her husband's return. She's French but she married an Englishman who works for Britannia called Moncrieff."

Mandy relaxed and the fingers stopped drumming.

"Where did you two have this adventure?"

"It wasn't exactly an adventure, it was in the bar at the Hilton. You're so suspicious."

"And don't you forget it." She moved her hand slightly up my leg which I found disturbing.

"Stop it, I'm trying to concentrate."

"I'm enjoying my supper."

"We haven't started yet."

"I have. Alright let's order."

We placed our order.

"Peter, did what Ms Moncrieff tell you help in any way?"

"It's too early to tell yet. It may have done, depending on what actually happened on the aircraft. I thought all her points were very valid. Before she worked at Gatwick she worked for DGAC in Paris and was attached to the EASA certification team for the 798. She told me all about her misgivings on the 798 avionic installation. She had a row with EASA after visiting Seattle when the aircraft was being certificated."

"Why did she have a row with EASA?"

"Because she was a new girl and the EASA engineers were hypnotised by Independant. She raised the very fundamental point that the pilot only sees what the auto-pilot sees so it's very difficult to monitor the approach independently, which is important if the approach paths are calculated by software."

Mandy considered this and then remembered I'd met Mike Mansell.

"How did you get on this morning?"

"Well we were briefing John Fairlane, the QC CrossRisk Insurance are using, and Tim Forrestal, their solicitor. Tim is going to the preliminary meeting on Thursday to meet with the Inquiries lawyers. I expect you know him." She nodded.

"I'll be there, Peter. It should be quite a short meeting."

"Are you sure? One of the issues will be whether the Inquiry will be in private or not when it comes to the flight deck voice recording; will everybody be allowed to hear it? Is anybody going to be allowed to hear it? Does the recording indicate how the hijackers got pistols and a bomb on board? Shouldn't all this be in private? My bet is that there will be a lot of argument but I'm hoping that some of the Inquiry will be in private so that we can hear the recording."

"Won't they produce a transcript?"

"They don't even do that normally and if they do they often miss out bits they think are not relevant. However this time, because of the Inquiry I think they will. That's why the meeting might take longer than you think. Deciding on the procedure." I looked at her. "And there's another problem. There's a D-notice out on the dead body they found in Sydney. Apparently he was due to be a passenger."

Mandy looked at me in amazement.

"A D-notice? That's ridiculous. It had better not apply to the Inquiry. Anyway how do you know?"

"I suspected there was one and Jim Akers confirmed it. He and our solicitor Tim are both trying to sort that out. Any ideas of what we might do to find out about this man murdered in Sydney would be very welcome. We need to know who he was for a start."

I could see Mandy considering the matter.

"Have to think about that." She looked at me. "When do we meet next?"

"How about Thursday? You can stay with me and tell me all about your meeting."

"OK. You can take me to Café Fish at six when they open and then we can go home. Pick me up from the office."

"Done."

Our meal arrived and we had a pleasant supper together.

"Now you're sure you won't stay?"

"I'd better not. I've got a lot to do and nothing to wear. Alright I know, but I've still got a lot to do. See you Thursday."

I saw her off to her train and then caught mine. When I got home I decided I'd better call Carol.

"I'm so glad you phoned, Peter. My solicitor has heard from Cathay and they have wired me £50,000 while they sort out the exact lump sum and pension due to me. It's a great relief. Please thank your solicitor friend for helping me."

"I will. At least that bit is good news. How are the children?"

"Tristram has gone very quiet. Wendy talks a little about the accident and her father. I think I am going to take them away to somewhere warm and have two or three weeks holiday. What do you think?"

"Carol, I think that's a very sensible idea. Why not go somewhere with lots of activity for youngsters? It doesn't have to be warm. You could take them skiing. The sooner the better. I'll call you in a couple of days."

We chatted a bit more. I rang off feeling rather guilty that we had not talked longer. As I went round the empty house doing this and that I reflected on the 798 accident. I hadn't really found out anything though the conversation with Anne Moncrieff might be important. The AAIB as directed by the Inquiry members would be working at the problems and getting data twenty four hours a day, whilst other people like myself who were vitally interested, would be completely in the dark except for what was leaked in the Daily Telegraph. It looked as if the truth about the hijacking was being blanketed by the D-notice. What a ridiculous situation.

CHAPTER 9

Diana

For the next three days I prepared some lectures, read some technical papers and wrote some letters to airlines trying to get more work. I left very early on Thursday and was at Mandy's office in plenty of time. She appeared looking like a girl who was being taken out to dinner and looking forward to it.

"I hope you didn't look like that in the office."

"Why not? You're a spoil sport."

"Well I know how I feel. I wouldn't like your clients feeling like that."

"You're jealous."

She looked pleased to see me and I hailed a cab for Rupert Street.

"How did the meeting go?"

She clearly wasn't in a hurry to tell me.

"I'll have a Kir Royale please, with plenty of attention."

The waitress, probably French, came over and took our order. We looked at the menu and made our choices. The girl returned with our drinks, bread and paté and I ordered salmon for Mandy and trout for myself.

"You were right, Peter. The meeting took a lot lot longer than I was expecting. The Treasury Solicitor people seemed to be in charge of the arrangements and of course there was endless discussion on how the Inquiry should proceed. In the end it was decided that the relatively non-contentious stuff like the police and firemen should start followed by the air traffic controller who was on duty.

"We then debated for hours about whether we should listen to the recording. AAIB said that it was unheard of for interested parties like us to hear the recording except for very special technical reasons. We countered by pointing out that this was not an AAIB investigation but a formal Inquiry conducted as a Court of law and we needed to hear the recording as evidence. AAIB then changed tack and said that we wouldn't be able to understand the recording because it was very noisy. We then asked for a transcript which was refused but, after a long battle, the Inquiry decided that a few people nominated by the interested parties could hear the recording and the transcript would be available for the second part of the Inquiry.

"The recording would be played at the Inquiry in private session without the press. A complete list of attendees for the private session was made, each organisation saying who they wished to be present and why. While still in private session the Inquiry would hear from the UK security experts and all of us would be excluded. It would be a very private session."

"Does the legislation permit that?"

"It refers to 'public interest' and presumably the Inquiry has every right to decide who will be present. Anyway, since the legislation is now outdated and this is a special inquiry they can almost do what they like. It was agreed that after the private session the Inquiry would go back into public session for some preliminary questioning of the AAIB inspectors. We all insisted that there should be a twenty four hour gap after hearing the recording before resuming the first part of the Inquiry so counsel could be briefed, which suited the Inquiry anyway because of their private security session. After the AAIB evidence had been heard, the first part of the Inquiry would be stopped. It would only be reconvened when the Inquiry felt that they were ready to take the rest of the evidence from the AAIB specialists and from the witnesses provided by the interested parties, RWA, GE, Honeywell etc. When the second part of the Inquiry was over, the Inquiry would prepare their findings for the Secretary of State, referring to likely causes and with recommendations for avoiding future occurrences."

"Well that's pretty comprehensive. They'll have to go to Sydney I should think to investigate how the hijackers got on to the aircraft with their weapons, though I'm not sure whether they can do that legally. I suppose they could get some people to come over. Of course, we don't know anything about the Hyatt body yet and the impact on the hijacking but I suppose they may have been told something. It's good news about hearing the recording. We should be able to understand exactly what happened."

"Isn't it rather unusual for everyone to hear the recording?"

"Well yes. But this Public Inquiry is unique and after all it isn't everyone who is hearing the recording. It's only the experts of the parties who are directly concerned and they should all be responsible people."

"The recording will get leaked, Peter."

"I'm not so sure. After all, the people who will hear the recording are known to the Attorney General." I paused. "Will you be at the closed session?"

"I don't know. I shouldn't think so. We may want to nominate an expert to listen."

We discussed it a bit more then I got side tracked looking at Mandy and she noticed I was noticing.

"I think we're ready for a night cap at home."

We caught a cab to the station and another home from Kingston. Mandy went upstairs while I made the coffee. This time I remembered to make sure the answering machine was on and I altered it to make sure it recordrd after one ring. Mandy appeared and we took our coffee into the front room and sat quietly for a bit enjoying the moment. I looked at her.

"You're making it very difficult for me to drink my coffee."

"You can have coffee any time. I thought you'd be pleased."

The phone rang for a moment and then the answering machine took over.

"Well you got one thing right but it's a bit bright in here."

I turned most of the lights out and put our coffee safely on the dresser.

"Wouldn't a bed be more comfortable?"

"Don't be so conventional."

I didn't argue.

***

We had to move quickly in the morning to get Mandy to the office on time. Dora wasn't coming until Tuesday so I didn't mind leaving the house looking a bit the worse for wear. I packed a few things for the week-end and we rushed for the station. I saw Mandy safely to the office, left my bag with her and went on to have a coffee and croissant in my favourite breakfast spot waiting for Mike to arrive; clearly insurance executives didn't start work at eight.

The Telegraph was full of the programme for the Inquiry and complaining of the iniquitous procedure of having a part of the Inquiry in private without the press being present to look after the public interest. Jim Akers in the FT said how necessary it was to have private sessions to prevent hijackers learning from the mistakes and successes of other hijackers. I finished my breakfast and went round to Mike.

"Have you heard about the Inquiry, Peter?"

"Only what Mandy told me. The private session sounded good because we'll be able to hear the voice recording.

"Yes, that is good. As you know the AAIB strongly resisted playing the recording or even providing a transcript but the Inquiry overruled them. Perhaps it was a judgement against them for leaking the recording. We need you there Peter because I'm sure you'll get more benefit from hearing the recording than Tim will. We put your name on the list as our technical expert."

"Won't John Fairlane be there?"

"No, I don't think so. We need him for cross-examination of the witnesses after we've briefed him. Then we shall have to have a meeting with John immediately after you've heard the recording."

"Will I have to give evidence, Mike? At the moment I've got nothing to say."

"Not for the first part of the Inquiry but you may learn something from the recording. I hope you'll have something to tell the Inquiry when the main part starts."

"You and me both."

After leaving Mike I went to the Royal Aeronautical Society to read some articles I needed from their library though I couldn't find some of the books I wanted as they were kept in a library at Farnborough, which I thought seemed a strange arrangement for a learned Society; however there was quite a lot of material I was able to look at on line. I was there for the rest of the morning and some of the afternoon and then went to the Royal Air Force Club to catch up with the periodicals, timing my departure to be at Mandy's office at 5.30. She didn't keep me waiting long and we were on our way in a taxi to Waterloo.

Mandy looked a bit weary but there was something else as well which I could not place. I knew she was pleased to see me and we leaned towards one another but I found I got the cheek and not the lips.

"Where are we having dinner?"

"I've booked a table at that place you like in Poole. The food's always good and they look after us well."

"Lovely." She held my hands, looked at me carefully, thought about saying something, changed her mind and then carefully kissed my cheek. We caught a fast train and then a cab to her flat.

"I need a shower and change and so do you" she said sternly. "Let's have a quick drink before we go out. I want to catch up with what you've been doing. Put your things in the other bedroom. I've missed you, Peter."

"Since this morning?"

"Since last night."

Mandy had first shower in the single bathroom and I showered while she dressed. It might have been quicker the other way round though I shaved while I was waiting. In fact I was ready just before Mandy and shouted through her door, asking her what drink she wanted. "I'll have a gin and tonic as it's Friday." came the muffled reply.

I prepared two gin and tonics, just in time before Mandy appeared.

"Call a cab will you, otherwise you won't be able to drink at all. Not that you drink much, I'm glad to say."

I obliged and asked the driver to be along in twenty minutes.

"What have you been doing to-day, Mandy?"

"Do you really want to know? It's so tedious in some ways but so important to the clients. How about you?"

"I saw Mike who didn't tell me anything new. Then I've been working at the Royal Aeronautical Society."

Mandy paused and again looked as if she was going to say something, but didn't. The taxi driver rang the doorbell.

118

"Come on, darling, drink up, we need to leave for Poole."

It was only a small place and we were put at a table near the back. We were not late but the place was quite busy. I ordered two more gin and tonics. We started talking of all sorts of things not connected with our work and again I realised how our lives were getting more and more involved. I thought that when this investigation was over I might ask Mandy to come away for a holiday and perhaps we needed to talk over the future. Perhaps I should sell the house for a start to lay the ghost of Diana. However, I sensed there was something on her mind which needed flushing out.

We decided to have coffee before we left since we were in no hurry. We got home soon after eleven.

"Peter. Let's have another drink. I want to say something."

I returned with two fairly stiff gin and tonics.

"Sit down over there." I complied with her request, wondering what was coming.

"I've had a client visit me to-day and it made me think about where you and I are going. We like one another a lot and we now know that we enjoy having sex together. But I'm not sure we should be making a habit of it. We need to decide whether we have any future. Peter, I see so many cases in my office of people who get into a tangle and I don't want it to happen to us. I know you like to forget all about it but we don't know whether Diana is alive and likely to reappear, or not."

She stopped and looked at me.

"Peter, you look as if I've hit you"

"Well you have really, metaphorically. You know I've done all I can trying to find Diana. I think the world of you and I thought our relationship was developing well. I feel a bit shattered. This is all rather sudden."

"Well let's sleep on it. I'm going up now and we can talk some more about the problem in the morning."

She came over, kissed me on the cheek and then went to her room. I never did understand women, or maybe I did.

***

In spite of Mandy's worries we had a lovely week-end together. The weather wasn't too bad for January and we managed to walk in the New Forest on Saturday. On Sunday I made breakfast and took the papers into Mandy's room. When we'd finished she got me to clear all the dishes away into the kitchen.

"Why don't you read the papers next to me in the bed?"

"It might spoil your New Year's resolution."

"Nonsense. Don't boast." There was a pause. "However I've decided I don't mind your trying."

Later she came out again with what was worrying her. "Didn't you ever find out where Diana went?"

"No. We'd been quarrelling for a long time and I was away a lot flying. I began to suspect that she was seeing someone else. One day when I got back from a long trip to Australia she had disappeared. I reported it to the police who suspected me at first but they lost interest after they found she was definitely alive after I had left. Her parents had not heard from her but she very rarely contacted them anyway. It was and still is a complete mystery."

"But you do see? She may come back. We can't ignore that."

"You may be right but I can't spend the rest of my life waiting for something that may never happen, and I don't want to lose you just waiting."

She rolled over in the bed and looked at me.

"Well it certainly is a problem." She thought a bit. "Peter, why don't you go on up to London now and get yourself organised for the Inquiry on Tuesday? If you come up with me early to-morrow morning you'll be rushing all day to-morrow."

Subconsciously I had been wondering how I was going to get everything I needed to do done on Monday and Mandy had now come up with a sensible solution. I nodded my agreement and got up and had a shower. Mandy got her car going and took me the station. We held each other for a bit and then I left to catch the train.

"Keep in touch, Peter." She waved as I disappeared up the steps.

The ghost of Diana which had stood behind us and which we had tried to put out of our minds was now out in the open. There must be a way of dealing with it legally. Surely Mandy must know. Why didn't she say? I was sure we both felt that there might be a real prize if we could find a way through. When we had said good-bye at the station we each had more confidence in the other than we had before the week-end. I decided to have another talk to my solicitor to find out how long one had to wait before the presumption of death. He had mentioned something to me at the time of Diana's disappearance but I had not taken it in. On balance I felt the week-end had been a success.

On Monday morning when I called Ted McIntosh, my solicitor, I explained my worries about Diana. "If she doesn't reappear is there anything I can do about getting a divorce? I seem to remember a year or so ago you mentioned seven years. It seemed a long time then, it seems much nearer now."

"Well Peter, let me ask you first has anything happened to change the way things were when we last spoke? In other words have you heard anything from her or have you heard anything from anyone else that leads you to believe she might be alive?"

"No I haven't. I left her to do a Britannia trip to Australia and I have never seen sight or sound of her since. As far as I could see at the time she had not taken anything with her. The jewellery that I had bought for her was still in her drawer and our bank account was untouched. I can only assume she died or was killed in some way, though how there was no trace is inconceivable to me."

"Well you've put your finger on it. You are presuming that Diana is deceased. The law says that if, after seven years from when she disappeared, there has been no change to the situation you may make a petition to the court to have it presumed that Diana is dead and to have your marriage with her dissolved."

"What happens if she reappears some time later and I have remarried?"

"You don't have to worry about that. Once you have gone through the necessary legal proceedings relating to death and divorce and your decree has been made absolute, then it does not matter if Diana reappears. It is the same as any other divorce that has been made absolute."

"So you're telling me to be patient and everything will work itself out?"

"I suppose I am really. Anyway keep in touch and you may think it sensible to check again about now to make certain that her parents have not heard anything."

I rang off. Presumably Mandy knew all the solicitor had told me by heart and I guessed she was nervous of Diana suddenly reappearing. I decided to call Diana's parents in Newcastle under Lyme. I think they secretly blamed me for her disappearance but we continued to have civilised conversations. Her mother answered.

"No, Peter. We've heard nothing at all. I've tried the police recently to recheck the unidentified bodies list from the time when she disappeared until now but there still does not seem anything that matches up. How are you managing?"

"I'm OK, but I must admit losing Diana is still a great strain and I find the uncertainty very upsetting. How about you?"

"Well we get along, but losing our only child is a great loss."

"I understand. Let me know if anything happens? Bye for now"

There was nothing more to be said. There never was any common thread between us except Diana and she had gone. In the evening I called Mandy and brought her up to date.

I went to bed thinking of the Inquiry. Presumably we would hear how AAIB's investigations had been progressing. It was vital to find out what had happened on the last few minutes of the flight of Alfa Juliet and my concern, judging by the leaks to the Telegraph, was that the investigation might be stopped prematurely without a proper technical investigation.

INQUIRY DAY 1

The Chief Constable

The weather was not very kind, raining hard and with a strong wind but still it was reasonably warm for the middle of January. I got up in plenty of time, went up to Town and had my normal breakfast of croissant and coffee before going to Mike Mansell's office. We left in plenty of time to get to the Queen Elizabeth Hall at 9.30, half an hour before the Inquiry was scheduled to start. The organisation of the Inquiry seemed good and we signed in as people who were parties to the proceedings. We went in to the hall and sat in the space specially provided.

The place was already filling up and I identified the area reserved for the public, the press, the places occupied by the counsel, the witness box and the Members of the Inquiry, placed on a fairly high dais. I saw Tim Forrestal but there was no sign of John Fairlane. Presumably he would only appear when there was something for him to do. At 10 o'clock prompt we all rose and Lord Justice Thomas appeared with the two members, Charles McGuire and Jeff Templeman. I looked for Chuck Osborne but he was nowhere to be seen. There were a few pressman but not as many as I expected.

It was always difficult at first to judge the age of someone wearing a wig but to my surprise Thomas seemed comparatively young for someone in such an eminent position, probably just less than fifty years old. He was quite short but had not run to fat, perhaps because he was abstemious or maybe just lucky. It must be very difficult to keep fit and trim as a judge, sitting long hours in court. Templeman looked a tough egg, six foot, heavy in build but not fat, slightly red in the face; I guessed the Chief Engineer had a drink or two during the day. McGuire looked very different from the other two, short, definitely running to fat, untidy suit, peering through thick glasses, every inch the stereotype of a professor. Time would tell how these three members of the Inquiry would perform and behave.

The proceedings opened with a statement from Lord Justice Thomas explaining that the accident was unprecedented in the UK bearing in mind the number of people killed and the location of the accident. The aircraft had crashed in the middle of a hijack and it was important to discover how the hijackers had managed to get on board the aircraft at Sydney. It was also vital to discover whether the hijack had caused or had contributed to the accident or whether the accident was due to some completely unrelated cause. He said that because of the serious nature of the Inquiry it would be conducted as a Court of law with counsel to examine and where applicable cross examine the witnesses who would be

123

giving evidence under oath. He anticipated that the Inquiry would be in two phases; this first phase would establish what had happened and, possibly, try to establish some indication of the cause of the accident. The Inquiry would then have to go into private session when the security aspects of the hijack were being discussed and when the voice recording was being played to the expert witnesses. There would be a gap while the Inquiry discussed with AAIB and others what extra work might be required and what additional witnesses would be needed. The Inquiry would then reconvene and hear the latest developments, if any, in establishing the cause of the crash; the information would come from the AAIB and any other witnesses who might be requested to appear by the parties to the Inquiry or by the Inquiry itself. He intended that the Inquiry would review all aspects of the accident, on the ground and in the air, to find the cause, to ensure that all the necessary lessons were learnt and to make sure that such an accident was unlikely ever to occur again. The Inquiry would then be closed and in due course the findings would be announced.

Lord Justice Thomas went on to explain that the Inquiry would hear first the reports from the emergency services, to ascertain how well they had performed and to see what improvements, if any, were required. It was the intention then to hear evidence from the AAIB to learn how far the investigations had proceeded. The witnesses would be examined by the chief counsel of the Attorney General and could then be cross examined by counsels on behalf of the organisations that were parties to the proceedings. He anticipated that the first two days would be spent looking at the emergency services and hearing the air traffic controller before calling the AAIB witnesses.

With the opening statement finished the proceedings started and the Chief Constable for the Metropolitan Area, Sir Robert Applegate, was called as the first witness. He was questioned by Janet Crowburn, the leading counsel for the Attorney General. Encouraged by suitable questioning, Sir Robert described how his officers had been alerted by calls from Heathrow saying that the aircraft G-RWAJ was transmitting a hijacking code and that the RWA Flight operations had had a message from the aircraft saying that the hijackers wanted the aircraft to be refuelled, some Government held al-Qaeda prisoners to be released and then loaded on to the aircraft which would then take-off for somewhere in the Middle East. Apparently the hijackers threatened to blow up the aircraft if their instructions were not complied with. By the time he had arrived at the police hijacking control room, RWA had told the office about the Foreign Secretary being on board.

Sir Robert went on to detail how the standard hijacking procedures had been implemented, how the crash crews and ambulances had been controlled and how the army and security forces had been integrated with the accident organisation. Furthermore, it had been arranged for the AAIB inspectors to have complete visibility of the accident site once the security and explosives experts forces were satisfied it would be safe to proceed.

Because of the hijacking every survivor needed to be checked by the security forces which made things very difficult and there was also a worry that there might be a bomb buried in the wreckage. The large number of bodies was another problem and in the event eight mortuaries were required to keep the bodies prior to the coroner's teams identifying the corpses. One difficulty was dealing with the people who lived nearby and also it was necessary to prevent onlookers trying to get to the crash site. The media were another concern as they kept on demanding unrestricted access which had to be refused.

Under the direction of AAIB the first crash recorder was found after eighteen hours but, despite intensive searching, it took another two days before the second recorder was recovered.

For the first forty eight hours the operation was an emergency one but gradually the emphasis changed to routine control as all the bodies had been removed and the AAIB inspectors were painstakingly examining the wreckage, which was then moved to a hangar at Farnborough to be arranged like the real aircraft in an effort to work out what had happened prior to the crash. When finally the AAIB had pronounced themselves satisfied that they had done all they could on the wreckage site, the A30 was reopened though the public was asked to hand in any further wreckage discovered later to the police.

When Sir Robert had finished chronicling the history of the ground response to the accident Lord Justice Thomas congratulated him and his enormous team for the very professional way the accident had been handled. He asked if Sir Robert felt that the response could have been improved if he had had more resources.

"No my Lord. We had a carefully worked out plan which had been refined as a result of other disasters such as the fire at Kings Cross and the Marchioness on the Thames. This plan had been dovetailed to match the Heathrow aircraft accident procedures and in the event we could do no more.

"I would like to pay tribute to the many, many firemen who risked their lives rescuing the survivors from the very hot wreckage and to the hundreds of people, police, ambulance men, army personnel, who worked for hours at a stretch dealing with this enormous problem. I would also like to pay tribute to the staff at the many hospitals involved and to the general public who co-operated with our plans to enable the rescue and investigation to be carried out so quickly."

Crowburn asked the Chief Constable if he knew the identity or the organisation of the hijackers.

"No, Ma'am. I was informed by the security forces that there had been an anonymous telephone call at about 6.30 that evening claiming that an aircraft would be hijacked and flown to Heathrow. Six high security al-Qaeda prisoners were to be released and put on board the aircraft. This warning had roughly coincided with the alert they had received from the airport. Unfortunately it had not been possible to trace the call. Apparently there had also been another telephone call in the early hours of the morning, allegedly from some outlawed IRA organisation, making it clear that the hijacking was none of their doing."

"Sir Robert, the hijackers apparently threatened to blow up the aircraft. Did you come across any bombs in the wreckage?"

"As I mentioned, we had a team from the Army helping us and apparently there was one badly damaged bag which had some explosive material close by. I don't know the details but the material had not exploded or ignited."

"Sir Robert, were there any weapons discovered during the search of the wreckage?"

"Well Ma'am, I believe there were some weapons discovered by the Army and security experts, but I am not familiar with the details."

There was a pause while Crowburn considered whether to explore the Chief Constable's answer in more detail. She leant down and spoke to one of her assistants, hesitated and then indicated that she had finished and it was clear that none of the other counsels were going to ask any questions. It was now lunch time; Sir Robert's evidence had taken well over two hours and the Inquiry adjourned. Mike and I went to a nearby pub to have a sandwich.

"Well Peter that's got the Inquiry on the road. I understand from Tim that Crowburn intends to call the duty officer at the British Airports Authority, the duty officer in the Heathrow fire section and the duty Control Tower air traffic control officer. He would have been the one who pushed the panic button alerting the fire station and indicating where the accident was likely to be. He will be the last witness to be called before the AAIB, since he will describe the air traffic landing procedure."

"What about the explosives expert and the weapons expert for that matter?"

"I think they will leave that until the closed session with security."

"Mike, do you think we need to go back this afternoon?"

"Not really. I think we should be here to-morrow afternoon to hear the air traffic evidence."

"You know Mike, I think they will be calling the approach controller before the tower controller because they have got to establish

126

the type of approach the aircraft was making. They may do it later but it would be a lot tidier if they got all the air traffic evidence over before AAIB."

"I'll check with Tim. He may want to check with the Inquiry's solicitor who they are calling."

Mike went back to his office but on impulse I decided to go back in to the Inquiry. In fact there was nothing really significant in the evidence but it was necessary for it to be given so that it was clear to the general public that all the emergency services had worked correctly. The Inquiry finished at five o'clock but there was still some more evidence to be given before the air traffic control evidence. I left just before the end and went home.

When I got back I went into the front room and switched on the television to watch the news. The Inquiry was mentioned but at a very low key. I had supper and read some technical magazines, then went to bed and watched the TV. I remembered that John Chester had told me that the relief first officer, Frank Mercer, had not been killed in the accident. Perhaps I should talk to him if he was getting better. Presumably AAIB must be talking to him if he was fit enough. Come to think of it, I hadn't spoken to Marcia Hodgson. That was something else I should do. I dropped off to sleep.

INQUIRY DAY 2

The Controllers

Next morning I went straight to the Queen Elizabeth Hall at about ten o'clock and sat next to Mike who was already there. I noticed that the seats reserved for the press were filling up. The airport fire officer was giving his evidence.

"He's the last one before the approach controller who will then be followed by the local air traffic controller on duty as you thought."

We listened to the fire officer and then the approach controller, Harvey Gates, was called. Janet Crowburn was doing the questioning. Gates explained that he had taken the aircraft over from the en-route controller in the Clacton sector and had positioned it for an approach on runway 27L. He cleared the pilot for a Galileo approach and the pilot asked if he could use the MLS instead but he had explained to him that the ATIS was incorrect and that the MLS was out of service. The pilot then requested a Galileo approach and he cleared the aircraft for the approach and to change frequency to Heathrow Tower.

Janet Crowburn decided to question Gates.

"Mr Gates. Why couldn't the aircraft carry out an MLS approach on 27 Left?"

"Ma'am as I explained the MLS was out of service. It was not transmitting so RWA 573 could not have used it, even if the pilots had tried."

"Now, the decision by the captain of RWA 573 to use the Galileo European Satellite System to land on 27L. Is that normal?"

"Well the procedure is approved though I can't recall it being used before in Category IIIC conditions because normally the MLS is serviceable."

"So in your view Mr Gates, there was nothing unusual in RWA 573 saying that they were going to do a Galileo approach?"

"It was unusual because, as I said, up to now the MLS has been working and pilots prefer to use the MLS. I checked with the approvals, saw it was permitted, and gave permission from an air traffic viewpoint. It was not my job of course to check if the airline permitted this crew to make this type of approach."

"Thank you very much, Mr Gates. That is very clear."

There was a pause to see if there was to be any cross examination but all the counsels present seemed to be content. The approach controller stood down and was replaced by the tower controller, Humphrey Barton. Ms Crowburn asked him to tell the story in his own words.

"RWA 573 came on to my frequency when it was at about ten miles finals at 3,000 ft and asked if the GBAS was serviceable. The cloud base was indeterminate and the transmissionmeter at the landing end of 27L was showing close to 20m. I cleared him to land, confirmed the GBAS was serviceable and passed the transmissionmeter settings. Everything looked normal at first. At two miles I thought the aircraft was low on the glide slope; I gave the pilot a warning and he then asked for a wind check. I asked the Met. Office since we only had surface wind in the tower and then passed the pilot the wind at 1,000ft. I tried to warn him again that the aircraft was below the glide slope but a Lufthansa aircraft kept on interrupting my transmissions. The height seemed dangerously low and though it was not my responsibility I called to tell the aircraft to abandon the approach but there was no reply. The next thing that happened was that the fire crew called and said they thought the aircraft had crashed short of the runway; I pressed the crash alarm button, spoke to the duty fire officer and told him the accident must be somewhere just short of the 27L runway. I told all the aircraft on frequency to go around and repeated that the airport was closed. I called approach control and told them that there had been an accident and divert all aircraft. There was nothing more I could do."

Barton looked very shaken as he finished telling the sequence of events.

"Thank you Mr Barton for that very clear description. I am afraid there are one or two questions I must ask you for clarification to the Inquiry. First of all transmissionmeter, what does that mean?"

"A transmissionmeter measures the runway visibility at its location and its reading; it is situated next to the runway and its readings are shown in front of the tower controller. In fact because visibility in fog is so variable there are normally three transmissionmeters for each runway, one at each end and one in the middle and this was the case for 27 Left. Aircraft landing and take-off minima depend critically on the actual visibility and that is why the readings are shown to the controller so that the controller can pass the information on to the aircraft captains. Of course, in the case of 27 Left the readings were for information only, since the aircraft was permitted to land in zero visibility, though had it been zero he would not have been able to taxi without a follow me van."

"Thank you Mr Barton. Another explanation please, what is GBAS?"

"The Galileo system can only be used for Cat III landings if its accuracy is supplemented by a Ground Based Augmentation System, GBAS. The system transmits accurate runway and satellite information to the landing aircraft."

"Thank you Mr Barton, for that. Now could you explain to the Inquiry what is your responsibility for monitoring the height of the aircraft on the approach?"

"Well in fact as I mentioned, the duty controller has no responsibility for monitoring the performance of an aircraft on the approach. The controller can see from the radar display whether the aircraft is lined up with the runway but has no accurate knowledge of the position of the aircraft relative to the correct glide slope. However, looking at the aircraft heights on my screen I did feel the aircraft was low and if you have heard the recording of the exchanges on the Tower frequency you will know I called the aircraft several times to pass on my concern."

"Mr Barton, we have not heard the tape yet but you mentioned that your transmissions were interrupted by another aircraft. Is that normal?"

"It shouldn't happen but sometimes aircraft transmit even though they are told not to call and that is what happened in this case."

"Surely it would have been better if you could have transmitted regardless of the other aircraft?"

"Yes it would have been but normally if there are two transmissions at the same time then both transmissions are garbled." I noticed that the seats reserved for the press were filling up.

"Thank you Mr Barton."

This time there was some cross examination. The counsel for Royal World Airlines got to his feet. He was all sweet reasonableness, searching to be educated.

"Now Mr Barton, I'm puzzled. Are you telling the Inquiry that in an emergency it is impossible for you to transmit if there is another aircraft transmitting?"

"It is always possible to transmit but it does not follow that the aircraft will always hear if there is another aircraft transmitting on the frequency."

"Are you telling the Inquiry that you knew that the aircraft was below the glide slope but it was not an emergency?"

"Aircraft do not always keep to the glide slope. They vary a bit. It is the crew's job to fly the aircraft, not the tower controller's. Our job is to control the flow of traffic, not to fly the aircraft."

The RWA counsel sat down and another counsel who represented the Air Traffic Controller's union stood up.

"Mr Barton, is it your responsibility to ensure that an aircraft flies an instrument approach correctly?"

"No, not at all."

"Thank you." The Counsel sat down.

There was a consultation between Crowburn and Lord Justice Thomas. It was only 11.30. Things had gone rather faster than anticipated and they must have decided to call Bob Furness before lunch. He was sworn in. Janet Crowburn got to her feet and went through the routine questions. Then she started probing.

"Now Mr Furness, you are the head of the Air Accident Investigation Branch. Who is your employer?"

"The Secretary of State for Transport. I report directly to the Department."

"Would you like to tell us what was the cause of the accident to RWA Flight 573, UK aircraft registration G-RWAJ or Alfa Juliet as I believe it is colloquially called."

"No, Ma'am. The investigation is still in progress. In fact Martin Foster, one of my senior inspectors was in charge of the investigation until the Secretary of State appointed the Inquiry and so he is in a much better position than I am to brief the Inquiry."

"How is it that you did not take on the responsibility of investigating this tragic accident yourself since it is the worst ever to occur to an aircraft on the UK register?"

"That is not the way we work at the AAIB. I always appoint a senior inspector in charge and leave it to him or her. I review the progress of all the accident investigations but do not handle any one in particular."

"In retrospect don't you think it would have been better to have handled this case yourself?"

"With respect, no I don't. By letting someone else do the initial investigation I am able to review the findings impartially."

"Well, let me come on to another matter. You do agree that there seems to have been a lot of leakage of information from your department to the press?"

"The contents of one channel of the cockpit voice recorder seems to have become public knowledge. I very much regret that and I am doing everything in my power to find out the source of the leak."

"How many people have heard this recording?"

"I'm not really sure."

"You're not sure?" Crowburn sounded incredulous. "I would have thought Mr Furness that with material as sensitive as this you would know exactly how many people had heard the recording."

"Normally I would have known and the number would have been five or six, not more. However, because this was a hijacking we had a lot of security people insisting on listening to the recording."

"But presumably you know all these peoples' names?"

"No I don't. The security people are almost a law unto themselves. I have interviewed personally everybody who might have known about the leak who works for me, but they have all denied giving the information to the press. It would hinder our investigation if we called in the police at this time to try to invoke the Official Secrets Act. A clear cut crime has not been committed. This is a civil accident we are investigating, not a military one. If the transgressor works for me and we find out who it is then he will almost certainly lose his or her job. However, it is my view that the leak did not come from my people."

"That's as maybe Mr Furness. But there have also been reports purporting to emanate from your team which give the reason for the accident as pilot error."

"I am aware of this and again I have interviewed all my staff individually. The number of people who could have leaked information of this nature is much larger than the number of people who have heard the recording and, in addition, some of the security people could have heard discussions within the building. Having said all that I do not believe that my senior inspector and his people have yet come to any conclusion as to the cause of the accident, so I regard the reports as incorrect as well as very unwelcome."

"Well no doubt the Secretary of State will have a view in this matter. The fact that the recording and other information has been leaked is one of the reasons why this Inquiry has been called and, of course, it has prevented your department from continuing the investigation except under instructions from the Inquiry."

"I have already said how much I regret the leaks but, once they happened, nothing could be done to mitigate the effect. In addition I am not convinced the leaks came from my staff."

Lord Justice Thomas joined in.

"Ms Crowburn, when are we going to find out what is on the recordings?"

"My Lord, may I suggest that we hear the next witness and then perhaps have a recess to discuss this matter. I would respectfully suggest that it may be in the public interest and in the interests of justice, that the recording is only heard in private session and only by the Inquiry and by the very few experts who need to hear it. You may care to consider before the second part of the Inquiry whether part or the full transcript should be made freely available."

"Very good, Ms Crowburn. Please proceed."

"That is all the questions I have for this witness."

Bob Furness left the witness box. He didn't look a happy man. The clerk said that the Inquiry would reconvene at 2 o'clock.

CHAPTER 10

The Recordings

Mike and I left the Hall and went to a nearby pub for a coffee and a sandwich.

"What do you make of all that, Peter?"

"Well, it is the Galileo approach which intrigues me. As you heard, the data transmitted by the Galileo has to be augmented by GBAS. You will need to call the telecommunication chief from Air Traffic Control to see what checks were done on the GBAS after the crash. It is vital to check that the runway position was correct quite apart from the satellite information."

"But if the data was wrong then wouldn't the pilots see that the aircraft was too low?"

"But how, Mike? As Anne Moncrieff pointed out, the same deviation goes in front of the pilot as goes to the auto-pilot. What is required is a completely independent check of the flight path, certainly for Category III approaches. Had the crew been able to watch the 27L MLS deviation down the approach they might have seen they were going low. But it was out of service and anyway Mike, we're running ahead of the game. We haven't heard the recording and learnt the hijack situation yet."

"What do you make of Bob Furness and the leaks?"

"Well he's right, isn't he? How could he hope to know who did the leaking when so many people knew what was going on? However, I'll tell you this for nothing. I bet the story that AAIB think that the accident was pilot error is probably true."

"You may be right. Let's get back in."

When we got back into the room the Inquiry had not reconvened and there was a delay of about thirty minutes. Then the Clerk of the Court appeared and announced that instead of calling the next witness the Inquiry would now go into private session for the experts to hear the voice recorder. The Inquiry would probably be back in public session on Thursday morning. The room was to be cleared completely and the solicitors were informed that only technical experts would be allowed to hear the recording, not all the lawyers. Some of the lawyers argued unsuccessfully that they should be allowed to listen but, after a lot of disgruntled murmuring, there were only a few of us who were approved as listeners. The process of clearing and re-entering seemed to take forever. We all had to sign the Official Secrets Act then be searched for recorders before we were allowed in. The only good thing was that we each got a special pass which we were told could be used for subsequent days if necessary. There were only about eight of us plus the Inquiry itself.

The Clerk made an announcement when we were all assembled to hear the recorder.

"As I'm sure you all know, there are four channels of voice recording on a modern flight data recorder, one for each pilot, the public address system and an area microphone which hears all noises and conversations on the flight deck. Apparently due to a fault on the recorder the area recording is very noisy and nothing intelligible can be heard. So we are going to listen to the Captain's channel which enables us to hear the captain's microphone and earphone communications which includes transmissions from air traffic, RWA operations and other aircraft. The recording we have here has been edited so that it only runs when something is happening. This was done to cut down the length of the recording, otherwise it would have gone on for two hours with a lot of blank time when nothing was happening."

I tried to contest this arrangement and asked that we might hear the full unexpurgated recording and I was supported by the other listeners, but we were told that the only recordings that were available in London were the abbreviated ones. I decided not to stir things up at this stage but to listen to what was available. However, I asked if there was a transcript available with the times of each transmission and we were promised that we could look at the transcripts later on or on the following day. We all sat at the front of the hall as the recording started to play. As Osborne had been told, the recording was noisy with an obtrusive low frequency whine, but I was easily able to recognize Harry's voice:-

Harry	*"Charles, did you speak with Eva. Was she awake?"*
Charles	*"You bet. She was fine."*
Harry	*"She's a lovely girl. Bursting with energy. Time you settled down."*
Charles	*"We'll see. That was a great evening we had at Maroubra with those two. I like that beach, and Caesars."*
Harry	*"Yes, I could see that. We certainly got through the wine. Well you and the girls did."*
Charles	*"I enjoyed the swim as well"*
Harry	*"Just as well it was warm or you both would have frozen."*
Charles	*"You're a fine one to talk. I'm afraid I didn't get a lot of sleep. Did you have a good time, Harry?"*
Harry	*"Very quiet, thank you."*
Charles	*"That's what they all say."*

Harry	*"Still we got back just in time."*
Harry	*"Are you OK, Dick?"*

Presumably Dick Tremlett the off-duty Captain was watching from the jump seat which surprised me as I would have thought he would be in one of the bunks. There was a click and then the recording restarted. Presumably there was a length of time with no significant transmissions which had been cut out.

Aircraft	*"RWA operations this is Flight 573. We have been hijacked. We have been told to land at Heathrow and then we are going to be given further instructions. If there is any interference with the aircraft after landing then the plane will be blown up with all the passengers."*
RWA	*"573 this is RWA Operations. Your message copied. Your transponder read by Eurocontrol."*

Presumably a reference to the hijack code which Harry must have selected.

Aircraft	*"Operations from 573, the hijackers have asked me to read the following message to be given to the Prime Minister. 'When the aircraft lands the following six prisoners are to be taken from prison and brought to the aircraft.'"* A list of six names followed, which I recognised were reputed to be members of al-Qaeda, and the recording continued. *" 'The prisoners will be loaded onto the aircraft, the aircraft will be refuelled and then the aircraft will take-off for the Middle East. Any delay greater than thirty minutes will result in first, the killing of the Foreign Secretary, and then the blowing up of the aircraft.'"*

RWA read Harry's message back.

Aircraft	*"Operations, please advise when refuelling is ready. The hijackers wish to know."*
RWA	*"573, will advise."*

Another click.

Harry	*"Would the Chief Steward come to the flight deck."*

`Presumably this was an announcement on the passenger address.

The next recording was Harry switching his microphone to the public address system.

> Harry: *"Ladies and Gentleman. I regret to inform you that we have been hijacked. We are carrying on to London as planned, where we shall refuel and then fly to somewhere in the Middle East. We do not know whether anyone will be allowed to disembark in London.*
> *"Please obey the instructions from our cabin staff and we will try to make the rest of the flight as normal as possible. I will keep you informed at all times. Thank you."*

The recording continued with some co-pilot conversations with the various air traffic centres as the aircraft crossed Europe.

Charles   *"Harry, shall I get the latest weather?"*
Harry   *"Go ahead."*

There was a pause. They must have switched the speakers off ready for landing as we could not hear the weather being transmitted by the ATIS, the transmissions were going straight into the headphones.

Charles   *"Harry that's real Category IIIC weather. Manchester is clear anyway if we need to divert."*

There was a click

RWA   *"573 from Operations, we've checked your fuel from your ACARS transmission and you are cleared to overfly Frankfurt and land at Heathrow with Manchester as your diversion."*
Aircraft   *"573 copied."*

The speakers had clearly been switched on again. Another click.

Aircraft   *"Operations, this is 573. Have you arranged the refuelling?"*
RWA   *"We're still doing that. You are being refuelled by tankers instead of by hydrants on the stands and we are making*

136

	sure that they have enough fuel for Karachi and that they can get to your parking position on the runway."
Aircraft	*"573 understood."*

There was a pause.

Aircraft	*"RWA Ops This is 573. I have been asked to establish whether the prisoners have been released and are waiting at the airport?"*
RWA	*"573 please stand by. Will advise."*
Aircraft	*"RWA Ops I have been told to remind you that the hijackers are going to blow up the aircraft if there is any delay to their instructions which I passed to you."*
RWA	*"573 This is RWA Ops. We have been advised that the prisoners are at Birmingham and in view of the fog it will take probably four hours before they are at the airport."*

The recording proceeded with very little other conversation. The aircraft crossed into UK airspace and the aircraft was cleared to descend. Charles called out the descent checks and then the checks for an auto-landing. Air Traffic slowly permitted the aircraft to reduce altitude in stages. Then we heard the weather being broadcast on the VOR. Ceiling indeterminate, visibility 30 metres. Harry was clearly doing the flying and told Charles he was going to do an automatic landing using the MLS.

Aircraft	*"Approach RWA 573 reaching 4,000."*
Approach	*"Roger Cleared procedural Galileo final approach 27 left"*
Aircraft	*"RWA 573 we'd prefer the MLS"*
Approach	*"Sorry RWA 573 the ATIS is incorrect. The MLS is out of service. What are your intentions?"*
Harry	*"Charles, did you know about the MLS?"*
Charles	*"Yes Harry. This means we won't be able to monitor the approach path on Galileo."*
Harry	*"Well that is not a requirement. The Galileo is self-monitored to death."* A pause. *"Charles, you had better set 27L into the MMRs for the Galileo approach."*
Charles	*"Yes Harry, have just done that."*
Harry	*"OK. Then you can select the Galileo system for the approach."*
Charles	*"Yes Harry, all done."*
Aircraft	*"RWA 573 Request Galileo approach 27 Left."*
Approach	*"You are cleared for Galileo approach and to descend on*

	the procedure. Maintain heading and call the Tower on 118.5"
Aircraft	*"118.5 RWA 573"*

Harry was obviously slightly concerned and spoke to Charles again.

Harry	*"Charles that is permitted, isn't it?"*
Charles	*"Yes Harry providing the GBAS is OK."*
Harry	*"We've got no warning so it must be OK."*

We heard the landing checks being carried out and then they were cleared to the final approach altitude. Harry told Charles to keep an eye on the Navigation Display as he needed to keep his display showing the Primary Flight Display most of the time.

Aircraft	*"Tower RWA 573 ten miles 27 Left. Confirm GBAS OK."*
Tower	*"RWA 573 hello. You are clear to land 27 left, wind calm RVR 20, 30,20 GBAS showing OK"*
Aircraft	*"Roger RWA 573"*

Harry said they were now on the glide slope and Charles was calling out the altitude and the distance to go, presumably from the Navigation Display. Apparently Harry's Navigation Display did not work so he could not monitor the aircraft approaching the airfield. As the aircraft got lower we could hear the automatic cockpit announcements from the radio altimeter.

Charles	*"800 ft. you are showing slightly right, but on glide slope."*
Harry	*"OK, I'm central on the glide slope. You check the approach on your Navigational Display. I'll keep my display in the Primary Flight Display mode. The rate of descent seems rather high. We must have a tail wind."*
Tower	*"RWA 573 two miles to go. You appear to be below the glide slope."*
Harry	*"Charles, I thought our rate of descent seemed high."*
Charles	*"Well we are right on the correct glide slope."*
Harry	*"Heathrow Tower RWA 573 copied please check approach wind speed."*
Charles	*"one mile, 300 ft, on centre line, on glide path"*
Rad Alt	*"200"*
Tower	*"573 from Tower, the wind is calm. You...."*

Another aircraft came on frequency and blotted out whatever the Tower was trying to say. All we could hear was the other aircraft's transmission when the Tower stopped talking.

Lufthansa	" 564 confirm Heathrow closed"
Tower	"Lufthansa 564 from Heathrow Tower. Airfield closed leave frequency immediately."
Rad Alt	"100"
Harry	"I can't see the loom of the lights yet."
Charles	"Still on glide path"
Tower	"RWA 573 ..."

Again there was a transmission blotting out the Tower, probably Lufthansa acknowledging Tower's instruction and asking for frequency.

Charles	"On centre line"
Harry	"Still can't see the ground"
Rad Alt	"50"
Rad Alt	"30"
Harry	"There's something wrong with the lights, I'm going around."
Rad Alt	"20"

A moment later we could hear Harry yelling and the background noise sounded louder, presumably because the throttles had been opened.

Harry	"Oh my God, we're hitting the road"
Tower	"573 you appear to be"

I looked at the members of Inquiry and the other listeners; understandably they all looked pretty shaken.

We then went on to listen to the first officer's and the Public Address recordings; like the captain's recording there was a nasty whine, perhaps even noisier, but they were still intelligible and did not add to the main recording we had heard. It was clear that the Clerk of the Court intended to close the proceedings but I asked that we might hear the flight deck area recording. There was some debate but finally it was agreed that we could hear this last channel; however, as the Clerk had said, it was impossible to make out anything intelligible as the whine was of a similar frequency to the other recordings but much louder and the recording was stopped after a couple of minutes. It was agreed that the recording should be given to some acoustic experts to see if any conversations could be recovered.

The Clerk of the Court drew matters to a close. "Gentlemen, you have all been allowed to listen to the recordings to help you in the evidence that you will be giving to the Inquiry. I think you can now all understand why we do not wish the transcript of the recording to be released at the moment. However, the transcript may be introduced as evidence in the second part of the Inquiry. I rely on you all to keep what you have heard to yourselves in accordance with the Official Secrets Act. To-morrow morning at the Treasury Solicitor's Office in Queen Anne's Chambers you may look at the transcripts of what you have just heard. There will be another private session of this Inquiry in the morning with the security experts. Then there will probably be another private session in Sydney after we have finished the first part of this Inquiry to find out how these people got on board the aircraft with their weapons. It is very important to do this because, as some of you must have realised, the fact that the hijackers had explosives on board is particularly worrying and we do not wish this fact to become general knowledge, but we must find out how it was done and what the explosive devices were. Good night to you all."

I left and decided I'd better have a brief discussion with Mike and Tim Forrestal. I called Mike and reluctantly we decided we'd better go to an office rather than the nearest pub. We agreed to meet at Tim's offices which were the nearest. He kicked off the discussion the moment we arrived.

"Well what did you hear, Peter?" He looked at me.

"I'm concerned about the recording."

"Why."

"It was almost impossible to hear the area recording. AAIB said the recorder had been damaged though they are going to see if experts can get anything out of the noise."

There was a long pause while the implication of what I had just said sank in. Mike looked at me.

"What's worrying you?"

"There's no conversation with the hijackers on the recording we could hear."

"What should we do?"

"Nothing we can do at the moment. I can't see how AAIB can blame the pilots when the effect of the hijackers cannot be assessed. By the way my first impression was how superbly Harry Hodgson, the captain, handled the situation. I believe that may be very important because on the run through of the recording we have just heard, it looks as if the hijacking did not cause the accident. Hodgson seemed right on top of the

140

job and he would therefore have been monitoring the approach. However, he made it clear he was relying on Charles to monitor the Navigation Display. The problem is that the aircraft heights for the distances from the runway which Charles called out at 300ft. and 200 ft. were correct yet we know from the controller that he thought the aircraft was below the glide slope judging from the aircraft position shown on his screen. If only the MLS indicator had been available to the crew for cross checking."

"But Peter," Mike could not contain himself, "they must have been under enormous pressure."

"Yes, you're right. But there is another thing that could be very significant. There has been no mention of the warning device in the Tower similar to the device they used to have, AFDAS, Approach Funnel Deviation Alert System. It should have given a warning to the controller that the aircraft was low."

"Peter, I don't understand. If it was there to give a warning why didn't it go off?"

"I'm not sure. The controller has to set the correct runway being used and then enable it. I would have thought Barton would have done that. It's something I want to look at. He didn't mention it so maybe he didn't switch it on and didn't want to admit it but I think that's most unlikely.

"Anyway whether the device was live or not, to be honest I'm a bit surprised hearing the recording that Harry didn't carry out a missed approach after getting the warning from the Tower. Maybe the hijackers wouldn't let him though it didn't sound like that."

Tim looked at me. "What do you suggest then?"

"Well I want to read the main transcript and I would like to check the recording of the other transcripts."

"Anything else?"

"Yes. Presumably we're going to hear Martin Foster, the AAIB senior inspector, who is dealing with the accident, albeit under instruction from the Inquiry members, before this part of the Inquiry is closed. If this is the only time he is going to give evidence he will need a thorough cross examination. Perhaps you should alert Crowburn about there being a special warning system in the Tower. It was strange Barton didn't mention it. She could ask Foster about it." I looked at Tim. "I may need to talk to you after I've read the transcripts to-morrow. How are we going to handle that?"

"Well Peter, I suggest that we review the situation at lunch time to-morrow. You should have read the transcripts by then. When we reconvene at the Inquiry on Friday should we ask about the transcript and the hijackers?"

"No, Tim. I think not for the moment."

"Why not?"

"I think we should wait until the situation becomes clearer."

We broke up and I went straight home and called Mandy who had only just got in.

"How did you get on, Peter?"

"I don't know. Unfortunately we couldn't hear the hijackers as the area recording had been damaged and was incredibly noisy."

"Couldn't you hear anything?"

"No, so I'm very curious to hear what the AAIB inspector says on Friday."

"Not to-morrow?"

"No. We're reading the transcript to-morrow and don't forget they're having a very private security session."

"You'd better get some sleep. When do we meet again?"

"Why don't you stay at my place this week-end?"

"I'm not comfortable in that house with Diana watching us and I'm not comfortable just being your mistress, enjoyable though it is in some ways."

"Well I don't know what to say. I don't want to lose you."

"That's nice, Peter and I feel the same way about you." There was a pause. "Alright, I'll stay at your place but I'm not sure about anything else."

She rang off. It really was a difficult problem. If only we could find Diana and I could get a divorce on the grounds of desertion.

***

In the morning I bought the Times, Telegraph and FT and studied them on the train. There did not seem to be any leaks of what was said on the voice recorder though the Telegraph was still complaining about the iniquity of having private sessions. Osborne took the opportunity to regurgitate the earlier leak of the recording, mentioning again the bit about the party in Sydney and restating the view of the AAIB that it was just pilot error. I was at Queen Anne's Chambers at 9.30 and went inside after showing my pass. We were all shown into a room where there were transcripts of the recordings. Each one was numbered.

In some ways it was easier to appreciate what had happened on the flight deck by looking at the transcript because there was a time written down for each transmission. However it didn't really help. I met Mike at the pub and he confirmed that John Fairlane had kept 5 o'clock free.

"Well Peter, did you learn anything new?"

"Not on the face of it but I'm still wondering if we're hearing everything."

"We must be. The Court wouldn't allow a miscarriage of justice."

"I hope you're right."

I left Mike when he went back to his office and wandered round the book shops in Charing Cross road. At the appointed time Mike and I met at John Fairlane's chambers and went straight in to his office. John looked at Tim who gave him a debriefing on the last two days' happenings.

"So if I understand you correctly, you think that both the voice recording and the transcript make it seem as if the pilots were monitoring their instruments properly and there is no obvious cause for the accident."

I joined in.

"From the excerpts on the recording it sounded as if the aircraft was making a perfect approach. What I can't understand is why the Navigation Display distances from the runway, which the co-pilot called out, did not show that they were at the incorrect height. I would have thought that the heights would have been far too low for the distance from the airport and this would have warned both pilots that the aircraft was below the correct glide slope. There could conceivably be shortcomings in the design of the aircraft during a Galileo approach or the Galileo airfield data could have been wrong. We have to find out if this data was checked and was correct. However, right now we need to judge how much we want to challenge the AAIB inspector to-morrow."

John looked thoughtful.

"What had you in mind?"

"Well I'm puzzled about the area recording. It was useless because of the background noise but it's just possible that some experts might be able to recover something I suppose. Will the inspector be recalled when the Inquiry is reconvened?"

"Yes, Peter, I'm sure he will be since the investigation is still going on and he will need to report to the Inquiry. If I am hearing you correctly you are going to do some more investigation as a result of what you have heard. You're not happy with the indicated heights and distances from the runway."

"Yes, there needs to be more investigation. There are some definite avenues which need more exploring and it is going to take time."

"Alright, I'll just play it by ear to-morrow."

Back home I pondered over the situation. Harry had behaved superbly. If there had been something wrong technically on the approach surely he would have noticed it. But if they were on the glide slope at the correct distance from the runway it just did not make sense.

Mandy called when she got home and I shared my thoughts with her. She told me that to-morrow was going to be very important and not to come to any conclusion until after Foster had given evidence.

"Are you coming to my office to-morrow?"

"What time do you finish?"

Blind Landing

"When you come round, about 5.30; you can wait if I'm not ready."

I retired to bed. I had a lot to do if I was going to earn my money with CrossRisk Insurance.

INQUIRY DAY 3

Martin Foster

The Inquiry opened at 10 o'clock and it was packed out with the press who clearly expected some excitement. As I looked round I noticed in the row behind us a pilot I used to know when I was flying with Britannia, Robin Turnsmith; I suspected he had already noticed me as he returned my smile of recognition.

There was an air of expectation in the Inquiry hall. Martin Foster was called and sworn in. He, understandably, looked a little nervous.

Janet Crowburn started probing straightaway after the initial identification questions.

"Mr Foster. You have been in charge of the investigations into the accident to RWA 573?"

"Yes, that's right, until the Public Inquiry was notified. Since then I have been working for the Inquiry."

"Well perhaps you will be kind enough to explain what happened and tell us in your opinion what was the cause of the accident."

"Well Ma'am we have not completed our investigation. The work of my team was delayed when the Inquiry was called."

"We understand that, but you had carried out a lot of work up to that time and I must point out to you that some leaks about the progress of the work have appeared in the press and have suggested you have come to a conclusion."

Foster's face flushed.

"The leaks didn't come from my team and we certainly haven't come to any conclusion. We have a lot more work to do analysing the recorders, quite apart from all the other investigations that need doing."

"Would you please tell the Inquiry about the investigation work you have carried out up to the present time."

Martin started by giving a factual account of the flight from the take-off in Sydney to the crash on the A30. He had projected on to a screen in the Inquiry Hall a picture of the flight path of the aircraft as it joined the extended centre line of 27L and the spot where the aircraft hit the ground, half a mile short of the expected touch down point. He said that the two pilot channels of the voice recorder confirmed that the aircraft was carrying out an automatic approach and landing in Category IIIC conditions using the Galileo satellite system as reference. He gave the names of the crew, their experience and their qualifications. He produced the relevant sheet of the technical log at Sydney showing the rectification of the Navigation Display and the Multimode Receiver. He explained that the aircraft was hijacked just less than three hours before landing.

145

"How do you know that Mr Foster?"

"Eurocontrol told Heathrow that the aircraft was transmitting the internationally agreed code for hijacking and in addition the Captain told RWA Operations."

"Now then Mr Foster. You have explained to us in detail the flight progress from Sydney to Heathrow but so far you have not told us what in your opinion might have gone wrong. Before you do that will you tell us if the aircraft was fully serviceable when it started its approach."

"When we were collecting evidence from Royal World Airlines we discovered from their operations room that RWA 573 had mentioned in one of the routine flight progress reports that the captain's Navigation Display was not working."

Jeff Templeman, one of the members, chimed in.

"Is that the same one that did not work when the aircraft landed at Sydney?"

"Yes Sir, it was a new box that had been fitted by NWIA in Sydney because the previous one did not work."

"Doesn't that suggest that there was something wrong with the aircraft installation and not the displays themselves?"

"Yes sir. Unfortunately so far our instrumentation has been unable to shed any light on this point."

"Mr Foster, would it matter that the Captain's display did not work?"

"It would have made it much harder to carry out the approach, Sir. We don't know the exact nature of the fault, whether it was possible for the captain to switch the Navigation Display format on to his Primary Display every so often to check the approach path. However, all the key information was on the Primary Display and we know he was getting full support from the First Officer who had both displays working."

Janet Crowburn tried to reassume control from Templeman and looked at Justice Thomas.

"May I carry on, my Lord?"

Lord Justice Thomas nodded.

"Now then Mr Foster. What in your opinion went wrong?"

There was absolute silence in the room as Martin Foster replied.

"We have analysed the records of the local Distance Measuring Equipment beacon, DME, and it is clear that the aircraft was below the correct approach path for the runway. The aircraft was not using the MLS on the runway in use, 27L, because it was out of service. The voice recorder makes it clear, as does the conversation with air traffic control, that the crew elected to use the Galileo. This is permissible if the correct selection is made on the flight deck."

Lord Justice Thomas turned to Janet Crowburn.

"Ms Crowburn, are we going to have transcripts of the cockpit voice recorder introduced as evidence?"

"If you think it advisable, my Lord, but if I may suggest, only when the Inquiry reopens since the recordings are still under examination."

"Very well Ms Crowburn."

Janet Crowburn returned to her examination.

"Mr Foster. You say you looked at the local Distance Measuring Equipment readings and it showed that the aircraft was below the glide slope. Where was the beacon? On the airfield?"

"No Ma'am. It was the DME located on the approach to 27 Right."

"Would the crew have been able to see these distances?"

"Yes Ma'am on the centre instrument panel."

"Would the crew have been able to do the calculation, in real time, on the approach?"

" No Ma'am. They would have to have done a lot of pre-flight preparation to calculate the correct heights from the DME distances."

" Well Mr Foster, was there anything wrong in the crew using the Galileo for Category IIIC landings?"

"No, Ma'am. We've checked that the crew were up to date with their simulator training."

Charles Maguire indicated he wanted to join in.

"Mr Foster, doesn't the Galileo approach depend completely on software? Can you explain the difference from an MLS approach."

"Yes, Sir. With MLS there is no doubt where the runway and glide slope centre lines are as they are determined by the radio antennae. With Galileo the runway information is downloaded from the GBAS and the deviations from the virtual centre lines of the glide slope and the runway are only found after extensive software calculations."

McGuire seemed satisfied and Crowburn carried on.

"Mr Foster, did the approach seem normal to the crew?"

"Well Ma'am, air traffic warned the crew that the aircraft seemed low on the approach at two miles from the correct touch-down point and the captain noticed that they were descending too fast so he asked for a wind check. However the first officer confirmed that the aircraft was at the correct height for the distance even though it was clearly well below that altitude. It is very strange that the crew did not realise that something was wrong."

"Could the presence of the hijackers have caused the pilots to lose concentration?"

"Yes, Ma'am. That could well be the case."

"Mr Foster. You seem unsure. You have heard the flight recordings. Surely you must have an opinion."

"Unfortunately the recording from the flight deck microphone is very noisy and we cannot hear the hijackers. We are trying to see if we can improve the quality of the recording. As I said we have a lot more investigation to do."

"Were there, in your opinion, any contributory causes to this accident?"

"No, Ma'am"

"We have read in the Daily Telegraph that the crew had been on a party before the flight. Was that in the recording? Wouldn't that have affected the crew's performance?"

The press were listening to every word. The hall was very quiet.

"There are rest bunks for the crew."

"You didn't answer my question, Mr Foster."

"I would not have thought so."

"Would you go to a party before a long flight."

"No, Ma'am"

"Mr Foster, will you be offering the transcript of the microphones as evidence?"

"It is not our normal practice to release the transcript of voice recordings."

"Do I understand that answer to mean that you are not going to?"

"Ma'am, this is a Public Inquiry and we are working for the members of the Inquiry. If the Inquiry wishes to have the transcripts in evidence it will of course be available, but we do not recommend it."

"Why not?"

"These transcripts are best interpreted by experts, Ma'am."

"Mr Foster, justice must be seen to be done. This matter will be raised again when the Inquiry reopens."

Crowburn looked at her notes.

"Mr Foster, you mentioned that the controller in the Tower told the aircraft at two miles that the aircraft seemed low. Is there any special equipment to warn the controller if the aircraft is too low?"

"Yes, Ma'am. There is an alerting system."

"Did it go off to tell the controller and is that why he warned the aircraft it was low?"

"We have examined the warning system and we do not believe it operated to give the controller a warning but we have more work to do in that area."

"Does the controller have to prepare it?"

"The controller does have to set it up and then arm it but it is not possible to check whether it was all done correctly. The equipment is working perfectly now and we have no reason to believe it was not working at the time of the accident. As I said we have more work to do."

Janet Crowburn turned to Lord Justice Thomas.

"My Lord. It would seem that there needs to be much more detailed investigations of the flight data recorder parameters and also the equipment in the Control Tower."

Thomas butted in.

"Thank you, Ms Crowburn. The Inquiry will be giving instructions to the AAIB the moment these hearings are finished."

"My apologies, M'Lord. May I respectfully suggest that I release this witness now and that he continues his examination when the Inquiry is reconvened when he can be cross-examined by counsel?"

The Inquiry and the law officers had discussions amongst themselves and then Lord Justice Thomas announced that the Inquiry would be adjourned to a date that would be notified but probably Monday 21st March. Foster left the witness box looking a bit uncertain, perhaps wondering how he had performed.

As we left I caught up with Robin Turnsmith.

"What are you doing here? Are you still with Britannia?"

"No, I left them about three years ago when I got married. I didn't like the long trips being away so much. I joined the AAIB after being trained at Cranfield. I'm helping Martin Foster."

A hundred things occurred to me to discuss with Robin but I decided it might be better to wait and try to talk to him when there was just the two of us. It was probably a good decision as I saw Foster coming over towards Robin who introduced me as he came up to us. He turned to Robin.

"Thank goodness that's over for the moment. How did it sound?"

"It sounded fine."

"Thanks. We'd better go back and look at the air traffic situation more closely. Have you heard anything from the people trying to get sense from the area mike recording?"

Robin shook his head and I said my farewells. Looking at Foster I did wonder how he would fare when the Inquiry re-opened if he hadn't got some definitive explanation of the accident by then and then it struck me that I too would have a problem as well if I hadn't got one!

CHAPTER 11

To Sydney

The four of us left the Queen Elizabeth Hall and returned to John's chambers where his secretary produced some coffee. He was obviously considering what we should all be doing next.

"Well that's that for the moment. Crowburn did a good job interrogating Foster and it's very helpful that AAIB are admitting that having the hijackers on the flight deck during the approach would make it hard for the pilots to concentrate. But the fact remains we haven't got an explanation of why the pilots didn't realise what was happening. We've got a week or two to think of something but it's not going to be easy." John looked at me. "What are you going to do?"

"There are a lot of unexplained things in this accident concerning the electronics which require investigation so they can be eliminated from the suspicious items list. There seems no obvious reason to suspect pilot error but to prevent any claims on CrossRisk we really need a proper explanation of what happened. Harry must have been under enormous pressure. If only the recorder had worked properly and we could have heard everything that was happening on the flight deck."

"You're not likely to get any help from AAIB are you?" Mike was inquiring and it was a good question which had been exercising me.

"Not sure if Foster will help. I'd love to know how Osborne got hold of the transcripts. Bob is normally very fair, he may help, but by chance an old colleague of mine is working for Foster in the AAIB. I'm wondering the best way of contacting him. Perhaps Tim you could arrange for me to talk to a member of the Inquiry if I need to. I'm not sure what the correct procedures are."

"Nor am I but I'm sure all rules would be broken to get at the truth."

"The other thing we mustn't forget is that Osborne is being told that the AAIB is suspecting pilot error which isn't in accord with Foster's evidence."

"You know if Foster is the source of the leak he wouldn't admit it, would he?"

I left feeling definitely uncertain of what to do and in due course appeared at Mandy's offices. She appeared looking like a solicitor who had been working hard all day.

"My bag is in the cupboard, Peter. Would you mind?"

We made our normal progress by cab and train, and then cab again in view of the bag, to my house. We were both tired but I had had the forethought to book a table at Simon's for 8 o'clock.

"Peter, my dear, once again I'm going to lie in your bath, Diana or no Diana, and I don't want you helping me. The only massage I need is from the jacuzzi. You can have a shower in the other bathroom and prepare two strong gin and tonics."

That was the nice thing about Mandy. I didn't have to guess what was required. Since we were walking to the restaurant I made the gin and tonics as directed and tested the mix was right. As usual I did not have too long to wait for Mandy despite her long day. She appeared in a dress that was definitely low cut and not too long. We sat down next to one another and she tasted the mix.

"What are you trying to do to me?"

"What are you trying to do to me sitting so close with a dress like that?"

"Perhaps you're right. You can't be trusted." She moved her body away so it wasn't pressed against me but the perfume remained. "I've decided we aren't talking shop until to-morrow. What do you think?"

"I have to tell you that for some unaccountable reason I wasn't thinking of shop, as you call it. I was looking at my watch and wondering how much time we had before we had to leave." She got up and sat on the chair opposite.

"I think I'd better sit here till we leave. I don't want to spoil my dinner."

She switched the TV on which was a mistake as there was a report on the Inquiry. Brian Tucker was being interviewed.

"Though a few experts listened to the recording on Wednesday, it was only allowed to enable the various interests they represented to be briefed in confidence. We're not getting the cockpit voice recorder transcript from AAIB until the Inquiry reconvenes so it's very difficult to come to any conclusion. The senior inspector, Martin Foster, made it clear that there was a lot more detective work to be carried out."

"But Mr Tucker, the Daily Telegraph is saying that the accident could be due to pilot error."

"In my view that sort of reporting is to be deplored. Something very unusual clearly happened and has led to a terrible accident. I agree with Mr Foster when he said that the presence of hijackers could affect the pilots' concentration carrying out the approach."

Mandy turned the TV off.

"You know, Mandy, listening to that recording reminded me of the Sherlock Holmes story. What was it called? You know the one. 'The strange case of the dog that barked in the night'".

"You mean the dog didn't bark in the night."

"Exactly, you remembered. The strange case of the hijackers that didn't talk on the flight deck."

"Well they obviously did but you weren't able to hear them."

"Yes, that's absolutely right. Let's hope the experts will be able to get something out of the area mike."

I held her coat as she put it on and we walked to Simon's. I helped her off with her coat and then hugged her before we sat down.

"I liked that, Peter. I'm glad I'm staying for the week-end after all."

It was a very pleasant meal and we discussed what theatres and exhibitions we wanted to see in the next few weeks. We walked home and as usual I made the coffee. Mandy came down and we took our drinks through.

"We'd better not turn on the TV or your wretched Inquiry will be on. You can play some soft, amorous music."

"How about Ravel's Bolero?"

"That's not quite what I had in mind. To much action after a long day. Some Frank Sinatra would be more restful."

***

We heard the papers arrive but did nothing.

"How wonderful, Peter. The whole week-end ahead and there is nothing we have to do."

We held each other tight, thinking our own thoughts.

"What were you thinking, Mandy."

"I was thinking, would it be greedy to have two poached eggs and how was I going to persuade you to cook them for me?"

"I was thinking how am I going to avoid having breakfast in bed, with all those crumbs."

"How very prosaic. Anyway the solution is now clear. You get up and cook my eggs and I'll come down in my dressing gown. I may get dressed later, I haven't decided yet."

We carried out Mandy's plan and sat at the kitchen table. I looked at the papers and read about the Inquiry. Osborne said that though Foster had made it clear that there was a lot more work to be done he still had reason to believe that the AAIB were coming round to the view that it was clearly pilot error, probably caused by hijacking interference and the fact that the pilots had only just got back in time for the flight.

Mandy appeared carrying a fax.

"When did you look at your fax machine last? This must have been here when we got in last night."

"To be honest I rarely look at my fax these days. Everything is email."

"Peter, in the office we still prefer faxes."

The fax was from Bill Baker.

Understand that the Inquiry on Alfa Juliet will be adjourned for a few weeks. Can you come out next week for a few days to talk with my 798 training captains on our proposed 798 training course? Would like you to travel Monday if possible. Please call me over week-end at home.

Best regards

I passed the fax over to Mandy.

"Can you spare the time, Peter? Surely you've got to prepare for the Inquiry."

"In a way you're right but I'd like to quiz the engineers over the unserviceabilities of Alfa Juliet. I want to be sure that they are not relevant. Going out to NWIA gives me a cheap way of doing it."

Mandy looked at me thoughtfully.

"And you want to check up on the party the night before?"

I grinned at her.

"You can read me altogether too easily. Yes, to be honest I do."

"Well just you be careful. When are you going to ring Bill?"

The kitchen clock showed 9.30, it would be 8.30 in the evening in Sydney.

"I'll call him now."

My telephone book was in my brief case. Bill answered straightaway.

"It's Peter Talbert, Bill. Thanks for the invitation and I can manage to travel Monday."

"That's fine. No worries. I took a flier and made a reservation. As RWA own 25% of us I've arranged for you to have a seat in business class on RWA574 leaving at 12 noon getting in 8 o'clock Tuesday night. I've booked you at the downtown Marriott. Please call RWA reservations in London and reconfirm the booking. Look forward to seeing you Wednesday. I'll get Jock Mansfield to collect you from the hotel at 9.30."

RWA found my reservation and I asked for an aisle seat. The tickets would be at the check-in in Terminal 3.

"Peter, I'd better go. You need to get ready."

"No. Don't spoil everything. The flight doesn't leave till midday on Monday so there's no problem. It won't take me long to get organised."

Blind Landing

"You've got your mind to pack as well. It's got to be full of 798 avionics and all those good things."

"Mandy, I've been thinking of nothing else since the accident. You know that. In fact talking about it to people who understand and can question my views on the flight deck will be very helpful."

She accepted the force of my arguments but the week-end somehow had lost its relaxed feel. I discovered she had brought some work with her and so after a walk along the tow path and a sandwich at the pub, she settled down to read some papers and I got the papers organised for my trip. Then I went upstairs and sorted out my clothes for Sydney's summer heat.

***

The alarm went off at 6.15. I got out of bed and went downstairs, put the coffee on and made Mandy some tea. She was already up when I returned with her cup. I went back into the kitchen and prepared breakfast. Mandy appeared shortly ready for work. I took her in my car to the station and held her for a moment.

"I'll miss you, Peter. I'm getting used to having you around."

"Me, too. I'll miss you. I'll call you from Sydney, Tuesday morning your time, before I go to bed. Take care."

I watched her walk into the station and drove home. I had a shower and put on the clothes I had put out ready the previous afternoon, blazer, thin trousers, and a sports shirt. I left quite a lot of Mandy's clothes as well as mine for Dora in the clothes basket. I closed my case, put my shaver in the holdall and carried the bags downstairs.

I called Jill and asked where the RWA crews normally stayed in Sydney and she told me it was the Hilton. I called Hilton reservations, made a reservation for a week from Tuesday night and emailed Bill asking him to let Jock Mansfield know that I would be in the Hilton and not the Marriott and would he cancel the reservation. I checked everything, bags, money and passport then I drove to Roehampton Lane and along the A4 to the M4 and Terminal 3 Valet Parking. Mike Mansell could pay for the parking as he was getting my flight for free.

At the check-in desk the girl behind the counter found my ticket. She told me the flight was fairly full but gave me my central aisle seat so I could move around easily. As usual It took the best part of an hour to get through the appallingly overcrowded security line; why the Government didn't force the airport authority to do something about it I could never understand, perhaps because the decision makers were always ushered straight through. I bought the latest best selling political blockbuster, a

154

VAT and duty free bottle of special Scotch for Bill, and some expensive chocolates for Mary Baker though the prices were no cheaper than the best buys at the local supermarkets but at least I hadn't had to carry the bottle from home. I reached the business lounge in reasonable time for the flight. However, I had barely sat down when my name was called out on the public address system.

"Mr Talbert?" I looked at the girl behind the desk and nodded. "Captain Falconer said that you would be very welcome to visit the flight deck but you would have to travel as supernumerary crew in the crew rest area for the whole flight. No-one, except perhaps a very special first class passenger, is allowed on to the flight deck from the passenger cabin during the flight. I need to tell the check-in staff at the gate what you are going to do."

Clearly a snap decision was required. I was looking forward to relaxing all the way to Sydney but clearly this was not going to be possible.

"Please tell the Captain I would be delighted to travel in the crew area."

"Fine. In that case you can go down to the gate now and I can get a message to the flight deck so that one of the pilots will meet you and take you to the aircraft."

I made my way along the concourse to the gate. As usual it seemed a very long way, though there were travelators to make it easier. When I reached the gate I gave my boarding pass to the man who seemed to be in charge.

"Mr Talbert, someone will be coming to take you on board. Suggest you go through to the far end and wait by the Upper Deck entrance."

I went through into the very crowded waiting area and squeezed my way between the rows until I reached the desks and glass doors leading to the walkways into the aircraft. As I got there I saw a First Officer coming through the Upper Deck door.

"Peter Talbert?" I nodded. The pilot spoke to the girl at the desk who checked my ticket and passport and then let me through. She re-opened the Upper Deck door using a keypad.

"Peter, I'm Josh Wilson one of the First Officers on the flight."

We shook hands and went through the glass door and started to climb towards the upper level of the aircraft. We made a turn, finally arriving at the Upper Deck aircraft entrance where a flight attendant was waiting.

"Peter Talbert will be travelling in the Flight Crew area so his seat will be empty."

The flight attendant let me through and we turned left through the Upper Deck. At the end of this section a man got up and virtually barred my way. He seemed to be acting in an official capacity, though not as cabin staff.

"May I see your passport and boarding card, please sir."

He reminded me of a policeman. I gave him my pilot's licence as well as my passport and watched him examining my documents.

"Do you have authority for Mr, er," he looked at my passport "Talbert to travel with you?"

Josh produced a piece of paper that looked like a computer form print out. The man scrutinized the document and appeared to agree with its contents. He turned towards me.

"Do you mind if I do a thorough search of you and your bag?"

It was clearly a rhetorical question as he immediately went over me with a fine tooth comb. That over, everything in my bag was inspected minutely. Finally he gave me the all clear.

Josh was waiting for me in the next compartment which looked like a First Class Area. The walls of this section were not parallel but gradually narrowed towards the front of the aircraft. At the end of the section we went through heavy curtains into what I recognised as a flight crew area. There appeared to be three bunks on one side and a table on the other with two seats either side. There was a Captain sitting reading a newspaper in one of the seats.

"We've made it, George," Josh looked at the Captain sitting down "this is Peter Talbert who will be travelling with us to Sydney."

George didn't get up but offered me his hand.

"Hello Peter, hope you enjoy the flight. I'm George Nesbitt the en-route Captain for this trip. What brings you up here instead of relaxing in the back?" He moved slightly. "Come and sit down."

"I'm going out to NWIA to discuss crew training on their new 798s and they organised for me to travel on this trip." I paused and turned back to Josh. "What was all that about just now?"

"Peter, that's one of the Flight Marshals that guard the front of the aircraft. We have to have them on all our flights now."

"I thought he looked like a copper. I suppose it is necessary but what has the world come to?" I paused. "But if there were marshals on the flight that crashed, how did the hijackers get control?"

George looked at me. "That is what we are all asking."

"Who employs these marshals? Does the airline?"

"You seem very interested?"

"I've been retained by one of your insurance companies to advise them."

George nodded. "Well Peter, I think we employ them though no-one wants to discuss the matter. Presumably we recruit and train them but I suspect they have to be approved by the Government security system.

They must have their own scheduling system somewhere, they certainly don't count as crew. They arrive from nowhere but always have the necessary papers, airline tickets etc to get on board and they always seem to sit at the front of the Upper Class. I guess they must be armed in some way but nobody wants to talk about it, or to them for that matter. There's normally two, one on each side."

He stopped for a moment and changed the subject "Why don't you sit down and make yourself comfortable? Are you hoping to go on the flight deck sometime?"

"Yes, I'd like that. I'm hoping Captain Falconer will let me sit in the jump seat going in to Sydney."

"Well he's pretty busy now getting everything organised for departure. You can discuss it with him when we take over. Incidentally, if you want to come up when I'm flying you will be very welcome." He looked at me. "If you've been retained by an insurance company and are going out to talk to NWIA about crew training you must be an expert on this airplane?"

I told George a bit about myself and what I was trying to do to earn a living. Then the plane started to shake in a very characteristic manner as the passengers came on board. In a surprisingly short time considering the hundreds of people going on board, I could hear the doors being closed and the aircraft being pushed back. The engines started and we were soon on our way to Sydney; I still found the whole concept of flying to the other side of the world non-stop absolutely amazing but perhaps it was because I had not yet actually done it.

George and Josh went to lie down on their bunks while I settled down and started reading the FT. Jim had written an article on the accident following the Inquiry and as usual had excelled himself. He said that the auto-pilot was flying the aircraft and that it was set up for a landing using the Galileo satellite system. The cause of the accident was not yet known and AAIB had a lot more to do to try to find out why the pilots thought the aircraft was on the correct glide slope. It was going to be very interesting to read the recording transcript when the Inquiry reopened and see the influence of the hijackers on the crew during the final part of the approach. If the hijackers had been talking to the captain during the last critical minutes of the approach it could have been a contributing factor, perhaps preventing the captain concentrating on monitoring the automatic pilot.

The puzzling thing Jim pointed out was that apparently the crew thought the aircraft was flying correctly down the flight path whereas it clearly was not. The loss of height could have occurred at the last moment but in fact the crew had been warned by the Tower controller that they were below the glide slope at two miles and they had noticed a slightly faster rate of descent than usual earlier on. Meanwhile he understood that the regulatory authorities, both the EASA and the FAA, together with Independant were reviewing the new system concepts that had been introduced in the 798, to make sure that nothing had been missed in the design.

One of the cabin attendants came forward and asked me what I wanted to eat. I chose roast beef which looked great on the menu. He brought it to me on a tray and left me to get on with it. Later the Chief Steward appeared to take my tray away.

"You're in luck. The VIP cabin is empty. You can sleep on one of the full length beds if you like."

"That's fantastic. I've got some work to do in Sydney so a good sleep will be a bonus." I looked at him. "Where do the marshals sleep?"

The steward look uncomfortable. Clearly it was bad form to mention the marshals. He leant forward and lowered his voice.

"They just put their seats back. They go horizontal. I think they take it in turns to sleep."

He rushed away not wanting to discuss the matter further but came back almost immediately and said that it was OK for me to go onto the flight deck. We went forward and he entered some numbers on a key pad by the entrance door to the flight deck. He then looked into a small camera which I had not noticed on the cabin wall. There was a click and he pushed open the door.

We went in, he introduced me to the Captain and then left. As he closed the door there was a very loud clunking noise which presumably was the door locking again.

"Peter Talbert? Didn't you give us a lecture on managing the systems, human factors and the pilot/computer interface on our training course?" I nodded. "Sam Falconer is my name and this is Fred Longshaw." He introduced me to the First Officer. "Sit down in the jump seat so that you can see what is going on."

I eased myself in to sit on the centre seat behind and midway between the pilots.

"Yes, I have been giving lectures to the 798 courses but my contract is nearly finished. As you know I specialise in the relationship between the human being and the computers on the flight deck --- 'Managing the Systems' I call it."

"Have you been up on a 798 flight deck before?"

"No. I've done quite a bit in the RWA simulators and also in Seattle. But however good the simulation and the visuals, the real thing is something different. It smells different for a start and there is much more activity behind the seats." I added wryly "And it's easier to get on to the flight deck."

Sam nodded but didn't actually smile.

"It's a cross we have to bear these days I'm afraid." He rapidly changed the subject. "What are you doing going to Sydney, if I may ask?"

"No problem. Bill Baker the NWIA chief training pilot has asked me to advise on their training course for the 798s they are getting and perhaps give some lectures. I'm going to suggest that a video might be a good idea so that it can be used on every course."

"What do you think about the accident to Alfa Juliet, Peter?"

"Terrible, and seemingly inexplicable. Did you read about the Inquiry in the papers today? What do you people think?"

"Well, Peter, we were all pretty shaken. The frightening thing is that accidents can normally be explained very quickly but this one seems different. I think most of us thought that a hijacking was impossible. I still believe that the highjacking must be the primary cause but I know there is a view that it may only have been a contributing factor."

Silence descended for a few minutes. We were probably all thinking about Alfa Juliet.

"Do you ever use the American GPS as well for navigation?"

"We can do but we have to select it. The default is the Galileo system. As you probably are well aware, the GPS output is sent to the Flight Management Computer but is not averaged with Galileo; we can select GPS instead of Galileo for navigation but we never do unless the Galileo goes wrong. The European system is so much more advanced and the integrity and self checking is so good that the GPS system is just not needed except perhaps if the Galileo fails. Anyway on the 798 we only have one receiver for the GPS system while we have three for Galileo which increases it's accuracy and reliability."

"Yes, it definitely should be more accurate."

"But Peter the FAA allows US carriers to make Category 1 approaches worldwide down to 200 ft using just one GPS augmented with corrections from their so called Wide Area Augmentation System, WAAS."

"I know but of course a much more accurate local correction system is needed for bad weather approaches below 200ft, and even then some local correction systems are not good enough at some locations. In fact I think there are local correction systems both at Heathrow and Paris but the US carriers aren't allowed to make GPS approaches at either place because the Local Area Augmentation System needs considerable improvement. Apparently the faults are only temporary and in my view FAA really ought to order the LAAS transmitters to be switched off but politically the US don't want their system to be seen to be inferior to the European system and they are trying very hard to fix the problems. RWA are probably very sensible to prevent the use of GPS on any approach, particularly now that Galileo is available with the accuracy enhanced by the GBAS when Category III landings are required."

"Nevertheless Peter, I'm glad that RWA did agree to have the GPS as a back-up for navigation to Galileo since, though there is no doubt that for normal navigation Galileo is superb, in fact we did have a problem with Galileo some months ago and were very pleased to be able to use the GPS."

There was a strident buzzing noise and Sam looked at a small screen to his left where I could see the face of the Chief Steward. He pressed a button on top of the screen and the steward came in with some coffee. It occurred to me that there must be some secret code so that the Captain would know if the person trying to get onto the flight deck was being threatened, though it would be a brave person not to use the code if he or she had a pistol or knife in their back.

In spite of having control wheels instead of side stick controllers, the view of the instruments and controls was superb. The navigation displays showed the aircraft moving steadily along the airway and the flight management display showed the expected arrival time at Kingsford Smith Airport.

"Did you notice, Peter, that at the moment we are using the 4D method of control; the automatic throttles are controlling the speed so that we will arrive at Sydney exactly at the flight plan time."

The autopilot was flying the aircraft and the model aeroplane on the display was sitting inside the flight plan predicted time box; the four throttles moved very slightly to adjust the airspeed to keep the aircraft there. I could see that the aircraft was being controlled automatically along the desired flight path at the correct height and, for the moment, the speed was also being controlled by the automatic throttle.

It occurred to me that the pilots' jobs on the flight deck had changed enormously through the years as the number of crew required to fly an aircraft on long haul flights had changed. The old flight engineers tasks were now automated in the aircraft systems. The radio operators tasks were also done automatically in many ways thanks to satellite communication with automatic position reporting and, of course, the navigators tasks were done by the Flight Management System. As a percentage of total flight time, the pilots spent very little time actually flying the aircraft. From a safety viewpoint the problem was the need for the crew to recognize and deal with any emergencies correctly; this was the challenge not only for the pilots but also for the aircraft designers and the organizations certificating the aircraft. This situation was always the one I was discussing with airlines when they were bringing their new aircraft into service.

As I drank my coffee, Fred drew my attention to a traffic advisory on the Traffic and Conflict Alerting System display, TCAS. An aircraft was ahead of us going our way but two thousand feet below. We were slowly overtaking it. It was an Airbus A330 of Cathay Pacific on its way to Hong Kong. Fred started talking to the Cathay crew which was something I always recommended to keep the crews alert.

"Peter, we are getting towards the end of our shift and the other crew will be taking over. Would you like to come back again later? If you like you can spend the last hour with us descending into Sydney for landing."

I leapt at the opportunity. "Yes please Sam. It would be very interesting. I'll get out of your way now and perhaps you could send a message back when you are ready for me."

I left the jump seat and returned to my seat in the crew compartment. I tried to put myself into neutral, reading my book for a bit. George and Josh got up, freshened themselves up and operated the security procedure at the flight deck door before going onto the flight deck. A few minutes later Sam and Fred appeared from the flight deck, had a quick meal off a tray and went to lie down. The stewardess appeared and asked if I was ready to lie down in the VIP Cabin. I agreed rapidly and settled down to sleep. In fact I managed to get about five hours so that when I woke up we only had three hours to go. We were 300 miles east of Darwin over the Gulf of Carpentaria. I went back into the crew compartment where George and Josh were having breakfast. It looked good and the stewardess brought me the same. I was only just finishing eating when she came back again and said it would be OK if I went back on to the flight deck. I packed up all my belongings so that I would not waste any time when I returned from the flight deck after the landing. The stewardess obviously knew the magic number on the flight deck door and we went in. It was dark by now and there were lots of lights from the ground 47,000 ft below.

"Good morning Peter. Where are we then?"

"26° S 145° E, if the front of the aircraft is in the same place as the monitor in the crew compartment."

Sam looked at his Flight Management System display and selected present position.

"Quite right, Peter. We're on schedule and will be letting down fairly soon. The weather's good at Kingsford-Smith, 10 miles visibility, no cloud, 15 knots from the south and a temperature of 28°C if you can believe that."

Sam got clearance to descend and wound the knob on the glare shield in front of him to the new cleared altitude of flight level 190. He then initiated the descent to 19,000 ft. and the throttles closed slightly. The Flight Management System took the aircraft steadily along and down the standard approach path, Sam gradually lowering the setting of the altitude controller as he received fresh clearances from the ground.

"I think we won't interfere to-day. We will let the autopilot do the landing." He selected the Galileo vertical position on the glare shield landing aid controller. "Oh, sorry. We can't. I see they haven't repaired the Ground Based Augmentation System yet. It failed a day or so ago. We will just have to use the MLS." He turned the approach selector one click anti-clockwise selecting MLS instead of Galileo.

We could see the lights of Sydney below and then the runway lights gradually emerged from the surrounding illumination as the aircraft got closer. Sam and Fred carried out the landing checks and Fred selected the landing gear down as we subsided on to the glide slope. The four throttles went back until the approach speed had been reached and then opened slightly to maintain the speed. The runway lights got closer and closer and slowly moved apart so that we could see the runway centre line markings. The radio altimeter called out the heights as the aircraft descended and at about 30 ft. the throttles closed, the stick came back and the aircraft touched down quite firmly. The aircraft pitched down, the nose wheels touched the ground and after a few moments Sam disconnected the autopilot and applied the brakes. It was a perfect landing. I looked at my watch, it was on schedule at 2000.

Sam taxied the aircraft clear of the runway and then followed instructions to reach gate C45.

"Thanks so much, Sam, for letting me watch that. It was great. Where are you staying?"

"At the Hilton until Tuesday unless the plan changes."

"I'm at the Hilton too so I'll probably see you. Thanks again." I went back to the flight deck area just before the aircraft came to a halt. We all had to wait until the passengers had left and then we filed out slowly from the top deck, the flight crew and all the cabin attendants. It seemed miles to customs and immigration but at least we did not have to queue like all the passengers. On the other hand the flight crew line was not insignificant once we were joined by the cabin staff since there were a lot of passengers to be looked after. The security and immigration departments had clearly done a marvellous job preparing for these large aircraft though there were always bound to be queues.

I said goodbye to the crew and became a civilian again. My bag, marked with its business class sticker, appeared quite quickly on the carousel and I walked through the customs line after having my bag x-rayed. I rang the Hilton courtesy phone.

"Just go to the hotel pick-up point and there is a coach every fifteen minutes. See you soon." the voice at the other end said. I followed instructions and realised for the first time as I left the air conditioned terminal how hot it still was at 9 o'clock at night. The coach appeared and I was at the Hilton in about 40 minutes.

When I checked in they told me there was a message from Matt Thompson. I took the elevator to the sixth floor and went to 617. It was like any other hotel room but it did have a magnificent view over the harbour. I unpacked my things and had a shower to freshen up.

I called Matt first but there was no reply and I left a message. Then I tried Mandy. Again there was no reply. She had obviously decided that sailing and the yacht club was the thing to do for the week-end and, unreasonably, I decided not to leave a message on her answering machine.

I lay down on the bed and thought about Alfa Juliet. Why didn't the crew realise they were below the glide slope? Why was the voice recording so noisy? Did the hijackers prevent the crew noticing some warning clue? There had to be an explanation. Richard's dying words weren't much help and the fact that NWIA had changed a display and a Multimode Receiver before departure didn't help either. As I dropped off to sleep I realised that Matt calling me might turn out to be a bit of luck because then I might have the chance to investigate the maintenance without seeming too inquisitive.

CHAPTER 12

Liz

When I woke up Sydney still had its heat wave. After a swim in the pool, a shower and wearing my lightweight slacks and shirt I went down to the breakfast room. Sam Falconer was having breakfast with a lady who turned out to be his wife. I went over and he introduced me to Sonia.

"Were you on our flight? Sam never mentioned it."

"Yes. I was in the flight crew area."

"How did you like the flight?"

"It was fine but awfully long. Still it's nice not to have to stop on the way. That was my first non-stop flight."

Sam invited me to join them for breakfast. They had only just ordered and the waiter laid a place in front of me.

"What are you doing to-day, Peter?"

"Jock Mansfield of NWIA is collecting me and we're going over to start work on their training course. What about you?"

"I'm taking Sonia over to Randwick where our daughter and her family live. Sonia's staying over for a week or so until I come out again."

The room was slowly filling up. Fred Longshaw was with Josh Wilson.

"Do the flight crews normally stay here, Sam? I see Fred over there."

"Yes pretty well. We rent the rooms all the time and our Operations Office at the airport keeps the hotel informed, tells them when they need to change the sheets, etc."

"Do the cabin crew stay here as well?"

"No, they're normally at the Oakford Executive Apartments or the Winyard Travel Lodge Plaza. You know there are so many of them that they make up a coach-load. It's a full time job for two people in the office arranging the accommodation."

Luckily Sam refrained from asking me why I wanted to know. I would not have wanted to tell him that I was checking up on Alfa Juliet's crew. After breakfast I excused myself and went upstairs and got my papers ready in my document case. At the news stand I bought the Australian. There were some London papers on sale which we must have brought out with us though I noticed the Mail was printed locally. The main local news was the cricket and whether the West Indies could score enough runs in their first innings to save the follow on. I searched for some news about Alfa Juliet and was disconcerted to read that we had brought two bodies back with us to Australia for burial on yesterday's flight. However, some of the other bodies could not be brought back yet because of difficulties with positive identification.

There was no technical news about the possible cause of the accident nor, I was glad to see, was there any more news about the cockpit voice recorder and the party in Sydney.

I considered what should be my next move and how to find out what Alfa Juliet's crew had been up to. I didn't know how long the crew had been staying in the hotel before they left for England and I didn't fancy asking at reception. Anyway they might not have known. Asking RWA's flight operations at the airport would be a possibility but that would alert them and it might get back to John Chester. I decided that I would try talking to the barman in the main bar at the lobby level at about 5.30 that evening before it got too crowded. Barmen always seemed to know what was going on.

Jock Mansfield came into the lobby at 9.30 prompt. That was one of the nice things about the airline business, everybody was on time or slightly early. We introduced ourselves and I got into Jock's Honda. We set course for the airport.

"When did you finish your course in Seattle, Jock?"

"On Friday night. We got in here 6 o'clock Sunday morning. It's quite a long flight, 16 hours. Not as long as from England but long enough."

"How was the course?"

"It certainly is a fantastic aircraft. They seem to have thought of everything. Mind you the systems are quite complicated, especially if anything goes wrong."

"Well I suppose that's why we're meeting to-day. Both Bill and I feel there's a problem in this area. How to keep the crews alert and ready to deal with any emergency."

We threaded our way through the traffic and arrived at the NWIA training block. Jock parked his car and we went into reception. The girl took my photograph with a camera she had hidden under the desk and gave me an 'unaccompanied' pass valid until Thursday.

"It is magnetised so you will be able to get in and out of this building but it won't work everywhere in NWIA."

We went up to Bill's office which was quite palatial. His secretary took us in and we were joined by Jack Phillips the other Captain in Seattle and Phillip Trotter who ran the Ground School.

Bill set the scene. "I've got Peter to come out here now that you two are back from Seattle because I believe we need to think more carefully than usual about training our crews for the 798. The accident to Alfa Juliet shows how difficult it is to prevent accidents. The sooner the investigators find out the cause the better. I suppose we all hope it will be the hijackers fault but it's just possible there may be more to it than that.

"Anyway, my concern is that we must have a training course that covers all our flight operations. The really long flights require two full crews and we have to ensure that the duty crew is ready and rested as they take-over the flight deck. All the systems including the navigation and flight controls are fully automatic, not only for normal flight but also when things start malfunctioning. The challenge for us is to devise a training program that enables the crew to deal with emergencies and situations which are not expected. I've heard Peter lecture on these issues both here and in London. 'Managing the Systems' he calls it, and the phrase he uses which I like very much is 'we must prepare for the emergencies that the designers have not thought of'. Remember our worst pilot must be able to fly this aircraft safely so this is what I want you four to think about in the next two days. Show me a training plan which faces up to the problem."

We talked a bit more and then the four of us went into a small conference room that had been booked for us. Jock produced the Independant training course and started discussing the strengths and weaknesses of the course. We gradually started to plan the NWIA training course.

"Is your aircraft going to be the same standard as Royal World Airlines, Jock?"

"No. We are going to match United and American exactly on the flight deck. I understand that RWA have a slightly different way of using the satellite positioning systems?"

"Yes, that's quite right. Your aircraft will have the capability of doing all four types of instrument approach ILS, MLS, GPS and Galileo while RWA can only use ILS, MLS and Galileo."

"Up to now we have not had any satellite landing systems, the 798 will be our first. We really like the idea of satellite approaches because they will work anywhere in the world using the latest GPS or Galileo satellites providing they have a local system to ensure accuracy.

"Well I'll arrange my talks to cover your installation."

We broke for lunch and went to the canteen. We carried on through the afternoon making good progress. I raised the subject of making a video which could be used for later courses and Jock agreed to get the NWIA expert over. Jock took me back to the hotel and he volunteered to pick me up again in the morning. Apart from the video we reckoned we would be through by the end of Friday.

I collected my key, left my things in my room and went down in the elevator as planned to sit at the bar. I ordered a gin and slimline tonic. The barman was dark, short and was called Mario, he sounded Italian. We chatted for a bit.

"Are you with Royal World Airlines?"

"No. I am working with NWIA" I didn't mind telling him since he was sure to find out. "That was a terrible accident to the 798."

"Yes. The crew had been staying here for several days before they left; we knew them very well because they always stayed here. You know Royal World Airlines put all their flight crew up here. It was a shame. Captain Hodgson was such a nice guy."

"Did you know Charles Tumbrill as well then?"

"Oh yes. He was much younger than Hodgson and always out for a party. In fact I saw them both on the Saturday night. Tumbrill appeared with a couple of girls and they were drinking at that table over there. It was quite early, about this time. He called for the bill and I heard him say that they had better be going to Maroubra as their reservation was for eight o'clock."

"Saturday night? But they left for the flight early Monday morning. Did you see them Sunday?"

"No I didn't. But they normally go to bed early when they are flying the next day. Not like some of them when they arrive."

"How do you mean?"

Mario went away again but returned after a bit.

"Can I get you a drink?"

"Not really when I'm working but if I may I'll put a large beer on your tab to have later."

"Fine. what did you mean about the crews not going to bed when they arrive from England?"

"You seem very interested. You a newspaperman or something?"

"No. I told you I'm working with NWIA but I used to fly myself with Britannia."

"Britannia stay here as well." He gave me another drink. "I was telling you, on Saturday night Tumbrill and Hodgson went off to the beach. On Sunday night I did not see the other crew but very early on the Monday morning as I was leaving I saw two pilots who had just come in from England checking in to the hotel with their bags. They were wearing slacks and short sleeved shirts so they must have got changed somewhere."

"Would you recognise either of the girls that were here on Saturday night?"

He looked hard at me. I was clearly showing too much interest. However he carried on.

"Oh yes. We see quite a lot of one of them. I think she works in the Royal World Airlines operations office. I haven't seen her since the accident."

"Is she Australian?"

167

"No, she sounds like a real Pom to me, like you. She is a brunette, smashing legs, good boobs, very nearly as tall as you. Don't know her name."

"Thanks a lot, Mario. I must be off now." I gave him a $20 note besides putting a generous tip on the bill.

I was glad to get upstairs and lie down on the bed even though it was only 8 o'clock. I had had to drink three strong gin and tonics to get what I needed from Mario. The phone rang.

"Mr Talbert?" I admitted to the operator that that was my name.

"I have a call for you."

Before I could prepare myself I heard Mandy.

"Peter, are you there?"

"Yes my darling. I'm safe and sound in bed."

"In bed! What time is it?"

"Well I've just drunk three double gin and tonics and bed seemed a good idea. I'm just resting."

"I take my eyes off you and you go on to the bottle. Are you alone?" she said suspiciously.

"No my dearest Mandy. I mean yes I am alone."

"You just said you weren't."

"Look. Your not cross examining me in court."

"All I am trying to establish is what time it is in Sydney and whether you are by yourself."

"It is 8 o'clock in the evening and yes, I am alone."

"The sooner they bring in TV phones the better. However I believe you ..."

"I should hope so."

"but only as far as I can see you." she finished.

"That's not very friendly."

"I'm not sure I'm feeling friendly. I'm feeling cross, lonely and I miss you" she said suddenly changing her tone of voice.

"Would it be trite to say I miss you too?"

"I am afraid it would be in your condition – as some of my clients would say – 'slightly pissed'."

"That's not a very ladylike thing for a young girl to say. I'll go along with 'slightly the worse for wear'."

"I don't feel ladylike and it was my clients talking. I'd better not tell you what I feel like, not that you could help in your condition."

"I only had three doubles and it was all in the course of research. I was chatting up the barman."

Mandy suddenly became serious. "How did you get on?"

"Rather well apart from the side effects. The party the Telegraph mentioned seems to have been the night before the night before the flight

168

if you know what I mean. The barman knew one of the girls, she works for RWA in operations. I guess all the crews know her as well, though not I trust in the biblical sense."

Mandy ignored my comment.

"That's good news. Anything else?"

"Not really. The crew that flew the plane in had a party after they got in but that is not going to help as far as I can see."

"Are you going to talk to the girl."

"Yes, if I can find her. I'll have a go to-morrow if I can but it looks as if I shall be working flat out for the next two days. I've also got to see the maintenance people. I'm booked for a Sunday morning departure which gets in late Sunday night but Sunday seems a long way away at the moment."

"Alright. Take care. Don't get into trouble and call me soon. All my love." She rang off and I suddenly felt lonely and sober. I got up and had a shower.

I thought about what Mario had said. Clearly Charles and Harry had had a beach party on Saturday night. Nothing wrong in that from a flight operations viewpoint though it might cause problems socially. The pilots must have been referring to the Saturday night party on the recording. Marcia Hodgson might be unhappy but from my point of view it was good news. However it occurred to me that it might be interesting to find the girl and talk over not only what had happened on Saturday night but if she knew anything about Sunday night. She probably knew the crew if she was in operations. How was I going to meet the girl?

I remembered I had not spoken to Matt. I called him and this time he answered.

"Matt, I don't think we've met. This is Peter Talbert. You left a message for me to ring you and I wanted to talk to you anyway. How can I help you?"

"Hi, Peter. I wanted to meet with you and chat over Alfa Juliet. What are you doing to-morrow?"

"Well Bill has mapped out a pretty full program for me and it's his party."

"I understand that. Why don't I come over to your place at about 6.30 to-morrow evening and we'll go out for a meal?"

"Sounds good to me. If we don't make contact before I'll see you then. How will I recognise you?"

"I'll be wearing a white shirt and red trousers, I'm 6 ft. tall and some people say I'm thin."

"OK. See you to-morrow."

It was now 9 o'clock. I was not too hungry but I decided I had better have something before I went to bed. I put some clothes on, took my book and went down to the coffee shop. I had a bowl of clam chowder, Australian style, some water followed by strong decaffeinated coffee. I retired to bed and slept through until it started to get light at about 6 o'clock. I managed my swim and breakfast next to the pool before Jock came and collected me. I asked Jock if he could take me to RWA Operations at lunch time.

"Yes, that's no problem. I've got the video man coming after lunch at 2 o'clock. I'll drop you off at Ops and you can go into the main airport for lunch if you want to. I'll pick you up at 1.45 from RWA Ops"

We did a good morning's work and I was in Ops at noon. There were several girls at the desk and I asked to speak to the duty officer. The girl I spoke to said that Ted Richmond was the man I needed and he would be back very shortly. I was wondering how to proceed when the girl, Barbara on her badge, made it simple for me.

"What are you people making of the accident?" She sounded as if she had definitely been born in Australia.

"We are appalled. Everybody is very shaken and very puzzled. Harry was a fine man and I knew him well."

"We knew them all of course. They were in and out of here all the time. We couldn't believe it. I think Liz was the most upset as she had got to know Harry quite well."

Ted Richmond appeared and introduced himself. I followed him into his office. I explained that I was working with NWIA and asked about getting back on Sunday. He looked at his computer and checked on the RWA allocated tickets.

"You have a firm booking for Sunday, that's fine."

"Could you tell me the Captain's name so I can contact him in the hotel?"

Ted consulted his machine again.

"Brad Wentworth. He came in last night."

"Thanks. Ted, may I talk about the accident?"

He smiled.

"Sure, go ahead. I guessed there had to be another reason for your coming here."

"I'm a friend of Harry's wife, Marcia. She's very upset and she asked me to talk to one of your staff who both she and Harry knew well. Apparently Harry saw her just before the flight. Is her name Liz or something like that?"

"Oh you mean Liz Ward. I'm afraid she took Harry's death very badly. I told her to take a week of her annual holiday but she's started working again now. I got her moved into reservations downtown so she'd get away from the crews."

"Marcia couldn't find her address. Do you think you could let me have it so I can tell Marcia?"

"Sure." He looked at his computer yet again and then printed out Liz Ward's address and telephone number.

"Thanks. I'll get out of your way."

I felt a bit guilty lying to Ted in order to get the information about the girl but I did not want to stir up any particular interest. Fortunately he did not behave as if anything I said was particularly unusual. I wandered over to the terminal, bought yesterday's Times and FT and had a tuna sandwich in one of the many eating places. The accident was no longer the main topic of news and I guessed the next bit of media interest would be when the AAIB preliminary report came out.

Jock picked me up and took me back to the training block. We had a discussion with the Video expert and decided that when I came out again to give a talk to the first course I would also make a video which could be used for subsequent courses. I made a mental note to discuss the financial side of this plan with Bill Baker.

We settled down again to finish the training plan and then I spoke to Bill to arrange to see him the following afternoon. Jock took me back to the Hilton where Matt arrived on time and took me to the Brasserie Restaurant in the hotel.

He passed me the drinks menu which had at least one hundred Australian wines.

"What are you having?"

"If you don't mind I'll stick to Scotch and water."

"That's fine by me. I'll have the same. Well Peter, what have you being doing?"

"Preparing the pilot training courses. Bill has kindly asked me to help since the 798 is a step change and a challenge for the flight crews. How about the engineering of the aircraft?"

"Typical Independant. Very well thought out and conservative in approach. My people are used to the Independant approach and we like all their aircraft. Let's hope the 798 will be as easy to maintain as our others. We've already got most of our spares and of course we're getting a lot of experience looking after the RWA aircraft. It seems very reliable."

"Matt, I had better explain. I have been retained by one of RWA's insurers to try to find out exactly what happened to Alfa Juliet. They don't want to leave it completely to AAIB. Do you mind if I ask you some questions?"

"Not a bit. But surely the accident was due to the hijackers?"

"Well, we've just been listening to the voice recordings and reading the transcripts at the Public Inquiry. The flight deck microphone was so noisy we could not hear the hijackers. It makes things very difficult to analyse as they must have been a distraction to the crew during the approach. I want to be certain that the maintenance your people did had nothing to do with the accident."

"Good. Well I did wonder what your interest was. Go ahead and I'll see if I can help."

"This aircraft that crashed. Was the failure of the Navigation Display unusual in any way?"

"Not as far as we were concerned. However, after the crew had filled in the tech. log, my avionics expert on the night shift functioned the unit and it worked perfectly. As you probably know NWIA policy is not to allow a 'ground tested and found serviceable' entry in the log so we actually changed the unit. We functioned the new unit on the aircraft and then we did an all night function on the unit we had removed. It worked perfectly and so we've placed the unit back in stores as a spare."

"Well as I am sure you know, Matt, the new display failed again shortly after take-off so it looks as if the aircraft installation was at fault rather than the display itself. Had the aircraft not crashed, there would have been an opportunity to find out what was really the matter."

"So I understand. Anyway I don't think the display had anything to do with the crash, do you?"

"I just don't know. It may have contributed to the accident. Who knows? The whole thing looks like a complete mystery. Tell me about the Galileo fault."

"Well as you know, to ensure the correct integrity for automatic landings the 798 has a triplex system with three Multimode Receivers. On Alfa Juliet the crew that came in reported that when they selected Galileo on the approach, one of the Multimode Receivers was giving a false reading. The engineer on the night shift decided it was a hardware fault and changed one of the Multimode Receivers. The engineer then did a full check and pronounced the aircraft serviceable."

"Well that sounds fine. Tell me, have the AAIB been on to you again?"

"No, it's surprisingly quiet. I would have thought that they would have flown somebody out to see the tech log pages at the very least. We did what they asked and faxed them copies."

Our conversation drifted away from the accident and Alfa Juliet and we talked about more general matters. Matt took me back to the hotel and I called Mandy's office and was told she was in court. I said I would try again on Friday. I slept well, waking up to another perfect day. I had my 7 o'clock swim and while I was dressing before going down to breakfast my phone rang.

"Peter. This is Brad Wentworth of RWA. I am taking you back to England on Sunday. How about having breakfast together?"

"Fine by me. See you by the news stand in ten minutes. I've got to make a phone call and then I'll come down."

I looked at the local directory and it gave the main police headquarters' number at Paramatta. They answered straightaway and, at my request, the operator connected me to the homicide department.

"I'm visiting from England. I wondered whether you had any more news on the body that was found in the Hyatt car park."

"What's it to you? What did you say your name was?" The voice was surly and didn't sound too helpful."

"My name is Talbert and I'm working on the aircraft accident at London Airport. I understand that the person should have been on the plane..."

I didn't get any further.

"I don't know where your getting your information from, Mr Tarbuck, but this matter is still under investigation. I suggest you get on with the technical investigation and leave police matters to the police."

I was left looking at a dead phone. Sounded as if the Sydney police were operating a D-Notice regime as well. Maybe they were sensitive that the hijackers had got on to the aircraft.

Brad was waiting when I got to the shop. He was about my height, 40 years old and looked very fit. We went over to the coffee shop but stayed inside rather going to the pool.

Brad came to the point straightaway.

"I wanted to meet you Peter. I know about your interest in the flight deck and navigation and I was looking forward to talking with you on the flight back on Sunday. However, out of the blue John Chester called me at flight operations before I left while I was picking up the flight plan. He said that he did not want you to go on the flight deck again. I thought I would tell you now rather than embarrass you on the flight."

I felt absolutely amazed and I suppose my face showed it.

"You look surprised."

"To be honest Brad, I am. I've known John for years and we've worked together at GAPAN and at RWA. I would have thought if he had a problem he would have had the courtesy to phone me."

"You know I think John is very worried about the crash" Brad remarked.

"Of course, but so are we all. John called me on the morning after the accident and we met for lunch but since then he seems to have got worried about something else and he is keeping it to himself. I must say I do appreciate your being so straightforward about this. It's very kind."

"Forget it. What are you doing to-day?"

"Well I'm having a day off. How about you?"

"So am I. I was thinking of going over to the Opera House for a conducted tour. Care to join me?"

I accepted with pleasure and we had a splendid morning looking at the extraordinary architecture and being shown all over the enormous complex with it's two theatres and many side rooms. We had lunch in one of the many restaurants on Circular Quay and then I went over to the airport to see Bill Baker. We agreed a deal over the video and I took my farewell. His secretary took me over to the terminal and I picked up a rental car and drove back to the Hilton to get changed. I got my map out and made sure where Liz Ward lived before setting out. I felt rather flat. I had taken a job halfway across the world when I really couldn't spare the time in order to try to investigate the crash of the 798. I had achieved precisely nothing and yet somehow I didn't believe that Harry Hodgson had made a mistake. He had handled the hijacking magnificently, he hadn't been rattled, there was something else in the equation that nobody had found.

I steered the car into the right area and found that the address was a small bungalow set in a myriad of bungalows. There were some lights in the rooms. I parked the car in the drive. A Siamese cat was sitting on the doorstep. I pressed the bell and I could hear a buzzer somewhere at the back. I heard noises and I could see through the opaque glass door someone looking through the spy hole. The door opened slightly on a chain.

"Yes?" came a female voice from inside.

"Miss Ward, I'm out from England working with NWIA" As usual I kept to the truth as much as possible since that way I didn't have to remember what story I had told. "I was a friend of Harry Hodgson. They told me in the RWA office that you knew him. I hope you don't mind but I got them to give me your address. I don't believe what they said in the press about a party the night before the flight. I wanted to find out the truth and if possible help his family."

There was a long pause and finally I heard the chain coming off the door which opened revealing a tall brunette, mid twenties possibly, longish hair, slim and alarmingly attractive. I could not decide whether this was due to her very short shorts and skimpy top or due to her superior look which seemed to say 'I know what you men want but don't hold your breath.' She eyed me carefully, looking me up and down. I noticed the whites of her eyes were red and it looked as if she had been crying.

"Come on in. What did you say your name was?"

"I didn't but it's Peter Talbert. I'm a specialist in electronics and the aircraft flight deck."

"Mine's Elizabeth but everybody calls me Liz."

When I entered the house I thought she might have been Australian but her accent was very English. She showed me to the living room in the back of the house which overlooked a very small garden and the other bungalows. It was very warm inside and the patio door was open. I sat on the settee. There were bits of clothing in the making, half sewn, in various parts of the room.

"Would you like a drink?"

I could have used a beer but the time didn't seem right for alcohol. I didn't want to miss anything and I was clearly going to have to concentrate and not start thinking of other things.

"A coke or something soft if you have one."

"You're sure? There's most things available."

"No, really. Coke would be just fine."

The room was quite ordinary and fairly tidy apart from the sewing. There were some recent English newspapers lying around as well as the Sydney Herald.

She returned with two cokes in long glasses stuffed with ice. She put them down and sat opposite me on a chair and looked at me enquiringly, waiting for me to begin.

"You know that somebody leaked the cockpit voice recorder conversation to the press just after the accident?" She nodded. "Everybody's assuming that the crew had been out partying the night before and consequently they might have made a mistake when landing. I don't happen to believe that and I'm trying to find out what really happened."

"I thought the accident was due to hijacking."

"We all hoped that, but now that some of us have heard the voice recorder and read the transcripts it's difficult to see that the hijackers directly caused the accident. So people are looking around again for another reason."

"Why did you come to me?"

"Well I spoke to the barman in the Hilton and from what he told me it appeared that Harry and Charles Tumbrill the first officer had gone out on Saturday with two ladies and he thought one of them worked for RWA operations in Sydney. So it was not very difficult to find you and here I am. Obviously, I want to find out how Harry and Charles spent Sunday night, hopefully in their own beds before the flight. What happened on Saturday is not important from my point of view."

There was a long silence.

"Harry was a fine person. He was a good friend. I miss him. And I've lost my room mate. I know life has to go on but at the moment things don't look too good."

"Your room mate? I'm afraid I don't understand."

"Are you on the level, Peter? You're not a reporter or a detective or something."

"No, I'm not a reporter or a detective or anything. However, I am dedicated to trying to save the crews' reputation. I don't believe that it was pilot error, pure and simple. I want to get at the truth and find out what really happened."

"Well that's fine by me. I'll try and tell you the story as best I can. I'm afraid I'm not in very good shape."

Luckily I knew what she meant and I kept very quiet.

"As you know I worked in the RWA operations office and obviously I got to know all the crews. It doesn't need a lot of imagination to guess that a lot of them tried to take me out and make passes. The married men were normally the worst. To cut a long story short, about six months ago Charles met my room mate Eva Pearson by chance, when she was visiting me in the office and persuaded her to go out to dinner. Eva was a NWIA trainee cabin attendant based in Sydney and was receiving training on the 798 getting ready for their new aircraft. Eva said OK providing I could come along as well." She paused and swallowed before she carried on.

"We agreed a time and Charles found the bungalow as you did. Harry was with him. We went out to a down town restaurant and had a good evening. Charles was smitten with Eva and she liked him a lot. Eva was about my age, maybe a little younger and like me she had known quite a few men. We enjoyed life." I noticed she used the past tense.

"Harry was different. He was happily married, teenage children of his own and he did not start chasing me all round the room, if you know what I mean." I nodded. I knew what she meant.

"After this first meeting we started meeting regularly whenever they came out. Harry and Charles often flew together but sometimes they came out at different times. Well, that Saturday they flew out together and this heat wave had already started. Eva suggested we went out to the beach and have a meal at one of the many restaurants. We drove round to the Hilton, had a drink, went out to Maroubra beach and ate at Caesars. It was marvellous out there and Charles could hardly keep his hands off Eva. By some strange chance NWIA had arranged with RWA for Eva and one or two other girls to travel on the very 798 which Harry and Charles were flying back to England on the Monday, in order to get some flight experience. The girls had not flown outside Australia before." She paused again, I think uncertain whether to carry on.

She leant forward and held both my hands.

"You are a straight guy? You're not going to tell this story round the world?"

The way she looked at that particular moment I would have done anything for her.

"I promise you this story will go no further unless you want it to."

She carried on holding my hands, leaning very close to me as if to make sure. I couldn't decide if she knew the effect she was having on me.

"For once there was no surf. The heat was getting to Eva and Charles in more ways than one and Eva, I think it was, suggested we should go swimming and the two of them rushed off down the beach. The moon was overcast and we could not see them. I asked Harry if he wanted to go swimming and he said yes. We went down on the beach and we took our clothes off and swam naked in the warm water. It was magnificent. Harry and I stood opposite each other with the water up to our necks. I held his hand and we walked back out of the water. I could see he was aroused. I told him it was OK by me but he suddenly turned away and went back to his clothes and sat down. We lay down a few feet apart drying off and then we got dressed.

"I liked and admired Harry but we'd never had sex together. If he'd wanted to that night it would have been OK by me." She stopped, let go of my hands and stood up. "Well that's about it. We went back to the restaurant and after a bit Charles and Eva came back looking as if they had had cream. Charles drove us home but both he and Harry seemed a bit impatient and were looking at their watches. I think they had a breakfast appointment. I never saw Harry or Charles again." She all but burst into tears and went out of the room. She returned a few minutes later holding a handkerchief.

"I'm sorry." She used the handkerchief again. "I know Harry was in the hotel on the Sunday night because he left a message on our answering machine and I called him back in the Hilton at 8 o'clock. He was in his room and he told me he was going to bed."

She came back from the past.

"Would you like another drink or something to eat?"

I looked at my watch. "When did you eat last? Why don't I take you somewhere for a meal? It's the least I can do." She looked undecided so I tried again. "Come on, Liz. When did you last have a proper meal?"

She hesitated. "I've only been grazing for the last week or so. I just haven't felt like eating."

Suddenly she smiled. "OK. You're on. Why don't we go to the same beach restaurant that we went to on that Saturday? It's a nice place. You'd enjoy it. Have a real drink." Before I could answer she disappeared. I could hear a shower going in the distance. I went into the kitchen, looked in the fridge. There was an open bottle of wine. I found some glasses and poured out the wine. Liz returned wearing a T-shirt and a very short skirt. She wasn't wearing a bra and her nipples showed through clearly. I gave her a glass of wine and we drank. We were very quiet. Alfa Juliet was certainly having an effect on both our lives.

177

Blind Landing

She locked up the house and we drove out to Maroubra beach. We barely spoke a word except when she told me the roads to take. I parked the car at Caesars but Liz suddenly changed her mind.

"Let's go to Frank's Bar over there." She pointed. "They have music and I need cheering up. Besides Eva and I were at Frank's the following night."

I didn't argue. I reversed out of the parking lot and drove to Frank's. I helped her out and we sat outside under a new moon in the tropical heat. I ordered some food and wine. There was no wind and surprisingly no surf.

"Let's dance." She dragged me unresisting to the small floor on the sand. I held her close but apparently not close enough. She pulled me closer. The music was slow. She smelt fresh and seemed to melt round me. The music stopped which was perhaps just as well and we went back to our table. Our wine was waiting for us. Not that I needed it. I was intoxicated already.

"You know, Peter, there is something else I haven't told you." Thankfully I forced myself back to Alfa Juliet. I felt rather guilty thinking of anything else. I was prepared to stay very close to Liz to hear the rest of the story. I listened gratefully, watching her every move as we enjoyed our meal.

"Eva and I slept most of the Sunday. We had agreed two weeks earlier in flight operations, on the spur of the moment, to go out with a Captain and a first officer from an incoming 798 flight the moment they landed. They had confirmed the arrangement by phone on Thursday. Eva had agreed before she knew that she had to report at 6.30 on the Monday morning. I tried everything but I could not persuade her to cancel the evening.

"The pilots turned up straight from the airport and changed at our place. They telephoned NWIA maintenance about some navigation problem they had forgotten to report. We came straight here at about midnight, danced, had a meal and probably too many drinks. It was the reverse of the previous night. Tony Giles, the first officer was my date, and he was all over me. Eva was thinking of Charles and being faithful and anyway Ray Robson, the Captain, was not proving to be much fun. I think she hoped that Charles would propose when they got to England."

She stopped her story, grabbed me and took me back to the dance floor. This time she held me very close indeed She whispered. "It was just like this on Sunday night. Tony and I went for a swim, shall we?" She looked me in the eye. "There's more to tell but I'll tell it my way."

We went down the beach. I felt events were happening that I couldn't control. The new moon was setting and it was getting dark. We sat down on the sand and she knelt in front of me, her breasts showing through her top.

She got up, took her skirt and top off and went into the water. I stood up, removed my clothes and followed her. I was determined not to miss the end of the story. We pressed against one another in the water. It was idyllic. We walked slowly back up the beach and we lay down naked very close together on the sand as the water dried off.

***

We stayed on the sand afterwards, next to one another, side by side, very close. I held her in my arms and she started to cry. I tried to comfort her. "It's alright. My life's in such a mess. And I think you're sweet." She paused then whispered next to my ear.

"I must tell you the rest of the story. I think it might be important. Tony and I returned to Frank's bar. Eva and Robbie were talking. We ordered a drink. Tony started to discuss something that had happened on the flight that apparently shouldn't have done. I can't remember what exactly. Robbie said something to the effect that he must call the chief pilot in England the moment he got near a phone. They started muttering about not filling in the technical log. We went back to my place soon after so that Eva could get two or three hours sleep. However before leaving Robbie called England collect but I went straight to bed and didn't listen. That's all I remember, I'm afraid. Is that what you wanted, Peter?"

"Yes, my dear. That's exactly what I wanted."

As I held her close I realised I would have to change all my plans. I needed to call Matt in the morning and find out what had really happened that night when the crew were working on the aircraft. There was now no point in going back to England on Sunday. I dropped off to sleep still holding Liz very close. She woke me. It was still dark but we could just see that dawn was breaking. She started kissing me very tenderly and it was fully light when we got dressed.

We went back to the car slowly. She gripped my hand very closely and I helped her up the beach. I drove her home and as we approached she kissed me again very quickly and leapt out as we stopped. I watched her open her front door and go in.

CHAPTER 13

Seattle

I got back to the hotel at about 6.30, collected my key and went up to my room. I rang RWA reservations and delayed my flight. Then I had a shower and sorted out my clothes for the laundry so that I would get them back in the evening. I told the hotel I would be leaving in the morning.

As I rested on the bed and planned my day I worried about Liz and felt in some way responsible. She had been a marvellous help to me in finding out what had taken place. I didn't feel I had taken advantage of her since she clearly wanted me to be with her. Unless she was a great actress she had enjoyed the evening as much as I did. However, I felt she needed help and a secure relationship but I didn't think I could be the person.

I tried to get Liz out of my mind and rang Matt in the office. It was Saturday but there was an emergency number and I asked the engineer on duty to get Matt to call me. He called me back almost immediately and I explained I needed to talk to him urgently about the accident. He agreed to see me straightaway in his office. I still had the car and drove to maintenance at the airport.

"Matt, was the display change and changing the MMR the only maintenance carried out on Alfa Juliet?"

"As far as I know. Why do you ask?"

"I have reason to believe that something else happened that was not recorded on the tech. log. Any chance of your checking with the night shift?"

"Peter, that's a pretty serious thing to say. Can you prove it?"

"No I can't Matt, but I would be prepared to bet money."

"OK. Give me a moment and I'll find out who the foreman was."

Matt started telephoning and apparently located the man he wanted. He also checked on some of the other people on that shift.

"We've had some luck. The night shift on the Sunday night are now working days and Tip Brewster the foreman is coming up to see me."

Brewster came in. He was a large red headed man and wearing the supervisor's uniform.

"Brewster. This is Peter Talbert from England. He is helping the insurers of Alfa Juliet and he says he has heard that your shift did more than routine servicing, changing the display and reprogramming the Multimode Receiver the night before it left for the last time."

"Matt, that's absolute rubbish." He glared at me in a very unfriendly manner.

"Brewster, think very carefully. If there was anything, don't be afraid to tell me."

"Matt, cross my heart and hope to die. There was nothing that you don't know about."

"OK. I'm glad to hear it. If you think of anything else please let me know. Thanks for coming." Brewster glared at me again and went out.

Matt looked at me and I looked at him. There was nothing to be said. However I did have one last idea.

"Matt. May I talk to the person who tested the new display on the aircraft and changed the Multimode Receiver?"

"Yes. I can arrange that. Would you like to talk to him without my being present? If there is anything going on that shouldn't be, you'll be more likely to find out."

I looked at him gratefully. "Yes Matt, I would."

"Well I thought you might want to talk to the guy. His name is Lance Stephens and luckily to-day he is in the avionics test house. I'll ask him to meet you in the empty office over the corridor. And Peter?"

"Yes?"

"Let me know how you get on."

I went into the empty office and there was knock on the door. A young lad appeared, about 22 years old, slight with large spectacles. We introduced ourselves. I told him I was interested in Alfa Juliet. He appeared slightly uneasy.

"Lance. I gather you checked the display and it worked OK."

"Yes. That's right."

"How about the display that you took out?"

Lance relaxed a little and started to warm to his task. He was obviously a very keen and able engineer.

"Well we gave it a very long and thorough test. It seemed absolutely fine. I left it running all the following day and it was still working perfectly the next night."

"What about the Multimode Receiver?"

"As you know they reported one was wrong and I could reproduce the fault using the Galileo test set which made it easier. It was clear that one of the MMRs was definitely faulty so I changed the box. I then functioned the complete system on Galileo and it worked fine."

"Now then Lance. Think carefully. Did you do any other tests on Alfa Juliet?"

Lance looked most unhappy.

"Is this conversation private and off the record?"

"I'll do a deal with you. I only want to know the truth. I won't tell Matt or anyone else for that matter unless it is absolutely necessary. I need to know the truth in case it's important. We must do all we can so that this type of accident will never happen again."

Lance hesitated and I looked at him.

"I know something went on but I don't know exactly what. It may not be important but I can only judge that when I know the truth."

"OK Mr Talbert. I'll trust you." He started to recall the work he did that night. "I checked the GPS system. Apparently the crew forgot to enter that they had a faulty GPS in the tech log and only remembered when they got into the hotel. They phoned engineering and reported the fault. I hadn't seen our foreman, Tip Brewster, at all. I don't think he had come in. The lead shift engineer Ron James got the call. He told me to check the GPS and if it was faulty to fit a new box. The GPS did not work properly so I got a new item out of stores and fitted it. The set worked fine."

"What happened then?"

"I wanted to sign the tech log but Brewster still had not turned up so Jack and I agreed to forget about the whole thing including the tech. log."

"What did you do with the faulty set."

"The box was manufactured by Honeywell and so we gave the set to the local rep who said he would send it back to Phoenix in the States to have it repaired."

"Do you have a lot of trouble with the avionics equipment on the 798."

"No, not at all. We keep an analysis of the faults and rectifications. Would you like to see it?"

"Very much. Is that possible."

"No problem." Lance went over to the computer at the end of the room and signed on. He selected what he wanted from the menu and seemed satisfied. He went outside to the printer in the office area and returned holding a piece of paper.

"Here are a list of faults on the RWA 798s at Sydney in the last two months. I've also given you a copy of the tech log pages for the Sunday night. Obviously I can't give you a copy for the GPS rectification that I did as we did not use the tech. log."

"Lance. I've got an idea. Does your system track material issued from stores? Could you let me have copies of the boxes issued when you were on?"

"Yes, I can get you copies of those sheets."

Lance returned yet again to the machine and finally returned from the printer with copies of the equipment issued from stores. I put all the papers together and put them in a plastic folder.

"Lance. Thanks very much for all of that. I don't know whether what you have just told me is significant as far as the accident is concerned. Probably not. However it might be. If I need anything more I'll let you know. Here's my card if you get anything. How can I contact you?"

Lance gave me his contact address.

"One other thing Lance. Did you do a 798 course at Independant?"

"No. NWIA only send their shift supervisors like Brewster to Seattle. The rest of us do our courses at United at Denver. I think they do that because it's cheaper."

"Well United clearly gave you some very good training."

I wandered back to Matt's office but he was not there, neither was his secretary since it was Saturday. I used Matt's phone. It was still afternoon in Seattle on Friday. I called Roger O'Kane at Independant. Roger had given me the original avionics design briefing on the 798 flight deck. He was in his office.

"Roger. It's Peter Talbert. I need help. Remember you briefed me on the 798 avionics some time ago. I need some more details. I'm going to be in Seattle on Sunday on my way home from Australia. Can you manage to see me?"

"Peter. It's good to hear from you. Isn't Seattle rather a long way home?"

He paused. Knowing him, I knew he was giving me a hard time. He was smart enough not to ask me what I wanted.

"OK. How about Monday morning? You know my office number. Call me when you get in Sunday. Do you want me to make a hotel reservation?"

"No thanks. I am not sure of my flight yet. I'll get the airline to do it. Thanks so much. See you soon."

I logged on to the computer on the secretary's desk. The Seattle flights left daily at 10 am so that they arrived in Seattle at 8 am the same day having crossed the international date line. I called NWIA reservations and booked a flight for the following day, Sunday. I would be in Seattle on Sunday morning. I requested the Red Lion Hotel at Bellevue and a rental car. The man in reservations booked me on the British Airways flight Monday night Seattle/London. I would pick the ticket up at the check-in desk. I remembered to get a message to valet parking at Heathrow letting them know my revised arrival time in London. There was not much else I could do. I called RWA and told them I did not know when I would be going back to UK. I drove back to the hotel and told the desk I would be leaving in the morning, then I went up to my room.

I lay on my bed and reviewed the situation. Alfa Juliet had had a new GPS set fitted and it worked. That bit sounded alright. But why had the 798 Captain called England? And who had he called? Presumably John Chester and presumably John Chester didn't want me to know. I was glad

Blind Landing

I had decided to visit Roger O'Kane to understand the installation in more detail.

The phone rang. It was Matt.

"How did you get on with Lance?"

"Do you really want to know?"

"Not unless you think I should."

"Matt. I will tell you something you should do. Find out what time Brewster came on duty on that Sunday night. Does he have to sign in?"

"Yes. Of course he does."

"Well you need to do some careful checking on your systems to make certain there are no loopholes. I'm off to Seattle to-morrow. If I learn anything relating to Alfa Juliet which requires investigation then I'll call you. If you find out anything please let me know. However do me a favour."

"What do you want?"

"Don't chase Lance for the moment or we may lose him and the chance to get to the truth."

"OK. Not unless the Brewster trail leads that way. Have a good time in Seattle."

I decided to call Liz. The phone rang for a long long time before she picked it up.

"Liz. It's Peter here."

"I thought you were going home to-day."

"I was until I heard your story. It was very important, thank you. Liz, are you alright?"

"Yes Peter. I'm OK."

"You don't sound too sure. Look, I know it's none of my business but do you have a family in England?"

"Why do you ask?"

"Well I'm concerned for you. I feel you need support. Especially now that Eva is no longer there. Can't you get someone else in?"

"Peter you're sweet. Don't worry. I'll manage."

"Liz. Come round and have dinner with me to-night. Make it early because I'm off to Seattle in the morning. We can eat in the restaurant or the coffee shop. Whichever you want and you can be home by 9.30. The information you gave me last night was very important and I'd like to see if I can help you in return."

"Peter. You did help me. You made me think about what I've been doing."

"Good, there's more to life than what we did, marvellous though it was. Come on. Come and talk to me and wear plenty of clothes so I can concentrate, if you know what I mean."

184

She laughed. "OK. You're on. Meet me at the front of the hotel at 6.30 and take me to the Guillaume at Bennelong."

I gulped. She had chosen one of the best restaurants in Sydney virtually in the Opera House. I hoped Mike would think it worth while. I went for another swim and had a sandwich by the pool. I kept looking at my watch waiting for Mike and Mandy to wake up in England. I went back to my room and at 6.15 I called Mandy in Bournemouth. A sleepy voice answered. "Hello"

"This is room service with your wake-up call."

"Well drop dead and call me in the office on Monday."

I looked at the silent phone. I called Mike at home.

"Good Morning. Did I wake you up."

"Yes Peter you did. However never mind. What's new."

"Good news or bad news?"

"Bad."

"You are going to have to pay for me to come home via Seattle."

"And the good?"

"I believe I am making some progress but I need to understand the 798 navigation system better, hence Seattle."

"Well I'm glad you're making some progress. Despite what Foster said at the Inquiry Osborne is still saying that AAIB think it's pilot error so it can't be Foster leaking the information."

"Not sure you're right there but I know how you feel. I do have some ideas which will take some time following up. I'll keep in touch and call you from Seattle. I'll be there Sunday morning and I'll try to contact you on Monday. Bye for now."

I decided that if we were going to eat in the Guillaume then I needed a tie. I showered, put on my smartest clothes and went down to the lobby. I watched through the swing doors as it was still very hot outside. A fairly elderly Honda appeared amidst the BMWs, Mercedes and rental cars. I barely recognised the driver. Liz was wearing a very smart lightweight blue jacket and skirt and dark glasses. It occurred to me that she probably did not want to be recognised which was why we were going out and not eating in the Hilton. I got in the car and she drove round to the Opera underground car park. She managed to find a parking slot near the exit; good luck like that never happened to me. I helped her out and she held my arm as I escorted her up into the opera house and towards the restaurant. I noticed that despite her disguise both the women and the men waiting to go into the Opera House eyed Liz very carefully.

As we made our way a free lance photographer asked if we would like a picture. I looked at Liz who did not refuse. I said alright if it was a digital and he could give us a quick print. He took our picture. I paid him $20 and he promised to send the photo to the restaurant.

Blind Landing

I looked again at Liz as we got close to the Guillaume. "I'm no good at giving compliments but Liz you look magnificent in that outfit. Where did you get it?"

She looked at me seriously. "Thank you. Real compliments are so nice. I made it."

"Really? I had no idea. You are very talented. Where did you learn that skill?"

"From my foster mother. She was an ace."

She leaned forward and kissed me very quickly.

As we entered I gave my name and we were shown to our table overlooking the Harbour and the Bridge. It really was a splendid sight. Liz clearly liked the ambiance and the waiter asked us if we wanted a drink. Liz asked for a Pimms which surprised me but not the waiter.

"You weren't sure if they'd have a Pimms?" I nodded shamefacedly.

"Well what have you been doing to-day, Liz?"

"Resting. Catching up with my sleep. How about you?"

"Trying to find out what really went on when they were servicing Alfa Juliet on the Sunday night. Then I booked a flight to Seattle and generally reorganised my life."

"Do you think you know why the aircraft crashed?"

"No, not yet. I'm just trying to eliminate all the reasons I can. This thing you told me about, it's sounds irregular but that's about all." I thought for a moment and looked at Liz. "Anyway, I didn't ask you out to-night to talk about the crash. I wanted to know what you are going to do with your life."

"Don't you like what I am doing at the moment?" She asked looking at me.

I couldn't decide how to respond and decided the safest thing was to ignore her remark. Luckily the drinks, nuts and the menu arrived. We studied the large choice. Liz chose a filet steak and I thought I'd have Moreton Bay Bugs.

"Liz, you need a plan. Are you going to have a career with Royal World Airlines? How long are you staying out here? Do you have any qualifications?"

"What a lot of questions, Peter. Alright, I know you are only trying to be kind but I have to work this thing out by myself. I did consider going back to England and staying with RWA but there are two problems. Firstly, I have no qualifications and the second is that I don't think I could stand the climate."

"How old are you?"

"Twenty five on a good day."

"Well, can't you try to get a qualification, either sponsored or supported by RWA?"

"Maybe, but the weather is so marvellous here. I'd much prefer a job in Australia."

"You could be right. I just feel you need to stop and think what is happening to you. Take a holiday in the UK. See your family. Discuss it with them."

"I only have a sister, she is married and lives in Christchurch, England. We were orphans, our parents died in a car crash when we were small. As I told you we were brought up by elderly foster parents who both died about two years ago, one after the other."

"Well go and see your sister. And I'll tell you something else. I'm no expert but if you can make clothes like that suit you're wearing you may be wasting your time with RWA. Think about it."

Our food arrived and we became more relaxed as we drank some wine. It was a good meal, in a superb location. We drank our coffee and then went down to the lobby.

"Liz, I'm going to walk back to the hotel. It's not far and it will do me good."

"When am I going to see you again?"

"Somewhere soon. Perhaps in England. Here's my card. Make sure you keep in touch. If you move or come back to England I'd like to know."

We went out and down to the car and I held her for a long time in my arms as we said good-bye. We kissed and her eyes were very full as we separated.

"Peter, look after yourself. You're a nice guy."

She got into her car and drove away without looking back. I walked back to the hotel feeling rather sad, lonely and inadequate. I went up to my room and there was a message to call Mandy. I got through to her flat but she wasn't there again. I left a message on her answering machine telling her my plans were changed and that I was off to Seattle in the morning. I put my things together ready, and in the morning I left the hotel at 8 o'clock.

I called Mandy at home from the departure lounge.

"Peter, sorry I was so rude when you called on Saturday morning. Where are you? I got some message you were going to Seattle instead of coming home."

"I'm just about to get on the NWIA flight to Seattle. I need to understand the navigation electronics better on the 798. There was some work done on the aircraft before it left and I don't understand if it matters or not. I'm off to see Roger O'Kane."

"When do you come home?"

"I don't know. It depends on Roger but I might get away Monday night. I'm booked on the BA flight Monday night arriving Tuesday midday. I'll call you from Seattle. Must fly."

I just had time to call Jim Akers.

"Where have you been Peter? I thought you had disappeared."

I explained that NWIA had done some servicing that was not written in the log but that he must keep this to himself for the moment as the significance was not known. I told him I was off to Seattle.

"Well you ought to find time to talk to Michael Noble. He is a friend of mine and the local editor of Aviation Week. Get him to tell you what is the word in Seattle. Call me if you ever get back to England. You probably know that Chuck Osborne is still saying that AAIB say that the accident is a clear cut case of pilot error and the pilots not monitoring the instruments."

"So I understand from Mike Mansell. See you soon."

As I went out to the aircraft I thought about what Jim had just told me. In spite of my discoveries in Sydney I felt that the chances were that in the end after all the investigations AAIB might well come to the conclusion that the pilots made a mistake. Certainly many unexplained accidents finished up by being attributed to the pilots which conveniently removed the blame from the regulators and the aircraft manufacturers.

The flight from Sydney was long and uneventful. The aircraft was a Boeing 747-400 and as usual the flight was full. The passengers in the business cabin seemed very varied but in the back of the airplane there seemed to be not only the regulation large number of Japanese tourists but also a lot of Chinese tourists as well. No wonder the long distance airlines needed so many of the large new aircraft.

I watched the CNN news on my video and then decided I had better write down my Sydney expenses for Mike Mansell before I forgot them. From experience I knew it had to be done fairly quickly after the expenses were incurred or I would miss some out even though I tried to keep all my bills and credit card vouchers. A lot of my expenses in this case were covered by NWIA but my car hire and entertaining Liz had to be laid at Mike's door. When I had finished this chore I started to read my book. However, my neighbour was a Seattle restaurateur who was returning from Australia having been round all the vineyards choosing wines. We spent a lot of time discussing the merits and demerits of Australian wines compared with US wines and he kept on reminding me of the excellence of Washington wines. He gave me his card and I promised to visit his restaurant in Seattle. In fact it was in Bellevue and I thought I might really give it a try since he seemed a real expert in his trade.

We settled down for the night and I managed to get about five hours sleep. We reset our watches and put them back a day. I found it difficult to be convinced that after I had been on the plane nearly sixteen hours and had left Sunday morning that it was still Sunday morning in Seattle, early Monday morning in Sydney and Sunday evening in England. All very confusing when trying to decide when to telephone someone on the other side of the world.

There decidedly wasn't a heat wave in Seattle. It was cloudy and raining and the temperature was 5°C. Just like home. I got through customs quite quickly but I had to stand in line at the Avis counter for about twenty minutes before I got a car. I crossed the bridge into the car park, found the car and managed to get onto US405. The Boeing and Independant Sunday shifts were already at work so it didn't take too long to get by Renton and across US90 up to Bellevue. I exited as Bellevue came into sight and found my way into the hotel parking lot, checked in and went up to my room. I called Roger at his home and we agreed to meet in his office at Renton at 10 o'clock to give him time to sort himself out on a Monday morning. Mandy was at home getting ready to go to bed.

"I'm in the Red Lion at Bellevue. How's things?"

"The Sunday Telegraph says the 798 accident was pilot error. The other papers seem to be copying the Telegraph."

"So I understand. I'm off to see Roger in the morning. I'll call you to-morrow."

"Well I'll spoil you. You can phone me before you go to bed and wake me up to get me to the office on time."

I rang Michael Noble. He was in and I explained that I was a friend of Jim Akers. He suggested we had dinner together in Kirkland where he lived, that evening. He would let me know the name of the restaurant and the time. There did not seem to be any point in ringing anyone else in England until I had spoken to Roger. I sorted my clothes out and had a shower. I didn't feel like sleeping so I went down to the car and drove over to the Olympic National Park west of Seattle. I went by ferry from Edmonds and then on the Hood floating bridge. It was a lovely drive on the peninsula and I drove down the west bank of the Hood Canal to Skokomish. I had a sandwich at one of the few places open in the winter and then drove home via Bremerton.

When I got back there was a message to call Michael Noble. He had booked a table at the Le Provencal for 6.30, quite early, but it suited me as I was short of sleep. I drove up to Kirkland the back way. It was misty and all the deciduous trees were bare. The Seattle winter was not unpleasant and seemed very refreshing after the oppressive Sydney heat. I managed to find the restaurant. Noble was already at the table which was just as well as we had not met. He was quite short 5 ft. 4 ins. but very wiry. We introduced ourselves. The waiter appeared and we ordered two beers.

Blind Landing

"I've known Jim for a long time. He's a very sound journalist and I like the way he gets technical help if he needs it. Sending you out here to do an article on the 798 technically was a good idea. Why did you come back again?"

"Oh I've been retained by an insurance company to look after their interests in the investigation of the 798 accident and I need to be sure I understand all the technical issues if I can. I'm seeing Roger O'Kane to-morrow to probe a little more deeply than last time."

"From what I'm hearing from London the AAIB seem to be favouring pilot error. I also understand that the second part of the Public Inquiry is going to start quite soon."

"I hope not, there's still a lot of work that we need to do. I agree that the papers are saying that the AAIB seem to favour pilot error but there is absolutely no reason for it, as far as I can see and that seems to be borne out by the evidence the AAIB inspector gave at the Inquiry. I must say I think it is scandalous the way the press seem to discuss what AAIB are thinking. To my knowledge that has never happened before."

The menu appeared and we concentrated on choosing our meal. We chose the house white, an Idaho Chardonnay, and a half bottle of a Californian burgundy.

"What is going to happen next then in your judgement, Peter?"

"Well as you said the Inquiry is probably going to start again very soon. All too soon as far as I'm concerned."

"Are all those likely to be found to blame able to represented?"

"Yes. They can have counsels and all the normal paraphernalia of a court. By the way I forgot to say that there are two technical experts members to help Lord Justice Thomas."

"It sounds a very high powered proceeding."

"Yes it definitely is. In order to hear the recording and read the transcript of the voice recorder we had to sign the Official Secrets Act. I think we'll be sent to the Tower of London at the very least if we say more than has been said at the Inquiry. You see the whole investigation is overlaid with the hijacking and the security aspects surrounding it. By the time I get back I imagine that the dates will be firming up, assuming the coroner's inquest is finished, though I expect Lord Justice Thomas wants to make certain the members feel reasonably certain of the cause before starting. AAIB expertise will still be crucial in this matter in my opinion."

"Well Peter, Independant will be there in force and they'll brief the best counsels in the UK if I'm any judge of the matter. I've been talking not only to the President of the Independant Transport Aircraft Company, William Parnell, but also to the CEO and they are understandably very concerned. The passenger litigation following the Inquiry will be horrendous and the sums of money will run into many billions. Not only

190

that, if Independant is found to blame then future sales of the 798 vis a vis the stretched Airbus A380 will be affected. There is a lot at stake."

"You're right. Of course, Independant are not the only people who are very worried. Royal World Airlines are clearly in the firing line and GE will need to be represented, though they will probably be in the clear. Then the pilots' and the cabin crew associations representing the families will be there and possibly some electronic manufacturers. The Inquiry could go on for some time depending on whether the cause is obvious or whether it is contentious."

"Peter, in reality whoever is to blame, an insurance company will pay."

"You're right, Michael. That's why CrossRisk Insurance have retained me as a consultant to try to ensure that the pilots are not held to blame. If they are then CrossRisk is liable."

Our meal arrived which silenced our conversation for a bit. The room was reasonably full and quite noisy which I liked. There was no view from the restaurant so the food and the conversation was important.

"When are you going back? If you hurry you can get the plane to-night."

"Thanks for the kind thought but I haven't seen Roger yet and I slept last night on an aircraft and to-night my sleep is going to be in a bed. I'm booked on the RWA flight to-morrow night. That will get me back on Tuesday morning."

"What did you do to-day?"

"I got some fresh air and tried to think things through. There is something we are all missing in this accident and I am determined to find out what really happened. Meantime I'm eliminating everything I can."

"Sounds good. Give me your card and if anything happens over here I'll let you know. Perhaps you could do the same for me. A bit of advance warning is always nice."

We finished our meal and I got back to the hotel at about 9.30. My room overlooked US405 and the traffic seemed to be streaming both ways without a break. But luckily I could not hear it. I turned the TV on in time to see the end of Larry King Live but Larry King was not doing it and his replacement did not seem as good. I got the TV guide out but there were so many channels I could not decide what to watch and anyway none of it seemed particularly interesting. I couldn't very well call Mandy before 10.30 so I watched the Public Broadcast Service which had an old BBC series on. At 10.30 prompt I was on the phone.

"This is your wake up call."

"How nice. I was expecting it and have been dozing. How are things with you?"

"Well I had a super drive in the National Park and a nice meal with the Aviation Week man here. I'm looking forward to seeing Roger tomorrow."

"Do you want me to meet you on Tuesday?"

"No thanks. It's a nice idea but my car is at the airport so I'll have to drive home. I'll be the worse for wear so I'll probably go early to bed on Tuesday night and be human on Wednesday."

"Give me a call when you get in. All my love."

I went to bed but woke up at 5.30 with the traffic still pounding up and back along 405. I managed to get some more sleep and then lay in bed making a mental list of things that needed pursuing. What was wrong with the GPS unit? Was the airfield position transmitted by GBAS correct? If that was wrong the accident could be explained straightaway. I needed to find out how Frank Mercer was and if he could tell me anything. I realised that I still had not worked out what Richard Trentham was trying to tell me before he died. What could he have possibly seen? Who did the stand-by Captain of Alfa Juliet on the inbound flight to Sydney talk to in England and what did he say? Come to think of it who was leaking information from the AAIB to the papers and why? In fact I had an idea about the voice recorder leak and I needed to investigate that when I got back. I decided I must try to talk to Robin Turnsmith. In addition I really ought to talk to Marcia Hodgson but what would I say?

There was no hurry since I had allowed Roger time to sort his office work out before I went to see him. After breakfast in the coffee shop I checked out and drove down to the Independant engineering parking lot at Renton and went into the lobby. The girl was the same one who was there when I was last out but she did not recognise me. I filled in the visitor's pass and she rang Roger. I sat down to wait.

Roger was very quick and he led me to a small meeting room near his office. He was about fifty years of age and a real expert in his field. He was employed by central engineering so that he was not on one specific Independant type but had experience of them all. He was fairly senior in the Independant engineering hierarchy but I could never fathom how that worked.

"Well what's the problem?"

"Well Roger the problem is the crash of the 798 Alfa Juliet. As I told you, I'm a consultant to one of RWA's insurance companies, CrossRisk, and it will cost them a bomb if the accident is due to pilot error. However, as far as I'm concerned I don't mind if it is pilot error or not. I just want to find out what really happened. I am dead scared that AAIB, encouraged by Independant, will take the easy way out and go for pilot error.

"I don't know if you have heard yet, Roger, but the Secretary of State called a Public Inquiry, probably because of the hijacking, the leaks from the AAIB and the seriousness of the accident. It's never been done before. The Inquiry has had its first session and it's now been adjourned."

"Yes we did hear and we think that it's a good idea. At least everything will be out in the open. Your AAIB investigations are very thorough but they're so secretive you have to wonder what's not being put in the report. Over here with the NTSB we are much more open as you know."

I did know. The United States National Transportation Safety Board was a very powerful institution with a lot of influence over the FAA and the regulators. It was my view that we needed something like the NTSB in Europe to keep the European Aviation Safety Agency under control."

Roger went on.

"Anyway, first of all let me reassure you that Independant always wants to get at the truth and would not support pilot error as a get out to bad engineering. In fact as you well know, most of the time if a pilot makes a mistake flying a commercial airliner it is generally the airplane designer who has made a poor judgement designing the flight deck/pilot interface or the man/machine interface as the media love to call it. The challenge for us is to make sure that the very complicated electronic computing on the aircraft can be understood by the pilots and can be easily controlled in the event of a malfunction. Of course, the problem is made immeasurably more difficult by having to cater for the wide range of pilot ability covering all our customers.

"Now then considering Alfa Juliet, as you might expect we have been helping AAIB in the UK in determining what might have happened to cause the accident. You already know that the analysis of the DME distances on the recorder showed quite clearly that the aircraft was below the glide slope and yet the crew did not show any concern, presumably because they were looking at the deviation computed by the MMR based on the Galileo positions."

I interrupted.

"Surely, they wouldn't have been able to see the DME distances if they were making a satellite approach?"

"Yes they would. The DME distances would have been displayed on a stand-by instrument together with the MLS on the left of the centre instrument panel." He continued. "Mind you to be fair, unless the beacon was lined up with the runway ahead of them the distances would have been unusable in real time."

"I agree with you completely, Roger. It's alright for us, sitting down in our office or lab to calculate what the true height should have been. Virtually impossible in the aircraft, even without someone holding a pistol to your head."

Roger carried on.

Blind Landing

"AAIB have not managed yet to analyse the Galileo deviation. They are not telling us very much but I think they are wondering whether the problem might be connected with the failure of the Navigation Display which the pilots did not appreciate. We feel sure that the hijacking must have been a significant contributory cause. At the Inquiry private session, where I know you were present, our man hearing the recording concluded that the only explanation was that the hijackers prevented the crew monitoring the instruments properly but of course the area mike wasn't working so he couldn't hear the hijackers. However, he couldn't understand why the Captain didn't notice something and, of course, he was very disappointed that the recording was of such poor quality. He told me that air traffic did tell the pilot that the aircraft was low. We are not really comfortable with the pilots having made a mistake but realistically we can't think of any other explanation."

Roger's words took a little time to sink in. If he knew about the recording and that there were no hijackers on it, it wouldn't be long before it leaked out. However, perhaps Roger was right. Even though the Galileo glide slope deviation looked OK, perhaps there was something that Harry should have noticed. Of course the hijackers interfering didn't give Harry much of a chance.

"Thanks Roger for bringing me up to date. I wondered if you could explain to me the difference between the Royal World Airlines navigation fit and the US airlines."

"Be glad to. As I suspect you know, the Independant 798 used a relatively new type of electronics box called the Multimode receiver, MMR The concept of this box, agreed between the world's major airlines, aircraft manufacturers and avionics manufacturers was that an airline, when it ordered the aircraft from the manufacturer, could choose which approach aids it wanted to be able to use. The choices were either ILS, MLS, Galileo or GPS. Nobody wanted to use GLOSNASS. The output from the chosen aid went to the MMR where the deviations were calculated and sent to the auto-pilot to control the aircraft down the glide slope and centre line to landing. With this design concept, we did not have to redesign the electronics every time a new airline ordered something different. OK so far?"

I nodded. Roger paused to let me catch up with my note taking, though in reality he wasn't telling me anything new.

"There were three launch customers for the aircraft. The two US carriers, American and United, wanted their new aircraft to have the capability of making approaches and carrying out automatic landings using any of the systems, though of course it was necessary to have local systems, GBAS or LAAS to augment the accuracy of the satellite signals for Cat III approaches. In fact, as you know US carriers are not as keen

194

about automatic landings as European airlines but nevertheless they recognised that they might need the capability. RWA, as the other launch customer, wanted to have automatic landing as standard from day one but they didn't want to use GPS because it was designed as a military system and could conceivably be downgraded or switched off at any time by the Department of Defense, notwithstanding that currently they are not doing so. They insisted that the capability of using GPS was physically prevented, something we had not anticipated.

"We tried very hard to persuade RWA to have the same system as the other launch customers so that when the GPS system became useable, all they would have to do, without any wiring change, would be to replace their GPS box which had one GPS receiver with a box containing three receivers. RWA refused and despite the MMR concept we had to make a change.

"The 798 uses three identical channels to achieve the required safety integrity on the approach and so in fact there are three Multimode Receivers sending steering information to the three channels of the auto-pilot and to the display. Consequently, the only way we could achieve what RWA wanted was to put a special approach selector switch in for them which only had three positions instead of four. We were able to do this without changing any of the wiring which was important for all the launch customers, to avoid special modifications forcing the costs up."

"Well that seems straightforward enough."

"We thought so and so at first did the European Aviation Safety Agency who were certificating the aircraft themselves and not merely validating the FAA type certificate. However, apparently there was some young engineer in the EASA who did not like our modification and though she was only an observer she tried very hard to stop the EASA agreeing to what we had done. I don't know who it was. All I know, I had to write a special review of the modification and let the EASA team leader have it."

"Roger. Do you have a copy of the report? It could be very useful."

"Sure. Anything else?"

"Yes. I've met the engineer you referred to."

"You're joking. How did you manage that?"

"She called me. Though she didn't say so in so many words, I think she thinks the accident is due to the Independant design and it's all the fault of the EASA who didn't listen to her."

"Why on earth would she think that?"

I explained Anne Moncrieff's concerns about the switch modification, the software certification standard and the lack of independent display of monitoring information to the pilot. Roger didn't look too pleased by the time I had finished. He looked at his watch.

"How about some lunch before Independant and Boeing fill all the eating places?"

"Is the Diner still going?"

"You bet. Let's go."

I told the girl at the Independant lobby desk I would be coming back and kept my pass. Roger drove us over to the diner and we sat down just in time; a few minutes later I noticed a long line had developed of people waiting to sit down.

Roger was interested in my non-stop flight to Sydney on the 798. Amazingly the nearest he had got to the aircraft was the simulator at Renton. I gave him my view that it was an awfully long flight but that if you really needed to go to the other side of the world quickly it was probably worth it. Like me he was interested in the challenge of keeping the crew ready for the unexpected, since the electronics tried to cater for both normal and failure modes.

I asked him about his prospects in Independant and he felt that he would not get much higher. The top management jobs were filled by up and coming youngsters who had been spotted early by the firm and given the necessary training. He was not complaining since, as an electronic engineer, he had had a fascinating life. He used to work for Boeing and had seen the digital technology develop from the 757/767 through the 777 and 787. He joined Independant when it was formed and so was the ideal person to design the avionic architecture of the 798. He represented the firm on international committees, like the Society of Automotive Engineers S7 flight deck committee, of which I was a member, and the standards committee of the Airlines. At international meetings he exchanged views with his old colleagues at Boeing, Airbus technicians and the regulating authorities of FAA and EASA. He knew instinctively what would be acceptable to the regulators.

After lunch we went back to Roger's office and discussed the 798 electronic displays.

" Alfa Juliet must have had something wrong with the display installation, Roger. The crew reported a failure on landing at Sydney but though NWIA could find nothing wrong with the unit they put in a new one. After take-off the display failed again on the captain's side. NWIA did a very long check in their shops of the unit they removed but it was perfect. I wonder if AAIB have found the unit in the wreckage and if it's operable. Have you heard anything?"

"Not a thing. I can't believe a display failure could have anything to do with the crash."

"Not sure about that. What about the monitoring of the approach. It would have helped there, wouldn't it?"

"Not really, Peter. The key glide slope deviation information is on the Primary Flight Display. It is so difficult to understand why the crew did not spot that the aircraft was way below the correct runway vertical approach path. Surely it has to be the hijackers interfering with the crew?"

"Well Roger, Harry did check that he was on the glide slope and lined up with the runway; Charles, his co-pilot, was checking and confirming all was well right down the approach. It's weird. I only wish we could have heard what the hijackers were doing and saying to the pilots. I can't believe they weren't saying anything." I paused for a moment deciding how much to tell Roger. "By the way there was something else. Did you know that there was a faulty Multimode Receiver when they landed at Sydney and the engineer changed the box? The engineer then checked the system out and all was well. I don't know whether this fault was significant but it is a remarkable coincidence."

"Yes, I had heard. Strange that the fault was on the MMR."

"There's something else I discovered in Sydney. There was something odd wrong with the GPS receiver when it landed in Sydney the night before which wasn't put in the tech log. The crew rang someone in England to discuss the problem."

"How do you know?"

"I spoke to the guy who worked on the aircraft. He could find nothing wrong but he changed the receiver anyway."

"Does your AAIB know?"

"No idea. Probably not as they haven't been talking to NWIA."

"Don't like snags like that."

"Nor do I. However just in case it's important I'm trying to find out a bit more."

We carried on discussing the problem for a bit and then I made my farewell armed with some more drawings and detailed descriptions of the 798 electronics. Roger said he would send on the report justifying the RWA approach to the switching modification which they had written for the EASA. I thanked him but I didn't tell him it would have to be a very special document to convince Anne Moncrieff.

CHAPTER 14

The Wreckage

I managed to get out onto 405 before Independant and Boeing employees filled the highway and set course for Seatac airport. It was too early for the flight but the executive lounge was as good a place as any to wait. Anyway I wanted a meal before going on to the plane so that I would be ready to go to sleep when we got airborne.

Looking at the incoming arrival time at San Francisco on my iPhone the flight appeared to be on time. Unless the aircraft had picked up some defects on the way from London there was not going be a problem. I did some work, the flight did come in on schedule and nine hours later we landed at Heathrow at two o'clock in the afternoon. I managed to get my normal five hours sleep which was not too bad and had some orange juice and coffee before landing. It did not take long going through immigration and while I was waiting in the customs hall for the flight to be allocated a carousel I rang valet parking to let them know I was on my way. It was my lucky day as my bag was one of the first to appear. I grabbed it and wheeled my luggage through the green lane and as I got outside I saw Mandy which was a real delight.

"What are you doing here? Am I pleased to see you. This is a marvellous surprise. You should be working. What will your clients say? Any news about the accident?"

"For once in your life stop asking questions and kiss me."

We embraced and I think she was as pleased as I was.

"I decided that I might just as well come and meet you. I fixed my diary, caught the tube and here I am."

"You've got no clothes."

"Some people are never satisfied. Anyway Dora should have done my washing."

"Well it's made my day."

We went out to the valet parking hut and I settled up for the car. It took a bit longer than usual as I'd left from Terminal 3 and arrived back at Terminal 5. We were home in 40 minutes. Mandy held my hand; as a distraction I wasn't sure how the police would rate it compared with phoning, looking at the satellite navigator or smoking a cigarette but I wasn't going to investigate.

I managed to keep awake until about 9pm and then we went to bed. However I woke up in the middle of the night; Mandy was sleeping peacefully and I tried not to disturb her. How was I going to get hold of the two pilots who went out with Liz and Eva on the Sunday night? It was going to be difficult if John Chester thought I was interfering. And then there was Robin Turnsmith, I needed to try and talk with him. It took sometime before I went to sleep again wrestling with all the issues affecting the accident.

In the morning Mandy left for the office and we arranged to talk later on when I'd sorted myself out. I decided to risk calling Jill Stanton. My luck was in because John was doing a trip in a 767 to Cyprus to keep his licence current.

"Jill? I am trying to find someone called Ray Robson, everybody calls him Robbie. He was a Guild member and they appear to have lost his address. Do you think you can help?"

"Yes I'm sure I can. I'll call you back as soon as I can."

Carol was my next call, really to assuage my guilt.

"Peter, I have taken your advice. We are all going skiing on Friday for a week. The children are very excited as they haven't been before. When are you coming round to see us?"

It was very difficult to refuse. She wanted to hear how I had got on in Sydney and Seattle. I said I might be able to manage the following night. I'd let her know.

I decided that, after what I'd just said to Jill, I had better check the Guild directory but all was well. There was no Ray Robson nor Tony Giles for that matter in the listing. However, there was a Frank Mercer. I could speak to him assuming he was getting better after the accident.

Jill called me back and gave me Ray Robson's number. I called the number and a lady's voice answered. He would be available that evening. I decided not to give my name in case John Chester had been talking to him. I tried Frank Mercer and again a lady answered.

"I'm a member of the Guild and I wondered how Frank was doing."

"He's on the mend thank you but he won't be out of hospital for another week."

"That's great news. My name is Peter Talbert. I give lectures on the 798 to RWA pilots on the flight deck/pilot interface. I'm involved in finding out the truth of what really happened at Heathrow. I'm sure Frank and I have probably met as we're both Guild members. When he feels like it, I'd welcome the chance to talk to him. I'm not very happy with what I've been reading in the press." I gave the lady my telephone number and rang off.

Mike Mansell came on the line.

"Good. You're back. Things are hotting up. I understand that there is a presentation at Farnborough by the AAIB this afternoon. Can you go to that?"

"I expect so but why have a presentation? Particularly as the investigation is now out of AAIB's direct control. I'll call Jim and find out what's going on."

"I understand that the coroner is still struggling identifying all the bodies but that AAIB are very well advanced sorting out the cause of the accident. It won't be too long before they reconvene the Inquiry. How are you getting on?"

"Mike, I told you this was not going to be easy. I am making some progress but I need time. The Inquiry seems to be proceeding at a most unusual, indeed unseemly, haste bearing in mind that we are dealing with the legal profession where more time means more money. I have to tell you that the way things are looking at the moment you ought to assume that there will be some element of pilot error in the Inquiry's findings. Can't you try and delay the proceedings?"

"I'm afraid not. For once the Government is proceeding full speed ahead. They want to demonstrate that when something like this happens they can act very quickly and effectively. I agree with you that at the moment we cannot refute pilot error, if that is what AAIB are going to say, even though they don't have evidence. We are really relying on you to get us out of this mess."

"Well do your best to get a delay. I need to follow some leads, if only to eliminate them. I'll call you in the next day or so, the moment I have some news."

"By the way, Peter, I meant to ask you. Did you try and talk to the Sydney police about the body in the Hyatt Car Park?"

"Yes, Mike, I did and got a flea in my ear, which actually makes me even more suspicious."

My next call was Jim who agreed to take me to the AAIB presentation if I was at the FT by 12 o'clock. He asked me how I was getting on but I put him off until we met as I didn't have a lot of time. I got ready, put on my raincoat and walked to the station. It was cold and there were frequent gusts of rain. It would have been quicker by car but I would never have been able to park the car at the FT so I suffered the rain. I read the Times on the train and was glad to see that there was nothing really new about the accident and that the papers were reverting to their normal diet of politics, sex and money, the actual order being dictated by the readership of the paper. At Waterloo I decided to try to get a taxi but, as an insurance policy, I started to go towards the footbridge to cross the river. I was in luck, managed to flag down a cab and got to the FT office with about ten minutes to spare.

Jim came down to the lobby and a car, an old but smart Jaguar, was waiting outside. I took off my coat and we got into the back. I couldn't help thinking how great it must be to work for a large company and Jim must have read my mind.

"Don't think I normally travel in this luxury. I had to attend an editorial meeting this morning and I have to be back this evening with the

200

story of this afternoon's meeting ready to roll. I plan to dictate the story on the way home in the car and I have got my secretary standing by to edit it straight into the system. If I had had to drive myself I would have run out of time."

"Well whatever the reason, Jim, it's great to travel in style."

We were quiet for a few minutes as the car started to thread its way onto the Victoria Embankment.

"Any fresh ideas yet, Peter? Do you think Osborn's leak about AAIB thinking the pilots made a mistake is going to be correct?"

"I hope not. The problem at the Inquiry, when it is reconvened, is that its members will find it very hard to go against the considered advice of the AAIB. Maybe we shall hear a bit more this afternoon but despite hearing the recording and reading the transcript of the cockpit voice recorder there don't seem to be any obvious clues. I'm puzzled why AAIB are giving us this briefing. They cannot and must not say anything that will prejudice the Inquiry.

"Of course one factor in the accident, Jim, is the weather. I hope at the Inquiry AAIB will give us a proper briefing on what the crew heard and the wind and weather at the time of the accident. There must have been something terribly wrong. I don't believe it was a simple mistake by the pilots. The hijacking has got to be relevant."

Jim did not reply. There was nothing to be said. We crawled along Cheyne Walk, left the river and finally got on to the Great West Road. We got by the Hogarth roundabout, crossed the South Circular Road and got onto the M3. The rain belted down for about ten minutes. We found our way to the Farnborough Airfield and went in to reception to get our passes and a pass for our car. The man behind the desk checked our identity very carefully before giving us our badges, all of which had been printed in advance. He showed our driver on the map the hangar we were to go to after the initial briefing.

We made our way to the conference room where Jim obviously knew a lot of the other journalists. He introduced me to Jane Franklin of the Times; from her writings I knew she was a very professional lady and I was surprised to see that she could not have been more than 30 years old. I could see Brian Tucker of Flight and we nodded to one another. I recognised Spud Mulligan, the European Editor of Aviation Week though I had never met him.

We sat down near the front and waited for Bob Furness to appear. He arrived spot on 2.30 looking very grim with two other people. Jim nudged me; he had seen what I had seen. Bob had arrived with Chuck Osborne and Martin Foster.

"Bob's probably tried to find out Chuck's source" he whispered.

Blind Landing

Foster was wearing flying overalls, presumably because he had been sifting through the wreckage, and sat down at the front, next to Robin Turnsmith who must have come in at the last moment as I had not noticed him earlier. Osborne made his way to the back of the room, not looking very comfortable.

Bob climbed onto the dais and looked around the room before starting.

"Good afternoon, Ladies and Gentleman. As you know the Secretary of State called for a Public Inquiry into the accident to RWA 573, G-RWAJ. The last such inquiry was after the Trident landing accident many many years ago. This Inquiry has meant that my department stopped investigating the accident on its own behalf and is now working for the Inquiry members. At their suggestion, in these days of almost complete openness, we are showing you in very general terms what we have been doing to establish the cause of the accident.

"I hope you find this briefing helpful. We cannot of course say anything substantive in view of the Inquiry. It is just to give you a background understanding of our capability and responsibilities. Our work is really detective work and, like a lot of detective work, it tends to be long and tedious since of course we are looking for the most minute clues."

He paused as someone's telephone started to ring.

"Please would you all switch off your telephones and pagers and all other hi tech devices. You will have plenty of time to report to your papers when I have finished."

He waited while everybody complied with his request.

"The accident to the 798 is the worst air transport accident we have ever had in the United Kingdom and it is absolutely vital that we find the true cause. Air Transport is so safe that the few accidents that do occur are always due to some unexpected cause and I am sure that this will be no different. Every possible cause has already been allowed for in the design of a new aircraft so we always have to look for the unexpected.

"Our modus operandi here is to appoint a senior inspector to be in charge of each accident and for this one, as you know from the Inquiry, I have appointed Martin Foster. Since he is doing most of the work he is our main line of communication to the Inquiry members."

Martin Foster got up so that we could all see him. He looked uncomfortable.

"Martin would normally be responsible for producing the report. However as I have indicated, the rules are now different for the investigation and reporting of this terrible disaster because we are having a Public Inquiry and we are merely assisting the Chairman, Lord Justice Thomas, and the members. Martin here has already started to present

202

evidence at the Inquiry and will therefore carry on when the Inquiry is reconvened.

"As you know, a meeting such as this is very unusual since it is normal practice to brief the press at the time the accident report is issued though we often issue intermediate bulletins. In this case we have a very undesirable development in that the conversation on the cockpit voice recorder has been leaked to the press. This is the first time that this has ever happened and, as you must realise, the leak could be causing untold grief to the families concerned.

"So far we have been unable to find the source of the leak and the Daily Telegraph is not co-operating with us, which I deplore." Bob looked straight at Osborne with obvious dislike.

"All I want to say at this time is that the conversations reported in the press do not give a true flavour of the actual dialogue and, anyway, there were more channels of information on the voice recorder than the one that has been leaked and published by the press. You have to realise that all this speculation as a result of the leak just does not help my team in any way. It takes the team all their time to get the complete information dump from the recordings including the voice recorder channels. I am sure you understand that they have no time to explain every move they are making and how they are getting on to you, the media.

"As I have said, in view of the Public Inquiry it is entirely inappropriate to make any comments on what may have happened. However, it is clear that when the pilots finally realised there was something wrong it was too late to overshoot and make a missed approach. Our job is to find out why they did not realise they were below the true 3° glide slope to the runway touchdown point.

"Our investigation is divided into several stages. We have to analyse the outputs from both crash recorders, we have to try to assemble the wreckage in a hangar in case that gives us some causal clues and we have to inspect all the maintenance and licensing records of the aircraft and the crews. We have to analyse not only the aircraft recorders but also the air traffic voice and radar recorders and the recordings which the airlines make. It is a huge task which has to be done in a very short time scale.

"In fact we have now analysed nearly all the hundreds of channels in the aircraft recorders and are getting a good idea of what was working. You will appreciate that this is a very demanding task since some of the traces can only be decoded with the help of the aircraft manufacturer. When we do know all the parameters that we need, we have to try to get simulator runs which match the traces so that we can ascertain the aircraft's true flight path.

"It will probably take us a few more days before we know for sure the exact path the aircraft took down the approach and what the crew saw.

This information may be crucial in determining what happened. We anticipate having all this ready for the Inquiry.

"There is a story in the press that the crew made a mistake. I have no idea from where this story originated. There are reports that the information is coming from the AAIB and I absolutely refute this. Clearly, the Inquiry has to find out the cause of the accident and whether it was indeed pilot error. If it was pilot error then the Inquiry needs to know if there were any contributory causes like poor flight deck design or interference from the hijackers. It will be up to the Inquiry to determine all the reasons for the accident. The problem is that if the true cause is not discovered, it may not be possible to prevent a similar accident from happening again."

There was dead silence in the room. Press men are not very sympathetic because, apart from anything else, they are being chased all the time for stories by their editors. However, I did feel that perhaps Bob had made his audience just think for a moment about what a very responsible task AAIB had and ask themselves whether the way they were reporting the story was really helping the vital task of finding the cause of the accident.

"I propose now that we go round to the hangar so that you can see the wreckage and the magnitude of our task."

We all left the meeting room and drove round to the hangar. It was full of crumpled pieces of aircraft and the large bits had been laid out in the shape of an aircraft. The AAIB had done a magnificent job in a short time assembling the wreckage. We were not able to get very close to the 'aircraft' because a rope barrier had been erected but we could get an idea of what the investigators were trying to achieve. I looked round the hangar and could see a pile of pieces, each piece numbered, in a separate area.

I made my way to Turnsmith who had come over with Bob Furness and Martin Foster. "Robin, what are all the pieces over there?"

"They are the parts we have not yet managed to identify and locate in the 'aircraft' we are building. Independant have given us a lot of help but it takes time to sort it out." He looked at me. "How are you involved with this terrible accident."

"CrossRisk are retaining me to look after their interests, not that I can do much. I did hear the voice recorders and as you know the pilots were convinced they were on the glide slope and the centre line."

Robin nodded and was clearly thinking what he might say.

"Yes, it's still a complete mystery. I hope we can find something definite."

"Can I look at the parts in the corner?"

Robin looked around, I suspect to see where his boss was.

Chapter 14

"Yes if we go quickly. We don't want everyone to come over."

He lifted the rope barrier and we went over to the parts. It was going to be a nightmare to find out where they all went. Besides metal structure, there were electronic boxes, some virtually complete and some shattered with their circuit boards completely missing. I could see cards with electronic chips lying on the floor and discrete chips gathered on special tables. Presumably the reference numbers on the chips would help the parts to be identified though it must be very difficult to find out which box the parts came from.

"If you look out of the window over there you can see the parts which the army has brought in and which we have not had time to arrange."

I thanked him and we went back to the others. Jim came over to me.

"What were you looking at?"

"I wanted to see how they were setting about dealing with the smaller stuff and in particular if they were going to sort out the avionics, you know the electronic computers. I suppose they will in time but from what I saw it's not going to be quick. They don't seem to be looking at the small components at all."

After about half an hour we drove back to the conference room and sat down. Bob Furness came back in and Martin Foster was back in his seat in the front row.

"Well I hope you have got some idea of the enormity of the task. This job will take a very long time, particularly if we have to become interested in the smaller pieces of wreckage.

"Do you have any general questions that I can answer? Please don't try to ask questions that will need to be answered at the Inquiry."

Brian Tucker of Flight stood up.

"How do you know that the Captain had selected Galileo for an automatic landing?"

"Brian, that's an Inquiry question. However, we know what crew said had been selected. We don't yet know what was actually selected but we hope to know once we have completely decoded the recordings and no doubt this subject will come up at the Inquiry."

"Was the GBAS flight checked after the accident?"

"No. There is no need with Galileo to carry out flight checking as we have to do with ILS and MLS. We can tell whether the Galileo and the GBAS is serviceable by the monitors and the equipment was shown as functioning perfectly. I think that is enough on that matter as I do not want to prejudice anything that is going to be investigated at the Inquiry.

"Next please."

"Why didn't the aircraft use the ILS if the MLS was not available?" This from Jane Franklin.

"The ILS has not been available on that runway for many years because it was not Cat III approved. The MLS replaced it."

"Did the aircraft have enough fuel? It had come all the way from Sydney."

"We have every reason to believe that there was enough fuel for an approach, a missed approach and a diversion to Manchester. Again this matter will be raised at the Inquiry."

"Were all the engines under power when the aircraft crashed?" asked Jim.

"We are analysing the engine parts but, from what we know now, all the engines had more than descent power when the impact took place, presumably because the crew had just initiated a missed approach. Again this is a matter for the Inquiry."

There were a few more questions and then Bob summed up.

"We have not finished this investigation and we are doing all we can to support the Inquiry. You will of course have the opportunity to hear the evidence at that time.

"Let me remind you once again that it is not unusual for there to be remarks on cockpit voice recorders that are not relevant to the accident. Please remember the families of the bereaved. Good afternoon."

Bob and Martin Foster left the room. I went up to Robin as we all slowly filed out and ran to our cars in the rain.

"How about having a chat about things in a more relaxed atmosphere"

"Fine, Peter. As you can imagine we are working all the hours there are but give me a ring and perhaps we can meet up somewhere convenient."

Jim turned to me as we got in the car.

"Peter, can we drop you off on the way home? We must be going somewhere near where you live."

"Thanks very much. If you go round the M25 and get on the A3 you will only have to make a very small detour to drop me off."

As we drove back Jim started dictating into a machine he had in his pocket. His article seemed to be stressing the fact that the cause of the accident was not known for sure but that the AAIB had inferred that in a few days they would have reached a conclusion which they could present at the Inquiry. Jim mentioned that Furness had strongly refuted the idea that pilot error was necessarily the cause of the accident but of course the article suggested that it might possibly become an explanation if no other reason could be found. Significantly, no mention had been made of the hijacking as a cause of the accident.

"Is there any special point that you feel should be mentioned?" Jim asked me.

"Not really. I'm amazed Bob is still standing back from the accident. Presumably it will be Foster that gives most of the evidence at the Inquiry. There is just one point which needs watching. You heard at the Inquiry that AAIB are having trouble finding out what had actually bee selected. From what was said to-day and what Chuck has written I'm beginning to suspect that AAIB are still not out of the wood in this area. That's between you and me, Jim. For the moment just keep an eye on what is being said."

Jim carried on dictating and as we approached the Kingston-by-Pass I showed the driver how to get to my house. I got out quickly, thanked Jim and saw them leave. Jim clearly had a lot of work to do before he was finished that night.

When I got in I decided to try Ray Robson again. A man's voice answered.

"Robson here."

"Captain Robson my name is Peter Talbert. We may have met. I give some lectures on 798 courses relating to the flight deck and the pilot interface, concentrating on managing the systems."

"Yes, Peter. I have heard your talks. They are very good if I may say so and I enjoyed them very much. How can I help you? You had better call me Robbie, everybody else does." He didn't sound very helpful even though he used the right words.

"Robbie, I believe you were the second crew on the London-Sydney leg on the flight before Alfa Juliet crashed. Was there anything unusual you noticed about the aircraft?"

"No, everything was quite normal."

"Robbie, are you quite sure? This accident is the subject of a Public Inquiry now you know, and it will not be possible to keep things that happened to yourself."

"You heard what I said." He began to sound unhappy and uncertain.

"Robbie I think I know how difficult your position is. I should tell you, if you don't know already, that I was out with NWIA last week. I am not going to press you any more now but I believe you should think very carefully about your position. It may be a lot easier to tell me what really happened before the Inquiry, than have it dragged out under cross examination."

"Are you threatening me?"

"No, Robbie, really I'm not. I just want you to realise that keeping things quiet between friends is no good in this situation."

I paused but Robby did not say anything. "Have you got something to write with? I'll give you my number and you can contact me if you change your mind. Think it over. I'm around, off and on. You can leave a message on my answering machine if necessary." I gave him my number and left him to stew overnight. I was pretty confident he would call me to-morrow. What I was not sure about was whether he would call John Chester.

I called Mandy at Bournemouth.

"What's new Peter? I know you've been busy. According to the Evening Standard AAIB had an open day. Did you go?"

"Yes I did, but really the visit was a waste of time because the Chairman is now in charge of the investigation and not the AAIB, though the AAIB's work will be crucial under instruction from the Inquiry members. Not surprisingly the AAIB were even more tight lipped than usual. I wondered whether Bob would take over from Foster because of the size of the disaster."

"Bit difficult for him because Martin was in the middle of giving evidence and a change of inspector would cast doubt on what had been said."

"Yes, you're almost certainly right, that must be the explanation. By the way, I did manage to speak to the second Captain on the flight into Sydney. He wasn't about to tell me the time of day but I think he was getting worried by the time I rang off. My guess is that he'll call me to-morrow but I'm not sure if he'll call John Chester first."

"Yes he certainly will, Peter. He will wish to clear his yard arm with John, saying he has no alternative. And let's face it, he hasn't. If he doesn't tell you what happened now it will be dragged out of him at the Inquiry. It probably will be anyway to corroborate your theory, assuming you will have got one by then."

"Touché. I still have not worked out exactly what happened though I have a glimmer of an idea."

"Well, when are we meeting next? I've kept to-morrow evening free from washing and doing my hair."

"I'm sorry I can't manage to-morrow. I half promised to go and see Carol before she takes the family skiing. How about Friday?"

"I'll have to think about it. I think I'm watching TV for the rest of the week. Keep in touch." She was gone. I definitely had the impression she didn't like my talking to Carol in spite of the fact that all I was doing was trying to help get Carol's life started again. Rationally she knew I was doing the right thing but she clearly didn't like it.

The phone rang. It was John Chester.

"Peter. I don't like the way you are pressurising my pilots and asking them questions. The AAIB are investigating the accident to Alfa Juliet and we must leave it to them. I know you are working on behalf of the insurance company but it is after all one of our insurance companies and I must ask you to stop interfering."

"John, I think I must tell you that I've made quite a lot of progress in investigating this accident. I suspect that when we met for lunch the day after the accident you did not tell me everything you knew. The problem for all of us now is that we are not dealing with an AAIB investigation. We are now in the middle of a Public Inquiry and it just will not be possible to hold things back. Let me say to you what I said to Robbie Robson, you need to consider your own position in this matter."

There was a pause as my message sank in. When he replied his tone was quite different.

"Peter. I could lose my job over this."

I tried to sound sympathetic.

"John. I don't know yet what Robbie Robson told you over the phone from Sydney but it is no use blaming yourself unnecessarily. You can't be clairvoyant. What he said to you and what you said to him may have been perfectly reasonable at the time. My suggestion to you is the same as the suggestion I made to Robbie. Sleep on it and give me a call if you want to tell me what happened. All I would say, John, is that it is much better that we know now before the Inquiry, it may save you being called as a witness." I rang off.

I looked at my watch. It was not too late.

"Carol, sorry I'm so late ringing you back. To-morrow night is fine. I'm looking forward to it. What time shall I come round?"

"Peter why don't we go out? My mother can baby sit and it will be a relief to get away. I'll make a reservation at a nice restaurant near here, OK?"

I was not at all sure this was what I wanted but I felt trapped.

"Fine, Carol. I'll be round at seven." Mandy must have scented trouble.

I was glad to turn the lights out and go up to bed. I suddenly realised that I had not really eaten anything all day but it seemed too late to start now. I dropped off wondering what John Chester knew that I did not.

CHAPTER 15

The Defect

A postman arrived with a special delivery. It was the report Roger O'Kane had promised me on the justification for the avionics architecture on the 798. I scanned through it; as I expected Anne Moncrieff would have seen it off in two minutes flat. In spite of my great respect for Roger, the report certainly didn't seem very convincing on a first look. But then he was supporting the party line; even if he had doubts he couldn't voice them.

I decided to call Matt to see what he had discovered. His secretary put me straight through.

"Matt. How did you get on with Brewster?"

"Peter. Thanks for tipping me off. Brewster had been coming in late, almost on a regular basis, and getting someone else to sign on for him. It should have been impossible but as so often happens, someone had worked out how to beat the system and Brewster took advantage. I've had to demote him and get the software firm who installed the signing-in system to plug the leak."

He paused. "Peter. How did you make out in Seattle?"

"Well I'm not sure I made much progress. I still can't think of any reasonable explanation to the AAIB story leak which says the pilots are to blame, though in my opinion the hijacking must feature in some way. Luckily the Public Inquiry has put a brake on the AAIB, which may give me time to find the true answer."

"OK. Well good luck. and keep in touch."

He rang off and I went in to the kitchen to make myself some coffee. I scanned the paper and was about to ring up Mike Mansell when John Chester came on the line.

"I've been thinking, Peter. You're quite right. I should have been quite open with you from the beginning but I was hoping that the whole thing could be hushed up. Clearly with the advent of the Inquiry, and now that you have found out that Robbie called me from Sydney, there is no way anything can be kept quiet. I suggest you come round to my office this afternoon. I'll have Robbie here and we can talk about it."

"I think I can manage that. If you don't hear from me I'll be round about 4 o'clock. Is that time OK?"

"Yes. That will be fine."

I called Mike to hear how things were going.

"How are you making out, Peter."

"Not as well as I would like. However, I am seeing John Chester this afternoon to find out the conversation that he had with the captain of the inbound flight to Sydney. It's obviously very important I find out what it was all about but I don't suppose it will change much. John had hoped to hush it up but he had no alternative once he realised that I knew about the conversation."

"Well, we'll have to have a meeting with John Fairlane our counsel fairly soon to get ready for the Inquiry. Let's try and fix a date to-morrow, OK?"

I put the phone down and immediately Robbie Robson came on the line.

"I gather you've spoken with John Chester, Peter. There's one thing I want to mention. Presumably you know how we spent the evening when we arrived in Sydney. Must John and everyone else know that we went out? You can imagine what my wife would say if she found out."

"I don't know. All I'm interested in is knowing what happened on the flight, what you did and what you said to whom. If you come completely clean with me it is possible that you may not be called as a witness in the Inquiry. Obviously if you are called, everything may come out. What have you said to John about the evening?"

"I just said that Tony and I were drinking in the bar when we remembered that we had a GPS snag."

"Alright but be careful. Have you spoken with Tony Giles yet?"

"Not yet. He is in Hong Kong or somewhere and I shall have to wait until he gets back and by then I shall be away."

"You've got a problem. I won't raise the matter of how you spent the evening but I must be frank with you. I wouldn't bet that it will not come out. See you later."

Robbie was obviously a worried man. It was impossible to advise him what to do for the best.

I decided I had better try and make my peace with Mandy, even though I had done nothing wrong arranging to have dinner with Carol. Still I did not want to lose Mandy. In my experience building an enduring relationship needed a lot of hard work, not that I had been particularly successful up to now with anyone else. Mandy's secretary asked who was calling and then said she was unavailable. That could mean anything but probably meant she did not want to speak with me. I had better try her at home in the evening but that was going to be difficult if I was out with Carol. I would try her from the car. I looked at my watch. and saw that it was nearly lunch time. I had no food in the house so I dashed round to the local store and got milk, bread, fruit, some cold meat and made a sandwich when I got home.

I finished my lunch and got ready to go to the airport. There wouldn't be time to get home before I went on to Carol's but that would not matter as I was wearing a suit to see John Chester. I arrived in reasonable time, unusually managed to find room in the visitors' parking area and got myself a pass in reception. Jill Stanton came down to collect me and took me up in the elevator to the office. There was someone in the outer office I did not recognise but who I surmised was probably Robbie Robson. He introduced himself and we waited without saying much until John Chester had finished a telephone conversation he was having. Eventually he buzzed his secretary and Jill showed us in. John got up and invited us to sit down at his office table. Jill reappeared with some tea and biscuits which helped to soften the atmosphere.

"Well Peter, how shall we start?"

"John let me put my cards on the table and then you must decide what you want to say. The day following the accident you called me and we had lunch. At the time I felt there was something you weren't telling me but that was clearly up to you. I wondered whether Jack Chiltern had warned you not to disclose anything to me or whether there was a security problem with the hijackers. Anyway, be that as it may I left with a question mark about what I was missing.

"I then phoned Bill Baker in Sydney to check on the maintenance that had been carried out on Alfa Juliet and discovered that the navigational display had been changed and that there had been a fault on one of the Multimode Receivers when Galileo was selected. Luckily, as a result of my conversation with Bill, he invited me out to Sydney to do some work so that I was able to speak to the engineer who did the jobs and he told me that he could find nothing wrong with the display that was removed. The Multimode Receiver was more of a challenge but he reckoned that the fault was in the approach path software section of the box and so he changed the box. The system checked out OK."

I stopped. They were giving me their full attention. Robbie Robson was now looking distinctly nervous. I carried on.

"I pressed the engineer and asked him if he carried out any further work on the aircraft and he told me that some time after the aircraft had landed he received a call from one of the pilots saying that there was a fault on the GPS which had not been entered in the maintenance manual. Apparently he found the fault, changed the GPS receiver and functioned the system satisfactorily but could not enter the fault in the tech log as the supervisor had not checked in. However, I managed to discover that there had been a conversation between a pilot and someone senior in the UK and it did not take me too long to work out that Robbie must have spoken to you John. I believe the conversation could have an important bearing on what happened subsequently and that is why I am so keen to hear the truth in this matter."

I stopped and looked first at John and then at Robbie. It was John Chester who spoke first.

"Peter, how did you find out about the conversation?"

"John, that's not relevant to the problem in hand and I do not propose to disclose my source." Robbie tried to look impassive but I could see he was less tense. He decided to join in.

"Let me tell you what happened on the flight. Somewhere over Singapore we got a GPS warning but when we checked the GPS position on the Flight Management System everything seemed to be alright at first. However, the warning persisted and Tony started checking the maintenance pages on the Flight Management System. He discovered that there was a warning coming from the No. 2 GPS receiver. We could not understand this since we only have one GPS receiver in the 798. We watched the performance of the navigation system very closely for the rest of our watch and everything seemed fine. In fact just before the other crew took over the fault disappeared and we thought nothing more about it.

"We went to our bunks for a rest and then after we had landed Tony and I went out to a bar in Sydney for a drink. We discussed the matter and decided that we had better snag the GPS, which we did by phoning maintenance, and I called John to tell him what had happened."

John Chester interrupted.

"I told Robbie that I would deal with the matter when Alfa Juliet got back and said that I was glad he had snagged the GPS. You can imagine how I felt when I heard that Alfa Juliet had crashed. I was sure then, and I am just as sure now, that the GPS fault had nothing to do with the accident but nevertheless I wished that I had asked Robbie to get the matter investigated more fully.

"I was going to tell you all about it, Peter, but somehow I felt it would be better not to disclose the matter to you since it was not important"

I sympathised with John in thinking that the GPS fault did not matter since, like him, for the life of me I could not see how it could be a contributory cause of the accident. However, he really should not have tried to keep things quiet but should have told the AAIB. In fact the occurrence of a No 2 GPS receiver fault seemed very strange and I decided to go home and think it through. I would probably need to talk to Roger O'Kane to find how it was possible to get a No 2 GPS fault when there was only one GPS receiver on the aircraft.

"I wish you had told me this story straightaway, John. It would have saved me so much time in Sydney and I might have got some details from the engineer. Even if you're right about the fault not being important it certainly requires more investigation."

The meeting broke up and as I set course for Carol's house I kept thinking about what John and Robbie had told me. A thought occurred to me as I arrived at Carol's house and before going in I opened my brief case and looked at the servicing folder that Lance had given me in Sydney. There had been a GPS receiver fault on Alfa Yankee about two weeks earlier and I mentally kicked myself for not noticing it earlier. I looked at my watch; it was too early to phone Matt but I could phone Roger before we went to the restaurant.

Carol's mother opened the door. She seemed quite active and I wondered if looking after the children was actually helping her. Apparently Carol was upstairs getting changed. Tristram was watching the television and Wendy was doing some homework. Presumably Tristram had done his but thankfully it was none of my business.

Carol appeared looking very smart wearing a blouse and skirt.

"Help yourself to a drink. What would you like?"

I chose my normal Scotch and water. Carol had a gin and tonic. Her mother joined us and had a glass of white wine.

"I've booked a table at the Running Stag. It's not too fancy but they look after you quite well."

Carol's mother asked me how I was getting on with my investigations into the cause of the accident.

"I'm making some progress eliminating all the things that didn't cause the accident. In fact you have just reminded me that I need to call an expert friend of mine in Seattle. Carol, may I make a call before we go out?"

Carol nodded. "When is the Inquiry going to reconvene?"

"I'm not sure exactly but it can't be long now, though the identification part of the inquest has quite a long way to go unfortunately. The problem here is that the AAIB normally goes on as fast as it can in parallel with the inquest but now that the Inquiry has started, the AAIB staff can only work as instructed by the members."

"What's your idea of what happened?" Carol's mother was not going to be deflected.

"Despite what has been said I can't think the pilots made a mistake. I'm still hoping something happened which resulted in them being misled completely."

I looked at my watch.

"What time did you say you had booked the table? 8 o'clock? Excuse me if I make my call now so as not to be late."

I went into the dining room and selected Roger O'Kane's direct number on my mobile; he answered straightaway.

"Thanks very much for your report to the EASA on the avionic architecture. I've only just skimmed through it. From my earlier conversation with Anne Moncrieff, Roger, I don't think your report would convince her but I'll show it to her if I may. Anyway, don't let's waste our time over that. I need your help again. I've discovered that on Alfa Juliet's flight into Sydney before the fatal flight, the crew got a GPS warning. Everything seemed to be working normally but when they investigated the Flight Management System maintenance pages they found that there was a warning of incorrect operation from No. 2 GPS, which seems impossible. Is there any possibility of a No. 2 warning from the RWA GPS?"

"My immediate reaction is 'no chance'. Would you like me to check with Honeywell?"

"Yes, that would be a good idea. However I believe that I may have a very simple explanation. I need to check it out but I have had an idea. You remember that I told you that there had been an undocumented GPS receiver change on the night before the flight. How about if NWIA installed the wrong GPS receiver box into the aircraft? I think they may have installed a NWIA satellite spare box which is of course fitted with three GPS cards. There could be a No.2 warning then if No.2 GPS had actually failed."

"But Peter, how on earth could Alfa Juliet have the wrong GPS box?"

"Well what you clearly don't know and I have only just noticed is that Alfa Juliet had a GPS failure going into Sydney a couple of weeks earlier and that the GPS was changed overnight by the NWIA maintenance crew. They may have installed the wrong box. I'm going to contact NWIA the moment they get to work."

"Well it wouldn't matter, the navigation wouldn't be affected. The MMRs don't care where the signal is coming from. What the MMRs do care about is if there is a GPS invalid signal when a GPS receiver card fails. That's why Alfa Juliet got the warning."

"Even if the GPS is not selected?"

"Yes. The MMR has to monitor all the time to ensure the pilot knows in advance which systems he can't use."

"OK Roger, that's fine. However, would you please check with Honeywell anyway that there is no other way the warning could come from a GPS box just fitted with one GPS card. We may need your evidence at the Inquiry."

I thought for a moment before carrying on. "However, just because the wrong GPS box was fitted, it doesn't explain the accident. I still think that it is a remarkable coincidence that one of the Multimode Receivers was changed just before the accident which was of course on a Galileo approach. If you have any ideas, Roger, please contact me straightaway. I must stop now and talk to Matt Thompson to tell him my theory and get his reaction. Bye."

I went back to Carol in the living room.

"How did you get on with the phoning, Peter? No, tell me later. We'd better be going if we are not going to be late for our table."

She said good night to the children and told them not to be late going to bed.

"Don't wait up Mother, though we're not going to be late."

I said goodbye to her Mother and we went out to my car and drove to the restaurant. As Carol had indicated, the Running Stag was not going to produce a gastronomic experience. On the other hand it was clean and the staff seemed very friendly. I ordered a gin and tonic for Carol but kept to water for myself as I was driving. We studied the menu.

"It's great to get away for an hour or two from the children and mother. I feel devastated without Richard and somehow I never seem to have time to think things through during the day. At night I just lie down and wonder what I should do. Anyway, thanks very much for the idea of going skiing. At least that gives us all something to look forward to."

"What are you going to do now? You can't just give up. You're still a young woman, very attractive and lots of energy. You've got an oriental language degree, you worked for Britannia as a trainee manager and you should be mapping out a career. It seems to me that you could be getting another qualification like business studies or learning about computers. Have you approached any airlines for a job? Britannia? Or you could start doing some translating for some agencies. With the Common Market being such a large part of our economy, there must be opportunities for you."

I finished my harangue apologetically. Thinking about it later I realised that I was very keen to get Carol started doing something constructive which did not involve her asking me what to do next. She was very understandably grief stricken at the moment but nature would reassert itself and it was difficult to ignore the fact that she was very attractive. Conveniently, the waiter came over to take our order.

Carol ordered a Tournedos, I settled for Steak and Kidney Pie and we ordered a carafe of red wine. The waiter disappeared and we resumed our conversation on what jobs she should be considering. We discussed what work she might do perhaps translating from home until the children were a bit older. I wondered if she had heard anything more from Cathay.

"Yes, thank goodness. I told you I've had one cheque and they have promised the other in about two weeks. Not that I know what to do with the money."

"I hope they are as quick as they say they are going to be. In my experience it all seems to take a long time. Anyway when it does come I suggest you try and get some reliable advice. But be very careful as there are a lot of sharks about. I'll ask my girl friend if she can recommend anybody. What about the house?"

"The mortgage was covered by an insurance policy on Richard's life so that will be paid off."

"Well, at least, it doesn't sound as if you are going to be destitute. You had better be careful or someone will marry you for your money."

She looked at me and I wished I had not said that. I poured out some more wine for Carol and water for myself. One whisky and a small glass of red wine were all I dared drink and stay within limits. Even that was more than I wanted.

We finished the meal and I took her home. She asked me in but I decided that it was probably better not to. Especially if her mother had gone to bed. I helped her out of the car and took her to the front door. I kissed her on the cheek and she came close so I had to hold her in my arms for a moment.

"Thanks so much Peter. You are such a help and strength."

She opened the door and went in. I felt relieved. I didn't mind giving help but I did not want anything else. I drove home and got back about 11.30 and though I was feeling tired I decided I'd better call Matt. He was in his office and I broke the news to him about the earlier GPS change.

"Matt, could you find out who changed the box and send me copies of the tech log and the stores issuing details. Also what happened to the box that was taken out?"

"Peter, I'll try. Why is it so important?"

"Matt I think the wrong box GPS receiver box may have been fitted; one of your spares and not RWA's."

"Would it matter?"

"Probably not but it's a strange coincidence."

I rang off and saw there was a message to call Mike but it was too late and I went to bed.

***

Mandy called at 7.15 prompt. I was in the shower. I got to the telephone, dripping wet, holding a towel, in time to hear her asking the answering machine where had I been last night.

"Good Morning, Mandy. It's lovely to hear from you."

"Don't 'good morning Mandy' me. I called you last night at 11 o'clock and you were not back. I am just beginning to be suspicious about the way you are consoling Carol."

"Now Mandy, my love, you have no reason to be suspicious. I spent all the evening trying to persuade Carol to get a job and start her life again. She's still young, very attractive, full of energy, a degree in languages, not destitute, she ought to be starting a new life."

"You told her all that? You are an innocent abroad. I can see that I will have to accompany you to future meetings to make sure she gets legal advice as well as career guidance."

"I'd really like that, my love. In fact I did tell her I was going to ask you to recommend a financial advisor. We said goodbye on the door step at about 10.30. I must have got home just after you called. Why didn't you leave a message?"

"I need a TV phone."

"You might see more than an innocent young woman should if you had a TV phone right now. I was in the shower when the phone started and I haven't any clothes on. I'm freezing."

"In that case I'm not interested. If you had a TV phone you would see me in the office drinking my second cup of coffee. We can't all lie in bed all day."

"Stop giving me a hard time, darling. When do I see you next?"

"Well, if you tried really hard to persuade me I might agree to come round to-night. I won't have to work in the morning."

"You're on. Are we eating in or out?"

"Haven't you learnt yet I don't make those kinds of decisions? However, I will give you a clue. Though I am only a solicitor I will need to be briefed on how you are getting on and that will need a lot of concentration from both of us."

The phone went dead. I returned to the shower and tried again but the phone rang again. This time it was Mike.

"Sorry to ring you so early but I wanted you to know we have an appointment with John Fairlane at 2 o'clock in his chambers. Can you make it? The Inquiry is expected to reconvene on Monday week. He has a brief from our solicitors but quite frankly I doubt that will do. You will have to give him a lot more information. OK?"

"Yes, that will be fine. I'll hang up now if you will call me straight back and leave the address on the answering machine, I can't remember where it is. You are the second person to call me when I was in the shower and I don't have a dry piece of paper."

"Fine. Must dash to the office. We are having a Board Meeting at 11 o'clock and I need to get ready. Everybody is very fearful about the Inquiry."

I went back to the shower again and this time managed to finish, shave and get dressed.

There was an email from Matt, *'Box was changed by an engineer who no longer works for us, Glen Lawrence. He now works for United in Chicago, details attached. Also attached are tech log sheet and stores issuing slip for GPS receiver. Trying to find what happened to faulty GPS receiver, may have gone to Honeywell office here. Brewster was the shift supervisor but he wasn't there again.'*

I had been considering for some time whether to call AAIB to inspect the avionic wreckage and after reading Matt's email I decided that I might as well have a go. I copied Fairlane's address and telephone number which Mike had given me and then called Bob Furness.

"Bob, this is Peter Talbert. You know I freelance for the FT on aviation matters. You may not know that I am also retained by CrossRisk Insurance in connection with the Alfa Juliet accident. Is it possible for me to look at the wreckage? I am curious about some of the avionic boxes."

"Well I would normally say 'no chance' for the very good reason that we would be in the middle of getting our AAIB report out. In addition I would want to know exactly what you were looking for and why. However, in view of the Inquiry I am not sure what rules apply. I tell you what, we're having to work week-ends on this job. Come down at lunch time to my office to-morrow. We can have a sandwich and then go over to the hangar and look at the reconstruction."

I agreed quickly and then called Mike.

"Sorry to disturb you before your meeting. Thanks for the information about Fairlane. Just for my diary what is the timing on the Inquiry?"

"Well the inquest will be wrapped up a week to-morrow as far as identification is concerned and then it will be adjourned."

"Surely they haven't managed to identify all the bodies already?"

"Well you're right. But they have done more than half. Of course they will be investigating the unidentified ones during the adjournment. Meanwhile the Inquiry re-opens the following Monday in the Queen Elizabeth Hall. Martin Foster will continue his evidence and be called to explain the details of the accident and give his opinion on the cause of the crash. What happens after that may depend on us, or more specifically you, and what you have been able to come up with. My guess is that Foster's evidence and cross examination will certainly take the whole of the first day by the time he's been cross questioned. Then there'll be a lot of expert witnesses called by AAIB and by the interested parties, like you for example."

"Fine. I just wanted to get a feel on the time-table and to discover how much time I have to try to find some sort of an explanation. See you this afternoon just before two at Lincoln's Inn."

I called Mandy but she was not available. I was clearly going to be late home from John Fairlane. Luckily, I had already given her a key and told her the alarm code so I asked her secretary to tell her to go straight to my house.

Blind Landing

I decided to ring Lawrence before I left to see Fairlane, hoping he would still be at home and I got an answer from a deep, man's voice.

"I am trying to contact Glen Lawrence. I'm calling from England."

"Who wants him?" was the very churlish and suspicious reply.

"My name is Talbert, Peter Talbert. I've just returned from Sydney and I understand that you used to work for NWIA."

"What about it?"

"You did a particular piece of maintenance on a 798 and I am trying to check on something that you did."

"I did lots of maintenance on the 798 when I was with NWIA. I can't possibly remember any details. Anyway I'm far too busy working for United now."

"Look, if I send you the maintenance page relating to the work would that help."

"What's it worth? My time costs money."

"If you give me your fax number and email address I will send you a copy of the page. I will call you again this time to-morrow night, if that suits you, and, if you would answer a few questions, I will send you $400."

"OK. You've got a deal." He gave me his fax number and email details. The moment he rang off I wrote a covering note and faxed him my note and the maintenance page. In addition I sent him an email with the page as an attachment to try to be certain he got the sheet and then rushed off to the station.

I walked to Lincoln's Inn and was there a few minutes early but so was Mike and we were shown in to John Fairlane's chambers. He welcomed us in. Tim was already there.

"Well the Inquiry reconvenes Monday week with Martin Foster still in the witness box. Before we discuss what he might say and what we need to do, Peter, what do we believe happened?"

"Well we know that Alfa Juliet did a Galileo approach. All perfectly kosher. I'm not happy that the GBAS was checked properly for correct functioning after the accident for this approach. I'm sure that you realise that if the airfield data transmitted by the GBAS was wrong, then all three channels would be wrong in the aircraft."

"But wouldn't the crew notice they were not on the correct flight path?"

"They might not. You see once the aircraft is on the Galileo approach, the centre line references for the display is the Galileo itself. The pilots can only see if something is wrong if they have an independent reference like the MLS but it is only displayed on the 798's displays as a back-up and of course, in this case, the MLS was not working."

"That doesn't sound too good, Peter. Surely the EASA should not have certificated that system?"

"That's what Ms Moncrieff told them when the 798 was certificated and they wouldn't listen to her. You need to call her as a witness, John but you'll also need an acknowledged expert as well."

"Won't you be the ideal witness?"

"Yes, I could be I suppose but you'll have to explain my background." I carried on. "The remarkable thing about Alfa Juliet is that the co-pilot called out the heights and distances which confirmed to Harry that he was on the glide slope centre line and yet the aircraft was far too low."

"Well did you learn anything in Sydney that might explain the situation?"

"There is something which may or not be relevant. When the aircraft flew into Sydney it had another fault which was not put in the technical log. The Global Positioning System had an intermittent fault which should not have happened on an RWA aircraft. To cut a long story short I believe that the wrong GPS box was fitted in Sydney, the box that was fitted had three receiver cards instead of one."

"Would that matter, Peter?"

"That is the really critical question and I'm not yet in a position to answer it. Hopefully, I will be able to by the time I go on to the witness stand."

"How do you know this?"

"Well, I found one of the girls mentioned on the recording. I also discovered that the other girl, Eva, was on the aircraft and was killed. As you know, the party referred to on the voice recording took place the night before the night before take-off. The girl actually phoned Hodgson in his hotel the night before the flight and he said he was off to bed. That same night the two girls did go out but with two of the incoming aircraft crew and the girl told me about a telephone call the Captain made to NWIA maintenance and another call to the UK. Once I had these clues, I was able to sort out what had happened."

"Well you've certainly done a superb detective job. Won't we need some witnesses?"

"Well John, it all depends on what line you are going to take. I think you will need the chief ATC ground installation engineer for Heathrow, the firm that makes the GBAS equipment, Microspot who provide the database for the MMRs and possibly the SRG airport safety regulator who is based at Gatwick. Those four will sow doubt on the Galileo. With regard to the wrong GPS box you'll need the maintenance guy from NWIA but he may not want to come. You also should try to find out from FAA the problem with the local LAAS augmentation."

"We'll also want the girl who told you about the party and the telephone calls."

"Why, John? You can call the Captain, Ray Robson, who flew the aircraft to Sydney and snagged the box. You can also call John Chester if you want to confirm he knew the snag."

"I know. But I want to be able to show that Hodgson was in his room the night before take-off and not partying on the beach."

I looked unconvinced and John realised that I wasn't about to agree but he decided not to argue.

"Well I'll think about the whole thing and then we can discuss it some more. Tim, for the preliminary hearing you had better assume that the NWIA engineer will be present, possibly the girl, Ray Robson, Peter here and John Chester. Peter will have to tell you how to contact all of these people."

John indicated that the meeting was over and we got up to go. As the others left John called me back and shut the door.

"Look Peter. This girl could be important. Why don't you want her called?"

"She's had a hard time losing her room mate and her friend, Harry Hodgson. Having to come to England and be exposed to all the glare of publicity as a good time girl would be terrible for her. Anyway, we don't know yet our favoured cause for the accident. I want you to win the case without calling her. If you can't, you had better let me know in good time." I paused. "Look, we're going to have to talk again before the Inquiry."

"Yes, we certainly are."

We shook hands and I left to go home. It had been a long day and I remembered that it was not over yet. It was 6.30 and Mandy was coming round if she wasn't there already and I realised I was looking forward to talking to her and hearing all her news. I saw her as I got off the train.

"Carry your bag, Miss?"

"How do you know I'm not married? Anyway I'm not tipping you."

"Don't worry. I'm doing it for love."

"That's what I'm afraid of."

But judging from the way she kissed me she didn't seem too scared. We were both tired and I got a cab. She unpacked upstairs when we got home and we celebrated with Kir Royale made with some sparkling wine.

"How did you get on to-day?"

"Well I finally managed to get through to the man who worked on Alfa Juliet and changed the GPS set at Sydney two weeks before the accident. I've sent him the details but I need to talk to him again. Apart from that I spent the whole afternoon with Fairlane trying to get him up to speed."

"What line is he going to take?"

"I don't really know. Anyway enough of my problems, what have you been doing to-day?"

"Do you really want to hear about divorce, conveyancing, wills, indecent exposure, you name it, I've got it."

"Sounds fascinating but not to-night."

"Why don't we have another drink and get smashed?"

I looked at her.

"Good Lord, your glass must be leaking. Anyway if you drink too quickly you won't be able to stand up."

"I don't want to. It's you that has to do the standing!"

"Ms. Arrowsmith, I think your clients are leading you astray."

I poured out two more drinks and took the telephone off the hook.

"You do realise I won't be able to resist temptation."

"I should hope not. We've got the whole week-end in front of us."

I looked at her.

"Ah. There's something I haven't told you. Do you want to know now or later."

"Definitely later. Turn the lights down and come here."

Mandy clearly didn't always like the conventional. I didn't really mind but it occurred to me later that perhaps a bed was more comfortable. I rolled over.

"You're leaving me. Why can't you lie still afterwards?"

"My end of the sofa is not fully sprung."

"You're always complaining. Alright you can call the Chinese takeaway for Nos 3, 10, 34, 46, 47 and 48."

"How on earth did you remember the numbers?"

"I didn't but they're the numbers I used on my lottery ticket this week. I expect I've won by now and we can live in Paradise."

"I'm certain you won't be in Paradise after you've eaten all those numbers from our local Chinese. And you'll be overweight."

I got up and rang the take-away.

"Please may I have Nos 3, 10, 34, 46, 47 and 48." I paused. "Well we like a lot of chop suey."

Mandy rushed over to disconnect the phone but discovered I wasn't on line.

"You bastard. Pass me the menu."

"Not when you haven't any clothes on."

"Stop making rules. I'll have sweet and sour chicken, spring roll and special rice. And if you go and collect it like that, I'll have another case of indecent exposure on my books."

We gradually sorted ourselves out and I brought the food back. I called Lawrence while Mandy dealt with the meal.

"Did you get my fax?"

"No but I got the email. I do remember the incident now. The GPS was reported as not working and I was able to confirm the fault. I got a spare from our stores and tested the box for giving correct inputs to the Flight Management System. There was not a lot of time as we had great difficulty finding a spare."

"Glen, did the spare come from the RWA pool or from the NWIA pool?"

"I've no idea."

"Well did you check the part numbers of the new and old receivers."

"No, why should I have done? They're the same aren't they?"

I decided to ignore his question since nothing would be gained by answering it.

"Did you do anything else, Glen, besides test the GPS for navigation?"

"No, nothing."

"That's fine. I'll mail you a cheque you will be able to cash in dollars. Let me have your mailing address."

I copied the information down and joined Mandy in the front room.

"Well the guy who changed the first GPS set at Sydney did not know that there was any difference between the RWA and the NWIA GPS boxes. Clearly they must have put in a NWIA box but it needs confirming. It's the only way they could have got a No.2 GPS warning in flight. I must try and prove it somehow though I don't quite see how it can be relevant. Perhaps I'm missing something."

"You were going to tell me something about this week-end before I interrupted you."

"You didn't interrupt me, you seduced me. Stop hitting me. What I was going to tell you was that I've got to go down to AAIB at Farnborough to-morrow lunch time and probably for the afternoon, Bob has agreed I can rake over the avionic boxes."

"Look, in that case I think I'll go back to my flat to-morrow and do all the chores, if you don't mind."

"And if I do mind?"

"In that case I think I'll go back to my flat to-morrow and do all the chores."

"Good, well that's settled. Seriously though, it's a pity but you do understand? I've just got to talk to Bob and count the boxes."

We ate our Chinese, watched the television and went to bed, still in the spare room. Even though Mandy was concerned about our not finding Diana, she was clearly taking a broad view. In the morning we had a leisurely breakfast and I took Mandy to the station to save carrying her bag. We embraced and as I watched her disappear into the station I wondered if I would ever find out what really happened on the aircraft.

CHAPTER 16

Return to Sydney

Back in the house I made a list of all the avionic boxes I needed to check in the AAIB hangar. Then I got the car out and drove to Bob's Office in Aldershot. At reception the girl on duty called upstairs and Bob came down himself to lead me up to his office. He poured some coffee from the percolator in the outer office into two mugs and put it on the table in his office before we sat down.

"Peter, let's put our cards on the table. I've been talking to John Chester and he let slip that you've been flying round the world investigating this accident. Have you found out anything? I'll be frank with you, we've not found any explanation for the accident and some of the team think that it was caused by the pilots not noticing something was wrong. I personally am by no means convinced that they made a mistake and I'm absolutely furious that there have been leaks to the newspapers. I will not demean your intelligence by pretending that Martin Foster does not believe it was probably pilot error but he absolutely refutes any suggestion that he was responsible for the leak, or for the original leak of the transcript of the cockpit voice recorder."

"Bob, it's quite true that I have been to Sydney and spoken to NWIA and also to Independant to check on certain design features. There's some new information which is probably quite irrelevant and quite frankly I don't understand. I would like to know how many of the avionic boxes you managed to recover, to check how they are identified and to see what part numbers they have. I'm also interested in how you are handling the avionic parts that came from the boxes that were smashed. As Martin Foster is still effectively on the witness stand and in view of what I have read in the press, it no longer seems the right course of action for me to talk to him. If you come round with me you can see exactly what I'm looking for and what I'm looking at. If I am on to something significant I will need to convince the members."

"That's fine. I'm tied up after lunch but I gather you know Robin Turnsmith. I've arranged for him to show you where we're up to. I'll call him up."

Robin must have been waiting for the call as he soon appeared and suggested we went over to the old Queen's Hotel for a sandwich before going to the hangar. We took both our cars to save my having to return back to the AAIB. Over lunch we discussed what we had both been doing since leaving Britannia and then inevitably we started discussing the accident. It soon became clear he felt that AAIB were missing something.

226

"We've had no luck deciphering the flight deck area microphone, Peter. What really puzzles me is why the warning did not go off in the Tower."

"It is odd but it probably wouldn't have made any difference since the controller did warn the pilots and they ignored his advice."

"He only told them they were low. He would have been much more forceful if the warning had been going."

"Yes, I agree. And the warning would have gone off a lot earlier, I think, though you must be able to tell if that's true since you've seen the DME readings of the actual flight path."

"I've looked at the approach path they did and the aircraft only really started to go low from about three miles."

"Robin, what happens if there is a disagreement on the cause of the accident in the AAIB?"

Robin looked at me and chose his words carefully. "I don't think we've ever had a case like that since I've been at the Board. This accident is of course unique in that whatever the formal position of the Board, the Inquiry members will have a casting view though I can't imagine they would overrule us ..."

I interrupted. "Assuming you have a unanimous view." I didn't wait for him to answer. "Who do you think let Osborne read the transcripts of the tapes? Who told him that AAIB favoured pilot error?"

He looked at me in a knowing manner.

"I was rather expecting we'd come round to that. As Bob said in Court, the problem is that so many people heard the recordings. I think Osborne couldn't have actually heard them, he was probably given a transcript."

"Same person who said the AAIB favoured pilot error?"

"Probably but not necessarily." He looked at his watch. "We'd better be going over to the hangar or you won't have enough time to do whatever you want to do."

We went down the road to the main gate and drove over to the hangar. It was open with one or two people moving wreckage and cataloguing the parts. The scene had changed even in the day or so since I had been there. A lot more of the electronic boxes had been put on staging and a lot of the boxes had been labelled. I asked Robin if I could start looking around.

"Fine by me. Are you looking for anything in particular?"

"Well for a start I want to check which avionic boxes you've found. Presumably your people are checking all the time with Independant and getting them to identify all the pieces of equipment."

"Oh yes. We have their people helping us but very often even though we can recognise the box, the part number will not be identifiable."

I produced a list of the important avionic boxes and showed them to Robin.

"It's going to take a long time to go through this list. If you would like to give me a copy of it I could get one of our people to mark up what we have found."

"OK, thanks a lot. If I write my email address on the list, could you send the marked up list to me? Meantime can I look at some of the electronic scrap that you have not been able to place?"

"Fine. I'll leave you to it. Call me if you think there is anything I ought to know. I'll send you the list, hopefully to-morrow. We should have it all on a database. The only problem might be identifying a box from the description you have given it since it may not be the same as Independant's description."

Robin went off and I started to look at the boxes. Luckily I had printed out two other copies of my list and I got one out of my briefcase. The boxes that had been identified had been marked on their cases by the AAIB and I marked my list accordingly. I could only find one Multimode Receiver and that was heavily impacted. I could not find the GPS box. All six displays were there but they were all crumpled. Both the Flight Management computers had been found and miraculously they looked as if they might work, hardly a mark on them.

I wandered over to two piles of what looked like scrap; presumably AAIB had been unable to find out where the components came from. At that moment I noticed Martin Foster had arrived, looking a bit doubtful.

"Peter Talbert?" I nodded. "We met at the Inquiry, I think. I'm a bit surprised you're in here. Robin tells me Bob authorised it. I know you're retained by CrossRisk Insurance but everything here is confidential."

"Martin, I know how you feel but there is an Inquiry on. It's not just an AAIB investigation. And to be frank the leak of the recording tapes and the alleged opinions of the AAIB hasn't helped matters. We have a right to know what is happening in your investigation."

"I'm not sure you're right, Peter. I think Bob needs to get legal advice or we'll have the world and his wife traipsing round here."

"Look it's almost certain that I shall be giving evidence at the Inquiry and therefore I believe I have a right to look at the wreckage. If the AAIB prevent me from making further visits then we shall have to make a submission to the Inquiry so that I am permitted to examine everything."

He looked at me carefully but said nothing.

"Martin, is it true you now favour pilot error as the explanation?"

"Peter, you wouldn't expect me to answer that question?"

"Why not? We're all trying to find the truth."

Martin looked as if he was going to reply and then changed his mind. I started to examine piles of material very closely.

"Oh we've looked at all that. There's nothing useful there."

"In that case you won't mind if I look, will you?"

I put my marked up list away and took out my notepad. Martin soon got bored and went away. In one pile there were small components which might be identifiable such as the very large scale integrated circuits custom made for firms like Honeywell, Collins, GE Aviation, Thales, and Microspot. I could see some identification on some of the parts and I decided that I would send the numbers to these firms to see if they could identify the parts and the boxes they came from.

In the other pile there were a lot of torn metal bits and a few badly damaged switches which had become detached from the many panels on the aircraft; presumably they were classified as scrap because AAIB was not able to identify where they came from. I looked at all the parts very carefully and would have liked to have spent more time trying to identify the scrap. I wondered whether Martin had come round to the view that the accident indeed was due to pilot error and consequently he had stopped a lot of the work identifying the small items. Presumably the Inquiry could be adjourned if the members needed more information.

It took me about three hours to finish my listings and by that time the AAIB staff were ready to leave. I made my farewells, drove home and spent the evening putting all the information into my computer, producing lists to send to the avionic firms, ringing my contacts in the United States firms to get the right names, email addresses and fax numbers, and finally sending the lists to the US firms and the UK product and technical directors. By the time all that was done it was 11.30. It was just as well Mandy hadn't stayed.

On Monday morning I phoned Lance at NWIA but he was still working on the night maintenance shift and was not available. I got transferred to Matt who was still in the office.

"Matt, you know the Inquiry will be starting the week after next. I believe CrossRisk Insurance will be asking Lance to come over and give evidence. We're not saying that the wrong GPS caused the accident but it will show that AAIB have not been very through doing their job. Do you have any problems with that?"

"Peter, I did know about the Inquiry and to be frank we are all very nervous about it. Clearly we don't like the idea of everybody knowing that someone in NWIA did some irregular maintenance on Alfa Juliet without signing the technical log. More importantly, we are bound to be found liable for negligence if the accident is due in some way to our poor maintenance. The sums of money involved are mind boggling. We're insured of course but that's irrelevant. It will reflect badly on NWIA and also on me as the ultimate supervisor. Having said all of that it is my view, and my MD supports me, that it is important to find out the real cause of the accident so I'm not going to try to block Lance travelling to London. Incidentally, we don't believe for a moment it can be due to the wrong GPS box. By the way have you spoken to Lance yet?"

"No I haven't. I've tried but he is working nights. I was going to try later."

"Well as you know, Lance is a very good lad and very sharp. He actually received the request from CrossRisk to be a witness this morning and his supervisor called me from home. Apparently Lance is very nervous about the whole thing and the need to give evidence. You had better treat him very gently or he may bolt."

"Matt, thanks for the advice. Do you think you could arrange to reassure him and get him to call me when he comes in this evening?"

"I'll do my best. Keep in touch if you discover anything else."

I put the receiver down and immediately the phone rang. It was Product Support at GE Aviation. They had looked at the list of components I had sent them and had recognised a few of the parts. They were going to send me a marked up copy of the list. I called Thales and spoke to their Product Support. They also had looked at the list but did not recognise any of their parts. I would not get anything from the USA until the afternoon or evening.

I went through my mail and opened a letter from American Airlines. They had accepted my quotation and wanted me to start as soon as possible. Would I please call them to make the arrangements. I looked at my watch. Only 11.30, far too early to call Dallas.

My printer started to eject paper. I looked at the first sheet. It was a fax from AAIB returning my list with all the boxes that had been found. I looked at the list when it finally arrived. They had done a good job finding well over half the boxes I had listed; the Galileo box had been found but not the GPS one. It was good of Robin to arrange the checking and return my list so promptly. I wondered if Martin Foster knew. My assessment was that Bob, mindful of the Inquiry coming up, did not want to have an argument in public that he knew he would lose. I sent a message back thanking Bob for the print out and for allowing my visit; I also asked him not to throw the scrap away but hold it in case more detailed investigation was required.

My phone rang. It was Lance. He did not sound too happy.

"Lance. Did you manage to find out what happened to the two GPS boxes that came off Alfa Juliet?"

"Yes Mr Talbert. The second set was functioned by the Honeywell people locally and they found nothing wrong. The set is back in our stores. The first set was apparently not to the same standard as the NWIA

GPS boxes and the Honeywell man has it in his repair shop until he hears from his office in Phoenix."

"Ask him to fax or email me the box type and serial number, please Lance. Did you check the reference and serial numbers of the set you took out of Alfa Juliet?"

"Yes. It was a NWIA box and the Honeywell man told me that it should not have been fitted to the RWA aircraft."

"Lance. Doesn't that mean that the set on Alfa Juliet was also a NWIA box?"

"Yes, unfortunately it does. It never occurred to me that there was something wrong. I checked that the spare I fitted was exactly the same reference as the one I took out."

Lance sounded even unhappier than he had at the beginning.

"Don't worry Lance. You weren't to know. I gather from Matt you have agreed to take a trip to England and come to the Inquiry?"

"Yes I am but I'm not looking forward to it."

"All you've got to do is to say what you did. Look, is there anything I can do to help you? When are you coming over?"

"I don't know yet. It's a week or so away. NWIA are going to meet me and arrange my hotel."

"That's fine. Lance, if anything changes in your plans please let me know." Lance said he would and I hung up.

I had some soup and cheese for lunch with some coffee and then I called American in Dallas and spoke to Tom Gardner who had written to me approving my quote. I introduced myself.

"Peter. We know all about you because we have a training captain, Jake Rodgers, on the SAE S7 Flight Deck Committee. To be truthful we got Jake to talk to the RWA man in connection with our requirement and your quote. I gather you are fully involved in the 798 accident inquiry. I won't ask you what you think happened."

"I don't know how you know that, Tom. I don't give evidence for a week or so and my involvement is not meant to be general knowledge."

"You know as well as I do it's impossible to keep anything secret in our business. Anyway I guess you're going to tell me you can't start straightaway until the Inquiry is over."

"Yes you're right. Is that OK? When do you get your 798s?"

"Not for six months and then at quite a slow rate. We'll be very happy to wait. Make sure you sort it all out before you come. Bye."

No sooner had I put the phone down than it rang again. It was Honeywell. They had got my list and had worked through it. There were a few LSI chips that they recognised as being their proprietary design and there were a lot more chips that were generally available. They were going to email me immediately saying which of the LSI chips were theirs and from which box they had come. I rang off. Honeywell was as good as their word and the email came through almost immediately.

I looked through the list; there was a chip from the Traffic Collision and Avoidance System, some chips from radio receivers but there was one chip used on their GPS card. No wonder that AAIB had not found the GPS box, it must have got smashed since Honeywell had recognised their custom LSI chips from the box. I was disappointed that there were not two GPS chips but in fact I had all the evidence I needed about the GPS boxes and the number of GPS cards from the evidence of Lawrence and Lance. However, none of it seemed relevant since the RWA aircraft could not do GPS approaches. There seemed no way that the wrong GPS box could cause the aircraft to crash on the approach. Perhaps I needed to get some more advice. The most likely cause of the accident just had to be the fact that the aircraft had been flying a Galileo approach and some wrong data had been fed into the Multimode Receivers like an incorrect airfield position. Alternatively, I supposed that the pilots might have been distracted by the hijackers and not spotted they were too low, but the recordings made that sound impossible. Of course there could have been some other reason which I had missed completely.

Mike Mansell called.

"Peter, John Fairlane has been on the phone. He says that he really ought to have the Australian girl available even if in the end she is not called. What do you think?"

"Well I'm not keen and I am sure she won't be. Leave it with me to think over. Can I speak to John direct?"

Mike gave me John's number but before calling I decided for better or for worse I had better discuss the matter with Mandy. She was busy with a client. I asked that she call me back. I got out the central London yellow pages and looked up 'Dressmakers' followed by 'Dress, blouse and skirt mfrs.' There were columns of entries. I decided I had better go up to Town and chat up some of the big stores in the morning.

Mandy came on the line.

"Darling, you remember that girl I told you about in Australia, Liz, who told me what really happened out there?"

"Yes I do. Go on." She had suddenly gone quiet.

"Well John Fairlane wants her to come over to England for the Inquiry. I know she won't be keen and quite frankly I don't think she will contribute much providing Robbie Robson is going to give evidence.

"I am going to call John Fairlane back to discuss it but I thought of a reason why she might agree to come. You see, what I didn't tell you because we were interrupted when I was debriefing myself to you, as you might say."

"I hope that is a figure of speech."

I ignored her.

"What I didn't tell you was that the girl, Liz, had a flair for dressmaking as far as I could judge."

"How do you know that, Mr Talbert."

"Well your Honour, I took her out to dinner as a thank you for giving me all the information and she turned up in a really smart outfit which I thought must have been incredibly expensive. She told me she had designed and made it herself."

"Did you check any of her other clothes?"

"Good point. No, there was no need since when I first met her in her house there were a lot of half finished clothes lying around, under construction you might say. The other reason was that I didn't have the opportunity as I left the following morning. Anyway I'm sure you wouldn't like me going through all her clothes."

"Too right."

"Mandy, what was going through my mind was that if she came over here with some samples, would it be possible to arrange for her to visit some of the good designers?"

"Possibly, but I'm not sure I can help you."

"Well I thought I might go and chat up the buyer in Harrods and possibly one or two other stores to-morrow to see if they have any suggestions."

"Yes, that seems a good idea. If the worst came to the worst she could visit the big designers on spec. and just knock on their doors. If the stuff really is any good she should be able to get a job, though the routine work is not very well paid I believe."

"Alright, I'll have a go to-morrow but meantime I'll talk to John. Bye."

I called John Fairlane in his office.

"Peter, you've obviously heard I really do feel that the girl in Australia should be available for the Inquiry. As I told you, we need to establish that the Captain was in his room the night before they left. What about it?"

"Well John, I've thought about it and I might be able to persuade her to come for an entirely different reason. Would you like me to call her?"

"Yes please. Mike will have to pay all her expenses but it is a very small insurance premium to pay when one considers the likely size of the claims."

"I will telephone her. But John, please don't call her unless you have to. The papers will be on to her like a shot because they will realise the sort of life that she was leading at the time. She is very attractive and inevitably if you call her some people are going to get hurt, especially Mrs. Hodgson and the Robsons."

"OK Peter. But I cannot promise. The stakes are enormous."

I put the phone down feeling very worried for Liz and for the damage she would inevitably cause. I wanted to call her straightaway but she would be asleep. I decided to call her at 8.30pm when she would probably be having breakfast. I started work on my American contract and apart from supper worked through until it was time to call Liz.

She answered the phone immediately.

"Liz, it's Peter. Remember?"

"Yes Peter. I'm not likely to forget you in a hurry."

"Hope I didn't wake you up."

"No. I'm a reformed character. I go to work on time in downtown Sydney and go to bed early. I'm having breakfast before I go to the office. How can I help you?"

"Liz. There is a Public Inquiry into the accident to Alfa Juliet and the insurance company who are retaining me, may want to call you as a witness."

"But Peter, how can I help? I don't know anything."

"Well you can explain that the reference about an evening out on the voice recorder was not the night before the flight but the night before that. I know it's irrelevant because they had plenty of time to sleep in the aircraft but nevertheless John Fairlane the counsel wants to make that clear. More importantly, our counsel wants you to make it known that Harry was actually in his room the night before the flight getting some rest.

"The other issue is of course the extra maintenance that was carried out that night before the last flight. You can testify about the conversations between the pilots and NWIA and Robson's call to someone in England."

I paused waiting for Liz to say something. There was a deathly hush.

"Now Liz I've been thinking. Don't give me an answer now. I have some unfinished business with NWIA and I plan to travel out on Wednesday, to be with you Thursday night. The Inquiry does not reconvene until Tuesday so I won't have to leave until Sunday. In fact if you agree to come you can travel back with me. I'll work Friday and we can spend some time together Saturday. I have an idea which may appeal to you about getting a job in England. What do you say?"

"Peter I really would like to see you again. However, I'm not sure about giving evidence. Wouldn't the papers make me out to be a good time girl? Anyway it would hurt Mrs. Hodgson and the Robsons if the story came out. You had better come out anyway if you've got work to do and we can talk it over. You can sleep here if you like. I haven't got another room mate yet. Tell you what. I'll meet you off the aircraft."

"Liz. That's a sweet offer but I am not going to accept. First of all we don't get in until quite late and you have to be working in the morning. Secondly I don't think I should sleep at your place. I don't want to be accused in the Inquiry of tampering with a witness."

"That sounds very interesting."

"No it doesn't. By the way, have you got some clothes that you have made, readily available to bring to England?"

"Probably, but I have not agreed to come to England. I will need a lot of persuading. See you Thursday night. Bye, Peter." She was gone before I could remind her that she was not going to see me until Saturday.

I went up to bed wondering what I had let myself in for.

In the morning I phoned Mandy at 8 o'clock in her office and told her what I was doing. She didn't sound over the moon but agreed that, all in all, it was the best thing to do.

"Won't you be very tired when you get back and the Inquiry coming?"

"Possibly, but the Inquiry does not start until the Tuesday and remember the flight is a long one so I should get some sleep and we land in time to go to bed. I'll get a good night's sleep when we get in and anyway I won't be giving evidence before Wednesday."

Mandy still sounded doubtful.

"I suppose it will be alright. However, if you learn anything you will need to brief your counsel. He won't want to get a surprise right at the last moment. When do I see you again?"

"Well you can come round to-night or the Sunday night of my return."

"No, my darling. I don't think so. If you are flying off to-morrow you need to get ready for the trip. Similarly on the Sunday night when you get back you are going to need some sleep. Let's make it the Monday." I agreed reluctantly and Mandy got on with her work.

I called Bill Baker at home. He was just leaving for the office. I asked him if it was OK to make the video on Friday and he said he would check and let me know by email. I called Mike at home and told him what I was planning. I also told him that I had had an idea and I needed to talk to Lance,"

"Well Peter you had better go. I assume that NWIA will pay for the travel and the video. I'll pay the extra for first class travel or you won't be fit for anything either in Sydney or back here for the Inquiry."

"Thanks Mike. I hope I can make it worth CrossRisk's while. However, if I persuade the girl to come back with me I think the best solution would be for us both to travel business class."

"Whatever, Peter. I know I can trust you completely in these matters."

"Fine. Would you send an advance of £10,000 for expenses? You owe me a lot already and I'll have the girl's tickets to pay for. I'll send you some more expense claims when I get back." Mike agreed and I rang off.

I called RWA reservations and booked myself out on Wednesday on the 798 non-stop and booked myself back on the Sunday business class. I paid with my Amex Card which only just covered the ticket. I then made a reservation for Liz to travel back with me in business class and said I would pay for the ticket in Sydney on the Saturday.

I called Hilton reservations and booked in for the three nights. I made one final call to Lance who still sounded very unhappy.

"Hello Mr Talbert. How can I help you. You only just caught me, I'm working days now."

"That's a bit of luck. I'm arriving Sydney this Thursday to do a job for NWIA. Can we meet Friday evening?"

"I suppose so. Where do you suggest?"

"I've no idea Lance. Do you know a quiet place for dinner?"

"Where are you staying?"

"I'm at the Hilton. Meet me in the lobby at 6 o'clock and we can take it from there."

"Fine by me. See you Friday."

Dora was doing her normal Tuesday magic and ironing some clothes.

"My paper says the Inquiry starts next Tuesday. Are you going to be there?"

I reassured her that I would indeed be there and would probably have to give evidence. She was clearly impressed and would undoubtedly tell the Fox and Hounds. I promised to let her know when I knew the actual day so she could read the evening paper.

I left straightaway to try to talk to the buyer before Harrods filled up. I was in the store at 9.30 and went up to the dress department. I looked around for suits like the one that Liz had worn at the Guillaume, inspected the labels and made a note of the names. A lady who had been watching me came over and asked if she could help.

"I'm looking for the buyer in charge of this department."

"Please wait and I'll see if she is free."

The lady disappeared and reappeared with a lady of about 40 years of age, very smartly dressed, slight and with brown hair.

"How can I help you?"

I decided that the truth was the easiest to remember.

"When I was in Australia a few days ago I met a lady who was wearing a really smart blue lightweight suit. It was so striking that I asked her where she got it because I was fairly sure she couldn't afford that sort of expensive outfit and she told me that she had designed and made it

236

herself. She's coming over to England next week and I was so impressed with her talent that I've suggested to her that she brings some of her work with her to show to someone with a view to getting a job as a designer. I was looking at the labels on the clothes you were selling and I was going to try to make some appointments for her at the various manufacturers."

I showed her the picture of us both, taken outside the Guillaume with Liz wearing the blue suit.

"Well you could certainly try that." She peered at the photo very closely and got a magnifying glass out. "That suit does look very good. I tell you what, I'll give you my card and she could come and see me. When might this be?"

"I expect it will be next Monday or Tuesday if that is alright. You really are very kind."

"No problem. You never know what can happen. It is one of the things that makes my job interesting."

I thanked her again and made my way out of the store using the stairs, that way I knew where I was going. Big stores always made me nervous as it was never immediately obvious how to get out quickly in an emergency nor, in my opinion, was it obvious where the nearest elevator or escalator was located. Out in the cold street it was blowing quite hard which always made walking in London so awkward as the wind varied the whole time, depending on the location and size of the buildings. There was no hurry and I carried on down Knightsbridge, under Hyde Park Corner and along Piccadilly until I reached Green Park. I caught the underground to Waterloo and went home.

Dora was still there and seemed in good spirits. Her daughter seemed to be doing well at school despite a lot of unsupervised homework. The Fox and Hounds debating club was clearly flourishing. I told Dora about my trip to Australia but reassured her that I would be back in time to give evidence at the Inquiry. Back in my office I finalised my script for the NWIA training video which took most of the afternoon, printed off two copies and made two spare discs as well. I checked in for the flight on line and then went upstairs to pack.

As usual it was always difficult to decide what to take when going from winter at one end to summer at the other. I decided to leave my coat in the car but take a pullover which I could use in the plane. As I was only going for three nights I did not need much but of course I was going to have to spend nearly two more days travelling in the aircraft. I would check one bag to keep down the weight of my old Lark carry-on bag. I called Mandy at home before I went to bed to reassure her that all was well. I told her about my visit to Harrods.

"Where's Liz Ward going to stay if she comes over?"

"I don't know, Mandy. I'm not having her here."

"Too right you're not. Can't she stay in a hotel? Doesn't she have any contacts in London?"

"I just don't know. It will be soon enough to find out if she decides to come."

"Well she can't stay here. There might be a conflict of interests in more ways than one."

I decided to ignore her remark.

"We have to face the fact that if she does give evidence I'm afraid it will be inevitable that the newspapers will be after her and try to get her life story. What is needed is a secure anonymous apartment in London. I think I'll get Mike on to the job since it is CrossRisk who want her to give evidence and they can pick up the tab."

"That seems a good idea. By the way is it alright if I go to your place to get some of my clothes? I think I must have left a dress I need."

"Of course. Why do you need the dress so urgently? What am I missing?"

"Trust me. Nothing you need concern your sweet little head about." She changed the subject. "Are you staying at the Hilton again?"

"Yes. I'll call you Friday morning your time when I get in. Bye, my darling."

I decided to call Mike though it was getting quite late. I explained the problem of Liz's accommodation.

"I'll call you from Sydney the moment I have news but you need to be getting a place organised in principle now. I am convinced the media are going to be a pain. The girl's no fool and she has already mentioned the problem to me. I need to be able to reassure her."

"OK Peter. I'll do what I can and send you an email which you will get when you arrive at the Hilton."

I finally got to bed and managed to sleep well. I set the alarm and left the house at about 08.45. I used valet parking again at Terminal 3 and let the man in the office know my return flight and scheduled arrival time.

I dropped my bag off, got directions for the first class lounge, confirmed I had the seat I wanted and then went through bag inspection and immigration. I found some magazines I had not read and also a thick novel off the shelves. I made my way to the lounge, got some black coffee and read the Financial Times. The flight was called but there was no rush for those of us lucky enough to be on the lower deck at the front of the aircraft. Just when I was getting nervous, we were finally called and made our way down the hall to the gate. A hostess showed me to my seat and took my blazer. I went into the toilet and put on some thin old slacks and my pullover and settled down for the flight.

We took off on time and I switched on my passenger entertainment system to watch the BBC news. There was nothing of special interest and

I switched the screen off. I was tempted to use the phone and thought of calling Mandy but there was nothing I could add to our last conversation. The steward took my order for drinks and I chose a tomato juice. I decided to read the paper and have the meal, whatever it was called, before doing any work. The food in first class was superb but I found it went on a bit. I managed to restrict myself to soup, fruit and cheese but it took a lot of will power. By the time I had finished my second cup of coffee three hours had gone by and I had finished looking at both the Times and the FT. I was very relieved when the hostess cleared everything away. On balance I preferred the faster business class service but I knew that the real benefit would come later. It was already dark outside.

I got out my work and finalised my plans for American using my small portable computer. I stopped and got my book out and read for a couple of hours. The aircraft Captain came round, I guessed he must have just gone off watch.

"Haven't I seen you before somewhere?" were his opening words. We soon established that he had attended some of my lectures during crew training. I gave him my card and he looked at it very carefully. I could see the penny drop.

"Wait a minute. Aren't you the guy who is investigating the accident to Alfa Juliet? The Inquiry starts next week, doesn't it?"

"Yes you're right, I am involved to some extent. I'm just fitting in a job for NWIA before the Inquiry."

"It really was a horrendous accident and we were particularly sad about the loss of our crews. The hijackers have a lot to answer for. As it happens my wife and I knew Harry and his wife very well. She is heartbroken and of course was very upset about the leaked voice recorder transcript. It is so unfair. She has no redress at all. She also feels that the story going about that it was Harry's fault is untrue and completely unsubstantiated."

"You are quite right. However I'm hopeful that at the Inquiry some light will be thrown on what actually happened. By the way, could you let me have Marcia's number? For some reason it is not listed on the Guild database. I think I would like to go and see her."

"Of course I can. Why don't you come up to the flight deck? I've got the number up there."

"I didn't know that was allowed." I paused as I remembered my previous flight. "Is it OK then if you're First Class?"

"Only if the Captain says OK. But you'll have to have a very stringent examination by a guard before you will be allowed into the VIP cabin and the flight deck area."

239

Blind Landing

"Well that's great. Perhaps I could come up for the last two hours and watch the landing. Is that alright?

"You bet. It will be a real pleasure. I won't ask you what you think really happened to Alfa Juliet though, as you can imagine, we all want to know."

"Thanks. To be honest it still isn't clear what happened. Actually another trip on the flight deck will be really useful before the Inquiry."

The captain went off and we were offered more food. I decided to have only a very small taste of whatever it was, since I had established over many years flying that it was vital to get one's stomach synchronised with the destination country as quickly as possible. What I would need to do would be to eat towards the end of the flight just before going up on to the flight deck. I stretched my legs and walked to the back of the aircraft. The flight was fairly full and most of the passengers seemed comatose after their meal. I went back to the front, got out my book and after a bit I started to doze. I called one of the cabin attendants who sorted out my bed, arranged the pillows, sheets and blankets. I lay down, put my eye shades on and felt myself dropping off. This was what first class was all about.

I woke up and looked it my watch. We had been flying for about ten hours and had reached Lanzhou, about 500 miles west south west of Peking. It was already light and I calculated that it was 10 a.m. in Sydney. I asked if I could have something to eat. Most of the other passengers were asleep and they were not planning to serve breakfast for some time. There was a stewardess who had come on duty and she offered to boil me two eggs, always a tricky operation when the cabin altitude was 8,000 ft and the water boiled at 92°C. However she did a super job and I really enjoyed my breakfast.

I tried to do some more work, not too successfully and then got out the magazines I had bought at the airport. The flight dragged on and I had some more breakfast when breakfast was being served to the other passengers, then dozed a bit. The time seemed to stand still. I looked at the map in the cabin and checked our position when we had three hours to go. We were just coasting in, a hundred miles or so east of Darwin.

I was in the middle of tidying up my things when the stewardess came down with a message that it would be OK for me to go up to the flight deck. I made my way up the stairs and was met by a marshal. He was obviously very unhappy that I should go on to the flight deck. The Chief Steward appeared and convinced him that it would be OK. He checked my ticket carefully and I showed him my pilot's licence. Then we all went through to the flight crew area where the marshal gave me a very through search. The Chief Steward then operated the keypad and we were let in. Justin Lockyer, I had discovered the Captain's name, looked

240

over his shoulder and beckoned me to sit down. The en-route first officer was on the jump seat but he got up when he saw me.

Everything seemed to be normal. We were flying at 46,000 ft. and .86 mach number. There was no cloud below us and we could see the inhospitable ground beneath. The sun was only just above the horizon in the west.

"What a super evening. What's the weather like in Sydney?"

"It's still hot but it has cooled a bit. There are some fires left in New South Wales but luckily this time Sydney seems to be in the clear. We should be landing spot on time."

"What sort of approach are you going to do?"

"Well they've got the GBAS running at last so I thought we might try an auto-land. Suit you?"

"Very much so. I want to watch your procedures again if you don't mind."

The flight proceeded normally and we got our descent clearance about 45 minutes out. Though there seemed to be a lot of traffic, air traffic control fed us into the traffic pattern without asking us to hold. Justin selected the runway to be used on the MMR controller and put the approach selector switch in the vertical Galileo position. The MMR positioned the aircraft for capturing the Galileo centre line and the first officer lowered the landing gear as the aircraft captured the synthetic Galileo glide slope. The navigation display showed the aircraft on the runway centre line and it seemed to be exactly on the glide slope. I glanced at the combined ILS/MLS indicator on the left centre instrument panel and was reassured when I saw that both needles were central so that we were on the MLS runway centre line and on the MLS glide slope. Not surprisingly, because of standardised crew drills, the altitude call outs from the first officer followed by the radio altimeter were exactly the same as the 573 recording. It was slightly unnerving. At 30 ft. the throttles started to close and we did a perfect landing on the correct spot. The nosewheel touched the runway and at about 80 knots Justin disconnected the auto-pilot and applied the brakes.

I thanked Justin and the crew and went back to my seat as we taxied in. I was first off the aircraft and got through immigration in record time. My bag, with a first class sticker, was already waiting for me on the carousel and I was through the customs door about twenty minutes after touch down. I decided I liked travelling first class.

As I came through the door I saw Liz waiting for me. She was wearing a very lightweight, semi-transparent mid length coat with a blouse and shorts underneath. She had a magnificent tan and I was sure it was not confined to the parts I could see. With her long legs she looked terrific and I guessed that most models would not mind looking as she did. She came up to me and I tried to kiss her on the cheek but got her lips instead. I tried to make sure it was a perfunctory embrace but it was not easy.

"I thought we'd agreed that you were not going to meet me, Miss Ward."

"No, Peter. You suggested that it was not necessary but I wanted to see you anyway. There are very few really nice men in my life."

"Thank you for that but you're a working girl and I don't want you to be late for work in the morning."

"That's very thoughtful of you but I can look after myself, thank you Mr Talbert."

We went over to the Avis desk to pick up a car. There was a line from the previous flight. As we chatted I realised that her coat was not just to stop her getting too cold in the air conditioned airport. Her blouse was almost translucent and I was sure I could see her nipples thrusting through the material. I hoped she was going to keep wearing her coat on the way home.

"Liz. Did you make the stuff you're wearing yourself?"

"Yes of course."

"It's a magnificent outfit but why don't you make bras as well?"

"Well they're a lot of hard work and I don't feel I really need them all the time. What do you think?"

"Now look, Miss Ward. We've got to sort something out. I really enjoyed that night on the beach. It was fantastic and I'll never forget it. But we've got to be sensible. You need to find a career and stop going out every night. I'm no expert but I feel you have a real talent for making clothes. I want you to show some samples of what you can do to some firms in England."

Liz thought about that, but there appeared to be something else on her mind.

"Peter. Do you have a girl friend?"

"You know I do. She's a lawyer and we are, what's the phrase, going steady."

"Well I think she's very lucky."

I made no comment and signed the necessary papers for renting the car. "You had better go home now, Liz. It was lovely of you to meet me but I think we both have got to get ready to work in the morning. Why don't you come to the hotel for breakfast on Saturday at 9 a.m. but please, for my sake, wear a bra. I'm only human. As Oscar Wilde said, 'I can resist anything except temptation.'"

We kissed good night but this time I got the tongue as well as the full lips. I could feel myself hardening against her. How I broke off I don't know. Liz certainly didn't help. I watched her go and then went to the

Avis park to pick up my car. It was still hot even though it was 9 o'clock at night. Still it was better than my last visit.

CHAPTER 17

The Harbour

I drove to the Hilton and checked in. There was a message from Mike saying that he had got an apartment organised for Liz in Chelsea Cloisters. I took my keys and went up to my room. It was still only 9.30 and I felt quite hungry. I had a shower, changed and went down for a snack in the coffee shop. Justin and the other Captain were already there and I joined them. I did not stay long and went up to bed and slept until 6 o'clock in the morning which wasn't bad in the circumstances.

I got up and went down for a swim. The sky was still absolutely clear and the pool water felt almost tepid. There was a light breeze for a change. I did ten lengths of the large pool and went up to my room to get dressed, then went down to breakfast without my lightweight jacket. I was finished by 7.30 and collected my papers and jacket from my room. I went to the parking lot, drove to NWIA at the airport and arrived at Bill Baker's office at the same time as he did.

"It's great to see you, Peter. You are looking fine. I can't believe you've just flown in from England. How was the flight?"

"Marvellous thank you. It takes a long time but it really is the way to travel. CrossRisk arranged for me to be upgraded to first class so I was able to eat and sleep as I wanted, which makes all the difference if you want to work the next day."

He looked at me.

"I reckon you have got other things to do beside make the video." I nodded. "When do you have to give evidence at the Inquiry? Do you know yet what really happened?"

"I think I may be giving evidence in the middle of next week, Bill, but you can never be sure when the legal profession are calling the shots. As to what caused the accident, I think we're all still groping for an explanation."

"Our papers say that AAIB have made their minds up that it's pilot error."

"Not sure if that's true or not. Maybe one or two in the AAIB believe that. That's one of the reasons I'm out here. I want to eliminate some theories and persuade some witnesses we need them to come to England."

"Well the best of luck. The video man should be here in a moment and then I'll leave you to his tender mercies."

The video expert arrived and we went down to a room he had set up for the filming. He had a mountain of lights and recording equipment which was quite beyond me but he also had some computer gear and a document scanner. He checked on what diagrams I had to go with the talk.

"What I suggest is that we scan your talk on to my special computer and then I've got some software here that will run your talk on a screen placed behind the cameras. What I would like you to do is to indicate when the diagrams are coming so that I can patch them into the tape."

We fed my talk through the scanner's document feeder and then I altered the narrative to match the diagrams. We had a trial run to make sure that I was able to talk to the cameras as the speech scrolled through. It took a bit of practice to be able to look convincing and read at the same time but I got used to it. Luckily, I knew what was coming and only had to do relatively small segments between the diagrams. However, it all took time. The video operator was an expert and knew what he wanted. By lunch time we had done twenty five minutes of the video and we went to the airport terminal for a sandwich. The operator had a beer but I stuck to coca-cola. I found time to go over to the NWIA ticket desk to take a gamble and buy Liz's ticket with my Mastercard.

We went back after lunch and gradually put the rest of my talk on to tape. The whole thing, not counting the diagrams, actually lasted one hour fifty minutes. I felt fairly confident that by the time the video operator had put the whole thing together it would look quite professional. The operator worked under sub-contract to NWIA and I asked him if I could have copies when he had finished. He pointed out that NWIA had the copyright so that I would have to negotiate with them. I called Bill and asked him about having copies.

"Well Peter. I would like to say OK but I will need to take advice. Of course the NWIA logo will be all over it so in some ways it will be a very good advertisement. I'll see if I can arrange a good deal for you. You can certainly have one copy for yourself but I'd rather you did not use it to show anyone else until I've sorted out the contractual position internally."

That seemed very fair to me and I drove back to the Hilton. I had decided before I left England that I needed to keep my cash flow under control so when I got up to my room I started to write up my expenses before I forgot. I planned to mail the completed sheet with the other sheet for my last visit back to Bill the moment I got back. I reflected that I also needed to get my expenses submitted to Mike pretty quickly or my bank manager would be after me.

I had a quick shower and went down to the lobby to meet Lance. He arrived on time wearing shorts, a shirt and no jacket, hardly surprising considering the weather.

"What would you like to do Lance? Why don't we have a drink here and then decide."

We went to the bar and sat down. The waiter came over and I ordered a whisky and water, Lance ordered a beer.

"Lance, I needed to talk to you because I want you to be ready when you come over to England. I don't want to spring any surprises on you."

Lance looked nervous.

"What do you mean, Mr Talbert?"

"You had better call me Peter, Lance." I carried on. "Well on that fateful night before the accident to Alfa Juliet you sorted out the navigation display and the Multimode Receiver with the faulty GPS. Those entries are in the log. It may well be that the cause of the accident will prove to be due to carrying out a Galileo approach and clearly people will be investigating that very closely. However, we need to make sure that there is not some other reason, or even fault, which could have caused the accident. Let me put this to you straight Lance. When you changed the GPS box did you do anything else?"

Lance looked slightly uncomfortable.

"Lance, you took out the GPS, checked the part number and fitted a spare from NWIA with the identical part number, right?" Lance nodded. "As luck would have it you were trained by United, not by Independant, and you did not realise that there were two different standards of boxes. What happened then, Lance?"

"I told you, Peter. I functioned the GPS and it worked fine. There was no supervisor and so I made no entry in the log."

"Is that it, Lance? Are you sure? Did you work on any other equipment? Find anything else wrong?"

"I told you, Peter, I just made sure everything worked according to the manual."

"OK. That's fine." I looked at him. "Lance one of the reasons I came to Australia now was that I wanted to talk to you before the Inquiry. You need to describe to the Inquiry, when you are asked the question about changing the GPS, exactly what you told me. Your supervisor should have been present and remember he had been trained in Seattle. He knew the difference between the 798 aircraft and the two standards of GPS box. Be quite straightforward about it. John Fairlane is the counsel who will be asking you the questions and he is a very reasonable man. He will ask you where you were trained and whether the RWA equipment standard was ever explained to you. There is really no reason for you to be upset. You will obviously be a bit nervous but then so will I."

"But you didn't do anything wrong."

"But neither did you, Lance, within your own knowledge base. You changed a box on an aircraft for an identical part and functioned it, right?"

Lance nodded, dubiously. We stopped at that point and I asked Lance again where he would like to eat. We decided that the coffee shop in the hotel would be fine and we went in and had our meal. He cheered up a bit during the evening but, understandably he felt very concerned.

"Do I have to come to England, Peter?"

"No you don't, but if you don't people may not believe the story of the wrong GPS being fitted. Lawrence won't come and give evidence and of course one can't really blame him since he was trained with United as well. Of course having the wrong GPS is not really important, is it Lance, since the RWA 798s can't use GPS except in a navigation mode?"

Lance nodded uncertainly. We finished our meal and I walked with Lance to the lobby and out to his car.

"When are you coming over?"

"Matt has booked me to travel on Monday. He has made all the arrangements in London as well."

"Well here's my card again. Give me a call when you get in or leave a message on my answering machine if I am out. We will need to keep in touch so that you will know when you will be called."

We shook hands and he drove off. I had hoped that talking to Lance would throw more light on the situation but I had got nowhere. I was not looking forward to giving evidence at the Inquiry. True I had made some progress but I had not come up with a solution. Perhaps pilot error for reasons unknown did look a real possibility.

I went to bed and slept soundly until 6.30. In the morning I had my usual swim and watched the news. I went down to the lobby at 8.45 to meet Liz. She arrived just before 9 o'clock looking very relaxed in a thin top and a 'not too short' skirt. I managed to kiss her on the cheek and noticed with some relief that she appeared to be wearing a bra.

"Let's have breakfast outside, Peter."

We went out to the verandah overlooking the pool. It was very pleasant, not too hot but we sat under an umbrella to keep out of the sun. We ordered breakfast, mine quite light, Liz's fairly substantial.

"It's not like this in England, Liz. You had better bring some warm clothes. I hope you have some."

"Peter, I have not yet agreed to come to England. I'm going to take a lot of persuading. Why don't we just have breakfast and not talk of unpleasant things for a moment. We can talk about the Inquiry later."

Liz changed the subject abruptly.

"What are we going to do for the rest of the day? It's far too good to stay here."

"What do you suggest?"

"Let's go sailing. We can arrange a bare boat charter for the day near here."

Blind Landing

I did not have much alternative but to agree since I was going to have to persuade Liz to travel to England and she was not about to give in easily.

"I'll need to buy a shirt."

"You can do that in the shops downstairs. Go up and get changed and I'll buy you something suitable. Meet you in the lobby."

I did what I was told but felt a bit guilty taking a day off, even if it was in a good cause, trying to make Liz go to England. I put a few things and my bathing costume in my Lark bag and went downstairs. Liz reappeared in a few minutes with a rather nice shirt.

"How much do I owe you?"

"$100"

"Australian, I hope."

She nodded and I paid her right away. It cost more than my regular shirts but that's because I rarely bought expensive clothes.

"Let's go in my car. I've got my things there."

We went over to her car and she drove to the marina where the chartering was taking place. The weather seemed almost too perfect. Just a light breeze and forecast to remain sunny. We went into the office and I convinced them that I could manage and paid a deposit. They obviously knew Liz so they didn't need much convincing. Anyway perhaps she was on commission.

"Don't go outside the Heads." the man said as we left.

Liz went to the trunk of the car and reappeared with a bag and a cold box.

"What's all this? You had it all planned."

"Well I knew I would need a lot of convincing. What's the phrase 'those that play together, stay together.'"

I hoped she was teasing me but I wasn't sure.

"Liz we're not going to stay together. You're a super girl and I think you're fantastic but our relationship would not work, long term."

"Alright Peter. Don't take the bait quite so quickly."

We reached the boat, a 24 footer, and put our kit on board. Liz disappeared below and reappeared wearing a bikini, leaving very little to the imagination. Her brown skin protected her from the sun. I put on my trunks and the shirt Liz had bought. I stood next to her, my white skin against her tan looked very incongruous.

"That's settled it, Liz. I don't believe in mixed relationships."

I could have bit my tongue off for even suggesting that there was a possibility of a relationship. Liz had clearly not missed the significance of what I said.

"I've got nothing against it. We'd soon be able to match the colours, if we tried hard."

We cast off and had an idyllic sail. Liz obviously knew the cruising area very well and we sailed gently across to the other side of the great harbour where we anchored off an island for lunch. I went down below and opened the windows to allow the breeze through the cabin and keep it cool.

"Take your shirt off and feel the warmth of the sun. Here I'll rub some oil on your back. It's a real blocker, just what you need."

The way Liz rubbed oil on my back was an experience, probably accentuated by the fact that she did not confine herself to my back.

"Will you put some on my back, my darling? Try and keep the oil off the strap if you can."

She passed me the oil and turned round. I tentatively rubbed some oil on her brown smooth skin.

"You can do better than that, Peter." She undid her bikini top and took it off.

"Does that make it easier? Don't be nervous. I won't eat you."

"It's not being eaten that I am nervous about, Liz."

She turned round and faced me and grasped the first finger of my left hand.

Her breasts were full and almost the same colour as her body.

"I really don't understand you, Peter. Most men I know would be all over me by now."

"I know, Liz. But I am trying not to be most men. You are a superb woman but I am not sure that satisfying my carnal desires as the saying goes is really very sensible in the long term."

"Well you know best. I must be losing my touch."

"That's exactly what I don't need, Liz," and I moved away.

"Alright let's sunbathe. There's just about room for both of us on the coach top. You had better put some more oil on."

I decided to swim over the side first. I found some plastic steps which fitted over the stern. The water was clear and not too cold, judging by my big toe. It looked superb but just as I was about to dive in Liz yelled at me.

"Stop, Peter, you can't do that."

"Why on earth not. It's ideal."

"Hasn't anyone told you about the sharks? You should only swim where you are protected. I'm not saying you wouldn't be alright here but you mustn't take the risk. We don't want you to leave bits behind here when you go home."

I looked around but couldn't see any sharks. Reluctantly I gave up the idea of swimming and lay down on the boat next to Liz. We had to lay our towels on the top to prevent the coach top burning us. It was not too easy to find room because of the numerous fairleads and jamming cleats but it was worth the effort. The weather was fantastic, with the breeze keeping us cool. Predictably Liz eased her bikini bottoms off to make sure that she browned all over. I decided I had better try to talk to her about coming to England.

"Not now Peter. Let's talk later when we are both fully relaxed."

We lay a bit longer and then Liz suddenly sat up.

"I'm hungry for food. Let's have lunch."

She got up, put her bikini back on and went down below. She brought up the lunch box. The sandwiches were delicious. I think she had bought them from a take-away. Shrimp, tuna and ham. There was also a bottle of white wine, not the greatest I noticed but, looking at the label, certainly not the weakest. We sat next to each other in the sun and England seemed a long way away. When we had finished Liz collected all the things and put them back in the box.

We went below. Liz had put the two cushions next to one another on the cabin floor but I put them back on the seats. We lay down and digested our lunch avoiding the heat of the day.

"My darling, you do see. I could never live in England again. This place has everything."

"Liz, for you that may be true but not for me. "

We both said nothing for a moment then to my surprise Liz opened the subject of the Inquiry.

"Peter, my love. I'm all sorts of things but I'm not a complete idiot. If I'm called to give evidence the newspapers will say I'm a hooker and hound me night and day. My life won't be worth living."

"But Liz, there is no-one who knows what went on except you. Poor Eva and Charles are no longer with us. My recommendation is that you say you went along to dinner because Eva asked you to go with her which in some ways is quite true. It will be clear when you explain that the dinner was on the Saturday night and not the Sunday night. The counsel will ask you to confirm that on the Sunday you called the hotel to thank Harry for the meal and that he was in his room. There's no-one to say different, unfortunately.

"With regard to the second night, again you went along with Eva and you must then explain about the telephone calls. I am going to make sure as far as I can that there is no cross examination since it would not be relevant. In fact I am going to try to ensure that you are not called at all but I cannot promise."

Liz was not convinced but did not turn me down flat.

"Where are you going to be if I come to London?"

"I'll be around. I've arranged for you to stay in an apartment in Chelsea Cloisters which is quite convenient. My suggestion is that you should travel back with me leaving to-morrow morning. We will get in late in the evening. I'll arrange for someone to meet us and take you to your apartment but I'll have to go straight home to prepare for the Inquiry the following morning. Do you know anyone in England?"

"I know a few acquaintances from RWA and my sister."

"Well give her a call and plan to go and visit her the following weekend. Look on the bright side. You probably won't have to give evidence and you are getting a free trip to England all expenses paid including a very generous daily rate.

"In addition I believe even more than ever that you have a real skill as a clothes designer. I have spoken to the buyer at Harrods, showed her that photo of the two of us with that blue suit you were wearing and she is prepared to look at some of the clothes you have made and give an opinion. By the way you didn't answer my question. Do you have any warm clothes?"

"Not really."

"Well I've an idea. On the Monday afternoon we'll go to Harrods together and you can buy some clothes. Wear something really gorgeous that you've made and try and keep warm on the way. Have you got a reasonably thick coat?" Liz nodded.

"After you've bought something we'll talk to the buyer, you can show her some of your work and see what she says. How does that sound?"

"That bit sounds alright though I am not sure your girl friend will like you buying clothes for me."

"Don't worry. Mike is going to pay for them. If I can prove this accident is not pilot error I will have saved his firm a fortune. Buying you a warm suit is the least he can do. Anyway, if you're going to appear in court you will need to have something to wear."

"You've convinced me about the suit but not about coming to England. Anyway my boss would be most unhappy for me not to turn up on Monday and be away, probably for the best part of two weeks."

"Haven't you mentioned it to him."

"Certainly not. He'd probably fire me."

Liz had given me a problem and I was not sure what to do for the best. I decided that I could talk to the duty officer in the evening when I got in. I sensed the wind freshening and we hastily went on the deck. There was a storm cloud heading our way and in no time flat the wind was gusting 30 knots. Luckily the anchor was quite heavy but I felt uncomfortable because the wind was on shore.

"Don't worry it's only a shower, Peter."

"I do worry. I'm going to reef the main just in case."

I pulled down two slabs and made sure everything was set. I started the outboard and waited to watch events. Liz appeared with a sweatshirt on top of her bikini. The storm looked quite extensive but the wind had slackened slightly.

"Liz I'll pull the main up, make sure the sheet is free. Then go ahead slowly until we're over the anchor and I'll pull it up. Open up fully and then I'll come back and get the boat sailing."

All went well but before I had got back to the stern after getting up the anchor Liz had got the boat sailing on the port tack and had unfurled the jib just enough so we did not heel over too much.

"You've done this before."

"Once or twice, darling. You are not the only person in the world who can sail."

We tacked backwards and forwards slowly across the harbour keeping away from the Heads and the deep water. Luckily the wind was from the South West so there was not too much swell coming in. As we made the marina the wind dropped and the heavens opened, rain falling like buckets. We tied up absolutely wet through, not that it mattered in that climate.

We waited in the cabin for about half an hour until the rain stopped and then we went into the office and I collected my deposit.

"We needed that rain. I only wish it was still raining. Did you have a good day?"

"Superb thank you. Everything is working OK"

We went back to the car and Liz suggested we went back to her place. I demurred and after some discussion she reluctantly agreed to drive me back to the hotel.

"Are you coming in for a drink?"

She was sulking.

"No, thank you. The least you could do after our lunch is to come back home with me and see I'm alright."

"I've told you before. You're very much alright but we must be sensible."

"I don't see why."

"Liz, life is more than just making love. We all need to have a plan. You said yourself that Australia was for you and I've told you, England is for me with all its shortcomings."

I changed the subject.

"My dear, go home and pack your best clothes. Here is the e-ticket for the round trip to England with open return . Your seat is next to mine in business class. The flight leaves as you well know at 9.30 to-morrow morning. I'll see you in the business class lounge."

"I'll think about it. I am not sure that I'm going to come. Anyway I haven't told my boss."

"Don't worry about that. I am going to do that now and you can call your office on Monday morning when we land Sunday night."

Liz looked very doubtful. Then she pulled herself together.

"Sorry to spoil everything, darling. It's been a lovely day."

She smiled and gave me a non-fraternal kiss and I watched her drive away

I collected my key and went up to my room. In spite of everything it was still only 6 o'clock. I called NWIA main exchange and got transferred to the duty officer. I explained the situation about Liz, the Inquiry and her travelling to England.

"She's likely to be away for about ten days depending on the Inquiry. You know you can never tell when witnesses are actually going to be called. I'll get her to call her boss at about 9 o'clock on Monday morning. Could you make sure you have explained the situation to him first thing?"

"OK. I'll double bank it by sending him an e-mail which he'll read when he comes in on Monday."

There was nothing more I could do. I had a snack in the coffee shop, watched some TV and went to bed. I got up at six, swam, had a light breakfast and checked out. As I drove to the airport I suddenly realised I had not rung Mandy. I looked at my watch, it was only 9 o'clock on Sunday night. I decided I had better try and put things right. I checked the car in with Avis, saw that I was in a wifi area, got out my pocket pc and called Mandy using skype. She answered straightaway.

"Have all the phones been down? I've been watching the news. As you hadn't called I thought there must have been an earthquake."

I ignored the sarcasm

"No, darling. All is well. I'm at the airport, just about to check in."

"Well I have to tell you, Peter, that I'm very curious about what you have been doing. I normally get better service. I hope the service didn't go elsewhere."

"You're clients are teaching you some rude remarks."

She ignored my comment.

"Well how did everything go?"

"Fine. I did the video. I didn't get anywhere with the NWIA engineer. He said all he did was to change the GPS box but, as we know, that is irrelevant on the RWA 798."

"How did you get on with the girl?"

"I think I've persuaded her to come to England but I just don't know. She's nowhere to be seen at the moment, I'm afraid. Look I'll call you from the lounge if you don't think it's too late."

"No, you do that."

I went to the check in desk but there was still no sign of Liz. I waited as long as I dared and then I checked in. I went straight through

253

immigration to the business class lounge but Liz was nowhere to be seen. I called Mandy as they were calling the flight.

"No luck I'm afraid. She's not here. Took fright. I'm sure John will be able to manage without her. Must fly."

I went to the gate and on to the aircraft. The stewardess showed me to my seat. Liz was already there.

She smiled a warm greeting, very smug.

"Well I do work for RWA. Why should I queue with the common herd?"

***

Liz and I arrived on time at 9.30 in the evening and it was still Sunday. It was a long, long flight against the wind, twenty two hours. We slept a lot of the time. We did not talk much. She was tired and very nervous and I did all I could to reassure her. The problem with the flight was that it was daylight nearly all the way because of the time change. I told Liz to stop fiddling with her watch and put it back eleven hours straightaway so that she had some chance of synchronising her stomach and sleep pattern with the UK. Not surprisingly, it was difficult to sleep even though all the blinds were lowered after about ten hours into the flight.

I had taken advantage of the latest satellite technology and had called Mike and Mandy from my mobile. I did wonder how much I would be charged for the call but comforted myself that Mike was going to have to pay. Mike said he would meet us. I told Mandy that Liz was on the plane and that I would call her again when I woke up.

It was a fine clear night but the temperature was -5°C when we landed. Liz had managed to find an old raincoat which did not look too bad and would help to keep her warm. She had put on a very heavy pullover before we got out of the aircraft. We were soon through immigration and customs and I was delighted to see Mike there, especially as Liz had taken me at my word and brought two bags, both full of clothes, most of them not wearable in an English winter. I could see that Mike kept on looking at Liz when he thought she wasn't noticing.

"What sort of flight did you have?" came the inevitable remark and we soon sorted that out. Mike agreed to take Liz to Chelsea Cloisters and settle her in her apartment.

"Do you need anything to eat, Liz?"

"Never again, thank you Mike. We've been eating all the way. I shall have to alter all my clothes when I get back to Sydney."

"Which reminds me Mike. Liz will need some UK clothes. Have you got a float for her? We can't really expect her to come all this way into a climate that does not exist in Australia and buy clothes she is unlikely ever to need again."

"I agree and I do have a float. Liz do you have a UK bank account?"

"I'm afraid not but I bank with the Australian & New Zealand Bank and they've a branch in London."

"Alright, I'll give you £500 in cash and I'll get my secretary to come to your apartment to-morrow morning at 10 o'clock to give you a cheque to pay in to your account. I'd appreciate some record of what you've spent sometime to keep our records straight. You can fax or email it to me when you get back to Sydney."

Liz nodded and I broke in.

"Mike, when are we going to see Fairlane?"

"9.30 in his office, OK?" I nodded. "Liz, if you need help telephone Mike's office. If you need me they will know where I am. To-morrow you need to get yourself some clothes. Mike's secretary can advise you where to go. Selfridges might be a good place to start. If I don't hear from you I will be at your place at 2 o'clock and I'll take you to Harrods to see the buyer. Mike will look after you now. And please Liz, don't forget to call your boss the moment you get to the apartment."

I gave her a perfunctory kiss but she squeezed my hand hard on the side that Mike couldn't see. I watched them go, Mike wheeling her bags. I went to valet parking, drove home, unpacked my clothes, made a pile of dirty washing and went to bed.

I woke early and called Mandy, she was just getting up.

"I'm home, my darling. Mike was there and took Liz to her apartment."

"Good. I have to say that I am curious to meet Liz. Could she join us for dinner to-night?"

I was not too keen on this line of talk.

"Not unless we eat near Chelsea Cloisters. She hasn't got any wheels."

"Well that's OK by me and then we can go home to your place."

"Fine. I'll call her sometime to-day and try and fix it. I'm taking her to see the Harrods buyer this afternoon. I'll take the car and leave it at the Chelsea Cloisters car park. She shouldn't be short of things to wear, she brought two large bags of clothes with her."

"You had better keep moving, Peter. Aren't you going to see your counsel sometime?"

"You're right again. Call you later."

I got dressed. The weather had not got any warmer overnight. Liz must be hating it. I switched on the TV and the forecaster had put snow

255

showers all over the map. I got rid of the car at Chelsea Cloisters and arrived at Fairlane's chambers just before 09.30 and for once Mike was not there but he arrived a few minutes later.

"How did you get on with Liz?"

"Oh fine. She's a nice girl and not unattractive."

"You noticed? I thought confirmed bachelors did not notice these things."

Mike ignored me.

"I managed to arrange the money and instruct my secretary before I left the office. That's why I am a few minutes late. By the way there're two thing I haven't told you, Peter. First of all your Lance Stephens has chickened out and won't be coming to give evidence."

"That's not good news. His evidence would have confirmed my story on changing the GPS set. I've got paperwork if it's needed but it's not the same thing."

"The other thing is that the NWIA insurers are in a real panic. They've obviously been warned by the airline that there may be a problem and I suppose it could bankrupt the firm if they have not made all necessary arrangements. The insurer is a UK firm, Pacific Aerospace Insurance plc, PAI, and they clearly want the fault to be pilot error, so CrossRisk Insurance, and that includes you, are not the flavour of the month with those boys. NWIA and Pacific Aerospace have applied, and it has been agreed, that they can be a party to the proceedings. It looks like an insurers' benefit since both ourselves and Hull Claims insurance are present as well as PAI. To be honest, Peter, that's the trouble with holding this sort of an Inquiry instead of leaving it to the AAIB. Everybody wants to be represented to defend their corners."

"How did my name come on the screen?"

"That's easy. Once they became a party to the proceedings they would see the witnesses who are scheduled to be called and who were 'promoting' the witnesses They will know that we are calling you because we are refuting that pilot error is in any way responsible for the accident."

"Well Mike I have to say it makes me feel very uncomfortable."

John called us in to his room. He had his copious notes in front of him.

"Well Peter, what's new since we met?"

"Just to recap on where we finished last, it was my view that it was a pity that the transcript did not have any conversation with the hijackers. We need to discuss that with AAIB and ask them how they can come to any conclusion without knowing what the hijackers were doing. Mike was going to organise the BAA, ATC and SRG witnesses. When I was in Sydney I thought I had persuaded the NWIA mechanic to come over to give evidence on the work he did, but Mike tells me he has changed his mind. However as you wanted, the girl who can say that the so called party was not the night before the flight, travelled with me yesterday and is now in London. Needless to say she doesn't want to be called as a witness and as you know I don't think she is needed.

"Now since we met last I have established that a few flights before the fateful flight, a NWIA maintenance engineer changed the GPS box in Alfa Juliet but he put the NWIA three GPS receiver card box into the aircraft instead of the single GPS card. His supervisor, who knew that the NWIA box was different from the RWA box was not on duty, even though his time sheet showed he was. The engineer who changed the box now works in the USA but he told me the story over the phone and we have paperwork showing the issue of a 'wrong' GPS box and the technical log showing it was fitted to Alfa Juliet."

"But Peter, that's good detective work but would it matter?"

"That's the problem. I don't think it does matter but I have to eliminate everything. Let me carry on. On the fateful night before the last flight the same supervisor was still not present. A different engineer changed the GPS set, a good engineer this time. Unfortunately he too, being trained by United and not Independant, did not know there were two standards of GPS boxes but he did check that the set he put in was the same part number as the set he took out. He functioned the set which worked correctly. The fact that he checked the part number for the GPS shows quite clearly that the wrong GPS was fitted some flights earlier by NWIA but let me stress, John, as I did last time we met, that bad GPS maintenance by NWIA ought not to be a factor in the accident since the RWA 798s can only fly Galileo approaches, they cannot fly a GPS approach."

"Peter, the story of the NWIA bad maintenance may not be significant technically but it is important, since it shows very clearly that Foster of AAIB did not do his job thoroughly because, unlike you, he did not investigate things properly. Unfortunately, we still haven't managed to find an alternative solution that explains what happened and therefore we will not be able to convince the Inquiry it wasn't pilot error. You are going to have to be very eloquent to persuade everybody that hijackers on the flight deck would have prevented the pilots monitoring properly."

"Yes, John, but the point is that the normal monitoring apparently would have showed nothing wrong. Now I'm fairly certain that when you question the Galileo experts you're going to find that the GBAS transmitter was not checked after the accident. The ATC man will say he didn't ask for it to be checked because it was not required and I suspect the SRG man will say the integrity of the system is such that it's not necessary to check it. My view is that the data should have been checked to make sure that the runway details for 27 Left were correct. If the data was wrong then an accident would be very likely. It seems to me you're going to have to do something akin to your normal lawyers' trick 'I wasn't there, I didn't do it, but if I was, and if I did, I'm sorry.' Certainly the hijackers must have prevented the pilots from concentrating and the Galileo was almost certainly wrong."

"Alright Peter, if that's the best we can do, so be it."

The meeting closed and I realized that in spite of all my investigations it was unlikely that I could prevent the Inquiry thinking that the pilots had made a mistake. It was going to be tough going for me when I went into the witness box.

CHAPTER 18

Liz and Mandy

While still in John's chambers I gave Liz a call. "How did you manage this morning?"

"Well, my darling, Mike's secretary came round and we went to my bank and put Mike's cheque in. I took a taxi to Selfridges and bought some warm trousers and a pullover. I took another taxi home. I don't feel equal yet for the London public transport system."

"Do you feel equal to coming out to dinner with Mandy and me to-night? We'd go to a place near you."

"That sounds fun, darling."

"Have you bought any food yet?"

"Just a little and I saw a small restaurant where I planned to eat if you stood me up, my love."

"Liz, to-night I think it would be helpful if you called me Peter, and not darling."

"OK, my love. I mean Peter. But it is not going to be easy, darling Peter."

"Stop giving me a hard time Liz. You know exactly what I mean. I'll pick you up at two this afternoon. Have your clothes bag ready. I'll order a cab to take us there."

Dinner to-night was going to be tricky. I had a brainwave and called Mike who had got back to the Office.

"Mike, what are you doing to-night? How about making up a foursome with Mandy and Liz? I'm going to book a table at Chez Augustine in the Kings Road for 8 o'clock."

Mike was delighted and he agreed that he would walk Liz to the restaurant. I said that we would meet him there. I called Mandy feeling a lot easier. I had come to the obvious conclusion that a threesome with Mandy and Liz had all the makings of an irrecoverable disaster. Even with four there would need to be no nodding off.

I called Mandy's office. I waited a few minutes and was put through.

"Chez Augustine's at 8 o'clock, darling. Mike, Liz, you and me. I'll be at your office at 7 o'clock and we can take it from there. My car's in position at Chelsea Cloisters so it should work out very well."

"I don't remember our including Mike in."

"I don't remember we included him out. He's a super chap and he seems to like Liz. He will make certain there are no awkward gaps in the conversation."

"How do you know I don't want awkward gaps in the conversation?"

There was no answer to that so I didn't give one.

"See you to-night, darling."

"Don't bet on it, Peter."

She hung up, but I judged only to keep me on my toes. I caught a taxi to Chelsea Cloisters. I was a bit early for the Harrods trip and, feeling slightly hungry, I went to the self-service restaurant close-by and as I went to sit down I saw Liz.

"Great minds. I was hungry, Peter, and didn't have any food in the apartment." She inspected my plate, "You haven't got very much."

"I'm planning on just having this for lunch as we're eating again to-night."

"No wonder you are so thin and gorgeous, my own sweet darling."

I was just beginning to know when she was teasing me. I ate my baguette and drank my coffee. Liz tucked in to her bacon, lettuce and tomato sandwich. She seemed to be able to tuck the food away without any effect on her figure which didn't seem fair. I went back with her to her apartment and waited while she sorted herself out. She was wearing what I guessed was the pullover and trousers she had bought at Selfridges. She looked great, but then most things looked great on her. I helped her on with her raincoat which rather spoilt the effect but kept the cold out.

"Where are your gloves?"

"I forgot to buy a pair. It was on my list but they didn't make the cut."

"Well we're taking a taxi so you should be alright but it's quite cold out and going to snow."

I carried Liz's bag and she locked up. We went to the front and a taxi was waiting. The traffic was heavy but we got to Harrods quite quickly. Upstairs in the same department where I was before, Liz started to look for a suit. I could see that this was going to take some time and I sat down to read the paper. I saw the buyer coming over.

"Hello again, Mr Talbert. I think I recognise the young lady over there buying a suit from the photograph you showed me."

"Yes. Living in Sydney she had no need for a suit to wear in our English weather."

"She is a very striking person. She could be model if she wanted to. That suit she found looks very good on her."

Liz came over and I introduced her to the buyer.

"That's a lovely suit for you, Miss Ward."

"Yes. I like it. In fact I'm going to buy it."

"Why don't you put on something you've made, my dear, and let me see it?"

Liz disappeared into the changing room and reappeared with a mid length dress which fitted her to perfection. I could see the buyer was

260

impressed. She went up to Liz and looked at the finish of the garment and the stitching.

"That's lovely. Have you anything else you want to show me. Have you a suit."

"Liz, how about the suit you wore in the Guillaime?"

Liz reappeared a few minutes later looking very elegant.

"Thank you my dear. I suggest you get dressed and bring the clothes to my office at the back when you have paid for the new suit."

Liz did all the paperwork and I carried the bag into the buyer's office. The buyer opened the bag and looked at all the clothes, pulling them out one by one and then laying them down in a pile. She and Liz then repacked the case.

"Miss Ward."

"Liz."

"Well then, Liz. Mr Talbert here was quite right. You are a very accomplished designer and also you are very good at making the clothes, not the same thing at all as you well know. However, there are probably quite a few things for you to learn to simplify turning design into production. I know that one firm we buy from is looking for a designer and I will give you the owner's details. Of course we buy from many firms and you have seen all the different labels. Would you like contacts at some of these firms."

"Yes, please. The more names the better really. I know I have a lot to learn but I feel I was well taught when I was growing up. I should have quite a bit of time while I'm over here on this visit to try my luck."

The buyer wrote the information down and we took our leave. Liz was profuse with her thanks. We stopped on the ground floor, Liz bought some gloves and then we caught a cab back to Liz's apartment in Chelsea Cloisters. I was glad to be relieved of all the clothes. In truth I had thought that there were more than was needed but in the event I was very impressed by the way the buyer had looked at them all.

"That seemed to go well, what do you think, Liz?"

"The buyer was very nice. And you were quite right, Peter. Though I knew I could make clothes, I never really believed I could make money out of it."

"Well you haven't yet. You need to make appointments to start visiting all these people. Be very careful they don't try to take advantage of you, particularly the men. Don't agree to anything on the spot. Suggest you should always say 'I'll think about it and call you back.' The good ones will understand and the others you don't need."

I stopped and smiled. "You don't need me to tell you that. Now what I do need to do is to find out when you might be called, so you can plan your appointments. Nothing will happen until after I have given evidence and that won't be until Wednesday at the earliest. I'll try and find out some more and let you know to-night. The next two days are clear anyway.

"About to-night. I'll go round to pick up Mandy. Mike will be round to pick you up at about 7.30. The plan is for you both to walk to the restaurant, it's only about half a mile but you'll need your gloves by the look of the weather. You've probably got time for a few telephone calls."

I kissed Liz good-bye, on the cheek, and went to Mandy's offices to wait. She was getting changed when I arrived and appeared looking like a young lady being taken out to dinner and not an aspiring solicitor with large spectacles. She was wearing quite a long dress and was carrying a warm camel coat and gloves. There had been some snow flurries during the day but, certainly in London, nothing had settled.

"Hello, my darling. You look superb."

"Thank you. You may kiss me."

I obliged and started to do a thorough job.

"That's quite enough, thank you. You are cutting my face to ribbons with your beard and getting me a bad name at the same time."

"Hardly, you must be the only solicitor in the building."

"Well you're wrong actually. Anyway, what sort of a day have you had?"

"I went to John Fairlane and briefed him on the situation."

"Is that all? No wonder you look so relaxed. Why don't you go into the men's room and freshen up?"

"You anticipate my every desire."

"Not if I can help it."

I had a shave with the electric razor I always carried in my brief case and threw some water on my face.

"Now that looks a lot better. Let me test if you've done a good job."

I started to oblige.

"Stop. You've passed the test. We don't both want to be wearing make-up. Let's see if we can find a cab."

I carried my brief case and Mandy's overnight bag downstairs and we went out into Fleet Street and flagged a cab down.

"Peter, I'm puzzled. I thought you had been working in Sydney. How do you explain your sunburn?"

"Well I didn't work all the time. I took the opportunity to sunbathe."

"So I see. Are you telling me, if I was brave enough to look, that your body is tanned as well?

"Not much. I covered it with sun blocking oil."

"How very sensible. How did you manage your back?"

"I didn't. I had to be careful."

Not for the first time I thought Mandy should have been a barrister. I changed the subject as best I could.

"What sort of day did you have, darling?"

"As usual a bit of everything except GE business which I am glad to say my boss is dealing with. When are you going to be performing?"

"Probably Wednesday morning, I'm not sure yet.

"Let me know. I want to be there."

We reached Chez Augustine just as a heavy snow shower descended on us. We rushed inside and checked our coats. Mike and Liz had not arrived. We went to our table and we both had a Kir Royale to celebrate my return. About five minutes later the other two arrived. They both had snow in their hair and Liz was full of excitement since she had not seen snow for many years. She was still wearing her rather ancient raincoat but when she took it off and gave it to Mike to have it checked we could all see that she was wearing a lovely long skirt and a low cut silk blouse which showed her figure and her sun tanned skin off to perfection. I could see Mandy appreciating the situation and framing a few questions for later. I made the introductions. Mike held Liz's chair as she sat down. I signalled for two more Kir Royales.

"This is a super place, Peter. I love French food."

Mandy cut in. "Miss Ward, that's a lovely outfit you are wearing. Did you make it yourself?"

"Please call me Liz. Thank you. Yes I did. The skirt was not too difficult but the blouse seemed to take for ever both in the cutting and the stitching. There was quite a lot of waste."

"Well it was clearly worth the effort. Very eye catching."

Liz grinned. I was not sure I liked the inference in the last remark. Mike rushed in.

"Liz showed me some of the clothes she brought with her. They look fantastic to me."

"Liz, did you have any luck following up any of the contacts the buyer gave you?"

"Yes, Peter, I called three or four of the big firms and have got two appointments for to-morrow."

The Kir Royales arrived and we toasted Liz's future as a dress designer.

"I think you are all being rather too appreciative of my skills and not sufficiently critical. The chances of being accepted as a designer must be very slim. Though I'm coming round to the view that perhaps I should have a go."

We all studied the menu. Liz announced she'd like Beef Wellington but it needed two people. Mike, who was clearly rather taken with Liz, agreed to have Beef Wellington as well. Mandy went for a tournedos and, as usual, I chose grilled sole on the bone. We all decided to have soup as a starter, presumably because it was cold outside. I chose a Pouilly Fumé to start the meal. I let Mike choose the red wine as it was not my speciality, he chose the house Bordeaux.

I was glad to notice that the atmosphere became more relaxed as the wine was consumed. I only had a half glass of white and a half glass of red as I had to drive back to Kingston and, perhaps more importantly, I knew that I would need a clear head to survive the meal.

Mandy started questioning Liz.

"How long have you been out in Australia, Liz?"

"About eight years. I went out on holiday and got various jobs but I've been working with Royal World Airlines for about five years, firstly in their operations office at the airport and now downtown in the ticket office. I like the job, the people, the climate, the sport and the chance of free travel. To be honest, I'm nervous of being offered a tempting job in England, I think I would miss Australia terribly. Have you ever been to Australia, Miss Arrowsmith?"

"Mandy, please. No, but I would like to."

"Get Peter to bring you. I'm sure you will both need a holiday when this Inquiry is over."

"I'm not sure I would want to go with Peter. It might be more fun to go by myself."

"You could be right there. Men can be a bit restrictive."

"Do you have a family over here, Liz?"

"Only a sister, Mandy. Our parents died when we were young and we were brought up by foster parents who died two and three years ago. It was my foster mother who taught me to cut and sew dresses."

"Well she certainly did a good job."

There was a pause as we ate our food and Mandy carried on.

"Do you sail at all? If you don't mind my saying so you look as if you spend every day sailing in Sydney Harbour."

"Not quite, but I do sail a little, not seriously."

"Peter will have to do a lot more sunbathing before he matches your colour, Liz."

I held my breath in case Liz had assumed that I had mentioned the sailing. I need not have worried. Liz was clearly a skilled campaigner.

"Peter tells me that you are an expert sailor, Mandy."

"Well I do a bit at week-ends but by the time I get home during the week it is too dark, too cold and too late to sail in the evenings."

"Well we have the advantage there. I can go sailing or swimming in the evenings during the summer and usually in the winter as well, no trouble at all."

She looked at Mike. "Have you been to Australia?"

"Yes Liz, several times, but all I have ever done is to work and investigate insurance claims. I need someone like you to show me round before I am too old."

"OK. You've got yourself a deal. I'll give you my telephone number and next time you come you can call me."

Mike almost simpered. He had Liz just where she wanted him. Mandy, not to be diverted, resumed her cross examination.

"Where did you take Peter to keep him amused, Liz, when he wasn't working?"

"You've got that the wrong way round, Mandy. After I told Peter about the RWA crews he was kind enough to take me to the restaurant at Guillaume as a thank you. It was so nice of him. That's when he noticed the suit I was wearing." Liz smiled sweetly at me.

Mandy agreed straightaway.

"Yes, he can be nice sometimes when he is saying thank you or when he wants something."

Mandy also smiled sweetly at me. I was not sure I liked their combined benedictions. I hastily plied them both with more wine. Mike, I decided, had had enough if he was seeing Liz back to her flat.

Mandy carried on, innocence herself. I hoped I looked impassive.

"Liz, how did Peter manage to persuade you to come to England?"

"To tell you the truth I didn't want to come. Of course the thought of getting a professional opinion on my clothes was tempting. However, if I have to give evidence I am afraid that the newspapers will get the impression that I am a good time girl, living on the beach. It simply happened that my room mate liked going out and needed a companion on those two nights. Did Peter tell you she was killed in the accident? It's really terrible. I miss her. She was a real friend."

Mandy was stopped for a moment and we carried on with our meal. Liz as the youngster of our party had crème brulée as a dessert. The rest of us went straight to coffee.

"Mike, do you think I will have to give evidence?"

"I don't know Liz. A lot will depend on Peter and whether the Inquiry believes his explanation. I promise I will try to prevent John Fairlane calling you if I can but I think you're right. The papers will try to make the most of the conversation on the recording and look for any parties on the beach."

We did not spend too long when we had finished as we were all working in the morning, even Liz. We put our coats and gloves on. It had stopped snowing but there was some snow on the road. We walked back to Chelsea Cloisters and Mandy and I said goodnight to Liz, Mandy shaking hands and I gave Liz a very light kiss on the cheek. We went to the car, I let Mandy in and walked round, took my coat off, put it into the back seat, and got in.

As we drove back to my house I tried to make light conversation. Mandy was very quiet and uncommunicative. I decided that least said, soonest mended. I parked the car, let Mandy in and then put the car in the garage. Mandy was boiling the kettle, clearly making a cup of tea before going to bed.

"We've both got a busy day in the morning, good night Peter." She headed upstairs with her bag.

"Wait a minute, Mandy. What's got into you? We've just had a nice evening and you are all het up."

"It may have been nice for you Peter but I suspect that you have not debriefed me fully about what went on in Australia on both your visits. Miss Ward is the sort of girl you would fall for in a big way if she fluttered her eyelids at you and everybody in the restaurant could not help noticing that she is, as some of my clients would say, well stacked."

"Liz is a nice girl Mandy. Don't give me a hard time just because you're jealous."

"Jealous? What have I got to be jealous of? That settles it. Good night."

She was off and I went to bed hoping that time would be the great healer but resolved to help time on its way by keeping Liz and Mandy as far apart as possible.

In the morning we went through our normal routine, I took the tea into Mandy's room but this time it seemed to me that Mandy had not pulled the sheet up quite as high as she sometimes did. Perhaps I was reading too much into little clues.

We had a subdued breakfast, I read the business section and she read the main paper. We put our coats and gloves on, it was still very cold, and walked to the station. I carried my brief case but Mandy carried her overnight bag as well as her briefcase. She refused to let me carry it. I clearly had misread the portents. We walked together to Waterloo. I went to Mike's office as it was still a bit early for the Inquiry and Mandy went to her office after offering a small section of her cheek to be kissed.

Mike arrived shortly after I did and we went up to his room. The telephone rang. Mike answered the phone.

"Hello Liz. How are you to-day?"

Liz seemed to be going on a bit.

"Yes he is. Hold on a moment."

Mike passed me the phone.

"Peter, thank you so much for last night. It was lovely. I really enjoyed myself. Mandy is so nice. She is very lucky and so are you."

I managed to restrain myself from all the comments that came flooding into my brain.

"Yes it was nice. Mike obviously got you home."

Mike looked uncomfortable.

"Yes. He took me to the night club by the apartments for a brandy before he left."

"You young things. I don't know how you do it. Liz, good luck to-day. Remember don't say yes straightaway to the first offer of a job. You need to shop around."

"I have no intention of saying yes straightaway to anything. Is Mandy staying with you this evening?"

"None of your business, Miss Ward."

"That means yes. Did I upset her."

"I can't possibly discuss the matter any further."

"You mean Mike is still listening. Well don't answer but if Mandy is in a huff you could come round to see me and discuss the matter, I'm free."

"Let me know how you get on to-day, Liz. Mike and I must go to the Inquiry."

Mike was looking at me and I hoped I did not look as flushed as he did as we went to the Inquiry.

INQUIRY DAY 4

Martin Foster

We went into the Inquiry at 09.45 and I noticed that the seats reserved for the press were filling up. The Inquiry started promptly at 10 o'clock. Lord Justice Thomas made an opening statement and then called for Janet Crowburn to resume questioning Martin Foster. She started by reminding Foster that he was still giving evidence on oath.

"Mr Foster, when you were giving evidence before the Inquiry was adjourned you told us that there was a lot more investigation to be done. Have you come to any conclusions yet?"

"Well we have now analysed all the data in the recorders and all the systems in the aircraft appeared to be working correctly at the time of the crash."

"Have you now analysed the Galileo deviations."

"No Ma'am, the data was not available for some reason nor could we get the output to the auto-pilot and pilots' navigation displays."

"But you have analysed the output of the MLS?"

"No Ma'am. We could not do that because it was not working. As I mentioned before, we were able to analyze the distance outputs of the DME beacon situated on the extended centre line of 27 Right and it was quite clear that the aircraft was too low."

"Well then have you established the position of the approach selector switch?"

"No Ma'am, for some reason the switch position wasn't shown on the instrumentation."

Janet Crowburn looked at her notes.

"We are all aware that the aircraft was too low. What I asked you before was whether it would be easy and a normal thing for the crew to use the DME to check on the aircraft's position relative to the runway and the correct glide slope?"

"It could have been done but it would be very unlikely. However they should have known they were too low."

"Mr Foster how could they know they were below the correct glide slope?"

"It should have been obvious when they looked at their displays even if their Galileo deviations were zero."

"Why Mr Foster? Does not the Primary Flight Display show exactly the same deviation as the autopilot sees."

"Yes it does, but the pilots should have noticed from the Navigation Display that they were too low for the distance out."

"Mr Foster, have you brought the transcripts of the voice recorder?"

"Yes ma'am."

"May I have them, please?"

She gave the transcript to the Clerk of the Court and then produced her own copy.

"Now Mr Foster, last time we met I asked you from the transcript, did the Captain tell the co-pilot to monitor the navigation display and he would be using the Primary Flight Display mode on the approach and you agreed?"

"Yes, ma'am."

"Mr Foster is it true from the transcript that the co-pilot called out the ranges and confirmed the aircraft was on centre line and the heights were consistent with being on the glide slope?"

"Yes ma'am."

"So how can it be possible then to say the pilots might have made a mistake? They checked as best they could and the instruments said that the aircraft was on the glide slope."

"Well the first officer must have been distracted by the hijackers. It is just not possible for the heights which he called out to have been correct."

"Mr Foster I asked you before and I must ask you again, how do you know there was not a fault with the Galileo or with the equipment on the aircraft?"

"We have no evidence that there was anything wrong with the aircraft's equipment or with the Galileo satellite system."

"But you were not able to look at the Galileo deviations on the flight data recorder?"

"No, Ma'am."

"And the pilots could not use the DME distances?"

"Not easily."

"Well what are you going to do now? "

"There is not much more we can do. As I said I believe that the pilots should have noticed that they were too low just as the air traffic controller did."

Janet Crowburn wanted to release Foster for cross examination by the other counsels but Charles McGuire, the software professor, indicated he wanted to ask some questions.

"Mr Foster, would you like to explain to the Inquiry very briefly the way the Galileo functions. I am not clear about the function of the GBAS."

"Yes, Sir. The Galileo receives signals from the Galileo European satellites including the latest runway information and there is software in the Multimode receiver which calculates the vertical deviation of the aircraft from a computed glide slope centre line and horizontal deviation from a computed runway centre line. It can only do this providing there is valid output from the GBAS ensuring that the satellite signals are accurate."

"Now Mr Foster, as you said earlier, it is true to say that the whole safety of the aircraft on the approach depends on the software calculations. The crew can never see the aircraft's true glide slope deviation. They only see the computed deviation that is sent to the auto-pilot. Do you think that's a good idea?"

"That's not for me to say Sir. That is a certification matter."

"But you would agree that the standard of the software is important?"

"Yes, Sir."

"Mr Foster what is the software certification standard in the Multimode receiver?"

"It is Category B."

"Is that high enough for such a vital calculation?"

"I'm not qualified to judge, Sir. The software standard is decided by the certification authorities. In this case EASA."

"Well Mr Foster, let's consider something else. Presumably the Galileo system would only have worked correctly if the position of the runway touch-down point, its direction and height had been entered correctly into the database of the MultiMode receivers?"

"No, Sir. For Category I approaches that is true but for Cat III approaches the runway position is taken from GBAS."

"Well Mr Foster, did you check that the airfield information transmitted by GBAS for 27 Left was correct?"

"Yes Sir."

"When did you check the information? Immediately after the accident?"

"It was checked soon after."

"Mr Foster, how soon after?"

"I will need to consult our records."

"How frequently is the GBAS data updated?"

"Whenever the runway direction is changed or when there is change in the runway information."

"If the data being transmitted was wrong would there have been a warning?"

"No, but there is an approved system for entering the runway information so that a mistake would be most unlikely."

"But the runway information could be wrong?"

"There are very careful checks to prevent that happening."

McGuire shrugged his shoulders, clearly not satisfied. Janet Crowburn indicated that the witness could be cross-examined. John Fairlane got to his feet.

"Are the transcripts of the four recordings you have given the Court complete? Have you edited the transcripts?"

"Yes Sir, they are complete and we have not edited the transcripts."

"Wouldn't you have expected to hear the hijackers?"

"Yes Sir, but the flight deck area microphone was not decipherable."

"Mr Foster, would you agree that if the hijackers had been talking to the pilots while they were making the approach in Category IIIC conditions it would have been very difficult for them to concentrate fully?"

"Yes, Sir."

"Don't you think it must have been very disturbing for Captain Hodgson to have to fly the aircraft and react to the hijacker?"

"Yes Sir, but the auto-pilot was flying the aircraft."

"But surely your point is that the pilots should have been monitoring the performance of the aircraft, whether it was on the glide slope, checking the aircraft's height against the distance from the airport?"

"The hijacking wouldn't have made any difference."

"That's your opinion?"

"Yes Sir."

"Mr Foster, have you ever done a real Category IIIC landing in a modern jet aircraft?"

"No Sir."

"Mr Foster, have you ever been hijacked and been responsible for 500 passengers."

"No Sir."

"In that case Mr Foster, the Inquiry will be able to judge how much importance should be attached to your opinions about the effect of hijacking when doing a Category IIIC approach and whether it would make the pilots make a mistake."

He paused. "Mr Foster, is it possible that the GBAS runway information could have been changed after the accident but before your checks were carried out?"

"I will need to consult our records, Sir. However the monitoring did not raise an alarm."

"Is that good enough? Shouldn't there have been a flight check? The alarm did not go off but the Tower controller could see the aircraft going low. I put it to you Mr Foster that you did not have the GBAS checked immediately because you felt there was no urgency as you had already become convinced the pilots had made a mistake.

"No Sir. The GBAS was checked. I need to find out the exact time when it was done."

John Fairlane looked at his notes. "You said that you have not been able to make the instrumentation work for the Galileo computed deviations but there was nothing wrong with the equipment?"

"That's probably a coincidence."

"Don't you think it a rather remarkable coincidence that the glide slope warning system in air traffic did not go off, that there was no Galileo deviations on the recorder and that all the indications on the flight deck were correct? Clearly there must have been a fault with the system you have not discovered."

"I don't believe so, Sir."

"Mr Foster, do you think you have done everything you reasonably could have done to look for possible avionic malfunctions?"

"Yes Sir."

John looked at his notes.

"Well then, Mr Foster, would you explain to us what investigations you or your team carried out in Sydney to find out the serviceability of the aircraft before departure?"

"We asked NWIA what work had been carried out overnight after the aircraft had landed at 8 o'clock the previous evening. As I have explained NWIA changed a Multimode receiver and the captain's Navigation Display."

"Was any other non-routine maintenance work carried out?"

"Not according to NWIA."

"Did you send anyone out to NWIA to check?"

"No Sir."

"Would you be surprised to learn that the Global Positioning System receiver box had been changed overnight?"

"Very. There was no entry in the technical log."

"Did you speak to the foreman of the night shift?"

"No Sir."

"I have a witness, a Mr Peter Talbert, who will show that some significant maintenance was carried out that night which was not entered in the log."

"I find that very hard to believe, Sir, without seeing some paperwork. Anyway the GPS is irrelevant to this accident."

"Oh Mr Foster, I promise you will see some paperwork. The witness seems to have done all the investigation that should have been done by your team. As to whether the GPS is relevant or not, it might be said that you and your team seem to be taking the easy option of saying 'pilot error' without being able to hear the effect of hijacking and without checking whether the total Galileo system was working correctly."

Foster was beginning to look uncomfortable, probably wondering what was coming next.

"Now then about this party and the voice recorder transcript which was reported in the Telegraph. Mr Foster, do you know how the Daily Telegraph got hold of the transcript?"

"No Sir."

"Are you sure?"

"Yes, Sir."

"Let me remind you that you are under oath. Do you know how the Daily Telegraph got hold of the transcript?"

"No sir."

"Was the transcript that appeared in the Daily Telegraph accurate?"

"I didn't check."

"Mr Foster, are you saying you didn't read the reports in the Telegraph?"

"I just glanced at them."

"Well then Mr Foster, what were the exact words on the voice recorder?"

"I can't remember."

"Then let me refresh your memory from the transcript."

Crowburn read out the relevant part of transcript.

Harry	*"Charles, did you speak with Eva. Was she awake?"*
Charles	*"You bet. She was fine."*
Harry	*"She's a lovely girl. Bursting with energy. Time you settled down."*
Charles	*"We'll see. That was a great evening we had at Maroubra with those two. I like that beach, and Caesars."*
Harry	*"Yes, I could see that. We certainly got through the wine. Well you and the girls did."*
Charles	*"I enjoyed the swim as well"*
Harry	*"Just as well it was warm or you both would have frozen."*
Charles	*"You're a fine one to talk. I'm afraid I didn't get a lot of sleep. Did you have a good time, Harry?"*
Harry	*"Very quiet, thank you."*
Charles	*"That's what they all say."*
Harry	*"Still we got back just in time."*
Harry	*"Are you OK, Dick?"*

"Now then Mr Foster what did you infer from that?"

"The pilots had been out on a party with two girls the night before."

"I see. If you thought the party would affect the crew's performance why did you not check what actually happened?"

"Well sir. It is obvious what happened. It should not have mattered too much as far as the landing was concerned since the crew had the opportunity to rest during the flight. However it must have broken the airline rules."

"In that case don't you think you should have investigated the situation more closely?"

Foster clearly knew he was going to be in some difficulty.

"I suggest to you Mr Foster that having found no obvious reason for the crash you started to blame the pilots and this last minute party supported your view. However you did not investigate what actually happened at all. Mr Foster, I believe that you have been rather slack in the whole of this investigation and your view that the pilots were to blame cannot be relied on."

"That is not so Sir."

"Well Mr Foster, we shall be telling the Inquiry in due course what we believe really happened. The Inquiry can then make its mind up how good a job you did."

Foster's initial air of composure was now gone as John Fairlane sat down having finished his cross-examination but his ordeal wasn't over yet. The counsels for RWA and the British Airline Pilots Association also cross-examined Foster and he blustered his way through trying to make the case for pilot error on the approach. The last counsel re-examining Foster was Hull Claims insurance who understandably tried to encourage Foster to rebuild his credibility since Hull Claims had no desire to pay for the whole loss and the claims from the dependants of those killed in the accident. However, Foster was not much help to Hull Claims. He left the witness stand looking rather worried.

There was a fifteen minute recess and then Crowburn called an AAIB electronics expert who spoke about the instrumentation and when cross-examined by Fairlane agreed that it was surprising that the Galileo instrumentation on the recorder did not work but had no ideas why not.

More witnesses gave evidence of the crews licensing and recent flight checks. Lord Justice Thomas decided that it was a good time to break for lunch. Mike and I went to a local pub we knew. Jim Akers had obviously been following us because he arrived about fifteen seconds later. He started questioning me.

"Peter, what do you make of all that. Crowburn and Fairlane have lowered Foster's credibility. However it is clear that AAIB will be saying that in some way the pilots are to blame for the accident."

For once I decided to keep my mouth shut. All Jim wanted was a story and for all I knew I might be on the witness stand myself later in the afternoon. I just nodded my head. I needed to be careful. We ate our sandwiches without discussing the case too much and returned to the Inquiry. To my surprise I suddenly saw Roger O'Kane being sworn in to give evidence. The Inquiry had clearly decided that it was necessary for them to understand how the automatic landing system worked and how all the flow of information took place. Roger gave a very good account of the system and explained how Royal World Airlines could select either ILS, MLS or Galileo. I noticed that he did not explain how the other 798s were arranged, nor was he asked. I sent a note to John Fairlane suggesting that he did not expose the differences between the aircraft until I got on the stand.

Roger's evidence took a long time as it was very complicated to anybody new to the various concepts. Only McGuire and to a lesser extent Templeman seemed to understand fully. But of course that was why they were there. The Inquiry adjourned when Roger had finished.

CHAPTER 19

The Robbery

I went up to Roger as we filed out of the Inquiry.

"Sorry I did not let you know I was coming, Peter. It all happened rather suddenly, I only got in this morning. I understand you're giving evidence to-morrow?"

"Yes, Roger. I'm rather nervous. I hope I do as well as you. What are you doing this evening?"

"Nothing much. Got any ideas?"

"Why don't we go for a meal somewhere? Mike, care to join us?" I introduced them to one another.

"Sure. Where shall we go."

"Let's go to Langans in Stratton Street. It's not too elaborate or expensive and reasonably quick. Let me check. Mike have you got your phone with you?"

I made the reservation and we agreed to meet Roger at 7.45. Mike and I went back to his office. We picked up an Evening Standard on the way. 'INVESTIGATOR CRITICISED BY INQUIRY' blared the headline. I noticed that it mentioned that Foster had been asked twice whether he knew how Osborne had got hold of the transcript. We agreed that Martin Foster had not had a very comfortable ride.

Mike turned to me. "Peter, what are you going to say to-morrow? I know Foster has been discredited but things don't look cast iron for us by a long chalk."

I didn't answer the question as an idea had occurred to me after thinking of Roger's evidence.

"Mike, can I use a computer? I need to send a message to Matt."

"He'll be asleep now."

"I know but I'll back it up with a text message."

I went to the machine Mike pointed at and sent Matt an email and texted him to check his email as soon as he could. Listening to Roger's evidence I had an explanation for what must have happened.

"Did you send the message OK, Peter"

"Yes. I've had an idea. The problem with this accident is that nobody wants to say what they actually did." I thought a moment. "If the worst comes to the worst and I'm wrong I do have some ideas to help denigrate the 'pilot error' even more and, of course, I've got some paperwork to prove the GPS change, but I'm not sure that will be good enough."

I broke away and called Liz.

"How did you get on to-day?"

"I got offered two jobs, quite well paid actually. I am seeing another firm and the small specialist firm to-morrow. Any news about my being a witness?"

"Not yet. To-morrow is the critical day. I'll call you this time to-morrow."

"Are you coming round this evening?"

"Not to-night I'm afraid Liz. I'm with Mike getting ready for my evidence to-morrow."

"That's a shame. I was looking forward to seeing you."

"Sorry, Liz. When are you seeing your sister?"

"This week-end. I'm travelling Friday night, back Sunday."

"Well call me if you need me. Otherwise I'll call you to-morrow."

I could see Mike had been listening to our conversation but he said nothing. We reviewed the plan for the next day and felt that we were as well prepared as we could be. I called Mandy but she wasn't at home. I told her answer phone when I would be giving evidence and that hopefully I would see her at the Inquiry. Mike and I left for Langans.

We arrived before Roger and ordered ourselves some drinks. Roger arrived about ten minutes later. He looked at me.

"Do you think you have an explanation, Peter?"

"Not sure exactly. However, listening to you I think I may know what might have happened. I'm waiting to hear from NWIA, hopefully to-morrow morning, our time. If I draw a blank, there is not much to go on except hijacker interference and the GPS being faulty. Whatever the primary cause of the accident, it looks as if it could have been avoided if only the pilots could have seen where they were relative to the correct glide slope. On any 798, whether you select ILS, MLS, Galileo or GPS the pilot can only see the same signals that are going into the auto-pilot. I'm not sure that's a very sound design, if I may say so, Roger."

"Well Peter, I understand what you're saying but it would be extremely difficult to do what you are in effect asking for, that is an entirely independent monitor by the pilots of the aircraft's position on the approach. Anyway, it's not a requirement. The ILS/MLS indicator is shown as a stand-by as you know."

"Well that's not much use when, as in this case, the MLS was not working. My guess is that a Category IIIC satellite approach woukd only be made if there wasn't an ILS or MLS. So it seems to me there should be an independent form of monitoring available for satellite Cat III approaches, certainly for the jumbos with so many people on board."

Roger decided to ignore my remark.

"The Independant solution which we adopted was to make absolutely sure that our system was immaculate and, after looking at it very carefully, the FAA and the EASA accepted our submissions. You remember Peter, I sent you a copy of our extra report on the subject which we wrote specifically for EASA after that new certification engineer said she was unhappy with the system."

"Yes I did get the report but remember I wasn't convinced. However you look at it, something seems to have gone wrong. Perhaps you'll have to look at the system again. Anyway, my immediate problem is to convince the Inquiry that it was not pilot error despite what the AAIB may say and that the Inquiry will have to look for another solution. The professor just loves the software in the Multimode receiver so he won't take much convincing."

"Yes he seems to. It's probably not relevant but I guess the software categorisation agreed by EASA is going to get some stick."

"You could be right, Roger."

"You know Peter, Foster may have a point. Accepting that the glide slope deviation was central, the displays should have been showing them as being too low for the distance. Surely they should have spotted something was wrong?"

"Well Harry didn't have a full time display but the first officer's distance and height checks sounded quite normal. Harry checked the deviation was central as Charles called out the ranges. Anyway to ensure that the display matches the approach aid when Galileo or GPS is being used you people make the display agree with the navigation from the approach aid. How would he know something was wrong?"

We gave up and stopped discussing the accident and went on to other things. We broke up at about 11.15 and I walked home from the station. I saw blue police lights flashing as I got close to the house and realised to my horror that it was at my house. I went up to one of the policemen who was talking to John Marchant, my neighbour. John introduced me. The policeman took me to the other policeman who seemed to be in charge.

"Central station phoned us about 45 minutes ago. We came straight round. Your front dining room window seems to have been the only entry point. Your next door neighbour here was down as a keyholder so we got him to let us in and cancel the alarm. We've had a look in but nothing much seems to have been touched. Would you like to have a quick look round?"

I went in and looked round the front room. The TV recorder and my silver tray were missing. I wandered into my study. All the papers in my vertical trays seemed to have gone. Nothing else seemed to have been touched. I called out to the police officer.

I explained what was missing to the policemen.

"Just a straightforward hit and run, Sir. Happens all the time. I guess the burglar could only have been in your house about one minute. He was lucky the neighbours did not catch him though nowadays people are afraid to interfere in case they are knifed or taken to court by the burglar. It's a strange world."

"Sergeant, have you taken any fingerprints?"

"No, Sir."

"Well I think you should. I know the evidence suggests robbery but I've just realised it may not be as simple as that. I am due to give evidence at a big aircraft accident Inquiry to-morrow and all my key papers have been stolen. I think I know a possible suspect so if there are any prints I could suggest a name."

"We don't normally bother too much for this sort of robbery, Sir. It would cost an awful lot of time and money if we took prints every time we had a case like this."

"Well Sergeant I don't want to be difficult but if you don't take prints I shall make a complaint, because this case to-morrow is very important. Perhaps you remember the accident, an aircraft landing in fog just after the Christmas holidays. Hundreds of people killed and injured."

"Of course I remember the accident. We were called in to help control the traffic. I read about the Inquiry this evening in the Standard. The accident investigator got rather a hard time didn't he? Alright Sir, let me call my Inspector and get permission."

He wandered outside and took out his phone. He was back in two minutes.

"Yes, Sir. That's fine, we'll have the fingerprints man round in half an hour. I'll leave you now if I may. There's not much more I can do. I'm on duty all night. If there are prints I'll let you know and you had better tell me who you suspect. Meanwhile try not to touch anything." He added as an afterthought "I think we've found your TV recorder outside on the grass with your silver tray. You may be right about robbery not being the prime motive, Sir. Perhaps you had better give me the names of the people you think might have broken in."

I gave him the only two names that I knew who could have leaked the information to Osborne, Martin Foster and Robin Turnsmith but there could have been quite a few more. I explained the background as briefly as I could and told him to contact me through Mike to-morrow if necessary or ring the Inquiry Hall.

The finger print man duly arrived. He took my prints and then he went into the dining room and living room.

"I've found some good prints in your study. I also found some prints on the window catch where the burglar broke in; he must have closed the window once he was inside. Your cleaner must do a good job as there are very few prints elsewhere. I'll be on my way."

The fingerprint man left me and I found a large piece of cardboard in the garage which I cut and fitted to the broken window.

Blind Landing

Whoever had taken the papers had been incredibly lucky to be able to get them and even luckier because I had no immediate copies. It was entirely my own fault which always made matters worse. I supposed I could get some replacements but it would take time since most of the papers would have to come from Australia. It occurred to me that I could get some from Anne Moncrieff. But the whole thing made me look so inefficient. There was nothing else for it, I called Matt in Australia and was lucky enough to catch him. I explained my predicament.

"Well I'll try to fax you and send you copies of the technical logs for the two nights in question in the next day or so. I am just going into a meeting with my MD and I am going to run out of time. I will also send you copies of the stores issuing certificates for the two GPS sets, the Navigation Display and the Multi Mode Receiver. I got your email yesterday and I shall be talking to Lance but goodness knows when. If anything comes out of it I will contact you."

"Matt, I really need all the paperwork for the Inquiry but I need you to talk to Lance very urgently. It's terribly important. Can you email the info as well? And text me."

"I'll do what I can."

Feeling very depressed I got to bed at about 1.30 and managed to sleep until 6.30. I called Mandy who I knew would be getting up.

"Hello Mandy. I'm in trouble."

For once Mandy didn't make the obvious retort. She must have sensed I was really in difficulty.

"What's happened, darling."

"I was robbed last night. I think it must be Foster. The only things that have gone are all the papers on my desk which I need for to-day."

Mandy was super. She didn't say 'I told you so.' She was straight to the point.

"You're right. Sounds like Martin Foster though surely he did not believe he would really gain anything. Poor chap, if it is him he must be desperate."

"That's what I told the sergeant. They found some prints. What am I going to do?"

"You are going to get dressed as quickly as you can and meet me for breakfast at that café opposite the Inquiry hall. Don't worry darling. I may be able to help you."

***

It was all very well for Mandy to tell me not to worry but I was panic stricken. Before leaving I copied down the number of my local odd job man so I could get the glass repaired as quickly as possible. I didn't think he would thank me if I called him at 6.45. I took my briefcase with me but I was woefully short of papers.

I got to the cafe at 8.30 a.m. and found Mandy already there reading the paper with a coffee in front of her, looking very smart, relaxed and without a care in the world.

"I don't believe it. How long have you been here? I can't believe you could have been so quick. You look magnificent."

She looked pleased.

"Well I managed to save time getting ready at home by not having breakfast. I was able to catch the earlier train. Have you read the papers?"

"Not properly. To be honest I'm too worried about losing the papers I need for the Inquiry. I did notice they seem to have given Foster a hard time. The Secretary of State will have to make some changes at the AAIB I should think when all this is over."

"Well settle down. You've got a long day ahead of you and you must have something to eat."

She beckoned the waiter over and we both ordered orange juice, scrambled egg, toast, marmalade and coffee, not that I felt like anything to eat. While we were waiting she opened her brief case and gave me a large envelope. I opened it and saw all the papers that had been stolen. I was speechless.

"You are a miracle worker. How did you get these? Did you steal them?"

"Peter, don't be stupid. You must be worried. Look again."

I did and noticed that the papers Mandy had given to me were copies, not the rather creased documents that had been in my tray on the desk.

"How did you get these copies, Mandy?"

"All very simple, my dear. When I went round to your house to collect my dress I decided the time had come to make copies of your papers which you seemed to like spreading, like confetti, all over your study. You know I didn't like the way you kept them in that stacked set of baskets on your desk. I took the papers to that place on the corner near the station, made two sets of copies, put one back in your tray, put the other set in my bag and then put the originals in our office safe."

She looked very smug.

"I could kiss you."

"Well you'll have to wait a moment while I conduct an investigation. Where were you last night? I called, ready perhaps to offer you a hope that sometime I might be ready to forgive you and you were out. I tried your mobile but there was no reply. I don't have to tell you where I thought you might be. I rang Mike to get Liz's number but he wasn't in the office or at home."

It was my turn to look smug.

"Serve you right. We wouldn't have answered anyway. We were having an orgy" Mandy started to rise. "All three of us. We went to Langans. Roger O'Kane the Independant man who had just given evidence, Mike and I. If you'd called me later you could have spoken to the policeman investigating the robbery and my next door neighbour as well as me."

"Alright then, you may kiss me."

I did as instructed.

"Do you think I should have the originals?"

"I'm having them sent over this morning."

"You seem to have thought of everything."

Mandy beamed. Our breakfast arrived and we glanced at the papers again.

"I see you're giving evidence to-day according to the FT."

"Trust Jim to get a plug in as well as a good story."

"Yes, that's what he is good at. Just as well he doesn't know about my robbery." I thought for a moment, "You know I almost feel sorry for Foster. He must have some real problem if it was him."

"Well, I suppose we'd better be getting over the road. At least we don't have to queue for seats. Look at that line over there. It must be more popular than that latest Lloyd Webber musical."

"That's only because the seats are free."

After we crossed the road Mandy stopped.

"Peter. I am sorry I'm being so touchy. I love being with you and everything. But I am nervous about the Diana situation. It could ruin our lives and, as for Liz," she smiled up at me and gave me an apologetic kiss. "I'm suspicious as hell and probably jealous."

Peter Talbert

Mandy and I signed in to the Inquiry and then separated after agreeing to meet outside for lunch. The press were there in force and as Chuck Osborne went by I pitched in to him.

"You know Chuck you have almost certainly ruined a man's career tempting him with money."

Chuck flushed.

"You've got that completely wrong. He was desperate to get some cash. It was his suggestion"

I turned away, my suspicions confirmed.

Spot on time my name was called. It was quite a sight, very different from the previous days. Every seat was taken and the press benches seemed overflowing. I went to the witness box and was sworn in. John Fairlane got to his feet. Everyone was looking our way.

John got me to explain to the Inquiry my background, my electronic engineering degree, my years as a pilot with Britannia. He got me to relate my subsequent specialisation on the interface between the flight crew and the modern computer controlled flight deck, with all the very sophisticated electronic displays integrating the enormous amount of information that the pilot had to assimilate.

"Mr Talbert you are an expert in your field? You are on the Society of Automotive Engineers S7 Flight Deck Committee?"

"In that very narrow area of expertise I suppose I am well known in the industry."

"Come on, Mr Talbert. Airlines round the world pay you to help with crew training. You are respected as an expert."

"If you say so."

John got me to explain how I got involved with Alfa Juliet. The call from John Chester, the call from an old friend whose husband was fatally injured, the call from Mike Mansell asking me to help establish the cause of the accident.

"Mr Talbert, I think you need to make your position absolutely plain. Mr Mansell asked you to help because his firm was at risk financially if the cause of the accident was found to be pilot error. What did you say to him?"

"I told him that I would be pleased to help with the investigation but I was only interested in finding out the truth, pilot error or no pilot error. However, I felt that the hijacking had almost certainly been the most likely cause of the accident either directly, or indirectly by having caused the pilots to make a mistake."

"Mr Talbert. You've heard the voice recordings and have read the transcript? Have you any comments?"

"Yes Sir. I believe that AAIB have written down what was on the three recording that they have. However, I wonder whether all four recordings have been tampered with by adding a low frequency noise and in particular the fourth recording of the flight deck area has been made completely unintelligible by the volume of the noise, presumably for security purposes so the hijackers could not be heard, and, of course, this has made it very difficult to assess the real cause of the accident."

There was complete silence and then a buzz went round the room. I looked at Lord Justice Thomas. If it was possible for a Judge to look uncertain, then he looked uncertain. It occurred to me that John must have been a bit surprised but he was the supreme professional.

"Mr Talbert, have you thought through what you are saying? This is a very serious allegation."

"Certainly, Sir."

"Why do you make this allegation?"

"Well Sir, I noticed that the Prime Minister in his original broadcast on the morning after the tragedy referred to two passengers being killed. None of that information was on the AAIB transcript. Then another thing I noticed was that the Secretary of State also referred to 'two hijackers being on the flight deck'. The Government clearly knew more than the AAIB."

"Mr Talbert, all this seems a rather wild accusation. What do you suggest happened?"

"Well Sir, as you know the crash recorder with all the flight parameters was found very quickly but I was surprised that the cockpit voice recorder took so long to be found so..."

That was as far as I got. Lord Justice Thomas ask Fairlane to stop questioning and then spoke to the Clerk of the Court who immediately announced that the Inquiry was adjourned for an hour. The room was to be cleared. Fairlane was told to meet the judge in his chambers. I was told to wait. The place was in an uproar and in the confusion I went over to Mike.

Mandy came over with a worried look. "Peter, you've really done it this time. You are the complete limit. You'll be sent to the Tower. I can't believe what you're implying actually happened. The Government couldn't have been that stupid."

"Well, the security people had plenty of time to hear the recording and to doctor it and remember, it was the security people who 'found' the voice recorder the following night." I pondered for a moment. "You know it has been said that Governments seem to have a sublime belief in their own infallibility. I suppose they feel that what they do must be right by definition and, anyway, they believe that maintaining security gives them complete cover to do anything they like."

John Fairlane came over.

"I shall be disbarred. Thomas said I should have warned him."

"What did you say?"

"'How could I, my Lord? I had no idea what he was going to say.'"

"Did he believe you?"

"I'm not sure. You've put him in a real fix."

"Why?"

"My guess is that he was given a full copy of the microphone area transcript but he was told not to use it because of the security implications, unless he felt that AAIB really needed the recording to get the right solution. Now he's caught with egg on his face."

Mike could not contain himself.

"He's got egg on his face? Think about the Government."

All of a sudden the Inquiry was reconvened and everybody trooped back. The press seats were full to bursting. Lord Justice Thomas made a statement.

"The Inquiry has just received a transcript which purports to be a record of the flight deck area recording. The Inquiry will go into private session to establish the authenticity of this transcript and to establish why it was not available to the AAIB. However to try to save time, the AAIB and expert witnesses will be able to read the new transcript. Will Counsel please advise the Clerk of the Court if they believe they have witnesses that need to read the full transcript."

CHAPTER 20

The Hijackers

We waited outside the Inquiry hall and it took two and a half hours before the private proceedings to read the transcript started; presumably copies had to be made and Lord Justice Thomas must have been considering how he was going to explain the arrival of the new transcript. There were just a few of us present, Furness, Foster, myself, Roger O'Kane and John Chester plus our respective counsels. John Fairlane was there to make a submission

"Mr Talbert advises me that if the Inquiry is going to get a true appreciation of the pressures which the crew were under it is necessary to actually hear the recording and not read the transcript."

The judge turned to Janet Crowburn.

"I agree with Mr Talbert, my Lord."

"Very well. I had rather anticipated this request. I understand that if you are prepared to listen from a loudpseaker rather than headphones we can start in a few minutes. I am told that the recording is like the earlier recording that AAIB produced, it skips the parts where there is no talking. If you want to hear the full four hour recording then I suggest we adjourn until after lunch and go to the Treasury Solicitors Offices where they can arrange a room with the necessary number of headphones for the experts."

Fairlane looked to me and I suggested to John that we heard the abbreviated recording now and then decide what to do. Lord Justice Thomas agreed, Fairlane together with the other counsels left and we settled down to hear the recording. The low pitched noise had completely disappeared and there was now a steady whine behind all the conversation which gave no doubt as to the realism of the recording. The quality was very clear and as before it started with the exchange between Harry and Charles talking about Eva.

Air Traffic came in with a call for RWA 573 which Charles answered. There was no further reference to the girls. We then heard a cabin attendant requesting admittance to the flight deck followed by the noise of the crew door being operated. Then there was a thump followed by a new menacing middle eastern voice being heard.

Ahmed   *"Captain, if you want to keep alive you will do exactly as I say. I have a special small pistol here and I will not hesitate to use it if you do not do exactly as I say. My colleague over there has his pistol next to the neck of the other pilot. We have two more people at the back of the flight deck here with your spare pilots and the Minister. We also have two*

286

more people preventing access from the rest of the aircraft.
We have shut the door so no-one can now get in.
"You will announce to the passengers that the aircraft has
been hijacked but that we are going to land as planned at
Heathrow. No-one will be hurt if everyone carries on
normally."

Harry	*"What is your name, Sir?"*
Ahmed	*"What does that matter?"*
Harry	*"It will be easier for me to talk to you if I know how you* *wish to be addressed."*
Ahmed	*"Call me Ahmed. Get on with the announcement, Captain."*

We could just hear Harry make the announcement talking into his
microphone.

Ahmed	*"Now Captain, you are to tell Air Traffic that the aircraft* *has been taken over and that, after landing, you are to stop* *on the runway and be refuelled for Karachi. Wait, Captain.* *You will say that if the aircraft is not allowed to proceed* *after landing at Heathrow then passengers will be killed* *starting with the Foreign Secretary. If there is any delay* *greater than thirty minutes the aircraft will be blown up."*
Harry	*"Ahmed, we are out of range of London Air Traffic. I will* *have to call our airline operations."*
Ahmed	*"Very well, Captain. You may do that."*

We heard Harry passing this information to RWA Operations.

Ahmed	*"Captain, you will call them now and ask them to arrange* *not only refuelling to Karachi but the necessary turn* *around facilities. No-one is to come on board the aircraft* *unless I have authorized it. In addition here is a message* *you are to read out and which they must repeat back to* *you, word for word."*
Aircraft	*"RWA Ops, this is 573."*
RWA	*"Go ahead, 573."*
Aircraft	*"As you are aware we have been hijacked. Please arrange* *for the aircraft to be turned around and refuelled for* *Karachi. No-one is to come on board the aircraft unless* *authorized. Assume the same passenger and freight load* *as we have inbound. I am to advise you that if the aircraft* *is not allowed to take-off after landing at Heathrow then* *passengers will be killed starting with the Foreign*

	Secretary of State. If there is any delay greater than thirty minutes the aircraft will be blown up."
RWA	*"Copied 573"*
Aircraft	*"I have been told to read out the following message. Please copy it down and read it back, word for word."*
RWA	*"Go ahead, 573"*
Aircraft	*"Operations from 573, the hijackers have asked me to read the following message to be given to the Prime Minister. 'When the aircraft lands the following six prisoners are to be taken from prison and brought to the aircraft."* The list of the six al-Qaeda terrorists followed. *"The prisoners will be loaded onto the aircraft at the front Upper Deck entrance, the aircraft will be refuelled and then the aircraft will take-off for Karachi. Any delay greater than thirty minutes will result in first, the killing of the Foreign Secretary, and then the blowing up of the aircraft."*

We heard RWA Operations reading the message back but there was no respite for Harry.

Ahmed	*"Captain, tell them to let you know when the fuel is ready. Also when the prisoners will be at the aircraft."*
Harry	*"Operations, please advise when refuelling is ready. The hijackers wish to know. Also when the prisoners will be at the aircraft"*
RWA	*"573, will advise."*
Harry	*"Ahmed. We have hundreds of people on this plane. They know we've been hijacked. I must reassure them if they are not to panic. The cabin staff must look after them. I need to talk to my chief steward before I talk to the passengers."*
Ahmed	*"Captain, is this a trick?"*
Harry	*"Ahmed. I am in no position to trick you. I want to give instructions to prevent the passengers getting out of control. May I ask for the Chief Steward to come here?"*
Ahmed	*"Very well."*
Harry	*"Would the Chief Steward come to the flight deck."*
Andrew	*"Captain Hodgson?"*
Harry	*"Andrew, you are aware we've been hijacked?"*
Andrew	*"Yes Captain. There appear to be two dead men in the front upper cabin who may have been the security guards for the Secretary of State. I think they've been shot in the*

head but the bullet wounds are very peculiar."

Harry
"Don't touch the bodies but cover them with blankets. Can you move the passengers that are next to them?"

Andrew
"Luckily they were on the front row with the Foreign Secretary who is now in the flight deck rest area. The rest of the passengers are in the rows behind."

Harry
"Good. I want you to carry on the rest of the flight with your cabin staff as normally as possible. I shall make an announcement on the PA."

Andrew
"Very good, Captain."

Harry
"Ladies and Gentleman. This is Captain Hodgson speaking. As I announced earlier, I regret to inform you that we have been hijacked. We shall refuel and then fly to Karachi. We do not know whether anyone will be allowed to disembark in London.

"Please obey the instructions from our cabin staff and we will try to make the rest of the flight as normal as possible. I will keep you informed at all times. Thank you."

Charles
"Harry, shall I get the latest weather?"

Harry
"Go ahead."

There was a pause. They must have switched the speakers off as we could not hear the weather being transmitted by the ATIS, the transmissions were going straight into the headphones.

Charles
"Harry, that's real Category IIIC weather. Manchester is clear anyway if we need to divert."

Ahmed
"Captain, why can't I hear the ground talking to us?"

Harry
"Ahmed we are not allowed to use loudspeakers when landing."

Ahmed
"Captain, turn them back on immediately or I will fire."

That seemed rather an idle threat to me but clearly Harry hadn't argued as we could hear Operations.

RWA
"573 from Operations, we've checked your fuel from your ACARS transmission and you are cleared to overfly Frankfurt and land at Heathrow with Manchester as your diversion."

Aircraft
"573 copied."

Ahmed
"Captain."

Blind Landing

Harry	*"Yes Ahmed."*
Ahmed	*"Is the weather alright for landing in London?"*
Harry	*"Yes Ahmed. The weather is foggy but we carry blind landing equipment."*
Ahmed	*"Is that safe?"*
Harry	*"Completely."*
Ahmed	*"Is the fuel ready?"*
Aircraft	*"Operations, this is 573. Have you arranged the refuelling?"*
RWA	*"We're still doing that. You are being refuelled by tankers instead of by hydrants on the stands and we are making sure that they have enough fuel for Karachi and that they can get to your parking position on the runway."*
Aircraft	*"573 understood."*
Ahmed	*"Captain, what are they doing?"*
Harry	*"Ahmed, they have to refuel the aircraft from tankers if we are to remain on the runway."*
Ahmed	*"Captain, are the prisoners ready at the airport?"*
Aircraft	*"RWA Ops This is 573. I have been asked to establish whether the prisoners have been released and are waiting at the airport?"*
RWA	*"573 please stand by. Will advise."*
Ahmed	*"Captain, remind the ground that we shall blow the aircraft up if there are any delays to our instructions."*
Aircraft	*"RWA Ops I have been told to remind you that the hijackers are going to blow up the aircraft if there is any delay to their instructions which I passed to you."*
RWA	*"573 This is RWA Ops. We have been advised that the prisoners are at Birmingham and in view of the fog it will take probably four hours before they are at the airport."*

There was no reply but I couldn't help wondering how Ahmed reacted to the news. The aircraft would have landed long before the prisoners could have arrived but of course there was probably no intention of handing over the prisoners anyway.

The flight proceeded with very little other conversation. The aircraft crossed into UK airspace and was cleared to descend. Charles called out the descent checks and then the checks for an auto-landing. Air Traffic slowly permitted the aircraft to reduce altitude in stages. Then we heard the weather being broadcast on the VOR. Ceiling indeterminate, visibility 30 metres.

Aircraft	*"Approach RWA 573 reaching 4,000."*
Approach	*"Roger Cleared procedural Galileo final approach 27 left"*
Aircraft	*"RWA 573 we'd prefer the MLS"*
Approach	*"Sorry RWA 573 the ATIS is incorrect. The MLS is no longer approved for Category III approaches and is out of service. What are your intentions?"*
Harry	*"Charles, did you know about the MLS?"*
Charles	*"Yes Harry. This means we won't be able to monitor the approach path on Galileo."*
Harry	*"Well that is not a requirement. The Galileo is self-monitored to death."* A pause. *"Charles, you had better set 27L into the MMRs for the Galileo."*
Charles	*"Yes Harry, have just done that."*
Harry	*"OK. Then you can select the Galileo system for the approach."*
Charles	*"Yes Harry, all done."*
Aircraft	*"RWA 573 Request Galileo approach 27 Left."*
Approach	*"You are cleared for Galileo approach and to descend on the procedure. Maintain heading and call the Tower on 118.5"*
Aircraft	*"118.5 RWA 573"*

Harry was obviously slightly concerned and spoke to Charles again.

Harry	*"Charles that is permitted, isn't it?"*
Charles	*"Yes Harry providing the GBAS is OK."*
Harry	*"We've got no warning so it must be OK."*

We heard the landing checks being carried out and then they were cleared to the final approach altitude. Harry told Charles to keep an eye on the Navigation Display as he needed to keep his display showing the Primary Flight Display most of the time.

Aircraft	*"Tower RWA 573 ten miles 27 Left. Confirm GBAS OK."*
Tower	*"RWA 573 hello. You are clear to land 27 left, wind calm RVR 20, 30,20 GBAS showing OK"*
Aircraft	*"Roger RWA 573"*

Harry said they were now on the glide slope and Charles was calling out the altitude from the radio altimeter, and the distance to go, presumably from the Navigation Display.

Ahmed	*"Captain, I can't see the ground. Is this a trick."*
Harry	*"Ahmed, shut up. I told you it's very foggy. You'll kill us all if you don't stop talking."*
Charles	*"800 ft. you are showing slightly right, but on glide slope."*
Harry	*"OK, I'm central on the glide slope. You check the approach on your Navigational Display. I'll keep my display in the Primary Flight Display mode. The rate of descent seems rather high. We must have a tail wind."*
Tower	*"RWA 573 two miles to go. You appear to be below the glide slope."*
Harry	*"Charles, I thought our rate of descent seemed high."*
Charles	*"Well we are right on the correct glide slope."*
Harry	*"Heathrow Tower RWA 573 copied please check wind speed."*
Charles	*"one mile, 300 ft, on centre line, on glide path."*
Rad Alt	*"200"*
Tower	*"573 from Tower, the wind is calm. You...."*

Another aircraft came on frequency and blotted out whatever the Tower was trying to say. All we could hear was the other aircraft's transmission when the Tower stopped talking.

Lufthansa	*" 564 confirm Heathrow closed"*
Tower	*"Lufthansa 564 from Heathrow Tower. Airfield closed leave frequency immediately."*
Rad Alt	*"100"*
Harry	*"I can't see the loom of the lights yet."*
Charles	*"Still on glide path"*
Tower	*"RWA 573 ..."*

Again there was a transmission blotting out the Tower, probably Lufthansa acknowledging Tower's instruction and asking for frequency.

Charles	*"On centre line"*
Ahmed	*"What's happening."*
Harry	*"For Christ's sake shut up"*
Harry	*"Still can't see the ground"*
Ahmed	*"Captain, tell me what's going on."*
Ahmed	*"Stop at once."*
Rad Alt	*"50"*
Rad Alt	*"30"*

Harry	*"There's something wrong with the lights, I'm going around."*
Rad Alt	*"20"*

A moment later we could hear Harry yelling and the background noise sounded louder, presumably because the throttles had been opened.

Harry	*"Oh my God, we're hitting the road"*
Tower	*"573 you appear to be"*

That was all and the silence in the room was frightening. I looked around. Everybody looked very shaken. Nobody said anything for a bit. I made a note to tell John that he needed to recall Furness and ask for his opinion of carrying out an approach with such interference from the hijackers. I also told the Clerk that I personally didn't think we needed to listen to the full four hour recording at the moment, but we should keep that as a possibility. However, we certainly needed the transcript with time added. Crowburn had a conference with the members of the Inquiry. It was decided that the Inquiry would remain in private session to discuss the authenticity of the new transcript and reconvene after lunch in open session when I would continue to give my evidence. However the full transcript would not be given out but the interruptions below 800 ft. would be added to the existing transcript. I couldn't be bothered to argue since I was pretty sure the media would sort it all out and force the rest of the recordings from the Secretary of State.

I could not believe the time. I got up and made my way to the door but I could see the press making a beeline for me. John Fairlane pulled me back and indicated I should follow him

"You'd better not appear at the front or you will get submerged by the media. Let's see if we can find another way out."

We escaped by a side door. Mandy had been watching and found us outside a few seconds later.

"How did you find us?"

"Peter, I work round here."

We set course away from the building. I had left my coat with Mike so I was freezing. Mandy had brought her coat with her. John made his excuses and disappeared. We took a taxi to Covent Garden and disappeared into one of the many small cafes.

Mandy looked at me.

"You've got yourself a problem, Peter, the way you've carried on. You're going to be front page news for the next day or so and the media will be after you. They'll want you to appear on TV. You had better make your mind up what you want to do."

"You know I don't like the media. They twist every word to get a story."

"Well you had better come home with me to-night. We can use the same escape route and then go to the station."

"Sounds a great idea."

"Now don't get any ideas. It will be a house of convenience, not of ill repute."

"Anything you say, Ms Arrowsmith. Please excuse me, I've just remembered I must organise a replacement window."

I called my building man and asked him to fit a replacement double glazing unit as quickly as possible. He had been listening to the one o'clock news.

"Are you the Mr Talbert they are all talking about?"

"Yes I am, but don't tell anyone."

My mobile phone vibrated. There was a text message from Matt.

'Peter, you were quite right. I spoke to Lance and finally he told me the whole story. Sending fax and email to Mike. Good Luck.'

We had left Mike in the Inquiry hall, presumably he must have gone to his office. I called him.

"Peter, I've got an email with some attachments from Matt. Do you need them?"

"Mike, have you looked at them? We needed them weeks ago. Now I understand why Lance was so nervous and didn't want to come and give evidence."

The first editions of the Evening Standard were out with 'COURT HAD TRUE CRASH RECORDING' on front page and the article describing how I had proved the AAIB recording had been rigged, presumably by Government Security experts, and that Lord Justice Thomas had the real recording all the time. We had a quick sandwich and caught a cab back to the Inquiry. Luckily we had timed it well as the Inquiry was due to start again and the media were all inside. Mike was waiting with John Fairlane.

"Peter, these extra papers from NWIA. Are they good news? Can you manage without a recess?"

"I think so John. If I get into difficulties then you had better explain the short notice to the Court and get one."

294

INQUIRY PM DAY FIVE

Peter Talbert

The Inquiry reconvened and to my complete surprise I saw Martin Foster coming into the building. He came up to me.

"It looks as if we may have missed some leads. Do you think you know what happened?" I nodded. "Well I'm sure you're about to tell us."

"Martin, someone came round to my house last night, broke in and took some papers."

He looked at me with amazement. "Who would want to do that?"

"I don't know. Luckily I've got the originals."

"Well I'll talk to you later."

As he went away I saw Osborne. "So it was Robin Turnsmith then?"

"Yes, I told you earlier he was desperate for money. Gambling and a woman I think."

I decided not to tell him that I had suspected Foster. We separated and I went back to the witness stand. Lord Justice Thomas announced that it had been decided that the new recording and transcript from the voice recorder was authentic. John Fairlane then reminded me I was still under oath.

"Mr Talbert, have you now heard the full recording?"

"Yes, Sir. As I expected the conversations with the hijackers are quite clear. The main hijacker was interrupting the crew all the way down the approach."

"In your opinion would it be possible for the crew to carry out an approach in the freezing fog with that level of interruption?"

"Not safely. It would be impossible to monitor everything, particularly with only one Navigation Display."

"Now then Mr Talbert, the crew were carrying out a Galileo approach. Do you have any comments?"

"The GBAS data being transmitted to the crew should have been checked immediately after the crash. Also the runway data should have been checked in the MMR databases. However, neither of those omissions was the reason for the crash."

There was a complete silence in the hall and then an air of expectancy from the press rows.

"Mr Talbert, that's an extraordinary statement. Do you think you know the explanation for this terrible accident? Wasn't the distraction from the hijackers the explanation?"

"In my opinion the distraction made the crash inevitable but it was not the primary cause."

"Would you please tell us what you believe caused the accident? Please start at the beginning of your investigations."

"Well Sir, I was never happy from the moment I heard the captain's recording. Captain Hodgson said he was on the glide slope when his co-pilot was reading out the ranges from his Navigation Display. They matched up perfectly."

"Matched up?"

"Very roughly the aircraft loses 300 ft. per mile on a standard 3° glide slope. So when the co-pilot called one mile range the aircraft should have been at 300 ft. and we know that it wasn't from the evidence of the air traffic controller. Clearly the range on the navigation display was wrong. AAIB seemed to have accepted that the Galileo calculated glide slope was wrong but failed to realise that the Navigation Display range was incorrect as well. Consequently, the pilots were misled. The challenge was to find why the electronics were wrong."

"How did you manage to do that, Mr Talbert?"

"Well I suspected that the problem was caused, like most accidents, by a combination of faults. With the help of an avionics expert who gave me some supporting documents, I had already identified a design feature which was undesirable. The expert gave me some papers which explain the point." I gave the material which Anne Moncrieff had given me to one of the Court's officials.

"Are you going to tell us what you both felt was undesirable?"

"In a moment, Sir. My problem at the time was to find what else had gone wrong."

I explained how I rang Bill Baker to find out what maintenance had been carried out by NWIA on Alfa Juliet and how Bill had offered me a training job which I accepted straightaway. Going to Australia gave me an opportunity to make some investigations myself, since I did not believe the reports that came out in the press about the pilots having been to a party the night before the flight. I told how I found out that Tumbrill had been friendly with a girl and how I had managed to find out the girl's room mate. I skated over my investigations as delicately as I could, telling the Inquiry how horrified I was when I discovered that Tumbrill's girl friend had been killed in the accident. John explored this in detail.

"Mr Talbert, let me understand this situation. Tumbrill's girl friend, a trainee stewardess, was actually on the fatal flight? Her name was 'Eva'?"

"Yes, sir. That's quite right."

"So the quote about 'did you speak with Eva' in the recorder transcript could have meant that Captain Hodgson was asking if Tumbrill had gone in to the back of the aircraft and spoken to his girl friend?"

I could feel the hall listening to my every word.

"Yes, that is exactly what I believe it did mean. As a result of my conversation with Miss Ward, Eva's room mate, it was clear that the four of them had gone out to dinner two evenings before the fateful flight. In fact I discovered that Miss Ward had spoken to Captain Hodgson to thank him for the dinner the night following, that is the night before the flight, and spoke to him in his room at 8 o'clock."

"You must have read the papers and know the interpretation put on that snatch of conversation. Do you have any comments?"

"Only that the conversation was clearly misunderstood and shows the danger of letting transcripts of voice recordings get in to the public domain."

"But the conversation clearly said that they had got back 'just in time'. What did that mean?"

"I'm not sure. Maybe that they had an appointment in the hotel. Nothing to do with the flight thirty six hours later."

"Mr Talbert did you learn anything else from Miss Ward."

"Miss Ward worked in Royal World Airlines Flight Operations department at Sydney so she met all the flight crews. She told me that on the night following the dinner with Hodgson and Tumbrill, Eva and she had a long standing arrangement to go out to dinner with the back-up crew which had just brought Alfa Juliet to Sydney. Miss Ward had wanted to cancel the dinner but apparently Eva felt it would be rude to cancel at such short notice. The crew arrived and immediately called NWIA maintenance about some problem with the Global Positioning System and the Captain called a senior pilot in England to describe the fault."

There was a murmur in the audience. I could see that this information was being copied at length by the press.

"Can you tell us what was the nature of the fault that caused a conversation with Royal World Airlines headquarters?"

"Well, Sir, may I first expand on what the Independant electronics witness said yesterday. He explained the avionic architecture of the Royal World Airlines 798. What he did not explain was the fact that the RWA 798 design is different from all other 798s because it has a different GPS box."

Again I could see the press writing away. I went on to explain the concept of GPS and how it could be used as a landing aid under some circumstances with all 798s except the Royal World Airlines 798s and that for this to be possible there had to be three GPS cards within the GPS box and not just one. I explained that to use the system as a landing aid there had to be a local system, LAAS, at each airport if Category III approaches were to be carried out. I then told how I contacted Captain

Blind Landing

Robson to find out exactly what was the fault they had on Alfa Juliet and who he telephoned.

"The fault was that there was a warning of failure of the No. 2 GPS card and of course, as I have just explained, the RWA aircraft only has one GPS card. His story in fact did not completely surprise me because I had already spoken to the NWIA mechanic in Sydney who had changed the GPS on Alfa Juliet that night. He had done a straight swap of GPS boxes checking that the part number of the box he put in was the same as the part number of the one he took out. Later I noticed that a week or so earlier Alfa Juliet had had a previous GPS fault and the GPS box had been changed by a less meticulous mechanic. The box taken out was a RWA GPS box with a single GPS card, the box the mechanic put in was an NWIA GPS box with three GPS cards."

There was a buzz of excitement. Lord Justice Thomas came in.

"Mr Talbert this is all very interesting but we are talking about a Galileo approach aren't we? NWIA may have fitted the wrong GPS box but what has this got to do with the accident?"

"You are quite right, my Lord, but irregular maintenance in the system we are looking at cannot be ignored. We now know that the NWIA engineer who fitted the box the night before the aircraft took off did a very thorough check of the system. He had not been trained on the Royal World Airlines avionic fit so being a first class mechanic when he did the full check on the new box he had fitted he discovered that it was not possible to carry out a GPS approach as laid down in the maintenance manual for the NWIA aircraft. He noticed that the approach selector switch on the RWA aircraft wouldn't select GPS but only ILS, MLS and Galileo. So he got a new selector switch out of the NWIA stores, fitted it, and everything then checked out correctly with the NWIA maintenance manual."

Templeman broke in.

"Mr Talbert, that's all very interesting but why would it cause the accident?"

"Well Sir, the RWA aircraft approach selector switch is wired so that only ILS, MLS or Galileo can be selected. All other 798s have a four position switch to permit ILS, MLS, Galileo or GPS to be selected for landing. The vertical position of the RWA aircraft selects Galileo, the right hand position MLS and the left position ILS. For all other aircraft the vertical position selects GPS, the right hand position Galileo and the two left hand positions ILS and MLS. What no-one had anticipated was that this change could be done during routine maintenance."

John Fairlane took over again.

"Mr Talbert, you have explained to us what you believe happened the night before the last flight. Would you now go on and explain the accident?"

"Well Sir, everything happened exactly as has been described by Mr Foster but, when the First Officer selected a Galileo approach, he was in reality selecting a GPS approach. Unfortunately, although there is a Local Area Augmentation System installed for Heathrow to correct the GPS inaccuracies, at the moment the LAAS does not work well enough to ensure an automatic landing and so Category III approaches using GPS are not permitted for airlines using the airport. Because of the incorrect switch, Alfa Juliet instead of doing a Galileo approach on 27 Left actually made a GPS approach and crashed because the accuracy of the GPS system was not good enough."

Again there was a buzz around the room. The press were working overtime.

"Mr Talbert, surely the crew should have noticed that they were below the glide slope?"

"No Sir, with respect that's not so. You may remember that I referred earlier to an unsatisfactory design feature. On all 798s the pilots only see the signal that is being used to drive the auto-pilot. If the pilots have MLS selected then they see the MLS deviation. If they have GPS selected, as in this case, they would see the deviation as calculated by the Multimode Receivers using the GPS position which, at London, we know is not accurate enough. The aircraft does have an MLS indicator which might be used as a back-up but, of course, the MLS was out of service. I support Mme Moncrieff in her criticism of the 798 certification by EASA.

"In my opinion the pilots flew centrally down a GPS calculated glide slope which was hopelessly inaccurate and took them straight into the ground. The pilots had no independent view of the aircraft's vertical position relative to the runway.

"In the case of Galileo, as Mr Foster of the AAIB explained, the Navigation Display would show distance from the runway touchdown point but the distances would have been incorrect because they were based on the inaccurate GPS system; the pilots would have been misled because the LAAS was not working correctly. On the recording transcripts we can see that they were checking the range and were checking not only that they were on the glide slope but also that they were at the right height for the distance being displayed. At 100 ft. Captain Hodgson said that the aircraft was on the glide slope. No crew could do more."

I could see that my point had got home to the press but McGuire couldn't restrain himself any longer.

"Mr Talbert you claim to be an expert. I have to say it all sounds very fanciful. Don't you think it is far more likely that there was something wrong with the Galileo software or database and the hijackers prevented the pilots realising what was happening."

"Well Sir, it could be. Of course immediate proper checks should have been carried out to find out if the GBAS transmitter was transmitting the correct navigational information to enable a Galileo approach to be carried out and also whether the runway 27 Left information was correct in the database. However, I found it very interesting that Mr Foster yesterday said that they couldn't get the Galileo deviations from the recorder. I believe Sir, that this was because the instrumentation could only work if the aircraft was fitted with the correct equipment and the correct approach selector switch. It is very probable that the instrumentation would not work with the wrong approach switch fitted."

I could see that I had scored a point. Certainly the press thought so but McGuire persevered.

"Have you any paperwork at all to support your theory?"

"Yes Sir. I have the technical log page for the first GPS swap. I also have the NWIA spares issuing slip for that night showing that the GPS fitted was not an RWA GPS but a NWIA GPS. There is of course no maintenance page for the critical night but I have two spares issuing slips, one for the GPS showing it was a NWIA spare and I now have just received a message from NWIA confirming that the wrong approach selector switch was fitted.

"Captain Robson will be able to confirm the fact that there was a No. 2 GPS fault and Mr Roger O'Kane will be able to confirm that the aircraft would work as I have described with the equipment that NWIA fitted. Presumably it will be possible at some stage to take evidence from the NWIA mechanic who fitted the wrong switch. Unfortunately he is not here to-day. In addition it might be useful to confirm with Mr O'Kane that the Galileo recorder information would not have worked on Alfa Juliet with the wrong GPS box and approach switch fitted."

McGuire seemed satisfied and John Fairlane got ready to resume the questioning.

"Mr Talbert. Thank you for such a clear explanation of the likely cause of the accident. Is there anything you would like to add?"

I looked at him and took something out of my pocket.

"I found this rotary switch in a pile of discarded scrap in the Farnborough hangar."

"Shouldn't you have given it to the AAIB team?"

"Yes Sir, I should, but they were regarding this switch as scrap and I was afraid it might not get fully investigated. It's very battered with wires hanging off it as you can see. Luckily I found a stores reference number on it but I have not had time to ask Independant to check it out. I believe this switch may be the approach selector switch, and that this switch is not used in the RWA fleet."

Lord Justice Thomas came in.

"Mr Talbert your evidence is remarkable and almost incredible. Can you sum up for us how you believe this accident was possible?"

"Yes My Lord, I will try. Because aviation is so safe, accidents these days are always a collection of unexpected occurrences all happening at the same time. In my opinion this accident happened firstly because the mechanics had only received training on their own airline's equipment, secondly because it was possible to change the aircraft modification standard during routine maintenance and thirdly because the pilots were looking at the same information as the auto-pilot. Had the GPS system been accurate when used with the LAAS system at Heathrow of course all would have been well, even though GPS was being used, but unfortunately it wasn't. The crew thought everything was alright because they could see they were on the centre line on the Navigation Display and the glide slope deviation was zero but it was a synthetic glide slope and it was not accurate enough using GPS as the sensor because of the innaccurate system. As with most accidents these days, it only happened because there were a chapter of earlier mistakes and, possibly, a deficiency in the certification requirements."

John came back in.

"One final question Mr Talbert. In your opinion were the crew to blame in any way for what happened to flight RWA 573."

"No Sir. Any chance they might have had of seeing something was wrong was almost certainly ruined by the presence of the hijackers."

"Thank you."

John Fairlane sat down. Janet Crowburn got up.

"Mr Talbert. You've told us an extraordinary tale. If the accident happened as you say, how do you explain that the AAIB did not discover it? Don't you think it more likely that the AAIB would find the true cause rather than you yourself, acting alone?"

"Ma'am I would prefer not to comment on what the AAIB did or didn't do. I did think when I started that, like the AAIB. the most likely cause was pilot error but I was fortunate in my investigations and I did not have any pre-conceived notions."

"Thank you for your very clear evidence on this very complicated subject, Mr Talbert. I have often noticed that people like yourself who claim to be lucky often work very hard indeed to achieve their good fortune. If there are no further questions you may step down."

However McGuire suddenly indicated he wanted to ask another question.

"Mr Talbert, I thought there was a warning system in the control tower which alerts the controller if the aircraft is not on the correct glide slope and on centre line?"

"Well Sir, I'm not an expert on the system. It is a development of an earlier system called AFDAS, Approach Funnel Deviation Alert System, but I believe it uses the positional information being transmitted from the aircraft and not from the secondary radar and so it would not have detected a fault."

"Surely that nullifies the effectiveness of the warning system?"

"As I said I am not an expert in these matters but secondary radar is slowly being phased out and reliance is being placed on aircraft transmitting their positions directly. The benefit of this method is that the update rate is much faster since the secondary radar sweep takes about six seconds. The other benefit I believe could be a financial saving in removing the requirement for airports to have secondary radar."

"Mr Talbert, surely money should not be a consideration in safety matters?"

"Sir, I'd rather not comment since it is outside my area of expertise but I believe these new monitoring systems can be modified to avoid reliance completely on the aircraft's position transmission."

McGuire indicated he had finished his questions and it was with great relief that I left the box and went over to sit next to Mike. Anne Moncrieff took my place and was sworn in. John got her to explain what happened during the EASA certification of the 798 and to confirm that the papers I had given the Inquiry were the relevant ones in her disagreements with the EASA.

"Summing up then Ms Moncrieff, you felt that it was wrong to have the three GPS cards in one box. You felt it was wrong not to have the Multimode receiver software classified at the highest safety level. You felt it was wrong that the flight crew did not have an independent display of the glide slope centre line on the approach. Finally you disliked the whole concept of the RWA special modification. Have you changed your mind at all since you wrote your letter to the chief certification engineer?"

"No, Sir. Unfortunately I believe that I have been proved right. If I may say so Mr Talbert has done an excellent job finding the truth."

McGuire asked a few questions but Moncrieff dealt with them all very easily. Roger O'Kane was recalled, sworn in and questioned by Janet Crowburn.

"Mr O'Kane, did you hear the evidence which has just been given by Mr Talbert?"

Roger nodded.

"With your detailed knowledge of the avionics on the 798, could the accident have happened as Mr Talbert suggests?"

"Well Ma'am I cannot comment on what happened when the aircraft was flying but if a three card GPS was fitted to a RWA 798 and the wrong approach selector switch also fitted to the same aircraft then the aircraft would be identical to all other 798s and would be able to carry out an approach using GPS as the sensor."

"What about Mr Talbert's statements about what the crew would see? If the GPS was inaccurate would the crew know that the aircraft was not on the ideal glide slope?"

"Ma'am, the pilots look at what the auto-pilot sees. If the calculation is wrong, then the pilots will not know. However my company took every step to ensure that the design met every known safety standard and the FAA and EASA agreed."

"But you had not allowed for the faulty maintenance as described by Mr Talbert?"

"There is a limit to what can be allowed for. Safety is all a matter of probability."

McGuire chipped in.

"Mr O'Kane, it is not just faulty maintenance, is it? The aircraft was carrying out a GPS approach the way any other 798 aircraft would do. The problem surely is that GPS is not good enough for Category III approaches and there has be an independent method for the crew to check what is happening to the aircraft relative to the runway."

"Well Sir, I cannot possibly comment on whether Category III GPS approaches are possible. My understanding is that with a Local Area Augmentation System it should be possible, but I am not an expert."

"Agreed Mr O'Kane but maybe the way the system is implemented in your aircraft needs examination. Perhaps the FAA and EASA need to take a good look at what the pilot can see."

Roger didn't have to respond because Crowburn got to her feet again.

"Mr O'Kane one final question. Would the Galileo instrumentation on the recorder have worked on Alfa Juliet with the wrong equipment fitted?"

"No Ma'am."

"Thank you, Mr O'Kane."

Lord Justice Thomas called Crowburn and Fairlane up to the bench. There was a long discussion and the counsels returned to their seats. Lord Justice Thomas said that the Inquiry would be adjourned until Monday with a possibility that there would be a further adjournment after that. More evidence was required from Australia as well as from the UK.

CHAPTER 21

The Dinner

John Fairlane came over to Mike and myself as people started leaving the hall. "I've just heard from Crowburn that apparently after you'd told Foster that you'd had some papers stolen from your house he called Robin Turnsmith at home when he did not arrive at the Inquiry; apparently Turnsmith was working with him on the Inquiry. Mrs Turnsmith answered the phone and was very distressed because Turnsmith went out last and she didn't hear him return; however she found what looked like a confession and suicide note on the kitchen table when she got up. Foster called the police and they managed to get some of Turnsmith's fingerprints from his house and they matched with the ones they found in your house. Do you know him?" I nodded. "Apparently Turnsmith did some betting and got overdrawn. He saw an opportunity to get some money by leaking information to Osborne. On an impulse last night he must have gone to your place to talk to you, saw you were out, and broke in. The police are looking for him now.

"Of course the Inquiry is adjourned so that Thomas and the other two can talk to Furness and decide what to do. They'll obviously want some statement from the NWIA engineer and that will take time to organise. They will want Robson and Chester to testify and also they will want some more evidence from Roger O'Kane to confirm your analysis and examine the switch."

He stopped and stared at me. "By the way you were sailing very close to the wind, pinching that switch."

"Why? It was scrap. 'He either fears his fate too much or his deserts are small, that puts it not unto the touch to win or lose it all.'"

He smiled and shook his head.

"Peter, that was Montrose just before his execution. You were lucky, you got away with it. By the way you will be pleased to know that the Inquiry agrees with my view that there is no point in calling Miss Ward since she can contribute nothing more and there is a danger of some counsels going on a fishing expedition.

"In my view now, the chances of CrossRisk Insurance being named as a party to any action claim must be very small."

"That's good John, but the dependants will need to get recompense from someone. The statutory minimum from RWA will be quite inadequate unfortunately."

John paused and Mike took over.

"Well NWIA are a target for claims, RWA another target perhaps for not ensuring that NWIA was properly trained but I think they might wriggle out of that. However the support contract between NWIA and RWA says that RWA must hold NWIA harmless for any servicing errors. I think one of the most interesting parties to be named might be the European Aviation Safety Agency. It is not normal for a regulating authority to be sued but some lawyers might take a view that they should never have certificated the aircraft with that avionic installation. Certainly that would be my view."

"For doing Cat IIIC approaches I agree."

Mandy had come over and heard most of the conversation.

"But would they get any money out of the EASA? Does it really have an independent legal existence? Court actions could go on for years."

"Well who can the dependants claim from? How about the EC?"

"Possibly if they can't claim from EASA, the airline and NWIA."

"Mike, what about Independant?"

"Well Peter, Independant are bound to be named because they are the aircraft design authority and clearly there is room for improvement on the aircraft. The quickest and best thing for the dependants, but not the lawyers, would be for RWA, NWIA, Independant and maybe EASA to agree their various percentages of any claim and make an offer to the dependants, but I am afraid it will never work out that way.

"Anyway that's enough talk. I think we ought to have a small celebration. I'll buy you all dinner to-night. John, can your wife join us?"

John said he would find out. He had a flat in the Barbican they used during the week and left to check. Mike turned to me.

"By the time we've finished dinner the press will have put their papers to bed so they won't be so persistent. However Peter I advise you to keep away from your house. By to-morrow evening everything should be forgotten. I'll tell you what we'll do. I will book two rooms for Mandy and you in the Savoy and we can all eat there. Is that alright?"

I looked at Mandy who nodded.

"Just as well I keep some clothes in the office. What time shall I meet you there?"

We agreed 8 o'clock in the bar lounge area. We chose the back route again to get out of the building but this time there was a photographer who caught Mandy and I leaving. Luckily there were no reporters. I went with Mike to his office where John joined us.

"Have you seen the latest Standard?"

The first Standard had the front two pages full of the accident. They had found an old picture of me from the Guild which made me look very young. 'EXPERTS PROVED WRONG'. There were detailed explanations of how the accident happened. The later Standard had a headline 'TALBERT TELLS THE TALE' with the front page devoted to

Turnsmith's disappearance. The accident explanation had been transferred to Page 2.

I called Liz and told her the good news. She had seen the first edition Standard but did not know about the adjournment and her being excused. She had not had quite such a good day as yesterday and was feeling a bit subdued. I tried to cheer her up without much success. She was fed up with the weather.

"When do I see you next?"

"Well not until after the week-end. When do you go and see your sister?"

"Friday evening still, back Sunday evening."

"The Inquiry is meant to be starting again on Monday but as far as I know I need not be there. I'll come and have breakfast with you on Monday, OK?"

"Fine, see you then."

I felt a bit mean but there was not much I could do. I left Mike's office and went round to Mandy's. I called Jim Akers at the FT. He had been looking everywhere for me. He offered me a good fee for an exclusive on my accident investigation. We agreed I would do it in the morning for the Week-End FT. He checked on one or two points for the article he was producing for the morning.

I decided to ring Frank Mercer. Catherine, his wife answered.

"I'm so glad you phoned. Frank has been listening to the news. He is still in bed but getting better rapidly, thank goodness. I'll take the phone in to him. I know he's very keen to talk to you."

There was a pause and Frank came on the phone. He sounded a bit weak.

"Peter, thank you for phoning. I've just heard the news. Well done."

"Frank, I though you must be in a very bad way and not able to talk because I was expecting to hear your story plastered all over the front pages. Have you been interviewed? What happened on the flight deck."

"Peter, would you believe I don't know? I was in the back of the Upper Class talking to a friend of mine when the two Marshals went into the VIP Area, there was a couple of thumps and then four passengers went forward into the VIP Area. The two Marshalls reappeared carrying guns and threatened us all as Harry announced the hijacking over the PA system."

"None of this appeared in the media, Frank."

"I know. I shouldn't have told you I suppose but you seem to know everything that happened. Some sinister guys came round to the hospital as I was getting better, flashed their badges, said they were Government Security and told me not to tell anyone the story I've just told you. Official Secrets Act etc."

306

We talked for a bit more and then I said I would come round and see him when things quietened down. I thought about what Frank had said. He had had a very lucky escape. So it was the Marshals who had the weapons. That would explain a lot. They could get them on board. It suddenly dawned on me that the dead man in Sydney was probably a bona fide Marshal and the other was probably 'bent'. No wonder security wanted it all hushed up.

Mandy finished tidying up her desk getting ready for the morning. No day off for her. I told her about the Marshals and Frank Mercer as we went round to the Savoy and checked in. Mike had done us proud. Our rooms were next to one another overlooking the river. The lad carrying our bags looked sideways at me when he realised that I didn't have one. Mandy told me she would need some time to get ready. I went down to the Strand and bought a few necessities and then went back to my room. I was just in time to hear a knocking on the adjoining door and opened it to discover Mandy in a slip.

"I thought I heard you. You can zip my dress up and then go and shower and shave."

I hesitated for a moment. I felt I was being dragged back into the past when Diana and I were together. I pulled myself together and kissed the back of Mandy's neck as she pulled her dress on which slowed things down. Then I pulled the zip up as requested. I freshened up and joined Mike, John and John's wife, Liz, in the bar area. Mike had already ordered a bottle of champagne. We opened it and were well into our second glass when Mandy found us. She was looking very elegant and, of course, without her spectacles.

"You might have waited for me."

Mike gave her a drink and ordered two more bottles. She sat next to me. We drank to our success. Mike cleared his throat and looked slightly embarassed.

"I hope you don't mind but I've asked two more people to join us. Roger O'Kane and Liz Ward."

I looked at Mandy who said nothing. I smiled reassuringly at Mike.

"That's nice Mike. They are both on their own in Town. I think it was a splendid idea. I don't know why I didn't think of it myself."

I looked at Mike who was pleased and at Mandy who looked like the Sphinx as she hit me under the table, unnecessarily hard I thought.

Roger arrived and was introduced to Mandy and Liz Fairlane. Mike looked at his watch. We were running a bit late. Then I saw Liz being shown to our table. She had obviously disposed of her raincoat and gloves, put her hair up and was wearing a fantastic dress which seemed moulded to her figure. Everybody in the room watched her progress to the table. She seemed not to notice, I supposed she was used to it. Mike welcomed her.

"Liz you look stunning. Who don't you know here?"

She was introduced to Roger, John and John's wife, who looked at Liz carefully, though whether it was with appreciation was hard to judge. Mike gave Liz a drink and was going to suggest we went to our table when the head waiter brought the menus over. We all relaxed in our seats again.

Liz Fairlane looked across.

"Miss Ward, I understand from Mike here that you design and make your own clothes. That dress you have on. Surely you did not make that yourself? It's wonderful if I may say so. Mind you, with your figure you have an advantage over me, but not Mandy of course" she added hastily.

"Yes I did make it. My problem over here is that my clothes were not made for this climate. Unless the rooms are warm I freeze and come out in goose pimples which spoils the effect."

"Why don't you get a job, Liz, if I may call you that? Please call me Liz, Liz, if that doesn't confuse every body." She grinned. "If I tried to buy a dress like that it would cost a fortune and John would go mad even though he is quite a successful QC."

"Liz, I'm going to. It was Peter here who really gave me the courage to go for it though I had been wondering about it for some time."

She smiled unreservedly at me and then more guardedly at Mandy.

"I've had some offers in the last day or two and I'm going back home on Monday to think about it."

"Can't you stay?"

"Not really. I've got a house to think about and to be quite honest, I'm worried whether I could ever live in the European climate."

We ordered our meal and the conversation broadened, savouring today's Inquiry and then going further afield. We went in to the River Room. Liz Fairlane sat on Mike's right and Liz on his left. Luckily Mike put Roger next to Liz and I sat next to Roger with Mandy on my left. John completed the table. Roger and I tacitly agreed not to talk electronics; anyway he was a bit down after the questioning from McGuire. Mike was a good host and the dinner went very well with the background of the activity on the Thames. The meal took quite a time and we did not finish until 11.30.

We all thanked Mike for a super evening.

"You must all thank Peter. He made it possible. Without him I have no doubt my firm would be bankrupt."

I felt pleased but embarrassed. Mandy squeezed my hand and then did her favourite trick of running her finger round my palm while I tried to make sensible conversation. We all agreed to call each other as necessary in the morning. Mandy and I went to the lobby with Mike and Liz. I kissed Liz goodnight, quickly, and we watched Mike and Liz into a taxi. We turned and got our keys from the desk. Mandy ordered a wake-up call at 7.15 with the FT, Times, Telegraph, Guardian, Independant, The Sun, Mirror, Mail and Express. She must have thought there was going to be something interesting in the papers. We went up in the elevator.

"You having a lie in to-morrow then?"

"I hope so."

She leant forward and kissed me as the doors opened to reveal some guests waiting to go down. Mandy appeared not to notice.

I escorted her to her room and kissed her good-night on the cheek. She responded suitably and disappeared. I went into my room, locked it with the bolt and opened the adjoining door to find Mandy waiting.

"I wanted to say good night properly."

"Well now you can say good-night improperly."

I was tempted to ask what her clients would say but I felt I knew the answer. We decided to sleep in Mandy's room so as not to miss the wake-up call. As I was dropping off to sleep worn out by the day's exertions, Mandy switched on the TV and started to watch Sky News. I could hear my name being mentioned and Mandy kept prodding me to sit up and watch. The always informed air correspondents were being grilled and had some nice things to say. Then they had a review of the following days papers except it was so late it was the morning's papers. My name and picture appeared to be on every front page and EASA and the AAIB got rather a roasting. Jim Akers of course pointed out the difficulties that now existed with the EASA issuing the type certificate instead of a National Regulatory Authority, half implying it would never have happened if the CAA had done the certification He also made the point that presumably the Judge had had the full transcript from day one, but was covered by a Public Immunity Certificate signed at least by the Secretary of State for Transport for one.

"Mandy, can I go to sleep now, my darling?"

"It seems such a shame to sleep when we are in the Savoy."

"Well what else is there left to do at two in the morning?"

"I wonder about you sometimes."

It was still dark when Mandy got up in the morning, put her dressing gown on and brought in the papers. She came back holding the papers but with her dressing gown open.

"Which would you prefer?"

"I'll start with the FT please."

"You've made the wrong choice and you know it. However you're right. I must get to the office."

She disappeared into the bathroom and I glanced at the papers. They were all full of the Inquiry and were very complimentary about the part I had played. As usual Jim Akers' report was by far the best. He even mentioned the switch I had taken from the AAIB hangar, saying it was the only way to convince the Inquiry that the AAIB had got it wrong.

"You had better get back into your room while I get dressed. Take all the papers with you and keep them for posterity."

I obliged but in fact I did not stay in bed but decided to get up.

"Darling, shall I ring down for coffee or shall we have something downstairs?"

"We don't sleep in the Savoy every night. Let's have a quick breakfast downstairs."

Mandy packed her bag and we both packed our briefcases. I felt rather tired with very little sleep and a bit dishevelled. I had put my trousers in the trouser press but there was not much more I could do. Mandy on the other hand seemed ready for anything. We went down and had a continental breakfast in style. We felt spoilt. Mandy had picked up some complimentary papers, I had put ours in my briefcase so it was almost bursting.

"I must say, my dearest, that they have done you proud. If you don't watch it you could become a celebrity."

"Not me. The papers will soon forget."

"Maybe but the Inquiry opens again on Monday. If you show your face it will be photographed. Talking of that have you looked at the Telegraph?"

She passed it to me. There was a picture of me and a smart looking Mandy coming out of the Inquiry hall.

"That will be bad for your business Mandy. The senior partners won't like it. You had better rush to the office and collect the Telegraphs."

"No point. The photograph has been syndicated to the other papers. Here it is again in the Mail. Anyway my firm won't mind. They will just be jealous, especially the ladies.

"I see that your ex-colleague Robin Turnsmith has still not been found. What a mess. Anyway when do I see you next?"

"That's up to you, my darling."

"How about coming to my place for the week-end. You know how I feel about ghosts and your house."

"Sounds good. Shall we catch the 6.30? I'll meet you at the platform entrance."

It was still very cold. We put on our coats and walked towards Fleet Street. I turned right across the bridge to Waterloo and Mandy carried on to her office. I was home by 10 o'clock. Dora was in and full of the Inquiry and the pictures of me and Mandy.

"You look a lovely couple. And you're famous. The phone has never stopped ringing."

"I hope you told them Dora that I had gone to Australia."

"No I didn't" she said indignantly. "I said I was expecting you home shortly and I was quite right. By the way, did you know they found a body in the river by Tower Bridge. They think it might be your accident man."

The phone went again. It was a bit of luck Dora taking all the calls since it had stopped to some extent my answering machine from being clogged up. As I picked up the phone I noticed that despite Dora there were ten messages on the machine and a lot more in Dora's writing. It was the BBC asking me to take part in Panorama on Monday night. The lady calling could hear I was reluctant and offered me a good fee. I refused saying the Inquiry was still on and I felt it would be improper to take part. That was clearly a concept the lady could not understand. We agreed to differ. She was obviously not going to be popular with her producer for failing in her mission.

I started work on the article for Jim Akers. The phone kept on ringing with media people and I kept on with the same reply. Then Liz came on the line.

"How did you get on with Mike?"

"Never you mind. Is breakfast still on for Monday?"

If Mandy was true to form she would be catching an early train. We agreed 8.45 and I said I hoped she had a good week-end with her sister. I returned to my article, struggling with the phone. Then Carol came on the line.

"You were magnificent. I was in the Hall."

"Carol, why didn't you tell me? You must have queued for hours. I could have got you in."

"It was not too bad. I got someone in to take the children to school and was there at 8 o'clock"

"You make me feel rotten. Anyway I hope you enjoyed it. How are you getting on?"

Apparently things had improved with the children after the skiing and Carol was doing some translating and looking for other jobs. She confided in me that an old friend of Dick's had called and taken her out. I got the impression there might eventually be something in it. I asked her to keep in touch.

I played the answerphone back while I was eating a sandwich I had bought at Prêt a Manger on the way home. They were mostly from the same people who had called me during the morning which was a relief. I rang my builder and he told me he should have a window by Tuesday. I went back and finished the article and put it in an e-mail to Jim at the FT. I packed for the week-end and then called Jim.

"Peter, that's absolutely fine. Just what I wanted. I like your point about a higher safety standard and operating rules being required for these large aircraft carrying so many passengers. We'll put it over your name if that's OK."

"Well just check with your legal people on my behalf that I can write that article bearing in mind that I was a witness and I suppose I could be recalled. I've refused to talk to the media."

I did my expenses for Mike and NWIA. I was going to be broke if I didn't watch it. There was a special delivery. I opened the envelope and found a very large cheque indeed from Mike and a note 'Just to keep you going. Final settlement later. Thanks for everything.' He must have moved like lightning to get that approved by his firm. I called American and we agreed provisionally I would be with them Monday week.

Bob Furness called.

"Peter this is a pretty mess. I shall be lucky if I keep my job. I just wanted to congratulate you on the magnificent job you did. I feel very ashamed of our poor efforts."

"Bob, you were let down by Foster and Robin Turnsmith. By the way, is it true they've found Robin?"

"I think so."

"Poor chap. I almost feel sorry for him. Has he got a family?"

"Yes, Peter, I'm afraid so. It really is an awful situation."

"Bob, I'm sure you don't need my advice but I think you should plan for the future. You've got lots of very good people in your team but these accident investigations can be terribly harrowing. They do need close supervision. I'm surprised Martin didn't realise that Robin was the source of the leak."

"You're right. That's where I went wrong."

"Anyway Bob, thanks so much for calling me. I do appreciate it."

I decided I had better call Marcia Hodgson. I introduced myself and said how sorry I was about Harry.

"Mr Talbert, thank you so much for everything you have done. My life is completely upside down as you can imagine but my children are marvellous. I knew Harry would not make a mistake like that and it was cruel of the AAIB. As for the recording it was disgraceful to start all that story for a straightforward dinner party. You were simply splendid."

I muttered a few platitudes and wished her the very best for the future. There was nothing more I could say.

There was a funny call from the Department of Transport later on. It was from a senior civil servant in the organisation. He tried to wrap it up but I detected that he was sounding me out to see if I would be interested in joining the AAIB. I stopped him in his tracks.

"There is a very capable chief inspector there already and I can see no reason why he should be changed."

I rang off, feeling rather annoyed. I diverted my phone to Mandy's number, locked the house and met Mandy at Waterloo. I told her first about the DOT call and she thought for a bit.

"The Secretary of State must be under terrific pressure to change Bob, Peter. You probably would be the ideal choice."

"No thanks. I don't think I want to be regimented, to have lots of administration and people working for me. I want to be free."

"So I've noticed."

I kept my head down and said nothing.

We walked to Mandy's flat and sat down and relaxed. I had been running around for weeks and at last I could relax, sit down and do nothing. Mandy disappeared and came back wearing shorts, a pullover and two gin and tonics.

"You'll freeze."

"Not for long. I've turned the central heating up and you can keep me warm."

"I'd like to take you out for a meal."

"That's very sweet of you but you really do need some rest."

"I'm not sure with your plan I'll get much of a rest."

"Well we shall just have to see." She smiled at me. "I've decided this week-end to do what my clients do for a change and shelve our problems, Diana and all."

I woke up in the middle of the night. It was cold. The central heating was off. I had my arms round Mandy, she was keeping me warm, or was it the other way round? I was wide awake. What was it that Carol had said? 'An old friend of Dick's.'? She had called Richard 'Dick'. On Alfa Juliet's voice recorder, 'Dick' was sitting in the middle seat. I had assumed it was Dick Tremlett, the off duty Captain but of course Richard Trentham must have known Harry from GAPAN. I remembered the visit to Richard in the hospital. What had he said? *'Peter. The hijacker...'* and *'I wanted to tell Harry...?'* It must have been Richard who was in the jump seat and who Harry had called 'Dick'? I remembered that Richard's shoulders were badly broken. By the shoulder straps? Another thought struck me as I suddenly realised what Richard might have wanted to tell me. He might have noticed something wasn't quite right. Perhaps he'd seen a warning written somewhere or perhaps a 'GPS' enunciation on Charles Tumbrill's display instead of 'Galileo'? I did not know enough about what the displays would show with the wrong boxes fitted and I was not about to ask Roger. Roger would have mentioned it to me for sure if he thought there had been something extra to see. As far as I was concerned the matter was closed. Nothing useful would be gained by further investigation. I finally got back to sleep.

We got up very slowly luxuriating in having nothing to do. Mandy finally got out of bed to make up a tray and have breakfast in bed and read the papers. I picked up the FT to read my article but the main headline made me wince "LARGE AIRCAFT NOT SUFFICIENTLY SAFE". The article was written by Jim Akers and really went to town on how, at the moment, large four engined aircraft were designed to the same certification standard as small aircraft like the Airbus 319 which only carried about 100 passengers. He had taken my remarks in my article on higher standards being required and started criticising EASA for not heeding the advice of experts like myself and Anne Moncrieff. He wondered whether in view of the size and complication of the new systems it would be advisable to re-introduce three crew members. Akers also felt that Category IIIC landings should not be permitted with these large aircraft unless there was an independent system the crew could monitor or until there was a system available so that pilots could see through the fog.

I could not really fault the article but I knew that the fall out would affect me since I would be accused of advocating putting up aircraft costs and operating expenses; the arguments were going to start and go on for a long time since airlines didn't like paying more than they had to and safety costs money. However, it was quite clear that if only the regulators had listened to Anne Moncrieff, all those people on RWA 573 would still be alive.

The phone rang. Mandy was still in the bathroom so I picked up the phone.

"Peter?"

I froze. It was a voice from the past which I had vainly tried to forget.

"You were marvellous."

I heard Mandy coming back and put the phone down.

"Who was it?"

"Oh. Just a wrong number."

ANALYSIS

Could it ever happen?

The current safety record for airliner flying is extremely good indeed but unfortunately major accidents still occur; therefore this safety record needs to be not only maintained but enhanced, particularly as larger and larger aircraft are being built and an accident to one of them would be a terrible tragedy. 'Blind Landing' is a fictional story about an imaginary accident which hopefully will never happen; its technology is set quite a few years ahead of the present day, May 2010, but the story is based on five safety themes which will be very relevant in the years ahead if the accident record is indeed going to be improved.

Firstly, the responsibility for overseeing the certification of modern aircraft in Europe has passed from the individual national authorities to a centralised organisation, the European Aviation Supervisory Agency, EASA, which is unmonitored. The second theme is the approaching use of satellite navigation systems to enable aircraft to land in very poor weather conditions such as extreme fog. The third theme, which affects the first two, is the all pervasive presence of software controlling not only the flying controls but the aircraft systems including emergency as well as normal operation. The fourth theme is accident investigation and the need to ensure that investigation authorities will be unaffected by commercial pressures. The fifth theme is questioning the logic of the present certification and operating requirements which basically are the same for all aircraft, regardless of size.

Certification of aircraft is a fundamental task to ensure the safety of air travellers. There is no such thing as absolute safety; taking into account statistically all of the perceivable risks, an aircraft has only to be 'safe enough'. In the past each national authority in Europe had either its own regulating organisation with a set of design rules which tried to ensure an acceptable safety level for civil aircraft or it used the rules of some other country. For example, in the United Kingdom the Civil Aviation Agency Safety Regulation Group, SRG, originally the Air Registration Board, had the responsibility for certificating UK registered aircraft and had its own *British Civil Airworthiness Requirements*. All the regulating organisations had similar requirements but, inevitably, there were important differences between the national authorities which often resulted in disagreements between them when they were certificating each other's aircraft. This was particularly true when the UK certificated United States manufactured aircraft, already certificated by the US Federal Aviation Administration, FAA, and the SRG introduced special conditions for certification of aircraft which it felt had not satisfactorily demonstrated compliance with BCARs.

Now that the EU has a supranational authority, EASA, to do the task of certification and regulation on behalf of all the individual European national authorities, individual countries have lost the responsibility for certificating new aircraft coming onto their own national registers and adding safeguards if they feel they are needed; furthermore, certification cannot be withheld by an EU country if EASA has certificated the aircraft. EASA's legal position is not entirely defined, in that it is not clear whether the Agency, for example, can be sued in the event of an accident for which EASA could be considered partly to blame.

The UK in the past had an organisation called the Airworthiness Requirements Board, ARB, which used to monitor the work of the Safety Regulation Group and this had the effect of ensuring that all decisions by the SRG were very carefully thought through. In the case of EASA, there is no equivalent of the ARB and history shows that an organisation without monitoring can sometimes take unwise and unsatisfactory decisions. Even with internal 'auditing' there is no guarantee of correct procedures, as can be seen in the EU itself and the way it operates; without proper independent technical monitoring the situation is particularly undesirable since safety is involved. In fact, the only check and balance on EASA is, surprisingly, the USA's Federal Aviation Administration; if the requirements of these two major certification organisations were to drift apart it would make the certification of each other's aircraft very difficult and there would be many arguments, perhaps even involving the World Trade Organisation, if protectionism was suspected.

Before leaving this point it could be argued that the FAA also is unmonitored but in fact the FAA is very much a part of the US Department of Transportation unlike the EASA which is in reality is completely stand alone organisation.

The second safety theme relates to the advent of satellite navigation and its increasing use for approach and landing, statistically the most dangerous part of any flight. The United States Global Positioning System, GPS, has been available for many years but it has never been satisfactory as a stand alone navigation system for civil aircraft, since it is basically a military system and does not meet civil safety requirements in the respect of failures, although the latest GPS satellites and the way they are being used has improved the situation considerably. The European Galileo satellite system is just starting and will eventually be operational; it is basically a civil system, suitable for sole source en route navigation. Conceptually, these satellite navigation systems can also be used as approach aids to airfields anywhere in the world, providing all the necessary airfield details have been entered in the aircraft's navigation system. Furthermore, the satellite systems can be used for landings providing the accuracy of the satellite information has been augmented with a local satellite measurement system and the latest runway data transmitted to the aircraft. GPS has a Local Area Augmentation System and the Galileo system, if it is to be used for CAT III approaches, will have a Ground Based Augmentation System, GBAS.

The situation is made more demanding because of the spread of software into the realm of landing aids. There is a huge difference between a landing system using ILS or MLS, with their vertical and horizontal radio beams as references, and a landing system using satellites. The ILS and MLS accuracies are determined by the positioning of the transmitting antennae, whilst the approach accuracy of a satellite system depends on the combined accuracy of the satellite system, knowledge of the airfield information plus the design and integrity of the aircraft on-board system software. On a satellite approach, the path in space for the aircraft to follow is computed entirely by the software in the aircraft and relies on the complete accuracy of the airfield information. The integrity of the software calculation therefore needs to be to a very high standard if satellite Category IIIC landings are to be made.

In addition, as an extra safety measure it is considered imperative that, as the expected use of secondary radar is being gradually reduced and replaced by using the aircraft navigation systems to report their positions, a reliable warning system is installed in the air traffic tower so that the controller can alert the pilot if there are significant departures from the centre line or the glide slope, even though the local air traffic controller is not responsible for the landing aircraft flying an accurate approach to the runway.

The third safety theme is software. The days of the aircraft controls following the position of the pilots' input lever, the control column, have long since gone. This is a situation well understood by aircraft designers and the certification authorities but, despite all their efforts, ensuring that software is 'absolutely safe' is not that simple. In particular in order to make aircraft as efficient as possible and therefore competitive, aircraft designers are relying more and more on computers and the software that drives them to manage not only the flying controls but also the aircraft systems. Both the normal and abnormal operations of the systems are being carried out automatically and the crew have to rely almost completely on the information being shown on the flight deck displays. The challenge for the designers is to make sure that every possible malfunction and/or failure is allowed for and that the crew will always know what to do in any circumstance. Furthermore, it is essential that the values of the parameters which are being fed into the computers to enable the correct response of the controls and the systems are as reliable as the software computations.

The fourth theme is accident investigation; it is vital that such investigations, the conclusions reached and any corrective action required be unaffected by external commercial or political pressures. European certification is now centralised but there has to be some concern over European accident investigation under this new certification regime, since the accident investigation organisations are national ones and are likely to remain so, because accidents are often appalling disasters and therefore it is unlikely that an EU national government would ever accept investigation by a supranational body under the aegis of the European Union. However, it is important to recognise that external influences on accident investigators are never far away due to the enormous financial and insurance implications of accidents and the concern of where the blame for the accident will be allocated. Whatever may be said to the contrary, a national European accident investigation authority, as distinct from a federal authority like the FAA, investigating an EU built aircraft is always liable to be under great pressures from the manufacturers, the airlines and from EASA. The current arrangements therefore could result in some very unsatisfactory conclusions and findings in the event of a serious accident.

The final theme of this book is to point out that at the moment the certification and operating rules for large transport aircraft are basically the same as for smaller ones. The unpalatable fact is that up to now all aircraft types have had accidents, for all sorts of different reasons. It is suggested that the rules for modern large transport aircraft, able to carry more and more people, may need to be reviewed to try to make the possibility of these large aircraft having an accident an even more remote occurrence. In the case of the operating crew only two pilots are required and they have not only to supervise the flying of the aircraft but also control the very advanced sophisticated systems; this is only made possible because the display of the procedures to be followed in the event of malfunctions which the designers have thought of are displayed on the flight deck. Whether two crew are able to carry out these completely separate tasks is a matter for the designers and regulators but it may be considered necessary to have more than two pilots on the flight deck, since inevitably there will be system failures and/or flight circumstances that will not have been allowed for. Furthermore, it may be deemed necessary for the equipment standard on these large aircraft to be to a higher standard; for example a synthetic visual landing system may be required so that the pilots can see the ground whatever the weather, though the new systems will have to be analysed in detail to make sure that there will be no conflict with the existing landing systems. Airlines may not like any of these changes but safety has to be paid for.

In summary it is considered necessary for designers, regulators and perhaps designated politicians to review carefully whether the current safety regime is good enough for the years ahead.

1. Should the work of EASA be monitored by independent experts?

2. What will be the minimum standard in the aircraft and on the ground for satellite landings in Cat IIIC conditions?

3. Is the software design for the systems and the matching crew operating procedures to high enough standards and is the input information to the computers which control the aircraft as immaculate as the software?

4. Is the accident investigation procedure in Europe sufficiently independent of the designers and regulators?

5. Is it really acceptable as aircraft get larger and larger to have just two flight crew to not only fly these huge aircraft with large numbers of passengers under all conditions but also to cope with all the demands of any systems malfunctions?

Aircraft design does not stand still. There will always be more and more technical challenges as aircraft become more efficient. This book takes a snapshot of the challenges in the immediate future. Peter Talbert will have to work hard to keep up!

ALB

May 2010

APPENDIX
Satellite Landing System

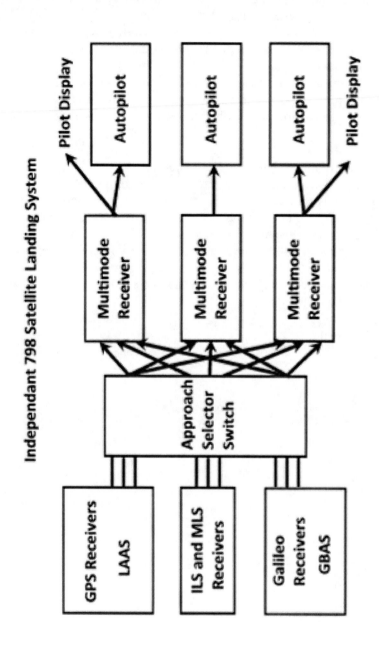

LaVergne, TN USA
07 July 2010
188684LV00008B/28/P